The Vast In Between

Carol Craig

© 2021 by Carol Craig
Published by Ingram Spark
1 Ingram Blvd.
La Vergne, TN, 37086

Printed in the United States of America.

Titles may be purchased in bulk for educational, business, fundraising, or sales promotional use. For more information, contact Carol Craig @ www.editinggallery.com.

Library of Congress Cataloging-in-Publication Data

Craig, Carol, 1957-
      The Vast In Between / Carol Craig.
         p.   Cm. -- Historical women's fiction
      ISBN 978-163625231-5

This is a book of fiction. Names, characters, places, and incidents are the product of the author's imagination or are used fictitiously. Any resemblance to actual events, locales, or persons, living or dead, is purely coincidental.

Edited by Sara Rolat.
Cover design by Darrin Brenner: D. Brenner Art & Design.

Printed in the United States of America
09 10 11 12 13 RRD 7 6 5 4 3

For Les, Sara and James, and Kaylee, the four lights of my life.
And to Parker, my fur baby.

"Truth lives on one side of life
Lies on the other
Everything else is the vast in between"

- Author Unknown

Truth is the lie we tell ourselves. Like a multi-faceted diamond, it can cut even the strongest of glass. During the Great Depression, for the coloreds awaiting rations, the facets were many. For there, lined up beneath the sign of an all-white family smiling in a brand-new car with the words "World's Highest Standard of Living, There's No Way Like the American Way," the irony could be no more apparent.

No, truth lay in the history rooted in the hardscrabble soil of Shardsburg, Alabama, where having a job as a cotton picker at seventy-five cents a day, meant the difference between eating and starving. And if lucky, the plantation would provide a little shack no bigger than a chicken coop lined with old newspapers extolling the virtue of white teeth and fresh breath. So, while eating a bowl of cornflakes, a child might stare up at the wall with the words "Lips that touch Camels shall never touch mine."

And so it was that into this world of hopelessness and poverty came a scrawny runt of a child who squawked piteously for any form of sustenance, be it food or love, which were on all counts in short supply that year. For 1932 was neither the beginning nor the end of the drought that followed the Roaring Twenties, but the vast in between. That long stretch that saw the gaunt faces of men and women lined up along streetsides as they awaited handouts. Children stirring the dust with dirty feet, long since gone the luxuries of bathing. In ragged dress or overalls, they rested, too weak to play "skip-the-hoop" or aggies. Instead, their large eyes told a story of hunger so keen that it caused the belly to swell so that it sounded uncannily like a ripe watermelon when strummed.

But this is not a story about the hungry child, nor of the many wealthy people who threw themselves off bridges when the stock market crashed, all their money gone. And it is not a story of hopelessness, despite what it might seem on the surface. No, this is a story of truth and lies. But truth and lies are subjective, are they not? And so, each of us must learn, which is the truth, which is the lie, and pray that we are not wrong.

1

COOKIE HAINES PEERED OUT OF the kitchen window of her parents' house at the woman pacing back and forth, back and forth, on the sidewalk next door. For all the world, she looked like a woman from an old black-and-white sepia photo Cookie had once seen. In the photograph, the woman was wearing a gunny sack dress, eyes protruding from a painfully thin face, skin burnished copper by the sun, children gathered at her feet.

"What are you staring at?" Mitzi asked, craning to see what her daughter was seeing.

But just as her mother bent over the farmhouse sink, the woman disappeared from view. Vanished. Gone.

"Nothing," Cookie said, grabbing a pecan sandy from a tray on the marble countertop in the sage green '50's kitchen. She took a bite of the buttery cookie. As she chewed, she thought of the woman. The way she had marched down the street only to stop to worry her hands together, her movements jerky, nervous, as though trying to make a decision of some sort. A hard one at that.

"Well, it didn't seem like nothing to me, little girl," Mitzi said, despite the fact that Cookie was all of thirty-three and still living at home.

Maybe that's why, at an age when most women in Montgomery, Alabama had a husband and children, Cookie was still "finding her way," as her father liked to put it when explaining Cookie to company. And yet they all knew why she had chosen a hermit's life, or more aptly been forced into exile, after the debacle of her engagement. Normally, she fought it with humor, but sometimes she wanted to shrink, disappear like the woman she'd just seen.

"I saw someone outside," Cookie said, frowning. "On the sidewalk. Her clothes were tattered."

"You're one to talk!" Mitzi said, running a hand through the air as if she were a television model selling a brand new Thunderbird.

And it was true. Cookie peered down at her overalls that she wore when working in the greenhouse. At her boots. She was nothing like her sister, Dipsy. No, her sister was everything Cookie was not -- fashionable, married with 2.5 children, one in the oven. Perfect in every way. Her skin was as flawless as her ebony hair with its Shirley Temple ringlets. Everyone loved Dipsy.

And no one would ever guess that Cookie was Mitzi's daughter, Mitzi who loved all things fashion as evidenced by her faux Pucci, pink and green psychedelic pantsuit. No, Mitzi Lee Haines was the epitome of sophistication. She often wore designer Givenchy knockoffs. Occasionally, she patterned herself after Audrey Hepburn, her hair swirled atop her head, her fitted black dress and pearls hiding the extra twenty-five pounds she had gained at Cookie's birth, which she'd never been able to shed. Even the faux designer sunglasses she wore when going out made her appear the height of elegance. So it must have come to her as a shock that Cookie was nothing like her. Cookie sighed in frustration. For years, Mitzi had tried to get Cookie to dress like her, but Cookie had refused.

She grabbed another pecan sandy as her thoughts scrolled back to one particular Christmas pageant when Mitzi had dressed them in matching red Christian Dior-type wool coats, complete with the signature cinched waistline, flouncy bottom, and huge bow at the waist. She'd been just eight at the time. Cindy Lou Ratcliffe had marched right up to Cookie and said, "What'd ya mom do, hatch her twin?" She and her friends had all laughed and pointed, hands over their mouths. After that, it didn't matter how many compliments her mother had received from the grownups. The ones that mattered, the girls from the rat patrol, as Cookie had come to think of them, had laughed. That was the last time Cookie had allowed Mitzi to dress her.

"For heaven's sakes, this is the 60's. I wish just this once, you'd let me dress you up. Make you pretty like the other young ladies your age."

Inwardly, Cookie groaned. How many times had she heard these exact same words over the years? And maybe she was just tired, or maybe she couldn't get the image of the woman on the sidewalk out of her mind and didn't want to look like her. To *be* her. Whatever the reason, right then and there, Cookie said, "Okay."

"Okay, what?" Mitzi asked, midbite.

"You can dress me." Cookie twirled in a circle. "Work your magic."

Mitzi paused so long that Cookie felt certain she hadn't heard her. Suddenly Mitzi squealed and said, "Oh. . . my. . . gawd!" Then she snatched Cookie's hands in hers and began dancing around the kitchen, swinging Cookie until she feared Mitzi might let loose and send her flying into the potted fern on its pedestal next to the window.

"And I've got just the thing!" Mitzi said, throwing up her hands as though the idea had just come to her. "I've been waiting for the right time to give it to you. Thank gawd you never gain weight. Stand still, don't move." Mitzi held up her hands like Moses parting the waters.

Cookie threw up her hands too, as though she was being robbed, and said, "Not moving. Right here. Go."

"You stinker!" her mother said, but laughed and then ran excitedly out of the room, talking to herself the entire way about young women who don't listen to their mothers and giggling over the prospect of finally changing her daughter into a proper Southern lady.

Cookie couldn't help but laugh. Mitzi always said that Cookie took after her father. Where Mitzi had blue eyes, Cookie had brown eyes. Where Mitzi was what Southerners liked to call "pleasantly plump," Cookie was skinny, or rather scrawny, all legs and sharp angles. She took pride in being different, whereas Mitzi put societal conformation right up there with God, Jesus, and Elvis Presley.

Cookie was in the midst of washing, then drying her hands with one of her mother's cotton tea towels, when she heard an unceremonious knock at the door. She frowned. "Now, who could that be?"

Through the curtain of the side door, she saw the silhouette of a person. Carefully, she opened the door a peep and peered out at the woman she'd seen moments earlier on the sidewalk. Like her dress, her farmer's tan and wrinkled skin bore the signs of a hardscrabble life. But what drew Cookie to her most was the utter look of despair that she wore like a second suit.

"May I help you?" Cookie asked, frowning.

The woman nodded, then heaved a sigh, as though born old. Her arms were no more than twigs, her brown skin hanging loose, her cheekbones protruding from a narrow face.

"Come in," Cookie said, ushering her in by the elbow, then steering her toward the kitchen table and food. Before the woman could even tell her why she was there, Cookie began plying her with leftovers from the refrigerator. "Our housekeeper, Beulah, makes the best meatloaf in town," Cookie said, as she set a plate in front of the woman along with a slice of fresh watermelon and a tall glass of lemonade. "Eat," she ordered, realizing that she'd picked up a thing or two from Mitzi, who was always organizing some charity or other.

"I just came here to. . ." The woman's voice trailed off. She looked at the food, then at Cookie, her eyes searching. But for what? Finally, hunger won out and she dug into the proffered meal.

"So where are you from?" Cookie asked, feeling a sense of déjà vu, as though she'd seen this woman before. But where?

"Shardsburg, originally," the woman said between mouthfuls. "A little place. Out in the country. A shack, really."

"Shardsburg. . . Shardsburg." Cookie rolled the name around

on her tongue as though by saying it over and over, it would provide some memory, but in the end, she couldn't place it.

"Northwest of here," the woman mumbled. "Near the border. My family's from out that way. We sharecropped for near on three years. Moved in town some years later."

Just then, Cookie heard Mitzi coming down the stairs, her voice tinkling with excitement about how beautiful Cookie was going to look once Mitzi got through with her.

At the sound of Mitzi's voice, the woman jumped to her feet, banging the table and nearly knocking over the chair. "I have to go," she murmured. "My name's Rachel. Rachel Aberdeen." She dug into the pocket of her plain brown dress and thrust a wadded piece of newspaper into Cookie's hand. "Hide this," she said, her eyes wild, her dark face lined with worry. "Don't let your mama or daddy see it."

The older woman rushed for the door and opened it. Just then, Mitzi came around the corner with a clutch purse in her hand while appraising a white frock with large midnight blue dots that would undoubtedly make Cookie look like a Dalmatian.

"This will look wonderful on you, Cookie," Mitzi said, glancing down at the dress.

But when Mitzi peered up, it was as though the world slipped into slow motion, for she let out a cry that was halfway between a gasp and a scream, both the purse and the frock falling to the ground in slow motion, as did Mitzi who landed on the floor with a thud.

"I'm sorry," Rachel said, her eyes imploring Cookie to hide the wadded piece of newspaper she'd given her.

Despite the fact that she owed nothing to this woman and everything to Mitzi, Cookie pocketed the faded and yellowing paper and said, "Go!"

Then, with a chill settling over her, she turned to help Mitzi up off the floor. But as she bent down to check on her mother, she saw that some business cards had fallen from her purse along with other paraphernalia. She pushed them to the side, but as she did, she saw a card that she had never seen before. One for a private investigator. A chill ran through her. Now why would Mitzi, of all people, need a private investigator?

2

FROM WHERE EBIE STOOD AT the window of his study, he watched as Rachel hurried down the walkway and out of sight, his world spinning. To steady himself, he held onto the rail of the wainscoting and forced himself to breathe.

E.B. Haines, Esquire, who everyone called Ebie, had always loved being a lawyer -- loved the smell of the leather-bound books passed down from his father, the feel of the full-grain calf-hide chair that swiveled according to his needs, and the wide oak desk with its stacks of manilla envelopes filled with requests. He loved the stand-up globe that stood next to the desk that would glow golden at the first blush of early evening as the sun's final rays shot through the transom windows. He loved the trill that the wrens made in the elm on a warm summer's day. He had imagined this life from the time he'd worn suspendered knickers and Stride Rite shoes. As such, he had followed the letter of the law to a tee. Only once had he gone outside the law. *Make that twice.* He turned away from the window of his study, the memories fading but not the fear that made his blood run cold. He heard a rustle and turned to see Mitzi, lunch tray in hand.

"Rachel's gone. You okay?" Mitzi said, as she entered the room with her customary tray of food, this time an egg salad sandwich, room temperature tea, and fruit medley soaked in cherry liqueur with shredded coconut, the meal prepared ahead by Beulah, their housekeeper. Beside the lunch plate were three cookies served on a silver-edged charger. Gingersnaps.

Ebie ran fingers through a lock of black hair that fell into his eyes at will. It gave him that brief moment to tuck his memories into a compartment that he had thought he'd put away forever. To face his wife. To tell her. . . what? I'm sorry? I'm not sorry? That this is the best thing we ever did? It had saved their marriage. She knew it and he knew it. And it had been a good marriage. It had completed the dreams he'd had as a child when he had sat across from Mitzi McCulloch, had imagined himself with the very outgoing, fun-loving Mitzi, who could turn heads even then. He had hoped that one day she would turn her gaze toward him. That she would one day marry him -- the quiet, studious, dark-haired boy who was much too tall, much too thin, and much too serious.

Mitzi seemed to read his thoughts, because she hurried over to his desk, sat the tray down and gathered her skirts before turning to him. "It's going to be okay," she said hurriedly, her eyes imploring him to believe.

He went along with the deception, just as he had all those years ago. It was easier that way. To forget. To pretend. To hope. As he had then, he went to her, wrapped his arms around her and felt her sink into him, a few pounds heavier, but still the beautiful woman he had married. The woman he had fallen in love with as a teenager. The woman who he would do anything for.

When she looked up at him, her eyes were filled with tears. Funny how soft she could be with him, and yet how strong she could appear to the outside world. Did anyone know. . . about this other side of her?

"I love you," she said, peering up at him, making him smile, even now. "It will be okay. You'll see. Rachel has done this before."

And it was true. Each time Rachel had sought them out, she had gone away, just as readily. For years. But she had always come back, had always nicked at their collective consciences. Hadn't allowed them to forget. To pretend. To hope.

"I've got to get back to Cookie."

Ebie nodded. As he watched Mitzi leave, his thoughts once again turned to that time -- to the Fourth of July picnic where it had all started. To Edna Farmer, the nosy matriarch of the Ladies of the South Cultural Society, a plump woman who wore peacock feathers in her veiled red hat. An ostentatious woman who ruled Montgomery's society with an iron fist. Who had pricked at Mitzi's fears.

"So when are you going to give Ebie that baby he's always been talking about, Mitzi? A little Ebie. Someone to play baseball with. An heir. Surely you don't expect a man of *his* caliber to wait too long before he begins looking elsewhere."

All those present at the picnic had laughed, agreed with Edna. All except Mitzi.

Over the next several weeks, Ebie had watched Mitzi crumble. The stalwart woman he had married had become a shell of her former self. When she hadn't known he was watching, he'd caught her rubbing her belly and looking down at the offending space where the child should be. He'd caught her buying items for "the nursery," small at first, then later, items that couldn't be overlooked. . . a rattle, a teddy bear, and finally, a crib. For "when." As if it were a certainty.

The color had begun to return to her face, and he'd heard her humming from the baby's room as she added a rocking chair and a quilt. He'd stood then, his back to the wall, lips pursed, tears in his eyes. He never cried. Had been taught early on that it wasn't the manly thing to do. But how could he not, knowing his wife was in such pain? Was it he who couldn't give her what she wanted most? Or was it her? Either way, he knew that without a baby, he would lose her. Their lovemaking had become more mechanical, more pointed, more fierce. With each passing day, he felt increasingly desperate.

Then the worst had happened. She began wearing maternity clothes and gaining weight. They had gone to the doctor. Had taken the pregnancy test. Nothing. And yet she refused to believe it. Refused to go back to wearing her normal clothes. And still she gained weight.

"Mitzi," he implored her one evening as they were preparing to sit down to dinner. "You can't keep doing this. You are *not* pregnant!"

But it was as if he had slapped her. For one brief moment, she just sat there, staring at him as if the offending words were even then floating through the air like mustard gas. Then, without warning, she let out a low wail and suddenly, she was like an animal, clawing at him, scratching his face. She screamed. And still he held her tight. Told her how much he loved her. That he would always love her, with or without a baby.

Then came the silence. A heavy silence that seemed to weigh the very air around him so that he thought he might be crushed by its oppressiveness. Months later, much to his relief, she finally became pregnant and for three short weeks she had been happy. For the first time in nearly half a year, he could relax. He found himself whistling, humming, smiling. Then came the miscarriage followed by a depression so deep that she had taken to her bed for days, never bathing, never eating. He was losing her. That he knew. Only one way to bring her back to the land of the living. But how? How could he find her a baby?

* * *

"Oh Lawd, Chester," Rayleen Williams said as she rocked in her chair on the rickety porch of her Shardsburg home, *yee-yah, yee-yah*, back and forth in a syncopated rhythm. "She's back."

"Who? That Rachel girl?" Chester said, placing a hand on his knee as he sat out on the front steps, his straw hat protecting him from the midday sun.

"Who do you think? Called today. . . again," Rayleen said, as she waved away the heat and flys with a fan she'd made out of a folded-up piece of paper. "Always tryin' to stir up trouble. . . absolving her guilt is more like it. And she ain't no spring chicken no more, shore as shootin'."

Chester snickered at that. Everyone around these parts knew Rayleen's husband, Chester. He was well over six foot tall, though it'd be hard to reckon, being how stooped he was at near on seventy. A big man, even by local standards, he nevertheless knew to keep his voice low and his head lower. More than once, that had kept them safe. Alive.

People had teased Chester that he'd married up, but Rayleen knew which one of them had won the real prize when they'd married, and it was her. Chester had kept her from runnin' off at the mouth and doing something stupid at near every turn. Papa had said she'd come out of the womb kickin' and screamin' and had never stopped. But she didn't scream for no good reason that she could see. No, she'd had plenty a' reason. *More* than plenty. She didn't like injustice. Didn't sit right with her. People oughtened to treat each other mean, but mean seemed to hang 'round every corner. Never knew when you'd turn the wrong one.

"Hey, you! Girl! Yeah you!" And then the real abuse would begin. Bad enough if it was a local "gentleman." Worse yet, if it was a police officer. And she, like a bottle being shaken, would try not to explode, try not to overflow in a tirade of anger when she knew she had more smarts in her little finger than some of them had in their whole damned body. But Chester was always there to gentle her. To put a quiet hand on her shoulder. He wouldn't have to say a thing. It was as if he could drain the festering rage from her with that one simple gesture. Remind her that she was better than that. To rise above it. But how long could a person rise, pretend that the injustices didn't exist? That the whole damned deck wasn't stacked in one race's favor, one *gender's* favor. Her mother would have told her to quit whining. To get on with living. That she could become someone if she really wanted to. Rayleen wasn't so sure. She thought of all the times that she'd tried and had met with a hurricane force wind. If she had tried harder, and lord knows she wasn't sure how that was possible, would she have succeeded? Could she have owned her own land, her own business, instead of sharecropping and getting deeper into debt year after year, no matter how hard they tried?

"Go somewhere else, if you don't like it here," she'd heard one particularly onerous white woman say when she couldn't pay her bill after a storm of locusts had come through and wiped out most of their crop.

"Go where?" she had wanted to say. "And with what money?" It's not like a person could just pick up an entire family, a colored one at that, and move up north with no money, no prospect of a place to call home. And as long as she owed every year for her losses, they'd damn sure never make it past the county line. No, life wore a person out. Made a person old before their time.

"You over there cogitatin'?" Chester said, reminding her that at least she wasn't alone in all this.

"Un-huh!" she said, pulling a bucket of snap peas over and shucking them into a bucket at her feet. She loved the earthy smell of them, a unique odor that she would recognize blindfolded.

"So what you think? Think that Rachel girl will get her way this time?" Chester picked at the dirt beneath his nails with a knife.

Rayleen almost wished she would. Bring this sad story to a close. Finally. But what would their part be in it? People found out what they had done all those years ago. . . well, what would they think of her and Chester? More importantly, what would people do once they knew their part in the whole depressing affair? Rayleen shook her head and sighed, then went back to shucking peas.

"I reckon it will happen when the time is right," Chester said in that deep, molasses voice of his that was rich with nuance. "And we did nothing wrong. We were given no choice."

Still, it didn't sit well.

"That's the truth," Chester said, tucking his knife away and staring off into the distance. "But Rayleen?"

"Yeah?"

"That little girl?"

"Yeah?"

"I'm glad we did what we did." He licked his lips. "And I won't apologize. That girl is alive 'cause of us. Leastways, I hope so."

Rayleen clucked, remembering the times she'd been asked to care for the infant when Rachel had needed to go to town for somethin' -- the dark eyes, the lightly colored skin, the shock of black hair. The look of love in the infant's eyes. Reminded her of her own babies. The way the baby had held her little hand out to Rayleen, fingering her chin, grasping her finger, exploring her eyes as though memorizing her face, as though knowing that their time together would be short. In some ancient part of her brain, did the adult girl remember their time together? Love Rayleen, even as she had then? No, that was too much to ask. But still she wondered about the child. Dreamt about her. And said a small prayer each morning that she was safe. Loved. Wanted. What more could a mother ask?

* * *

Rachel made her way to the nearby park where she had gone to lick her wounds over the years. It had been her sanctuary in the storm that was her life. She dug out a bag filled with bread crumbs from her old DeSoto and nearly stumbled to the bench seat that sat next to the pond where ducks and geese squabbled amongst themselves or made quiet reassuring noises when they were settling in for the evening. Once there, she recalled the many times she had seen Cookie over the years -- watched her grow into the beautiful young woman she was now.

Rachel's thoughts reeled back to Cookie as a child, of Rachel standing, fists balled around the metal fencing, staring at the school playground hoping to get a glimpse of her. Then seeing her in her white bobby socks and saddle shoes, her little pink dress, knobby knees revealing the rapid growth of a child in the process of becoming a preteen. Rachel had clutched the fence until her fingers nearly bled, the shaking beginning in her hands and spreading throughout her body until she stood there sobbing. Invariably, someone would come to pull her loose, to warn her to be on her way. Then soon, she would get the call from Ebie's lawyer with threats to stay away as per the signed agreement. But what more could they take from her? She had already lost everything the day the tornado hit her little corner of Shardsburg.

As she fed the ducks and listened to their contented quacks, her throat constricted at the memory. Too many times her life had circled back to that moment. One mistake compounded by so many afterwards. But now it was time to pay the piper. Time to tell Cookie the truth. To tell her that her mother was dying.

3

COOKIE GROANED, BUT ALLOWED MITZI to position her in front of the mirror in the hallway. For her part, Mitzi was still acting as though nothing had happened, as though a strange woman hadn't just entered the house, given Cookie a folded-up piece of paper and then summarily hightailed it out of there. To Cookie's amazement, her mother hadn't missed a beat after she'd come to. Instead, she'd ordered Cookie to help her to her feet, then for Cookie to go to her room and get dressed while she fed Ebie his noonday meal. Cookie knew not to ask about Rachel, so instead she had asked about the card she'd found from the Private Investigator.

"Oh that?" Mitzi had said, waving her hand through the air as though it were nothing. "Picked that up at one of those trade shows your father is always taking me to. Some vendor trying to sell his wares. I meant to throw it away."

"Ah. . ." Cookie sighed, wishing she could ask about Rachel, but she knew that until Mitzi was ready to talk, wild horses couldn't drag it out of her. To try to get her to crack before she was willing would spell disaster.

Cookie had only to recall the "Givens Fiasco" as it had come to be called when Mitzi and her best friend, Lucille Givens, had a row. No one was allowed to speak about it or risk spending the summer in solitary confinement, consigned to their bedroom. Cookie had made the mistake of bringing it up over supper one evening and had ended up in this very room, for a week. Fortunately, her father had come to her rescue and cajoled Mitzi into conceding a partial victory. For Cookie's part, she exited her room appearing paler than the other kids, who had all been outside enjoying the sunshine and newly mowed lawns. All because Lucille had borrowed a pair of Mitzi's favorite amethyst earrings, given to her by her grandmother, and then lost one. Well, Cookie wasn't sure what Mitzi had "lost" this time, except maybe her mind. Still, she knew to steer clear of any discussion of Rachel until Mitzi was ready to talk.

"Don't you look stunning," Mitzi said as Cookie exited her room, yet again, this time on a happier note. "Turn around, but no peeking. I want to do something with that mop of yours," Mitzi added, fiddling with Cookie's fine brown hair, "now that the rest of you looks so nice."

With that, Mitzi ushered Cookie into the dining room where she proceeded to put Cookie's hair up in a beehive and gave her boots to match the dress. Then she placed her hands over Cookie's eyes and led her to the hall mirror, warning her to keep her eyes closed.

"Now, open them."

Cookie gazed at herself in the mirror, not sure whether to laugh or cry. For, there she stood, all five-foot nine inches of her, wearing a white dress with big midnight blue spots and a matching pair of spotted boots. "I look like a Dalmation!" she moaned.

"No you don't." To the decolletage, Mitzi quickly added dangle earrings with a black-and-white ball at the end, and cats-eye sunglasses, complete with little fake diamonds in the corners.

Cookie didn't know whether to meow or bark. Or simply buzz. She felt like a damned menagerie.

"You look lovely," Mitzi said, her smile just the tiniest bit forced.

"You *do* realize I have to water my plants in the greenhouse," Cookie said, knowing that not enough time had passed to mention the visitor to Mitzi. Not until she'd cooled down a bit, which should be about the middle of the next century, knowing her mother. "I'm a tad overdressed, wouldn't you say?"

Mitzi frowned, her blue eyes nearly teal when she was concentrating. Finally, she snapped her fingers and said, "I've got it. Hang tight!"

With Mitzi safely away, Cookie's hand moved automatically to her jeans, which she'd laid out on the sofa. She felt for the paper with Rachel's information on it. Fortunately, she'd had the foresight to keep it in her pocket. After all, *Nosy* was Mitzi's middle name. Whatever this Rachel woman had wanted Cookie to hide, she'd meant to keep it from Mitzi, although why was anyone's guess.

Before Cookie could dig the paper out of her jeans pocket, Mitzi startled her with the words, "Aha! I'm back."

Cookie flinched. The woman walked around on cat's

paws, for cripes' sake! Even as a child, Cookie would be playing quietly in one corner of the room and up would pop Mitzi like a proverbial jack-in-the-box, scaring the living daylights out of Cookie. How many times had she dissolved into a puddle as a kid, after one of her mother's surprise entrances?

It's high time I buy that woman a bell!

"Look what I found!" Mitzi proudly held up a see-through rain poncho, the kind they passed out at baseball games.

Cookie backed away, hands in the air. "Oh, no. You don't expect me to wear *that*. In the greenhouse?"

"You are *not* getting that lovely frock wet, young lady!" Mitzi scolded, her nearly black hair spilling around her head in curls.

Before Cookie could protest further, Mitzi stood on her tiptoes and began shoving the poncho over Cookie's head and shoulders, careful not to muss her hair. When Mitzi was done, Cookie peered at herself in the mirror. After the shock had worn off, she began to laugh.

"Now I look like a Dalmatian wearing a raincoat!"

Mitzi studied her, head cocking to the right then the left. But even Mitzi, who was known to ignore the biggest lie, couldn't fight her on this one. Instead, she giggled. In those moments, Cookie could see the child in Mitzi, one of those pudgy little Southern girls who always wore a smile, and who could somehow make even the most churlish of adults laugh. Sure, Mitzi was messy. . . complicated, but something about her made Cookie smile, as though she carried a ray of sunshine with her wherever she went. Even when she was being snarky, she did it with flare, a certain "bon vivant." Cookie loved her, pure and simple.

"Oh, darlin', forget the raincoat and let me fix you one of my famous mimosas before you go outside."

That was Mitzi's answer for any problem. A mimosa. And Cookie had to say, they did take the edge off. While her mother toddled off to the kitchen to make them one, Cookie quickly grabbed the folded, wrinkled brown paper out of her jean's pocket and stuffed it into her oversized Dalmatian boots. She just prayed she wouldn't make crinkling noises as she walked.

*　*　*

One hour, and three mimosas later, Cookie stumbled into the vintage greenhouse with its distressed white wood and gabled windows. It reminded her of a church. And the thought was not lost on her that this *was* her church, the wet smell of loam, houseplants. . . and what? An indescribable earthy smell as ribbons of water cascaded down the insides of the glass. The greenhouse was where she came to escape. To think. Here, she had collected unusual plants that intrigued her, plants that were unique like her. She always felt as though she had fallen to earth from a different planet, a human comet from outer space. Only in the greenhouse did she feel grounded, as though she belonged.

It was here that she had escaped, following her excommunication from Montgomery society. A cold shiver ran up her back at the memory. She was twenty-one and slated to marry the handsome, charismatic Jared Ostrum from Mobile, Alabama -- a tall man with a permanent tan and perfect white teeth. He had been everything her mother had hoped for in a marriage. Her family's wealth, his family's name in cotton. For Mitzi, the match had been perfect.

But it wasn't.

Even now, the memory caused her to reel, to force back

23

a burbling of terror that edged the back of her throat. She'd bought the dress, had sent out the invitations, and even purchased the flower arrangements. But the worst of it all was the announcement in the paper. It had been big news -- had kept tongues wagging for weeks. Cookie rubbed the goosebumps running up her arms.

Then it happened. Two days before they were slated to be married she'd found *the* letter and a photograph. From his real family. His other family. The one in Mobile. A beautiful wife, three kids -- three, five, and seven.

Even now, her throat tightened and her pulse quickened at the memory. Cookie had read the pain in the other woman's words, the loss. Prior to discovering the letter, Cookie and Jared had talked about children. He'd wanted her to get pregnant as soon as they were married, on the first night, if possible. It had seemed almost an obsession with him -- to seal her to him forever. But then she'd come to realize their engagement was a sham.

Disconsolate, she tore at a dried begonia leaf. It had shriveled like her heart. She'd had to call all of her family's friends, nearly two hundred of them, and repeat the now familiar refrain over and over again, that she was forced to cancel the wedding because. . . Finally, she could do it no longer and Mitzi had stepped in. But gossip had burned up the telephone lines. At church, she'd heard whispers, people staring when they thought she wasn't looking. Or even when she was. After that, she had stopped going to church. Had turned to her garden, to her greenhouse. Gone were the clothes she had started wearing to please both her mother and Jared. Instead, she'd found comfort in her old overalls with all its rips and tears. Her plants didn't judge her. She turned to them now, relieved to put the past behind her.

Carefully, lovingly, she tended her *mimosa pudica*, her sensitive plant as it was called, for its leaves would fold up at the slightest touch as she had those many years ago. The leaves would quiver, as though timid, afraid. Then there was the pitcher plant, the *darlingtonia californica*, a carnivorous plant that would eat insects, the plant producing a sweet slimy goo to entice insects who, once caught, would slip into the mouth, fall down into the maw where acids would devour the insect whole, which was exactly how she had felt -- as though she were being eaten alive for having trusted so completely. As though she should have somehow known. But she had been naive, sheltered. The world had seemed an open place, a kind place. It was as if she'd been wearing blinders all these years to awaken to a nightmare. She'd understood nothing of this world she'd been born into and its mores. She'd simply trusted people to have her best interests at heart, and she theirs.

She turned from her pitcher plant to her Venus flytrap, that even now had encaged a fly with leaves that snapped together like a steel trap, its green fingers acting like a mini jail for insects. And just like with the Venus flytrap, hadn't her world shrunk since the failed wedding, become like a jail in a sense? For months, she'd refused to leave home, not that anyone would have spoken to her anyway. She tapped the spring-loaded end of the Venus flytrap and watched it snap shut then moved on to her chain of hearts. Like the plant, with its trailing runner of heart-shaped leaves, *her* heart longed to reach out but was afraid. The few times she had tried, she'd met with rancor. Eventually, she'd stopped trying.

Once again, she turned to her plants for support, to her

favorite, the prayer plant, whose red-veined leaves folded at night so that they looked like praying hands. It held a special place in her heart because it had not only led to her first foray into gardening, it mirrored her plea for acceptance, human kindness, compassion.

Well, she could do nothing about any of that now. Feeling at home only in the greenhouse, Cookie dipped her head to avoid the green-and-white spider plant with its "baby spiders" that hung by runners from the mother plant. She knew where she was headed -- to the potting shed at the back of the greenhouse, a room unto itself with a C-shaped set of potting tables. Rows of clay pots sat beneath the table on one side, sand, loam, and peat moss on the other. Here, she could hear her mother's stiletto heels should she decide to come in search of Cookie.

Taking a seat on the hard red metal chair, flecks of paint missing to reveal the rust underneath, Cookie fished out the paper that she prayed was still intact.

She hadn't been able to get a good look at it, but now, as she unfolded it, she could see that it was a yellowed newspaper clipping that read "September 07, 1932." It had been printed just a few years after she was born. The headline read: *Toddler Goes Missing: Father Suspect.*

Toddler? What toddler?

She continued reading.

Shivers of anxiety ran down Cookie's arms. Who was the toddler and how did it relate to her? She paused, digesting what she had just read. Did this woman, Rachel, want her father, a lawyer by trade, to investigate the lost child? If so, why hadn't she given the clipping to him, or told Cookie to do so? None of this made sense.

Cookie laughed at all the thoughts swirling in her head. For all she knew, the woman could be a nut. No use fretting over something that might not be there. But then why had Mitzi reacted the way she had? Cookie frowned as she began transplanting some fuschia starts. Mitzi usually claimed that *Cookie* was the one prone to imagination, not Mitzi herself.

Of course, there *had* been notable exceptions when Cookie *hadn't* been imagining things. Like the time she had seen a man skulking around the yard and had sworn she'd seen a flash of light. Her mother had poo-pooed Cookie's story, but later, in the alleyway, they had discovered a flash bulb on the ground, right where Cookie thought she'd seen the flash. Mitzi hadn't allowed her daughters outside for weeks afterward. Gradually, Cookie and Dipsy had been allowed in the yard again, but only if accompanied by an adult. Then there was that time she'd seen a car following her, day after day, until finally, she'd told her mother. At first, Mitzi had thought her daft, but seeing the real fear on Cookie's face, Mitzi had grabbed her by the arm and literally dragged her into her father's study.

"Why, what have we here?" her father had said, lowering his plastic framed glasses until they sat near the end of his nose. He stared studiously over them, as was his habit, so that it gave him a rather professorial appearance, despite the fact that he was a lawyer.

"Your *child*--"

It was always "*your child*" when Cookie had done something stupid or was lally-gagging, as her mother liked to put it. As though the stupid half of Cookie could have nothing to do with Mitzi and everything to do with her father, despite the fact that her father was one of the best lawyers this side of the Mississippi.

"What has Cookie done now?" her father asked with just a gleam of humor in his eyes.

"She's seeing things. Thinks a black car has been following her," Mitzi said, her voice quavering.

But even as her mother spoke, Cookie could sense that this was part melodrama for Cookie's benefit, so that she could see how silly she was being. Yet, Cookie knew Mitzi well enough to know that she was just as worried as Cookie herself.

For the briefest moment, Cookie had seen a glance pass between her parents that spoke of fear, dread. Then her father turned to her and said, "Not to worry, Pumpkin. You go play now."

And just like that, she was released into the wilds of her backyard jungle, albeit with their housekeeper, Beulah, in tow -- into the prettiest jungle in town with its thickets of boxwood, all trimmed into neat little rows, hedging in roses of all kinds, from the peach-colored Austins to the Cherokee Roses. Beds of lilac and penstemon, hydrangea and foxglove bordered the lawn. It was a virtual paradise for birds and butterflies, but especially for little girls who loved to get lost among the flowers.

She'd even made a tepee of sorts out of old grapevines, clematis climbing up the sides. There, as a child, she would sit inside the imaginary tepee with her empty half shell walnut "boat," a johnny jump-up blossom acting as a pretend person seated inside. Then she would set it adrift down a "river" of small pea gravel that she'd absconded from the greenhouse. She'd even made a canopy of "trees" that she had planted along the river made of snapped-off twigs with leaves. She had topped the scene off with a series of log cabins that she'd made with popsicle sticks. Lastly, she'd snuck one of Mitzi's tea towels from the kitchen, the one with wisteria vignettes sewn into it, and placed it in the center, so she could have a place to sit as she moved her village around at will.

Cookie thought of all this as she stared out over the garden remembering that little girl who hadn't changed much in the years that followed. Now, seated inside the greenhouse, her eyes drifted to the newspaper clipping and she read the name of the father who supposedly stole the child: Allister K. Byrd who went by the nickname Byrdy.

Cookie frowned. The woman who had delivered the newspaper had gone by a different name. . . what was it? *Think, think.* She rubbed the dull ache that was beginning to form at her temples then suddenly sat upright and snapped her fingers. *Aberdeen!* That was the name of the woman in the kitchen. Rachel Aberdeen. Was that a maiden name, or had she simply delivered the clipping on behalf of someone else? Cookie didn't know, but she aimed to find out.

But how?

She had just begun to read the rest of the article when she heard a scraping of feet on the walkway and jumped. Deftly, she stuffed the paper back into her boot and peered up, thinking that once again Mitzi had snuck up on her silent feet and caught Cookie unaware. But no, when she peered up, it was into the eyes of her younger sister, Dipsy.

4

THEY WERE SITTING IN LAWN chairs on the grass out back where the sun lay low on the horizon, heralding the nighttime that was just now edging out the sunset. The smell of corn added a sweetness to the air that made Rayleen think about her childhood. Back then, they had followed the crops -- worked for white farmers. Never knew where you'd end up. Once, the five foot by eight foot shack they'd been given was situated so close to a pigsty that they'd all ended up with the runs for weeks. They had finally left that place and its misery for some other poor picker, all of them a good ten pounds lighter. Another time they'd been offered a converted chicken coop as shelter. Her mama had cut an especially large gunny sack in half and had strung it down the middle of the room so that each of them could enjoy a little privacy at night. She recalled the faint glow of candlelight, the smell of tallow, the flickering shadows at night. During the day, they had cooked whatever they could manage to hunt or forage over a wooden fire outside in a large dented pot or on an iron skillet. There was no government assistance back then, just a decade of grinding poverty. Her stomach had been round and ripe from malnutrition. Without thinking, she rubbed her belly.

"You never said why Rachel called the other day," Chester said. The cinnamon flavored toothpick in his mouth scented the air.

Rayleen could never get over the fireflies that danced in her yard this time of year. They were like a thousand twinkling stars lighting up the night sky, filling it with a joy that could come only from nature. People. . . now they were another beast altogether.

"Get a load of this, Chester," she said, waiting until she had his full attention. "Rachel asked if we would take them in."

"Them?" Chester quizzed, the whites of his eyes blazing in the early darkness.

"You know. . ."

All Chester would say was "Hmm." For several moments, they sat in silence, each with their own thoughts. "And what'd you say?" he finally asked.

"What do y'all think I said. Heck no! We been down that road before. I seen that show already and I know how it ends." She wiggled her shoulders for emphasis.

Chester laughed that deep throaty laugh of his. "You are somethin', girl," he said, scratching behind his ear. "Still, I never felt right about all of that."

Silence once again stretched between them. If truth be told, it was Chester with the softer heart. Of course, he didn't get hitched like she did with all the work that come with a soft heart. You learn, soon enough, not to take in more than you can handle. No, she'd done her time. She'd cared for that child, the lot it did for her. But in her quiet moments, in darkness such as this, she would picture that child, feel that tiny hand on her cheek, and she would smile. But just as quickly she would harden to the pain that had come afterward. No, she was right to say no to Rachel. She just hoped Chester could understand and love her anyway.

* * *

"Dipsy?" Cookie stood so fast that she tore her raincoat on the sharp edges of the red Griffith patio chair. There, in the greenhouse, stood her sister, all five-foot-five inches of her, dark hair curling around her shoulders. She was wearing a lime-green paisley, sleeveless dress, nylons and white heels.

"Howdy there, girl," Dipsy said, but upon seeing Cookie in her new "Dalmation" getup, she stopped and frowned. "Oh my gawd, Cookie? Is that *you*?"

"Mitzi," Cookie said by way of explanation.

Dipsy giggled. "Mama finally got to you, huh? She finally turned you into her. You poor thing!"

Cookie glowered, but she couldn't hold it for long. Instead, she gave a nervous laugh, hoping Dipsy hadn't noticed her shove the clipping down her boot.

But Dipsy -- the girl who never missed a thing -- waggled a brow and stared at Cookie, hands on ample hips. "You're looking like you could spit feathers. What's up?"

Dipsy, like Mitzi, was shorter than Cookie and had a bit of pudge around the belly. And, like their mother, she wore the height of fashion, albeit the real stuff, not the homemade version that Mitzi wore. No, Dipsy had married money, as they liked to say here in Montgomery. One had only to look at the three-carat, rose-cut diamond ring on her finger in its platinum setting to see that.

"What a surprise to see you," Cookie said, ignoring Dipsy's comment while giving her sister a polite hug. The smell of gardenia wafted from Dipsy's hair, its color reminding Cookie of the brazil nuts Mitzi served at Christmas time. "What brings you here?"

"Mama's offered to babysit the kids while I get my hair done." Dipsy's deep blue eyes flashed her excitement for a day away from her brood. No doubt it would involve a bit of shopping while in town. Her house was situated on the outskirts east of town where all the old cotton plantations were located. The irony was not lost on Cookie that the polyester Dipsy was wearing had been the downfall of the plantation system.

"Where's Kent?" Cookie asked, picturing Dipsy's tall, thin, moody-looking husband with salt-'n-pepper hair. Dipsy had married up, as they liked to say in the South, which meant he was an older man, a widower with an established career.

Dipsy shrugged. "You know Kent. Always working."

And yet Dipsy's words seemed stilted. It was probably just Cookie's imagination, a hangover from the odd day she was having, what with Rachel, three mimosas, not to mention the strange getup. Clearly, Dipsy's family arrangement worked for her and her husband. In fact, her sister had never seemed happier than when she'd married Kent. Whenever Cookie pictured herself with a man, she envisioned a different relationship, one where they shared responsibility and where they needed fewer material things. Mostly, she just wanted to be happy.

Her thoughts turned to Wilbur, the tow-headed boy who had fawned over her during their teenage years. He spoke in an old man's cadence and had never married. She bet dollars to donuts that he was still a virgin. For years, he had pursued her. Then there was Winn Cowel. Although shy and awkward, he had been her best friend growing up. But Mitzi had thought him not upwardly mobile enough, after having lost his father, and had therefore forbidden their friendship. Instead, Mitzi had pushed her toward Jared. Cookie shuddered at the thought of the man she had almost married to please Mitzi. No, she was happy puttering in the garden and greenhouse, and living in the guest house out back. It gave her enough autonomy to pursue her dual passions: gardening and writing. She sold her houseplants to a local indoor plant store and had experienced some success with her poetry. To her immense surprise, she had finaled in the Snowflake's Poetry Contest, which was an odd name for a poetry contest considering Montgomery hadn't seen snow in years, if ever.

On a whim, Dipsy said, "Why don't you come with me while I get my hair done?"

"Huh?" Cookie asked, not sure she'd heard right. After all, Dipsy never invited Cookie to go anywhere with her in public.

"It'll be fun. Just us two. We could even get our nails done afterward." Dipsy cocked her head as though hopeful.

Normally, Cookie would have said no. Especially since she wanted to do some digging to find out more about Rachel, and the best place to do that was in the study where all of their family's personal documents were kept. Perhaps this Rachel person had something to do with one of her father's old cases. Should Cookie show the clipping to him? She bit her lip, recalling the fear on the woman's face and the admonition to keep it to herself. No, maybe Cookie should do as Rachel asked, for now. No use causing a stir when this could be nothing, just some crazy down-and-out woman needing attention. *Then why did Mitzi faint when she saw Rachel?*

Dipsy snapped her fingers in Cookie's face as Cookie's thoughts drifted further afield. "Cookie? Are you listening to me? Do you want to come with me to get my hair done or not?"

Cookie hesitated. Seeing her sister's forlorn expression, Cookie said, "Tell you what. Give me twenty minutes, then I'm all yours." Her father was meeting with a rare Sunday morning client and shouldn't be back for at least an hour. It wouldn't hurt to take a few minutes to see if this was indeed one of her father's old cases. And the best place to search was his filing cabinet. If for some reason he came home early, she could always say she was looking for her birth certificate, which wasn't far off, as it was high time she got a driver's licence, and she would need it when she did.

* * *

Funny how seldom Cookie had ever entered her father's study, which had become an extension of his work life, and as such was considered private. A sanctuary, of sorts. Normally, she loved the smell of cherry tobacco, the walls lined with bookshelves, law books intermingling with rare antiquarian books, her favorite being those with gilt edges, or better still, those with fore-edge painting like the one of a clipper ship. As a child, she had asked to see it over and over. On the rare occasion that her father had given in, he had worn white cotton gloves, giving the viewing a ceremonial feel. She had never forgotten the anticipation, the childish delight, and had vowed one day that she, too, would have such a rare and beautiful book. Perhaps it was that which had begun her love of books.

For the next ten minutes, she plowed through files, finding nothing. She was about to give up when she discovered a manila envelope thrust to the side. She peered inside and saw the words "Shardsburg" written on a deed. She glanced at it, then quickly tucked it in her boot along with the news clipping. To be safe, she found her birth certificate and was just about to close the file drawer when she heard a rustle and turned.

"What are you doin' in my study, darlin'?" her father asked, his filled pipe cradled in the palm of his hand.

Cookie jumped, nearly slamming her hand in the drawer in the process. What was her father doing home early? "I-I needed my birth certificate," she stammered. As if to prove her point, she quickly snatched it up to show him.

"What for?" he asked, entering the room and propping himself on the huge oak desktop, his eyes scanning the room lined with books on history and law, business and architecture, as if to assure himself that they were all still there.

Cookie shoved the drawer of the file cabinet closed, birth certificate in hand. "I thought I would finally learn to drive," she said, wishing she already knew how.

"Well, now, that's mighty enterprisin' of you, young lady," he said, tweed patches on the elbow of his suit making him seem especially professorial today. "Still, you should have asked me before going through my files. I have client files in there and they're private. Understand?"

Cookie felt the weight of his displeasure and nodded, her

eyes on the oak tongue-and-groove flooring.

Ebie lifted her chin, scrutinizing her, then gave a short laugh. "Glad to see you finally taking the initiative to get your driver's license. Can't always count on Beulah to drive you. She's gettin' up there in age, you know."

Beulah was a short, heavyset little powerhouse who did everything for the family: housekeeper, babysitter, grocery shopper, and errand runner. And when Cookie was in a pickle, she was her driver too. To Cookie, the stalwart woman, who often wore a black dress that matched her skin, and a ruffled white apron, was as much a part of the family as every other member, only she had a family of her own. Cookie had been to her house a handful of times when Beulah had stopped amid errands to check on a sick child or to drop something off at home. It had always come with the promise that they would "keep this to ourselves." Beulah had finished it up with a treat. An ice cream cone or a penny candy. Back then, Cookie hadn't recognized it for what it was -- a bribe to win her silence. But Beulah needn't have worried. Cookie loved Beulah and had thought of her like a second mother, despite the difference in their skin color.

Fortunately for Cookie, Beulah popped her head through the doorway of the study at that precise moment and saved her from having to answer any further questions from her father. "Oh, there you are, Cookie! Dipsy's waiting on you and she's fit to be tied."

"Sorry, Daddy! Gotta run!" Cookie inhaled the sweet scent of Old Spice as she gave him a quick peck on the cheek.

As she was about to leave the room, she bobbed her head to Beulah, who recognized it as her thanks for rescuing Cookie from an awkward situation as she had so many times over the years. Beulah just shook her head and raised a brow, her shoulder-length hair ironed into a neat little bob.

"Wait!" Cookie's father called after her. "Who's going to teach you to drive?"

Cookie stopped her exit, considering. "Beulah will teach me."

"What?" Beulah hissed, grabbing her arm. "Are you crazy, girl? I can't teach you to drive!"

"Sure you can," Cookie whispered in return. Then to her father she said, "We'll be fine!"

Beulah clucked her disapproval as she followed Cookie down the hallway. When Cookie turned to Beulah, the woman nearly ran into her, Cookie had stopped so fast. "Tell Dipsy I'll be a minute. I have to use the bathroom."

"She ain't goin' to want to hear that," Beulah admonished, still shaking her head and clucking.

"Just tell her. . . *please!*" Cookie added, sheepishly.

Then she made a detour to the bathroom with its honeycombed shaped cream-colored subway tile on the floor bordered by pink ceramic tile on the walls. Once there, she unfolded the deed. It was yellowed with age and had tears at the edges, but what had attracted her to it in the first place was the geographical name heading the deed and the property therein. *Shardsburg.* The word sent a shiver of excitement racing up Cookie's arms. Attached to it was another document, a sharecropper's document.

The name on it?

She had to sit down before her knees buckled, the porcelain throne the only seat available.

Allister K. Byrd, aka Byrdie.

Before she had time to process what she'd read, a loud rapping on the hardwood door sent her scrambling. She stuffed the document back into her boot and pretended to flush the toilet.

"Just finishing up," she yelled.

"Hurry! I'll miss my hair appointment," Dipsy called. "Fran promised to do your nails."

Inwardly, Cookie groaned. Fran wore one of those updos, the kind with all the frou-frou that made even a good-looking woman look like a wedding cake, tiers and all. She loved nothing more than the color pink and to add "sparklies," as she liked to call the glitter that she sprinkled liberally on clients' nails.

Can this day get any worse?

It was bad enough her mother had put her hair up in a beehive. At least that was a modern hairstyle. She closed her eyes and cursed, then yelled, "Coming!" She took one last look at herself in the mirror and, to her surprise, smiled. She looked like one of those go-go dancers out of Hollywood. That should win her the right man, all right.

Dipsy nearly fell into the bathroom when Cookie opened the door. "You going to keep that raincoat on in public?" Dipsy demanded pointing out the rip in the back and the fact that the entire thing now looked like a see-through wedding train trailing the floor.

"Oh, right," Cookie said, lifting it over her head, glad to be free of it. She felt like she'd been wrapped in a shower curtain.

In one day, she, who never did anything to write home about, had hidden a newspaper clipping in her boot and stuffed a deed in there too. And now, horror of all horrors, she was about to get her nails done too.

Twenty minutes later, they pulled up to Daisy's Dos in

Dipsy's big black Buick with pecan-colored leather seats. Cookie was about to get out of the car when Dipsy stopped her. "Wait," she said, grabbing Cookie's arm. "Before we go in, I have something to tell you."

Cookie paused to take stock of her sister, her expression. . . what? Desperate, maybe. "I thought you were in an all-fired hurry to get here, rushing me out of the bathroom and all!"

"I know," Dipsy said, refusing to look Cookie in the eye.

Cookie had never seen her sister like this. . . Dipsy who was always the sunny one, the life of the party, the perfect hostess -- "hostess with the mostest," as Cookie called her in private.

"It's just that. . ." Dipsy gulped.

This *must* be serious if *Dipsy* was at a loss for words. Cookie frowned. "Whatever it is, you can tell me," Cookie said.

For all of Cookie's faults -- and there were many, like the fact that she felt comfortable amid clutter, or didn't care that she fit into "perfect" society, or wasn't good with money -- she loved her sister. And Beulah. And Mitzi and her father.

"Okay," Dipsy said tentatively. "Here goes." She took a deep breath. "Kent left me."

Cookie sat stock still as she absorbed what her sister had said, the shock of Dipsy's words leaving her breathless. "Have you told Mama?" They both knew this was serious if Cookie had called Mitzi mama.

"No. I'm working up the courage. I thought maybe getting my hair done and going shopping. . ." She burst out crying, the "ugly" cry, not the polite little girly cry that she used when trying to win Mitzi's favor.

"Oh, gawd, Dipsy. You don't go spending money when

you're about to get divorced. Even *I* know that and I'm no good with money!"

That only made Dipsy cry louder and harder, her eyes swelling, her lips pushed out in a pout.

"It's okay, honey," Cookie said, wrapping her sister in her arms. "I can help. With the kids. Whatever you need." But Dipsy was howling now. If Cookie was any more helpful, they'd have the cops at their car door wondering what was going on. "There, there," she said, patting Dipsy on the back. "We'll get your hair done, then I'll take you out for an ice cream. I'm sure there's some way to fix this. You just have to have faith."

But Dipsy's bawling had started to draw the attention of passersby -- a mother and her baby, and a middle-aged man in a bowler hat. After some minutes, the sobbing subsided and Dipsy said, "Do you really think so?"

Cookie clasped her sister's hand and said, "I know so. In fact," she added, "I have just the thing for you and I know where to get it."

5

FRANTIC, MITZI RUMMAGED THROUGH THE stack of papers she kept hidden in the upper drawer of her chifforobe. Her fingers touched the frayed edges of the yellowed envelope. *Rachel Aberdeen.* For years, that letter had nagged at her subconscious, had filled her nighttime dreams, had left her with guilt for something that in her heart of hearts she knew was a right decision. Right for her, right for the Williams family, and right for Cookie. But had it been right for Cookie's biological mother? That's the question Mitzi had never been able to answer. Had her own happiness superseded Rachel Aberdeen's?

Well, despite Ebie's determination to keep his head in the sand and pretend the woman didn't exist, Mitzi had gone on offense from day one. *She* had kept track of the woman's whereabouts. And come hell or high water, she *was* going to speak with Rachel. Mitzi pulled out the list of the many places the woman had gone since leaving Shardsburg and the number of the private investigator Mitzi had used to locate Rachel over the years. Guilt pressed in on her for having lied to Cookie about the business card, but it couldn't be helped. Too much rested on keeping the private investigator a secret. Fortunately, Mitzi had followed her mother's wise advice and had kept a bank account of her own so that Ebie would never know she had hired the P.I. It was the only major secret she had kept from her husband over the years.

Nervous, she marched over to the bed and sat on the chenille bedspread. With reluctance, she lifted the receiver of the phone that sat on the nightstand and dialed. Her heart thrummed in her chest as she listened to the rings. One. Two. Three. She was just about to hang up when a woman's breathless voice came over the phone.

"What?"

The woman's rudeness shocked Mitzi into silence. From out of the upper story window, Mitzi saw Ebie leave the house wearing his suit and appearing focused. *What's this all about?* Ebie always told her when he was leaving the house. She frowned as she watched him march down the sidewalk.

"Yoo-hoo! Is anyone there?" The woman on the other end of the line tapped the phone.

"Yes, yes," Mitzi said, feeling harried. "I was looking for Rachel. . . Rachel Aberdeen?"

"She's moved," the woman said then yelled at the children making noise in the background.

"Do you know where she went?" Mitzi twirled the phone cord that had twisted together at each end.

"Do I look like her keeper?" the woman asked, now snarling

at a man in the background who seemed to have lost his watch.

"No, of course not, but I need to find her--"

The other woman cut her off with a curt, "Well, good luck with that. I have problems of my own." With that, the phone went dead. For several minutes, Mitzi sat there, listening to the dial tone. Rachel Aberdeen was gone. But gone where? On a sigh, Mitzi pulled out the number of the private investigator. Time for reinforcement.

* * *

Maximillian Frye had always wondered why the great E. B. Haines had chosen him as his personal lawyer, a man who could try his own cases, should he need to. A man who could have asked one of the partners in his firm to handle any need he might have. Yet, he had more than a suspicion *why* E. B. had chosen him.

He peered up at his black Howard Miller banjo-shaped Dorchester clock that stood next to his built-in bookcase and checked it against his watch. E.B. Haines was never late. Never. Something must have kept him. Max buzzed his secretary.

"Jane?"

"Mr. Haines is here," she said, before he could get a word in edgewise. Sometimes Max could swear the woman was psychic.

"Good, send him in."

Seconds later, the door opened to Ebie Haines who stood next to his secretary, Jane, her hair in a stylish flip and wearing a pencil skirt and high heels. She held a file in her hand, which she handed to Ebie before turning and shutting the door behind her. An uncomfortable silence ensued, but only for a moment, as

Ebie had obviously long since learned that the best way to garner information from his clients was to play the "aw-shucks" card. Show 'em the down-home side of a good Southern gentleman.

Max stood and came around the large mahogany table to shake the lawyer's hand. "How are you doing? To what do I owe the visit?"

Ebie had been very mysterious when he called earlier that day, refusing to give a reason for their talk over the phone. "I'll tell you when I get there," he had said.

Now, seeing the ashen face of the tall, lean lawyer who had always seemed larger than life, he wondered anew what had brought him here.

"So, Ebie, take a seat," Max said, offering him the Arts and Crafts style chair with its buttercream leather seat. "What brings you here today?" He took a seat opposite Ebie.

"Well, Max--" Ebie hesitated, hands steepled on the table, as though deciding how much to tell the lawyer. "I have a bit of a dilemma."

"Oh?" Max knew not to push.

"Yes. It has to do with Cookie."

"The adoption?"

Ebie nodded.

"It's a little too late to un-adopt her," Max said with a grin, trying to lighten the conversation, but the normally jovial Ebie didn't bite. Max knew Cookie had been a handful, what with her independent streak and her unwillingness to act like a proper Southern belle. "Is there a problem?"

On his right hand, Ebie tapped each finger with a thumb, a nervous gesture if ever there was one. His eyes appeared sunken, as though he hadn't slept well. He tapped the file and then pushed it toward Max who already knew what was in it. He had been Ebie's lawyer for years -- soon after Ebie and Mitzi had married. In fact, it had started with the adoption.

"Max, I need your word, your absolute *word*, that what we say here is confidential."

Max froze at the words. No one, but no one, needed that kind of guarantee except someone who had done something unlawful. And the very last person on earth he would suspect of that was Ebie. There wasn't a more honest man around.

"You have my word." Max used a hushed tone, hoping to instill confidence.

"I may not have told you the entire truth about the adoption." Until now, Ebie hadn't looked Max in the eye, but at that announcement, he peered up, his brown eyes never wavering.

"How so?" Max leaned away from the table as if to lend distance, when what he really needed was a moment to process what he'd just heard. The beginning of a confession. From the most decent person he knew.

"She wasn't the Williams' baby."

Max let out a long, slow breath. In some ways, that absolved him of guilt. The Williams were colored. He had always guessed that to be the reason Ebie had chosen him to act as his counsel, rather than one of his colleagues. The story behind the adoption had been a sordid one. A Negro daughter, a white boy, the baby white. Keeping it would never fly in the white *or* colored community. It had been the only sensible choice. . . for a childless white woman to keep the child. To raise it as her own. But even so, it was dangerous. . . for the child, for the Haineses, and for Max. For all their sakes, the secret had been kept. But now. . .

"Whose baby was she?" he asked, leaning forward.

Twenty minutes later, Max stood at the window, watching Ebie leave and wondering how a man could carry a secret for that many years without anyone finding out. But more than that, he wondered what it did to a man to have to carry it. Well, whatever the consequences, he knew one thing for sure. Ebie was a good man. An honorable man, who'd faced a dilemma and had chosen the only option he could. The one that had saved two lives, maybe three.

6

IN COOKIE'S FAMILY, THE WORD divorce was spoken in the same tone one might reserve for cholera or mumps. It was a disease best left for other families, not theirs. So for Dipsy, the traditionalist of the family, to even suggest such a thing was dire indeed. No, to Delphinia Josephine Haines, who was nicknamed Dipsy after she'd fallen in the Tallapoosa River and Cookie had dived in to rescue her, divorce was not an option. For months after the river incident, five-year-old Dipsy would howl at the sight of any water, baths included. It had caused Beulah no end of grief.

"What will I do?" Dipsy asked amid tears as they sat out front of the Daisy Do Beauty Parlor in the black Buick. "And with a baby on the way!" She began bawling again in earnest.

"Are you sure the marriage is over?" Cookie asked. "I mean, have you given reconciliation a try? Marriage counseling?"

"Oh, gawd, Cookie." Dipsy reeled backward in her seat, as if to physically remove herself from the very suggestion. "Mama would have a fit if I went to counseling. She'd be the laughingstock of the DAR. I could never do that to her. . . to Kent."

The weight that had sat on Cookie's chest ever since she'd first learned about Dipsy's plight lightened. "Okay, then why don't you give it time. Think of this as temporary until you work things through."

"You think so?" Dipsy sniffed back tears.

"Definitely."

Dipsy sat in silence for a moment, then peered up at Cookie, her makeup smudged. "You're so lucky."

"What do you mean?" Cookie asked, puzzled.

Dipsy hemmed and hawed, then finally blurted out, "Well, you have a career, talent. I always feel so. . . so inadequate compared to you. You're so brave. You don't care what people think of you. You do what makes you happy. I. . . well, I'm *Mama*." She started blubbering again.

"You're not Mitzi," Cookie chided. "You're just finding your way, that's all. We all are. Heck, I feel inadequate compared to *you!*"

"You do?" Dipsy said, pausing to blow her nose which had turned a healthy shade of red.

Cookie nodded furiously. At least Dipsy had the guts to tell Cookie about her trials, while Cookie had yet to say a thing about hers. "Of course. We always want to be what we're not," she said, placing a hand on Dipsy's shoulder. "That's why each of us marries. To find the person that takes up the slack for our inequities."

Dipsy laughed. "When did you get so smart?"

"I'm not. Far from it. That's why I'm so damn humble!"

They both laughed and then put their foreheads together as they had as children when they were having a hard time.

"So, what are you going to do?" Cookie asked.

Dipsy shrugged. "Stay with Mama and Daddy for a while until I figure things out."

"But Dipsy," Cookie said, clasping Dipsy's hand between hers, "don't give up just yet. You owe it to your family and to this little one," she said, patting Dipsy on the tummy, "to try. Okay? Then if it doesn't work out, I'll be behind you, 120-percent, okay?"

"Okay," Dipsy said, dabbing at her nose. "I will."

Leaning across the seat of the black Buick with its brown leather interior, Cookie threw an arm around her sister. They were beginning to attract attention inside the Daisy Do. Through the windshield, Cookie could see Fran with her cake-like "do" bobbing her head back and forth between the large white letters of the establishment.

"Looks like we have company," Cookie muttered beneath her breath.

"I guess we can't keep them waiting much longer," Dipsy agreed. "We're already ten minutes late for our appointment."

Cookie, who had always been the instigator of the bunch, according to Mitzi, had an idea. A wonderfully awful idea.

"Hey, Sis, what do you say we blow this beauty salon?"

"W-what?" Dipsy blubbered. "We can't do that! We have appointments. Commitments."

"Sure we can," Cookie said. "I'll send our beauty operators a check and you can reschedule. Let's go get us a pistachio nut ice cream cone with a cherry on top! We can take it down by the river and throw sticks like we did when we were kids."

Dipsy frowned. Then a slow smile formed on Dipsy's face. Suddenly, she plugged the key into the ignition and fired up the Buick, putting it into reverse. A big puff of smoke bellowed out of the tailpipe as she put it into drive, Cookie howling her approval.

Twenty minutes later, ice creams in hand, Cookie watched the water flow by as they walked along the waterfront. She thought of all the times they had snuck out as children, Dipsy complaining the whole way that they were going to get in trouble if Mitzi caught them. But still she came.

Their pace slowed as they rounded the bend. Cookie could see the bridge arcing out over the wide, calm, Alabama River, born out of the Coosa and Tallapoosa Rivers. The breeze smelled of wet and rotted wood, of moist sand and the knobby-kneed Cypress trees that lined the riverbanks. But mostly, it smelled of her childhood. Of freedom.

"Dipsy," Cookie said, stopping and turning to her sister. "I have something to show you, but first I need to find what I came here for."

"What?" Dipsy asked, a puzzled expression on her face.

Cookie laughed, because Dipsy had a dollop of green pistachio nut ice cream on her nose. Cookie pulled a tissue from her pocket. "Hold still," she said, licking the tissue as she had seen her mother do countless times, then dabbing at the ice cream on Dipsy's nose.

"That is so gross!" Dipsy said, but giggled.

Once Dipsy was cleaned up, Cookie took hold of her sister's arm and dragged her to a spot along the riverbank where she snapped off a twig from a tree with round leaves, serrated at the edges. She handed it to Dipsy. "Here!" she said.

"What is this?" Dipsy asked, scrunching up her nose with distaste.

"Hazel, for reconciliation. Maybe it will bring you luck. . . with Kent." Cookie held the sprig out to Dipsy, who stared at it a moment, then accepted it, depositing it in her handbag. "Now, let's go eat our ice cream." Cookie herded Dipsy to a bench at the top of the bank, surrounded by potted geraniums and a wide lawn. For a few moments, they sat in silence, until Cookie could stand it no longer. She turned to Dipsy and said, "Now, I have something to tell *you*."

"Mmm?" Dipsy said as she dug through her purse and pulled out a shiny silver tube. She opened it and applied a pale shade of lip gloss to her lips.

Cookie reached into her dotted plastic boot and pulled out the yellowed newspaper clipping, unfolding it as she went. "A woman stopped by today. From Shardsburg."

"Oh?" Dipsy said, her mind obviously elsewhere.

"She gave me this. Told me not to tell Mitzi or Ebie." She held the paper out for her sister and watched as Dipsy leaned in to read the news article.

"Stolen baby?" she said, shaking her head in confusion. "I don't get it."

"Look at the baby's birth date." Cookie pointed to a spot on the paper.

"June 1930. So?"

Dipsy, who could be a bit dense at times, stared wide-eyed, a comical expression on her face, part pygmy owl, part river otter.

"The child was a toddler. *I* would have been a toddler then," Cookie hissed.

"You think *you* were the stolen baby?" Dipsy read on. "And

you think you were stolen by this Byrdie guy?"

Cookie shrugged. "I don't know, but I was looking through Daddy's files and found this." She dug into her bra and pulled out the sharecroppers deed.

"My, my! Aren't you full of surprises," Dipsy said, still not getting the full implication of what Cookie was saying.

"Read the location on the deed." Cookie tapped at the yellowed papers that were tattered with age. For years Cookie had known Ebie owned properties up and down the valley, but this was the first time she had heard of him owning property in this particular location.

"Shardsburg!" Dipsy's eyes darted to Cookie.

"Now read the person's name on the document."

Dipsy frowned, her eyes quickly scanning the document before suddenly alighting on one particular spot. She gasped. "It's daddy's name."

"Not that one." Cookie scrolled her finger down to another name. To Byrd's name.

Dipsy dropped her cone to the ground, her purse falling open onto the bench seat, makeup scattering everywhere. Just then, a huge yellow lab came running over, its owner chasing it and calling, "Stop, Chick. Down, boy!"

But the lab merely ignored its owner as it gulped down the ice cream cone in three quick bites. Then he jumped up with his front paws, licking at Dipsy's face as she struggled to push him off her, all the while laughing.

"Cookie?"

Cookie looked up in time to see Winston Cowel, tall, thin, and gangly with dark hair and a smile that made her forget all about her ice cream cone. Winn. She had known him since grade school, had been there when he skinned his knees playing dodgeball, had watched him grow from a shy young boy to a strapping young man who took his role as head of the household seriously after his father died. Better yet, he was just about the only person she knew who had a thumb as green as hers.

"I'm so sorry," the young man said, panting and gulping air as he grabbed the dog and placed it on a leash. "I'm trying to teach him manners and haven't been too successful so far. Here, let me buy you a new cone." He reached in and handed Dipsy a ten dollar bill, a ridiculous amount for the lost cone.

"No, no! I shouldn't have been eating it anyway," Dipsy said with a sigh. It seemed that she was forever on a diet.

"You keep it," Winn said, still admonishing the dog for his misdeeds. "For damages done." He tossed the money toward Dipsy's purse, then winked at Cookie. He turned around and left before either Dipsy or Cookie could say a thing.

For a moment, Cookie sat in silence, her thoughts on Winn. She had adored him from the first time she met him. She had always wondered what would have become of their friendship if Mitzi hadn't intervened -- talked her into marrying... She closed her eyes, refusing to think of that awful man at a time like this. Instead, she opened her eyes and turned to Dipsy, who was still mulling over what Cookie had shown her, the name on the deed -- the same Byrd from the clipping.

"So you think maybe this story in the article has something to do with you?"

Cookie nodded.

"What are you going to do?"

Cookie shrugged. "I don't know. Go on with my life, I guess."

"You can't!" Dipsy cried, taking Cookie's hand in hers. "You have to go to Shardsburg. I mean, for goodness sake, what if you are the stolen baby."

"I'm sure I'm not. I mean, what are the odds?" She licked at her cone, savoring the taste. "Still, it's all a little weird, the article, the deed. The woman telling me not to say anything to Momma or Daddy. But *Shardsburg?*" Cookie shook her head, her eyes trailing Winn and his big yellow lab, Chick. "I've got plants to water. I have deliveries to make. Deadlines to meet." Besides, she wasn't sure she *wanted* to know about the past. She liked being Cookie Haines. She liked being Dipsy's sister. But most of all, what would it mean for Cookie if she wasn't who she thought she was? What then? She shuddered at the thought.

Dipsy squeezed Cookie's fingers. "You *have* to go." Then to sweeten the pot, she said, "And I'm coming with you. Besides, Mitzi is always complaining she never gets enough time with the grandkids. Now she can. It'll be fun!" But just as suddenly as she'd lit up, a shadow from a scuttling cloud crossed her face and the worry returned. "I do need to get some loose ends wrapped up at home first, but I can go in July. Besides, it will get my mind off Kent while I figure out what to do. . . if we're not back together by then," she added, her words hopeful. She grabbed Cookie's sleeve. "*Please!* Before we go, we can do research at the library on our way home."

Cookie heard the wheedling tone in her sister's voice and cringed because she could never say no to her sister. And now, seeing tears start to form in her sister's eyes as she no doubt thought of Kent, their unborn baby, and their possible failed marriage, she breathed a sigh. Still, *Shardsburg. . .?* She wasn't sure she was ready for what she might find. And yet how could she not go?

She groaned. "How about we compromise. I'll go with you to the library, then we'll see what's what," she murmured as she stared out over the glistening rush of river that hid snags that could suck a swimmer under its steely waters. And perhaps that's what she feared most. That by going to Shardsburg, she would be sucked into a life not of her design. And yet she would never know unless she went. She just hoped that whatever she found didn't destroy her.

7

COOKIE FELT THE FAMILIAR EXCITEMENT settle in her chest as the Cooke County Library came into view with its red brick facade, narrow lawn, and row of azaleas in front. As a child, she had thought the library was named after her, and her mother had been too kind to explain to her that it was named after a wealthy industrialist instead. Much of her childhood had been spent at the library, looking up the care and feeding of houseplants. She had scoured through books, preferring glossy-paged ones with photographs. Even now, she could recall pouring over books with plants such as the iron cross with its hairy leaves -- a large cross in the middle of each leaf. The *aphelandra*, or Zebra plant, with its green and white foliage and large yellow bracts with red stamens shooting from each corner of the bract. The *ficus benjamina* or weeping fig with its ovate leaves that fairly danced off their stems.

Her endeavors, which had their roots in the books she had discovered in the library, had found their way into her garden, like the arbor she had talked Mitzi into having built. Cookie had planted a wisteria vine to grow up the arbor, which had grown so unwieldy that the blooms, even now, hung in lush lavender cones of fragrance. From the legume family, the wisteria's tendrils clung to the arbor while its lacy leaves reached skyward, forever searching for the light. Just the thought of everything she had gained by coming to the library each week had her humming. Cookie wrapped her arm around Dipsy's as they entered the library, the smell of books comforting, like the smell of warm baked bread in the morning, or the feel of an old worn sweater that had seen its owner through hard times. The smell of books instantly shed any worries that she had harbored. Just as the greenhouse was her church, the library was her home. Each gave her a sense of belonging, of existing, as if here, in these places, she was known.

"What have we here?" said Pearl Laugherty, the only black librarian in the state, who had recognized in young Cookie a burning thirst for knowledge. Through the years, Pearl had plied Cookie with books, understanding instinctively what interested her, what did not. It was as though she'd seen into Cookie's soul and understood her intuitively.

Pearl removed her reading glasses that were held around her neck by a seed-pearl chain. Little red indentations dug into the side of her nose where her glasses had been, and her small brown eyes appeared myopic without the familiar lenses. Her newly graying hair kinked tight to her head, while her face was jowly and sagged with age, but to Cookie, she was the angel who had rescued her from a life of boredom. Who had seen Cookie's thirst for knowledge not as unbecoming a Southern woman, but as a beacon in the darkness of an otherwise drab life for women who were expected to become wife, mother, housekeeper, helpmate. Who had been pigeonholed since birth by their very sex. Who, like children, were to be seen and not heard.

As if she were a mind reader and recognized Cookie's need for comfort, Pearl grabbed Cookie up in a bearhug, then did the same to Dipsy, who squirmed and made faces at Cookie over Pearl's shoulder. Cookie couldn't help but laugh.

When Pearl was through hugging Dipsy, she pushed her away and looked her up and down. "Why, aren't you a sight, Miss Dipsy. I haven't seen you here since you were knee-high to a tadpole. Where've you been?"

Dipsy stammered. "Well, I married--"

"That Kent fellow, I heard," Pearl said, clearly having kept up with the goings-on around town. "And I see you're with child. Three months?"

"How did you know?" Dipsy said, her eyes clicking over to Cookie's in amazement.

"I've had a few of my own, Miss Dipsy. Eight, to be exact. I know when a woman is with child. Besides, I can see it in your face. You glow like a lightning bug." She patted Dipsy's baby bump and said, "Wait! I have just the book for you." She disappeared behind a long row of books and reappeared a few minutes later with a musty smelling paperback that had taken on the odor of smoke from a former reader's home. "Sorry about the smell, Miss Dipsy, but this here's the best book on raising a child."

Dipsy scoured through the text, then said, "Could I put the book on your card, Cookie?"

"Why, sure," Cookie said. "By the way, Miss Pearl, do you have anything on the Haines genealogy? Or anything about Shardsburg in the early 30s? Where should we start? Journals, census records, maybe?"

"Let me take a gander through my Fiche files." The librarian turned and strode to the bank of files inside the oak file drawers with gold slide handles, then to the Fiche files behind the counter. It took her no more than a few minutes before she was off to search for books or manuscripts in the archives section. Moments later, she returned with a large musty pebble-bound book and handed it to Cookie.

Just then the door swished open and Henrietta Willoughby entered in a pale blue A-line dress, her hair done up in a chiffon. Although only a year older than Cookie, Henrietta acted more like her mother, Ginger. Snooty. Normally, Cookie would have laughed at the comparison. But in that brief moment, it was as if a subtle shift had occurred, as though Henrietta had brought a breath of cold air in with her, for Pearl stepped back, her face suddenly a mask of indifference.

"Ms. Willoughby." Pearl plastered a fake smile on her face as did Henrietta, the youngest to ever head the garden club, a very exclusive club that allowed in only well-heeled white women. No Jews or Blacks need apply. For that very reason, Cookie had refused to join.

"Pearl?"

For a few moments, the two women stood like two prizefighters gauging their opponent. Pearl was the first to look away. Cookie noted just a trace of gratification from Henrietta, an ever so slight upward tilt of her chin, her eyes narrowing to two self-satisfied slits.

Henrietta turned to Cookie. "So, Cookie, Mitzi tells me you would be a great fit for our garden club. Your mother's clearly not aware of our standards, but we could help you with that."

Heat rushed up Cookie's face so fast that she feared she would need a hose to put out the flames. She stuttered and stammered a weak retort, speed never her strong suit.

"What my sister is trying to say," Dipsy said, linking arms with Cookie, "is that she's *so* busy with her greenhouse that she couldn't possibly find the time."

"But we could help you with your business." Henrietta leaned in closer as if to impart some monumental piece of wisdom. "We *know* people. I mean *really* know people," she added with a lifted brow in reference to Cookie's failed walk to the altar.

"No thanks," Dipsy said in such a cheery voice that even Henrietta had no comeback for that. "Besides, my sister and I are about to embark on an adventure. Very hush-hush!"

"Ooh!" Henrietta squealed, her face so close to Dipsy's now that Cookie could smell the cinnamon from her toothpaste. "Anything *I* should know?"

The woman winked. *Winked!* Cookie willed herself not to laugh.

"Sorry! State secret!" Dipsy said, sealing her lips in a zipping motion and throwing away the key.

Henrietta pursed her ruby red lips into a tight straight line then looked down to the heavy tome Cookie held in her hands. "Census records? Looking for anything in particular?"

Cookie shared a harried look with Dipsy whose eyes made it clear she should walk lightly where Henrietta was concerned. For years, Henrietta had been Cookie's nemesis, the proverbial fly in Cookie's ointment. Always trying to best her in everything she did. Cookie had never understood what drove Henrietta to target her. She just knew that when the wedding had been called off, Henrietta had been the first to tell all of Cookie's friends, to plant the seed that her family had known that Jared was a bigamist but hadn't told Cookie because they'd been afraid she would become an old maid. Better to have her married off to a bigamist than that. And yet Cookie knew Henrietta was lying. Knew Cookie's parents wanted only the best for her. But like chokeweed, in Cookie's lowest moments, her worries would grow and she would wonder.

No. Henrietta's wrong! None of us knew.

"Well, let's just hope you're in that census, because you sure don't look like the rest of your family," she said with a short burst of derisive laughter.

At the suggestion, Cookie nearly dropped the book she was holding. Although she had never questioned Mitzi openly, it had bothered Cookie that there were no pictures of her before age four. What mother didn't keep photographs of her firstborn child? Her mother had chalked it up to a flood in the basement, and yet Dipsy's baby pictures had all survived the flood. Besides, who kept *all* of a child's photos in the basement? It had made her feel invisible somehow. Unwanted.

"Maybe we should look up *your* records," Dipsy said in challenge.

"Wha--? N. . . no!" Henrietta stammered, hand over her heart. "Why, I never!" She was so beside herself and befuddled that she left without ever looking for a book. Once the door had closed behind her, all three women burst out laughing.

"State secret?" Cookie said, turning on her sister with a gale of laughter, tears forming in her eyes. "Where on earth did you come up with *that* one?"

"Hey, women like her just want to feel important. Now she does. Plus, you'll be the talk of the town. Every Tom, Dick, and Harry is going to want to buy your plants now without you ever needing to join her silly club. But first, we've got some research to do!"

For the next hour, they poured over book upon book, starting with the census rolls. Cookie searched until she found her name.

"See, there you are," Dipsy said, her chin bobbing up and down in confirmation. "1940. Daddy, Mama, you and me. We're all there. And Henrietta's full of it. You do too look like us... well, Daddy, leastways!"

"So that's a dead end," Cookie said. "Except that the census is ten years after I was born, so it really doesn't *prove* anything. Let's keep looking." She was beginning to lose all hope that they would ever find anything about Shardsburg and the baby when Pearl dusted off a particularly old, particularly musty smelling book that made Cookie sneeze. "What is it?" she demanded, scanning the title dubiously, "*My Year as a Sharecropper, A New Form of Slavery.*"

"Look where it's from," said Pearl, pointing over Cookie's shoulder as she read the nameplate of the autobiography.

Beneath the name Franny Whiteside, a name Cookie had never heard, were the words, *Shardsburg, Alabama.* "Well, at least it's something." By the look of things, Shardsburg was a small town back then. According to the written account, it consisted of a clapboard store with a wooden porch and porch rails, two stories. The owner of the store lived on the second story. It also had a small gas station and a church. Not even a bank.

That is small!

She read the words aloud to the pair. "'A train ran behind the store on raised tracks.'" But as far as Cookie could tell, the town had no train depot. The nearest city was Birmingham. Mostly, the town was set up for sharecroppers and landowners, according to what Cookie had read so far. "'Typically, in a town such as this, the person who owned the land also owned everything else in town.'"

"So does this mean that Daddy owned the store and gas station in Shardsburg?" Dipsy asked Cookie, her dark brows set in a frown.

"I have no idea," said Cookie, and yet something about the place seemed familiar.

"You ought to find out, don't you think, Miss Cookie?" Pearl said.

Cookie read on. "'Because of the distance to the nearest city, sharecroppers would often be forced to buy their seed, their tools, and their food from the landowner, the cost placed on a tab to be added to the bill at the end of the season. As for the use of the land itself, sharecroppers paid by giving the landowner a portion of their crops, the exact percentage and price set well before the crops were ever planted. Due to poor weather or insects, the land seldom produced enough to pay back the cost of production.'"

"Tsk, tsk," Pearl said, shaking her head behind Cookie.

Cookie continued to flip through the pages, not sure what to think anymore. As she passed a page, something caught her eye. She turned back one page and skimmed down with her finger until she saw what had interested her. "'Byrdie and his wife Rachel are said to be bereft at the loss of their missing child.'"

A direct quote attributed to the Charlottesville Newspaper. But as Cookie read on, she saw that Franny Whiteside had added a word or two about the incident. "'For a couple worried about their stolen child, they sure skipped town awful fast, and both in different directions. Folks around these parts wonder if there wasn't some hanky panky going on. Many 'round here wonder if the child's even alive. But we all keep our mouths shut. No use stirrin' up a hornet's nest.'"

Cookie turned to Dipsy, whose eyes had grown wide. Funny how, after all these years, and despite the fact that they didn't know the toddler, the news of the loss still had the power to shock. And then, without warning, Dipsy's mouth withdrew into a frown and her lips began quivering, and suddenly, she was lost in a puddle of tears.

"Oh, honey," Cookie said while Pearl ran to get tissues. "It's okay. I know everything's a mess for you right now, but it'll get better. I promise. Does Kent know about the baby?"

For a moment, Dipsy hesitated, then she burst out crying anew, shaking her head with vigor. "How could I? I mean what if he stayed with me just because I was pregnant, not because he loves me?"

"Are you sure he *doesn't* love you?" Cookie said, running a finger along Dipsy's hairline like she did when they were kids, when, as the big sister, Cookie would always comfort her baby sister when she cried.

"No," she sniffed through the nasal sound of her voice. "It's just that he used to bring me flowers. He used to care about my opinion. But now I'm... *fat!*" She nearly spat the word. "And I'm always tired because of the kids and the house. I never get any sleep, Cookie. I'm exhausted. It makes me grumpy. And I make him grumpy. It's just that I never knew how hard it was to be a mother. I don't get to read anymore. He's out in the world meeting exciting people, and I'm at home, just a boring housewife!"

Tears fell in fat droplets down Dipsy's chin. Pearl returned at that moment with a tissue and held it out to Cookie, who wiped Dipsy's tears then handed the tissue to Dipsy for her nose and waited for her to blow.

"Well, let's do something about that, Dipsy," Cookie said when Dipsy was done blowing into the tissue. Cookie bent down to force her sister to look her in the eye. "We can change it."

"We can?" Dipsy snuffled.

Cookie nodded. "You just need a housekeeper, and a babysitter, and date nights. . . *lots* of date nights."

"Kent will never go for those kinds of extravagances. He believes in pinching pennies."

"But--" Cookie frowned. "Your clothes. . ."

"Goodwill."

"Really?"

"We live in a rich area. People don't wear their clothes for very long."

Cookie was trying to wrap her head around this new information. "And the kids?"

"I sew," Dipsy said. "You don't think I could live with Momma all those years and not know how to sew, do you?"

"I did," Cookie said.

Pearl laughed and patted Dipsy's shoulder. "Well, aren't you something, child." She shook her head and clucked, but clearly she had a newfound respect for the resourceful woman.

Cookie hugged her sister. "Let's just forget this whole thing about a missing child and work on you."

"Oh no, Cookie," Dipsy said, still sniffling, "I can't. It's just that I can *picture* that tiny baby." She rubbed her tummy. "So helpless, needing a home. And here I am with one of my own on the way. And I wonder what a mother would do for love, what lengths a mother would go to keep her child healthy and happy. Safe. Then you see something like this. . ." Once again, she broke down in sobs for the baby, for the current shape of her life.

It took nearly a full half hour to calm Dipsy enough to get their things and go. Cookie thanked Pearl as they exited the library. When they climbed into the car, Cookie said, "Are you sure this is a good idea? Us going to Shardsburg, I mean. We don't know what we'll find there, if anything, right? And July might not be a good time for you," Cookie concluded, eyeing Dipsy's stomach.

But to Cookie's surprise, Dipsy turned on her with a look so fierce that a mother bear couldn't be any prouder and said, "Catherine Leigh Haines! You are *not* backing out on me. We're going to find out what happened to that baby and we are going to bring that young woman home, dead or alive." Her voice broke, but her resolve had not. "And who knows, if Kent and I haven't had a chance to sort things out by then, maybe time away will help me figure out who *I* am. For you to find out who *you* are. Don't you want to know, Cookie? Really?"

And maybe that's what Cookie needed, that proverbial kick in the pants to get her to face her fears. Cookie's throat swelled at the strength of her sister's conviction. For Cookie's entire life, she'd felt different, softer, more fragile than either Mitzi or Dipsy. As if, like a dandelion puff, she could just disappear into the wind forever, as though she'd never existed. Her likes and dislikes so different from the others in her family. Her love of gardening, her dislike of fashion, her less social lifestyle. And yet she loved her family members for their differences. She just hoped that they felt the same about her. No matter. Like Dipsy, she needed to know the truth about that long ago child.

"You're right, Dipsy. We're going to find that young lady and bring her home to her family, whoever that is. And we're going to figure out who *we* are, as women." Then she paused, an unnamed worry bubbling up to the surface and spilling over onto her lips. "But what if that child *is* me? Will you still love me, even if I'm not your biological sister?"

Dipsy cocked her head as though Cookie had sprouted an extra eye. "Of course I will, you dope!" Then she leaned over and hugged Cookie, because that's what sisters do.

Lies blow in on even the softest of winds or the harshest of gales. But in Shardsburg, Alabama, in March of 1932, they blew in with the most massive of tornadoes, one so ominous that it filled the sky in an upside down volcano. Like a drunken sailor, the slow whirl on the horizon made its way toward town, weaving right, then left, and back again. Filling those who saw it with awe. Terror.

According to old-time wisdom tornadoes were portents, omens of things to come.

Yes, it was in this year of disasters that the black funnel touched down, its mouth so wide that it swallowed counties whole. Swallowed up homes. People. The child who squawked piteously. . .

Thirty-eight people died, two hundred and fifty injured. For sharecroppers, all hope of paying back the landowner was lost, and so, too, interest accrued. Any chance of escaping this new system of slavery, gone.

But change blew in on that same wind. Change that would improve lives for decades to come. Yet for the child, it was too late. Her fate was already sealed. Only time would reveal whether for better or for worse. . .

8

STONE STANCHIONS SUPPORTED THE ROOF of the two-story ranch-style home, while a huge willow tree graced the front lawn. Borders beneath the windows were a lush mix of delphiniums, hydrangea, foxgloves, and azaleas. And all along the borders, in neat little rows, grew pink and white caladium, the sun shining through them so that they appeared translucent, like small shards of stained glass. But it was the fragrant aroma of the star jasmine and heirloom roses that made Cookie think of home. No matter where she went or what she did, those smells brought her back here.

But as she and Dipsy walked up the wide steps to the wrap-around porch, Henrietta's words returned unbidden. *You don't look like the rest of your family.* It was true. Cookie looked nothing like Mitzi or Dipsy, but she'd always thought she detected traces of her father in her looks. His high cheekbones, his ruddy undertone. His dark hair.

No, Henrietta was just an unhappy busybody who had been nipping at Cookie's heels ever since Cookie had won the star role of the introverted Laura Wingfield in *The Glass Menagerie* during her sophomore year in junior high. Henrietta had been given the role of Amanda Wingfield, an aged, angry Southern belle whose husband had abandoned her. She'd had to wear a graying wig and matronly costume, whereas Cookie had worn an apricot chiffon accented with lace, one of Mitzi's designs. And Cookie had to admit, her outfit *was* stunning. Cookie shrugged. Perhaps that's where the rivalry had started.

As they entered the beveled front door to the house, Cookie could smell brownies in the oven. On the way home from the library, Dipsy and Cookie had formulated a plan to go to Shardsburg to search for clues about the lost child. But they wouldn't be able to go until at least mid-July, possibly later. Dipsy had her charity work that she needed to finish up and her prenatal visits to the doctor. If she went on this trip, Cookie could prove to herself that she was a Haines, through and through, and Dipsy could take her mind off her current troubles. That decided, they marched through the living room, into the dining room and finally the kitchen. Cookie braced for the talk they would have with Mitzi.

"What do you mean you're taking a road trip together in July? It's humid in July," Mitzi said when Cookie told her, both kids at their grandmother's ankles as she poured over the Montgomery Times where an advertisement read: Dr. Thatcher's Worm Syrup. It followed up with the odd claim that it "tastes and does good; children like it." Below Mitzi, three-year-old Russell kneeled, tying and untying her shoelaces, while six-year-old Rita Mae sat licking out the remaining batter from the bowl of brownies, chocolate smattering her lips as she tested her recipe.

"Just look at your shirt," Dipsy admonished with a laugh. "Give me that bowl and go wash up." She snatched it up before Rita Mae could protest further and tapped her on the rear to get her going. "And you, Russell, get up from under there and leave your grandmother alone."

As the two kids were leaving the room, Russell tugged on the collar of his sister's navy dress, while Rita Mae yowled in protest. Mitzi shook her head at the children's antics, then returned to the matter at hand.

"And why do you girls want to go on vacation together in July? That's one of the hottest times of the year." Mitzi stood and nearly tripped on her shoelaces. "That boy!" she muttered with a touch of exasperation.

Cookie bent down and untied Mitzi's shoelaces, then redid them the right way. "Weren't you the one always begging to take care of the kids? Here's your chance."

"Hmm. . ." Mitzi said, absentmindedly. "I know, but. . ."

"But what?" Dipsy demanded, hands on hips, the usually demure, complacent Dipsy suddenly having grown a backbone. "Here's your one and only chance. Take it or leave it."

Mitzi's eyes grew wide, clearly taken aback by this new tone of Dipsy's. For a few moments she stammered and stuttered, then at last she said, "Fine. I'll talk it over with your father. If he says it's okay, we'll watch the grandkids, but you'll need to bring clothes for them."

"I have some in my car," Dipsy said, to Cookie's surprise, as though she had been planning something like this all along.

While Dipsy was gone to collect Russell and Rita Mae's

things, Mitzi turned to Cookie and said, "Okay, what's up? Give!"

"What?" Cookie said with her best wide-eyed expression.

"Oh, girl, don't give me that." Mitzi slapped the newspaper down on the table as though swatting a fly. "I can read you like one of those books you're always pouring over at the library."

Cookie balked, then frowned, sniffing the air. "Do I smell something burning?"

"Don't try to change the subject," Mitzi said, seconds before she ran with a shriek toward the oven, which was even now beginning to smoke. She opened the door with a hand mitt and fanned the burned brownies, a sour expression on her face.

Smoke filled the large kitchen. Cookie rushed over to one of the windows and shoved it open with a loud squeal from where a former paint job had left the track sticky. Mitzi dropped the overly hot brownies onto the stovetop with a loud thud. Then, standard Mitzi, she began to laugh. She laughed so hard it brought tears to her eyes.

"What's so funny?" Cookie demanded, worried that Mitzi really had gone off her rocker this time.

"Don't you remember that time you made me Mother's Day pancakes? You were eight. Do you remember what you said?"

How could Cookie forget? She had turned the burner on high and hadn't remembered the part about greasing the iron skillet. She had wanted to surprise Ebie and Mitzi, but instead a cloud of smoke wafted into their bedroom just as Cookie wandered in wearing her white nightgown with spatula in hand.

"Happy Mother's Day!" Cookie and Mitzi said in unison.

"You were quite the cook," Mitzi said as she fanned the brownies, then tested them with a butter knife. "Ooh, not bad. A little crispy on the outside, but the insides are holding together."

"I'm better now," Cookie said, hoping in vain to defend her baking.

"Not much!" Mitzi blew on a small square she had dug from the middle then took the teensiest bite. "Ooh, again, not bad. I think I like them a little burnt. Comes with age. Everything tastes a little better with charcoal on it."

Cookie shook her head. How could she ever live with the idea that this woman was not of her blood. She was just so. . . so *funny*. "Oh, Mother!"

"Don't 'oh mother' me, and don't think you're off the hook, young lady. I want to know what all this is about." She pointed a mitted hand at Cookie. "Your sister never drops in unannounced and then she offers to let me take care of the kids? I usually have to promise my first born to get even a night with those kids. Afraid I will *spoil* them! As though one brownie and some Frosted Flakes in the morning are going to do irreparable harm."

"Wouldn't your first born be me?"

"You know what I mean, Miss Smarty Pants! Besides, those children love me."

And it was true. Whenever they were at "Nana's," as Dipsy urged them to call her, it was as though they'd been set free. They loved the wide open backyard, the greenhouse, cooking with Nana. In private, Mitzi referred to herself as Nana Baa-nana. Mitzi was possibly *the* most irreverent person Cookie had ever known. Despite all of Mitzi's annoying traits, Cookie adored her for her free spirit and kind heart. And maybe that should have been a clue. Because what mother and daughter got along so well together? It wasn't. . . normal.

"Mitzi, I think Dipsy should be the one to talk to you about her situation, not me."

"You think I don't know?" Mitzi huffed as she dug out a spatula and five small plates, placing burnt brownies in the center of each of them. She topped the brownies with whipped cream. Mitzi leaned in and whispered, "No one will know they are burnt this way."

"You don't think the smoke is a giveaway?" Cookie couldn't resist adding. "And what do you mean you know? What do you know?"

Raising an eyebrow, Mitzi glanced toward the doorway to be sure Dipsy wasn't nearby. Then she turned to Cookie, once again speaking in a whisper. "I know about her and Kent. They were fighting when I was on the phone the other day. And they've been apart too much. It's not healthy for a marriage." She handed Cookie a plate and a fork.

Cookie took it, fork poised. "So you're okay with this?"

"I didn't say that. Those two love each other. I know Dipsy loves Kent. And whether Kent realizes it or not, Dipsy's the best thing that ever happened to him, but it's hard to see when you're busy fighting wars."

"Wars?"

"Oh honey, you really *do* know nothing! All business is war. For new territory, for maintaining what you've worked so hard to establish. Your grandaddy owned the Good Deal Hardware Store here in Montgomery. Kept that place for nearly forty years until that big box store came in and wiped him clean off the map. Worst day of grandaddy's life. But he picked himself up, dusted himself off and was good as new, and you know how he did it?"

Cookie's mouth was stuffed with burnt brownie and whipped cream, so she merely shook her head.

"Mama snapped him up in her arms, nursed him back to his

old self, and together they scraped up enough money for a new business in a new field. And you know what?"

"W-hat?" Cookie said through a mouthful of brownie.

"Oh, honey, don't talk with your mouth full."

"But you asked!" Cookie protested, gulping down what was left of the bite she had taken. She walked to the refrigerator and pulled out a bottle of milk. She tipped it back, chugging it.

"Good gawd, Cookie!" Mitzi said, marching over and taking the bottle from her, a single sploosh running down Cookie's chin. "You weren't born in a barn. Who raised you?"

Cookie merely said, "Moo!"

Any other mother would have seen this as a challenge to her role as queen of the kitchen, but good-natured Mitzi swatted her with the oven mitt and laughed. And it came to Cookie in that moment that Mitzi was one of the few people who got her humor. Who understood it. Understood *her*. How lucky was that? But what if Mitzi had stolen her from another mother? What then? She couldn't go there. Not yet. Maybe never. And besides, it probably wasn't even true, for cripes' sake.

"You're still not off the hook," Mitzi said, breaking her from her reverie.

"Oh?" Cookie asked, absentmindedly staring out the window at Dipsy's kids who had been ushered into the backyard to play.

"Why the sudden need to travel, and where are you going?"

Fortunately, at that moment, Dipsy entered the kitchen through the side door. Seeing the smoke and clearly feeling the tension, she let the screen door slam behind her. "What?" She turned dark eyes from Mitzi, whose pupils were wide, to her sister. "Cookie?"

Cookie didn't know what to do.

"Well, say something. I--"

Just then the phone rang. For several seconds no one moved as it jangled on. Finally, Mitzi ran to grab it. She mumbled a few unintelligible words then turned to Cookie. "It's for you."

Cookie mouthed the word "who"?

"Pearl from the library," Mitzi mouthed in return.

Dipsy and Cookie exchanged harried glances, then Cookie grabbed the phone. "Pearl, is that you?"

"I found something," she said without preamble, her voice hesitant. "About Shardsburg. There was a tornado, Cookie, a *huge* tornado."

A tornado? But she already knew about the tornado from the clipping and from Franny's book. "I know, that's what it said in the book."

"No, you don't understand," Pearl hissed. "This was the storm of the century. Wiped out most of Shardsburg. Left a path of destruction for miles."

Fortunately, the phone was next to the door that led to the stoop outside. Cookie sensed that this was a conversation best kept private. She breezed through the doorway, leaving the door open just enough to allow for the phone cord. She seated herself on the top stoop, head down.

Pearl spoke in a hushed voice. "Thirty-eight people died."

Cookie paused, considering this. "So, maybe the toddler died?" But if that were true, it wouldn't make sense that the parents had claimed her missing in the article. But what *had* happened to the child?

"I don't know about the missing toddler," Pearl said, "but I do know the article said that the town all but closed up after that and most people moved away. So what will you do now?"

Cookie cradled her head with her left hand. What was she expecting to find? The article probably had nothing to do with her at all and she was simply chasing windmills. *Cookie Haines, the windmill chaser.* A real life Don Quixote.

"Cookie? You there?" Pearl said.

"Uh-huh," Cookie replied, suddenly feeling sad, nostalgic, but for what? Everything felt topsy-turvy, like those dolls her mother had made her as a child, one side Little Red Riding Hood, the other side The Wolf. Which life was hers? She frowned, unsure if she wanted to find out.

"Go." Pearl paused, as though afraid to continue. "Take it from me, Cookie. I didn't know my momma until I was closing in on forty. This child may have nothing to do with you or your family. Who knows? But don't wait long to find out or you'll wind up like me with a lifetime of regrets. Besides, whatever happens, you've still got your family. But if you don't go, you'll always wonder."

Before Cookie could ask her another question, the line went dead. Cookie set the receiver down on the stoop and breathed deeply of the humid summer air. . . of the freshly mown grass. Pearl was right. She would always wonder about the truth. And yet, like Laura in *The Glass Menagerie*, she had a fragile side that she showed to few people. Worried, she wrapped her arms around her knees.

"Okay, I'll go," she whispered into the wisteria-scented air as she walked the phone back into the house and rested it on its cradle. But before she could answer Mitzi and Dipsy's questioning looks, the phone rang again. "Now who could that be?"

9

"WHAT DO YOU MEAN YOU have a job to do?" Dipsy said, as she stood in her childhood bedroom, packing to go home.

Cookie's eyes wandered the length of the room. In the center stood a four-poster bed, cream colored with gold accents, courtesy of Mitzi, whose skills at rehab were famous, or more to the point, infamous. Case in point, the fuzzy red "powder room" that Mitzi had wallpapered. It looked like something out of a late 1800's whorehouse. Cookie chuckled at the memory. Mitzi had even paired it with a gold-leafed mirror and stand, and a matching gold chair. Unpretentious, it was not.

Absentmindedly, she picked Tillie, her matted, much-loved bunny from childhood, off the dresser. She had told everyone that Tillie had a sister Millie and that they liked tea and cookies. For years she had cried over Millie only to be told that the bunny was a figment of her imagination. She fingered the glass eyes, the fallen ear. One of the kids must have brought it to Dipsy's room.

Fortunately for Dipsy, unlike the powder room, Mitzi had chosen a much tamer pale pink chenille bedspread to complement Dipsy's white four-poster bed with matching dressers and end tables. Dipsy's awards were lined up on the dresser, her ribbons and medals hung over the mirror: for the third-grade spelling bee, for horsemanship, for penmanship and God only knew what else. Dipsy had been the golden child, the daughter expected to accomplish the most. And she *had* in Mitzi's eyes because she had married well and had 2.5 children and a beautiful home. Cookie. . . well, Cookie was Cookie, according to her father. To Mitzi, she was a "kick." She kept Mitzi entertained, but they both viewed Cookie's work as a hobby, which truth be known, maybe it was. Maybe that's all it would ever be. Still, she wasn't ready to wave the white flag just yet.

"I received a phone call. . . after I finished talking to Pearl." Though Cookie couldn't say why, she felt shy telling Dipsy about the call from the botanical garden, as though by talking about it, she might jinx what could be a potential business venture.

"And?"

"It was from the Birmingham Arboretum."

Dipsy shoved a pair of dungarees into her bag, then paused. True to form, Dipsy owned the largest piece of luggage Cookie had ever seen. "Where they have the herb and flower gardens?"

Cookie nodded, trying to hide her excitement, but it slipped out in a high squeal of delight. "They heard about the topiaries I've been working on from Henrietta Willoughby and wanted a brochure."

"Henrietta did that for you? Now there's a surprise. I wonder what she's up to. Do you *have* brochures?" Dipsy asked, her packing temporarily forgotten.

"No," Cookie said, "and I don't have time to print any either."

"Do you have photographs at least?"

"That, I do."

Dipsy tipped her head as though deciding what they should do next, and then said, "Oh hell--"

"Dipsy!" Cookie's sister never swore, not even as a teen. Whenever Cookie had sworn, Dipsy had been the first to go to Mitzi, tattling all the way, and the first to be standing in the background, arms crossed, leg out, mouthing "ha-ha, serves you right!"

"Don't tell Mama," Dipsy pleaded as though they truly were eight again.

Cookie crossed her heart and pretended to poke a finger in her eye. "Promise."

"Okay, then, show me your topiaries," Dipsy said, following close on Cookie's heels as they marched out to the greenhouse.

Immediately, as they opened the doors, a rush of humidity encased Cookie, the smell of loam and moisture filling her lungs. The smell never failed to calm her. It was as if she had been born with a green thumb, intuitively understanding what a plant needed to be healthy.

"The topiaries are in the lath house," Cookie said, pointing toward a door at the left side of the building that led to the area where the shade plants were housed, or those being acclimated before going into the ground outside.

They exited the greenhouse and walked down a short walk until they reached the lath house. The air instantly cooled, the light dimmed to a pleasant level, as if hiking through the underbrush of a rainforest.

"There," Cookie said, leading Dipsy around a supply of maidenhair fern and begonias on cedar tables to an open area with nothing but pea gravel and larger plants that wouldn't fit on the tables.

"Oh my gawd!" Dipsy said, her blue eyes widened in wonder.

Seen through Dipsy's eyes, Cookie viewed her handiwork: the giant heart done in pink begonias, a giraffe nibbling on a tree, a Shetland sheepdog, and last but definitely not least, one that looked like a Fourth of July fireworks display. She had used silvery artemesia to climb up the shooting stems of the display, each "tip" finished with a bright array of pink, purple, and red firework flowers, so that it looked as though it were a shower of flowers. She had never seen it done before in any book she'd read or garden she had attended. It spoke to her sense of patriotism.

Dipsy whistled. "Oh my gosh, Cookie. You've found your calling."

"You think?" Cookie flushed, embarrassed by the attention.

"But how are you ever going to get them to the gardens? You don't drive and you don't own a van."

Cookie tugged on a tendril of hair that had fallen loose from her beehive that was held up with bobby pins and enough hairspray to keep it in place for a month. "I don't know. Up until now, my customers have picked up their own plants, but those are small mom and pop shops. This is different."

"You need to learn how to drive, girl. *And* you need that van."

"How am I ever going to be able to afford one?" Cookie asked, picking up the clippers she kept handy in the lath house and absentmindedly trimming anything that was beginning to brown.

"First things first," Dipsy said, poking her forefinger into the plant bases, one by one, testing the soil for moisture. "This one needs water." She frowned. "How come you never grow cactus or succulents?"

"I'm too nurturing." Cookie laughed. "I always want to take care of them but they need to be left alone."

"At least I know what kind of plant to get in the future," Dipsy said wryly.

"You?" Cookie asked. "But you raise children--"

"Which is why I only have time for cactus or succulents." Dipsy made a face. "Once the kids are in school, maybe I'll have more time for. . . for *sleep*!" Dipsy released a long, slow moan.

Cookie set the pruning shears down and came over and hugged her sister. "I didn't know things were so hard for you."

"Well, I'm not the first mother to be exhausted, and I won't be the last. I always think if men did what we do for even a year -- take care of the house, cook, clean, take the kids to all their functions, and play hostess -- they would. . . would what?" Dipsy yawned.

"Give you a raise?" Cookie reached up and plucked a dead leaf off of one of her hanging plants.

"Not that men's lives are any picnic," Dipsy reminded her, "at least the laborers. An office job wouldn't be so bad though, and I *could* go for a martini lunch. But first things first. Follow me." She beckoned with a curled finger.

"Where are we going?"

"You'll see," Dipsy said mysteriously. As they entered the house through the side door to the kitchen, the kids were seated around the table eating a late afternoon snack. Each of them clamored for Dipsy's attention with "Guess what Nana helped us make?" and "We made a mosaic goldfish in a pond." For her part, Mitzi was standing over the stove, spatula in hand, flipping grilled cheese sandwiches.

"I called upstairs for you two to come down to eat, but no one answered. Where have you been?" Mitzi was now dressed in a blue-and-white seersucker jumpsuit with a pair of two-tone t-straps, red costume jewelry flanking her ears and neck. She waved her spatula like a baton.

"No time," Dipsy said, grabbing Cookie by the arm.

"The cheese sandwiches will be cold by the time you. . ."

Mitzi's voice trailed off as Cookie hurried to follow Dipsy, who seemed to be on a mission. Dipsy ran up the stairs, her short legs taking the stairsteps two by two until she reached the second landing. Off to the right was a small door that led to the attic. Cookie had avoided the attic, its interior the stuff of her dreams and more often her nightmares. In her mind, it had a rather haunted quality that she preferred to avoid, especially after she'd caught a rat peering out as a child. Mitzi had hired a carpenter to add a small door to the attic after that. No, the attic was off limits and Cookie meant to keep it that way. She halted at the closed doorway, refusing to enter. But before she could protest further, petite Dipsy bent down and pushed the child-sized door open, then nearly crawled in, pulling Cookie after her.

It took several moments for Cookie's eyes to adjust and her heart to stop pounding. Through the open transom that looked over the street, a ray of light filtered in on a musty haze. To her surprise, the room had been turned into an art studio complete with an easel and stand that contained an array of oils, pastels, and watercolors along with brushes of varying sizes and shapes and in various stages of use. But what really drew Cookie's attention were the numerous paintings scattered about. They were amazing. The jewel tones were done in vivid hues of cerulean blue and fluorescent yellow, deep reds and royal purple.

"Mitzi?" Cookie said, certain no one else would have chosen such bold colors. Not in *this* house.

Dipsy merely nodded, then tilted her head to the side as she inspected the new painting on the easel, one that reminded Cookie of a Van Gogh, only with a more modern twist. Although the one on the easel wasn't nearly as sophisticated as most of the other paintings Cookie had seen, more child-like in its rendering, it still held a certain appeal. What surprised Cookie most is that Mitzi had used some of Cookie's plants from the greenhouse as inspiration.

"But why hasn't she ever said anything about her artwork? And how did you know and I didn't? And why didn't you *tell* me?" Hands on hips, Cookie faced her sister. She knew she must look like a petulant child, but the world that she had so carefully crafted for herself seemed to be tumbling down around her, brick by brick.

"Think about it," Dipsy said as she bent down and picked up a portrait of a woman dressed in blue, holding a colorful whirligig at a fair. Bubbles floated in the background. "Mama disappears every day after lunch. What did you think she was doing?"

"Taking a nap." Cookie leaned down to peruse the canvases in one corner of the room. It struck her just then that she had always presumed this room to be dusty and full of cobwebs as it was when she was small. Or maybe she'd been told that to keep her out. "Hmm."

"Well, Mom wasn't taking a nap. She was up here painting."

"But why the military secret? They're just paintings, for god's sake. Albeit kind of amazing. She always was creative, but I would have never guessed she had *this* level of talent." Cookie frowned, taking in the scope of Mitzi's creativity. There was something subtle about the characters and the bold choice of colors. The odd composition, as though she were painting a narrative that revealed something more than the sum of the parts. And yet some of them seemed far less developed than the others.

"What do you think this one means?" Dipsy said, holding up an especially provocative piece. In it were almost cartoon-like characters, each holding something odd, unique. A scepter. A crown. A key and a lock. And yet the main composition was of a dark-haired young woman, who hesitated in front of a doorway, as though afraid to enter. As if what was on the other side might not be to her liking. Yet, how would she know unless she entered?

"The unknown," Cookie said.

"Precisely," Dipsy echoed. "It's always hard to cross a threshold because you may never be able to turn back. It changes you."

For one brief moment, Cookie felt certain that Dipsy was talking about herself. About her choices. And Cookie could understand that because she had been given a key to a door that she wasn't sure she wanted to open. In fact, if she could, she would throw away the key and never go further, but something had shifted. It's as though everything in her life had collided into this one prescient moment. Dipsy taking a time-out with Kent, Mitzi talking Cookie into trying on clothes that she had heretofore shunned. The look Mitzi'd had when seeing Rachel Aberdeen at her door. And Rachel herself. Even Cookie's father had seemed more preoccupied than usual, as though he, too, understood that they were at a watershed moment. She toured the room, looking through the stacks of paintings, searching for something to make sense of her life. Toward the back of one particular stack, she stopped, a chill racing through her.

"Dipsy?"

"Hmm?" Dipsy said absentmindedly, as she studied what looked like an older painting.

Cookie's heart stilled. "Do you see what I see?"

"What?" Dipsy's eyes drifted lazily to follow Cookie's gaze. For a moment, the picture didn't seem to register, but then Dipsy gasped. "Oh my gawd, Cookie. What *is* that?"

It was an older painting Cookie had found at the back of the stack. The colors weren't nearly so bright, and the style looked like something from the thirties. It was an outdoor scene done in almost sepia tones of a sharecropper's hut, of a black family seated on the front porch of a very dilapidated building. The children were dirty and barefoot, the adults appeared tired and worn, their faces prematurely aged by the whip-hot Alabama sunshine. And still, Cookie read family, unity, into their expressions as though despite everything, their love for one another had withstood the test of time. But what stood out most among this Southern "idyll" was a woman. Her features were different. Her skin baked by the sun, but golden, not brown, her eyes hazel, freckles dotting her nose. She wore a simple, tired shift and heavy leather sandals. But what caught Cookie's attention most was the baby she held in her arms, raising a ruckus, its skin wrinkled like her mother's, only Cookie saw it for what it was. Malnourishment.

Dipsy whistled, then clucked, as though the whistle weren't enough to fully encompass everything she was feeling. "Do you think that's the stolen baby?"

Cookie shrugged, yet she couldn't help but wonder as she studied the woman carefully. Her image was somewhat shaded by the overhang from the porch, so only the features below her forehead were visible, her jawline shaded as well. Yet, there was something about the eyes, the nose.

"Do you think the woman is a mulatto?" Dipsy said, no judgement in her voice.

"I don't know. Maybe, maybe not." As Cookie knew only too well, genetics were a tricky thing. Traits could go underground for years then pop up three generations past. General Carter, as they had called their neighbor for as long as she could recall because of his upright manner and marching gait, had coal black hair. And yet he had produced three redheads from his mother's side of the family. Then there was that kid from Montgomery, who had two parents, one blonde, the other brunette, but the child's hair was kinky black and his skin the color of a walnut. His great-great grandparents had owned a cotton plantation, be that as it may. So who knew? And occasionally, a seemingly all-white child could have two black parents.

"Let's face it," Dipsy said with a wry smile, "we're all just like grandma's jumble cookies. . . one great big mix."

"Why did you bring me up here, Dipsy?" Cookie said, training a gimlet eye on her sister.

Dipsy held up a finger, then went rummaging through a stack of medium-sized paintings until she found what she was looking for. "Aha! Here it is," she said, dusting it off.

"What is it?"

"Take a look," Dipsy said, crossing the room and handing it to Cookie.

It was Cookie's turn to whistle. "Oh my gawd, it's perfect!"

"That it is!"

For there, on the canvas, was a painting of the botanical garden's giant greenhouse with flowers in bloom and wide steps leading up to it. It would be perfect for showcasing the photographs of her topiaries. If she placed them correctly, it would appear as though they fit right in with the landscape. She would need a frame, but that would be the least of her worries. As if Dipsy had read her thoughts, she marched over to a metal divider with all sorts of frames in them. She dug through until she found a black one.

"Take a look at this!"

Cookie gasped, for there, on the black frame etched into a gold plaque were the words "Birmingham Arboretum."

Dipsy dusted the frame off with her fingers, blowing the last of the grime off in a swirling cloud. "Mitzi had hoped to sell this painting and frame, or donate them to the gardens one day, but she never got up the courage to ever sell a painting. She didn't think she was good enough."

"Good enough!" Cookie turned to her sister. "Dipsy, she is *talented*!"

"You know that and I know that, but tell her." Dipsy placed the painting within the frame, bringing it to life in an instant."

Cookie frowned, puzzled. "But why did she tell you all this and not me? I live here, for cripe's sake."

"I know, Cookie," Dipsy said, suddenly reluctant to say more. "It's just that. . . that, well, you're so talented, Cookie. And she trusts your opinion. If you hadn't liked them, you would have been honest with her, and I don't think she could have taken that, you know? Mom may wear her big girl cape sometimes, but she's really a softy, when it's all said and done."

Cookie had never imagined Mitzi in this way. She had always seemed so sure of herself, so "take charge." In Cookie's mind Mitzi could have led a cavalry, if she'd set her mind to it.

"Okay, I get that, Dipsy, but why didn't *you* tell me about Mitzi's paintings? Tell me that!" Cookie couldn't say why she felt so betrayed by this, but she did. That she had been left out in the dark for so long -- that she had been deemed unreachable. Worse yet, that she had been deemed *an outsider*. She turned to the painting of the black sharecroppers and the white woman. Had *she* been that baby? Had the woman in the painting been as much of an outsider as Cookie was in her own family?

Dipsy peered down at her emerald green peep-toe heels that she wore to appear taller, as if unwilling or unable to face Cookie, all the while stroking her matching green shirt dress with its wide Peter Pan collar.

Seeing that nothing was forthcoming, Cookie gave an exasperated sigh. "Are you going to answer me, Dipsy?"

"Okay," Dipsy said, her expression hardening even as tears formed in her eyes. "You want to know the truth? I was jealous! You have Mitzi all to yourself. It's always Cookie this and Cookie that. . . well, I wanted something that was mine. . . all *mine*!"

"Oh, Dipsy," Cookie said, placing a hand on her sister's shoulder.

Dipsy shrugged Cookie's hand away. "Don't!" she hissed. "Don't treat me like the little sister! Like I only matter when it affects you!" With that, she broke into tears and rushed over to the door, bent down and disappeared through the opening.

For several minutes, Cookie stood there, stunned, the sting of what her sister had said still fresh. Had it always been her and Mitzi? Had Dipsy felt like *she* was on the outside looking in? Cookie rubbed her arms, wishing she could halt the march of time.

91

10

FROM HER PERCH IN THE attic, Cookie listened to Dipsy's footsteps as she pounded down the stairs. How had Cookie not known that her sister felt like an outsider when it came to Cookie's relationship with Mitzi? Dipsy had always seemed so sure of herself, so confident. Cookie took one last look at the paintings and sighed. Well, she knew one thing. She couldn't sit in this dusty old attic stewing. She grabbed the painting of the arboretum and the frame that went with it, all the while listening for Mitzi. Fortunately, she could hear her downstairs playing Chinese Checkers with Dipsy's kids, the marbles bouncing off the tin star. Poor Mitzi. She always lost at marbles.

For a brief moment, Cookie thought of going after Dipsy, but she knew her sister well enough to realize she would want to be left alone for a while. . . to sort things out. And truth be told, Cookie needed the same. With a snort of frustration, she finished putting the painting of the arboretum in the frame, then wrapped it in one of the many quilts Mitzi had strewn around the attic for just such a thing. Then she crawled through the low opening, careful to be sure Mitzi was still downstairs with the kids. She knew she should ask Mitzi before taking the painting, but she also knew the answer would be "no" followed by a long lecture about taking what didn't belong to her. Cookie didn't have time for that. She needed to get the painting with pictures of her topiaries to the arboretum before it closed. Her sales pitch shouldn't take more than half an hour. Afterwards, she would place the painting back in its rightful place. Then in two months time, if Dipsy was speaking to her by then, they would drive to Shardsburg.

Cookie hurried to her room, working frantically to place the photo cut-outs of her topiaries onto the painting, attaching them with sticky putty. When she was finished, she inspected her handiwork. She just hoped the Birmingham Arboretum would look past her somewhat amateurish job and see the topiaries as they might appear in the gardens. And if she were to say so herself, they looked amazing! She said a silent prayer, then packed the painting up in an oversized tote. Now for the hard part. Beulah. She had been lying low ever since Dipsy's two children had arrived, complaining that she had enough work with her own three kids. She had muttered and fumed, and yet, like Mitzi, she was all bluster and no bite. Okay, maybe a little bite, but for the most part, Mitzi and Beulah were mirror images of each other, each belonging to a different world and yet the same, somehow. Each a ferociously protective mom. Each finding a niche in a world meant for men. Each with a life of duty and service to their families.

Cookie grabbed her tote with the painting inside and tiptoed down the stairs, avoiding the third rung to the bottom which squeaked and groaned whenever any weight was put on it. Fortunately, she could hear Beulah humming in the library, while inside the kitchen, Mitzi was once again marshalling the troops. "You! Russell, sit on your bottom, and Rita Mae, stop swinging your leg."

Cookie took the opportunity to hail down Beulah who stood with a feather duster in her hand, all the while perusing a *Life* magazine with John F. Kennedy on the front. When Cookie whispered her name, Beulah jumped.

"Good lord, Child, you scared the bejesus out of me. What'd y'all up and do that for?" Beulah, who, on a good day, was round faced and rosy cheeked, appeared harried today, her normally neat hair spiralling out of her bun in an array of curlicues that made her look as though she were about to take flight.

"Shh!" Cookie hissed, placing a finger to her lips and glancing over her shoulder in the direction of the kitchen. "I need a favor."

Beulah paused. "A favor?"

"I need you to drive me to the arboretum."

"In Birmingham?" Beulah said, a tad too loud for Cookie's taste. "That's almost an hour and a half from here.

"Keep it down," Cookie whispered. "I don't want Mitzi to hear."

"Oh, girl," Beulah said, setting her feather duster down on the coffee table. "That don't sound good. Every time you say something like that I know you're about to get me in a mess of trouble, and I don't want no trouble, Miss Cookie."

"But it's important. You know I wouldn't ask--"

Beulah put up a hand. "Let me stop you right there. You

want me to drive you to the arboretum and you can't tell your mama *why*?"

Cookie groaned. Couldn't Beulah help her out just this once without Cookie having to go into a lengthy explanation? "I have a potential job. Dipsy's mad at me, so I can't ask her. And if I go to Mama she's going to ask too many questions. I don't have much time," she added, checking her watch. "Besides, if I sell the arboretum on my ideas, I'll need time to get everything together in the next two months before Dipsy and I go out of town on vacation."

"Out of town?" Beulah placed her hands on her hips. "Where you going?"

Cookie felt the tiniest bit of relief when she saw Beulah start to untie her white apron. That meant she would at least listen to her.

"To Shardsburg. It will take too long to explain. . . unless, of course, you want me to tell you on the way to the arboretum." Cookie shrugged noncommittally. "It *is* pretty juicy."

Beulah gave her the death glare, and while Cookie might deserve it, this could be her one and only chance to start a business. A *real* business. One that would earn her a living so that everyone wouldn't always have to explain Cookie like she was the crazy aunt they kept in the attic.

"Okay, Missy. I'll bring the car around front. But you're going to tell me everything, young lady, and you're going to start from the beginning."

It spoke to their years together as part of a cobbled family, despite Beulah having one of her own, that they could speak so freely to each other. Cookie knew it wasn't the same in most families here in Alabama in the 60s, but she was immensely grateful that they'd been an exception to the rule, an anomaly that she chalked up to Mitzi's unbending sense of fairness and Beulah's nurturing personality.

Several minutes later, they were settling into the old blue-and-white Nash Rambler station wagon. Beulah retrieved her "Sunday-go-to-meeting" hat and her gloves, then turned to Cookie and said, "Okay, Missy. Start at the beginning."

For the next hour, as they drove down the highway, Cookie recounted all that had happened over the last couple of days, telling Beulah about Rachel, about Mitzi's strange reaction, about Dipsy and her husband, even about her find in the attic.

"Oh, yeah, Mitzi's been at that for years," Beulah said, peering through the rearview mirror at the cars behind. "She's not very good, if you ask me."

"She is so, good. And you knew about her artwork, too? Am I the *only* one in the dark about nearly everything in this household?" Cookie demanded, feeling angrier than she had in a long time.

"Appears so," Beulah said, reaching over and patting her leg as she had when Cookie was a little girl crying over some perceived slight. "But don't you worry none, Child. You'll always have me."

Cookie felt like a five year old all over again as tears welled in her eyes. "Really?"

"Of course. You don't think this is just a *job* for me, do you?"

Cooked shrugged.

"Are you kidding? I have enough work at home taking care of a husband and watching after three grown kids. Oh, heck, no. I would have given this up for lent long ago, if I hadn't thought of you like one of my own. No. . ." She shook her head. "I love you girls."

"But--"

"Haven't you noticed I'm not a spring chicken anymore?" Beulah said with a laugh. "My back aches, and my knees hurt. My kids have all flown the coop. Believe me, I can think of better things than cleaning y'all's house and my own. No, I've stayed on because I'd miss you girls. Someday you'll both be gone, and then I'll give my notice. Until then, I reckon I'll stay."

As Cookie was pondering that, she checked her watch to make sure the arboretum was still open. Forty-five minutes and counting until it closed at 6:00. They would need to hurry. Before she could consider that further, Beulah turned off the highway onto the ramp that led to downtown Birmingham. "Oh Lawdy," she murmured beneath her breath. Cookie looked up in time to see a sea of dark faces before her. "What's going on?"

"Don't your mama tell you nothin'?" Beulah said, clucking like a laying hen. "But then I suppose she wouldn't want to worry y'all. Course I shoulda been thinkin' more clearly, what with you surprising me with this cockamamie story about needin' to go to the garden. I've just been so preoccupied, and Harold hasn't been feeling too well, and. . ."

"Beulah!" Cookie admonished. Everyone had peculiarities, Cookie knew, Beulah's being that she ran off at the mouth everytime she became frazzled. Cookie's being that she didn't. No, she grew deathly still when *she* was fretting over something. "What is this?"

"The Civil Rights protest! Oh Jesus save us! With all this rushin' around, I forgot all about it," Beulah said, stomping on the brake and careening forward in her seat as the station wagon ground to a quick halt.

Cookie grabbed Beulah's hand in hers and held tight, because at precisely that moment, Cookie saw what Beulah had seen: a group of police officers, some with fire hoses, while one urged a snapping and snarling black-and-tan German shepherd to attack a colored boy, college age, lean and clean-cut. As Cookie watched in horror, the throaty growl of the shepherd drowned out the cries of the protesters. In that moment, it was as if everything were moving in slow motion. . . as though she had a 360-degree view of the world: the colored grandmother in the flowered skirt whose face revealed her disgust; the many black men, most wearing hats and dressed far better than the officers attacking them, turning toward the commotion, fear and concern registering in their sober expressions. Across from the 16th Street Baptist Church, sat the black-owned Jockey Boy Restaurant, with the words Coca-Cola written in a flowery scrawl, an ironic backdrop to the protest.

"Quick!" Cookie urged. "Drive!"

Beulah inched the Rambler forward, and when she was finally able, turned at the corner ahead. Unfortunately, this street was just as blocked as the last.

"We've gotta get out of here," Beulah muttered, her dark features now ashen. "Oh, Gawd, there's Trixie."

Cookie knew Trixie from the many times she had stopped by the Haines' house over the years when Beulah needed advice about some special cleaning project. For her part, Trixie was the Erma Bombeck of the colored community in Birmingham. When Cookie got gum on the couch, or when Dipsy spilled grape juice on the light carpet, Trixie knew just what to do.

"You mind if we take her with us?" Beulah said, leaning forward and tapping on the glass to get Trixie's attention. "Can't leave her here, not with this mess."

Cookie readily agreed. They pulled up alongside her, engine running and rolled down the window.

"Psst! Trixie, climb in," Beulah said.

Trixie, who was dressed in a tan dress with silk stockings, ribbed at the back and high heels, of all things, said, "I'm stayin' put. Nobody's goin' to tell us we can't march peacefully." No sooner had the words left her mouth, then up by the cinema house where the marquis read "Suspense! Excitement! Susan Hayward in *Back Street and Damn the Defiant*," two police officers had a tight grip on a young black woman in a dark dress.

"Trixie!" Beulah begged. "We gonna fight this; we are, but you done your part. Now get in!"

"No!" Trixie hissed. "I'm stayin'." Then thinking better of it, she added, "But could you lend me your shoes? These shoes are rubbin' my heels raw."

Beulah looked down at her own work shoes. "They're size nine," she offered without hesitation.

"Fine. But lend me your socks, too."

"Really? What the. . .?"

"Just do it!" Cookie hissed. "I'll buy you some new ones on the way home."

Beulah looked at Cookie as though she'd lost her mind, but took them off and handed both the shoes *and* the socks to Trixie. "For the cause," Trixie said, even though Cookie could tell that it had cost Beulah.

Trixie handed her high heels to Beulah through the open window. "Thanks, honey," she said, leaning in and giving Beulah a hug. "I'll buy you a big fat root beer float for this when it's over."

"It's me who should be buyin' you the float," Beulah said, though it sounded rather begrudging. "Now, how do I get out of this mess?"

Trixie pointed down a side street. "Go right, three blocks down, then take another right. That should get you out of the worst of it."

It was almost closing time when they reached the Birmingham Arboretum. Beulah pulled the Rambler up out front, her feet still bare as she refused to wear the heels. Cookie reached over and gave Beulah a hug, then said, "Wish me luck."

"Luck," Beulah said with a half-grin.

"Thanks! I owe you big time."

"You're not the first and you won't be the last," Beulah said.

Cookie nodded. Then she grabbed the painting from the back seat. "This shouldn't take long."

Beulah just snorted. "I'll go park the car and wait for you." Then she put the two-toned station wagon in gear, a puff of smoke belching out the back.

With a reluctance bordering on fear, Cookie said a simple prayer, then steeled herself for what lay ahead.

11

COOKIE RACED DOWN THE WIDE steps that led from the arboretum's mammoth greenhouse to the parking lot below. "I will not cry. I will not cry. I will not cry," she whispered beneath her breath, steadfastly refusing to look at any of the visitors to the garden as she traipsed down the steps. Beulah must have been watching for Cookie because she pulled up at the base of the steps in the blue-and-white Rambler just as Cookie's feet touched the sidewalk.

"Oh, honey," Beulah said when Cookie opened the car door, unable to hide her tears any longer. "Come give Beulah a hug."

Beulah wrapped Cookie in her generous arms and let Cookie sob onto her gray sweater. A honk from a white and teal sedan that pulled up behind the station wagon sent Cookie scattering to fasten her seatbelt, while Beulah struggled to put the Rambler in gear.

"Hold your horses!" Beulah muttered to the impatient man who threw his hands up in frustration. "So, what happened?" she asked once they were on the main road.

Cookie peered out the window, unwilling to show Beulah any more of her tears. She sniffed and then thanked Beulah when she tapped her shoulder and handed her a handkerchief. Cookie blew unceremoniously into the linen, then wiped her eyes with her fingers.

"Well?" Beulah said, putting on the blinkers as they headed north.

"They didn't like it. Thought it doesn't fit with their style and I'm too unknown--"

"And you're a woman," Beulah said, as though that explained everything.

"Maybe," Cookie said as she watched the scenery pass by in a blur of wide lawns, pink peonies, and large chestnut trees. "It's true they've never had a female contributor. But worst of all, Henrietta was there."

"Henrietta? What was *she* doing there?" Beulah's eyebrows came together in a deep frown. She'd never liked Henrietta. Said the girl was always stirring up trouble, too hoity-toity for her own good.

"I don't know, but she says she did a little checking."

"Checking into what?" Beulah demanded, looking out her rearview mirror before changing lanes.

"The church census."

"The church census? What on earth for?" Beulah glanced over at her for no more than a second, but that's all it took for her to nearly rear-end the car ahead of hers. She slammed on the brakes and tsked. "Lord A'mighty. This traffic will be the death of me."

Cookie steadied her hand on the dash, then chose her next words carefully. "I ran into Henrietta at the library. I was going through the census to make sure I'm in there. And I found my name, in 1940."

"So? That's good, right?"

Cookie fidgeted, peering out the side window as she searched for the right words. "Henrietta checked the *church* records. I'm not in the church census until 1936. Neither are Mama and Daddy," Cookie said in a rush. "If Daddy and Mitzi lived here their entire lives like they'd said, why did they only show up on the church rolls in 1936? The census is taken every ten years, but the church records are prepared yearly."

"Maybe they didn't go to church until you were old enough to attend, or maybe they went to another church." Beulah kept her eyes on the traffic, hazarding a glance only when the traffic had stopped once again at another intersection.

"But wouldn't they have said something?"

Beulah turned on her blinker. "Even if they did attend another church, what does that prove?"

"Well, that I may not be Daddy and Mitzi's. That they may not have officially adopted me before 1936."

"First of all, Missy," Beulah growled, taking Cookie's hand firmly in hers as she waited for the light to turn and cars ahead of her to move, "that's a huge leap to take. And secondly if they *did* adopt you, so what? You still love them, don't you?"

"Of course."

"And nothing can change that, can it?"

"No." Cookie shook her head fiercely.

"Then there's nothing to talk about," Beulah said, releasing

Cookie's hand and patting her knee just as the light turned green.

"But," Cookie blinked back tears, "Henrietta just happened to let it slip to the gardening committee that I may not be mama and daddy's. And they specifically wanted to work with someone from Alabama, preferably someone from this area." Her words trailed off in a near whisper.

"Speak up. Use your big girl voice," Beulah said, brooking no argument. "So what are you going to do about it?"

Cookie frowned. "What do you mean?"

"I mean, what are you going to do about it? Cry? Complain about how unfair it is that they don't take you seriously because you may or may not be from here? Because you're a woman and you think differently? Or because you're not 'pure' enough, or whatever dumb reason they come up with to exclude you? I never let that stop *me*."

Cookie didn't know what to say. It dawned on her that Beulah had probably dealt with this sort of thing nearly every day of her life. And yet, what alternatives did Cookie have? If the door was closed, the door was closed.

"Oh, honey." Beulah shook her head and "tsked," her disappointment evident from her tone. "Me and your mama didn't raise you to roll up in a ball like one of those pill bugs you were always playin' with as a child." She reached over and tapped on Cookie's chin. "You hold your head up, girl. If the clubhouse is closed, you make your own clubhouse, let people come to *you*."

"What do you mean?" Cookie turned to Beulah, giving her full attention to the elderly woman.

"I mean you set up your own shop like my oldest son did. And you advertise. And you take any help you can get from family and friends. Or better yet, get a permit and sell from your greenhouse. That way it won't cost you anything, except for whatever rent your momma and daddy charge. That, and you'll need a till. It's too bad you don't have more space though, for more greenhouses and a parking lot. Still, it's a start."

Cookie felt her blood stir and her excitement grow. "Do you think I could do it?"

Beulah laughed and patted her knee. "Oh, honey, you can do anything you set your mind to. And Dipsy could help."

"But Dipsy's got a family. . ."

"For now." Beulah lifted a single brow.

"So, she talked to you?"

"Honey, *everyone* talks to me," she said, tapping the brakes, "even your mama. It's what I do. Listen. You might learn a thing or two if you tried it once in a while."

Cookie winced because it was true. Just as Beulah was a listener, Cookie was a talker, or more precisely, a doer. It's just that she found life so interesting. She'd always had way too much curiosity. Once, Mitzi had said Cookie could never get bored because she always had her nose in a book, her foot in the garden, and wore her heart on her sleeve. And it was true. Nature fascinated her. It was where she felt whole. Without it, she would shrivel up and die as surely as if she'd been put into solitary confinement. That's why she had never lasted long in jobs where she was stuck indoors all day. To her, it had felt like a slow death. And books were where she traveled to other worlds, lived different lives, learned new things. But what caused her problems was the fact that she *did* wear her heart on her sleeve, and as such, she was easily taken advantage of by people who saw her as giving, caring, a nurturer. *A target. A rube.* They could use her naivete for their own purposes. She would have to get over that if she were to go into business.

"So what are you going to do?" Beulah asked, refusing to let her stew and fester.

"Well, first, I need to build my inventory, if I'm going to make this a real business. Then in July, I have a trip to make with Dipsy--"

"And me," Beulah said as she peered through the rearview mirror.

"W-what?" Cookie said, not sure how she would feel about having Beulah along should she discover that she was indeed the missing child from the article. But then again, Beulah, of all people, would love her no matter what she learned. Be her biggest supporter and fan.

"Why not? I fit better in that neck of the woods than you two girls. I can open doors for you."

It was true, Cookie knew. Former sharecroppers were generally black, or poor whites who had no doubt worked alongside blacks in some capacity or other. Beulah might get them to speak about things they wouldn't with either Cookie or Dipsy.

"You've got exactly five minutes to think it over, 'cause we're almost to your house," Beulah said. "And you're gonna have to come up with an explanation for why I'm taking the rest of the day off." She showed off her teeth in a wide smile. "And then you gonna have to come up with an explanation why I'm goin' to take a week off in July. And when we go, you're gonna come pick me up at my house, say nine o'clock. That work for you?"

Cookie had to laugh. If Beulah wasn't so darned right about everything, Cookie might actually be mad at her for putting her on the spot. But years of living with her and knowing how much she loved Cookie meant that she also knew Beulah was doing this as a way of insulating her from pain, should she learn anything unforeseen about her past. Because no one was more caring than Beulah. One of Beulah's motherly hugs could shore her up against the harshest of losses.

"Nine o'clock it is," Cookie said, giving Beulah's hand a squeeze as they pulled up to the sidewalk a couple houses down from hers. As she got out, she bent down and said, "And thanks, Beulah."

"Oh, girl," Beulah said with a brush of her hand. "We been together too long for that. You just get your fanny in there."

Cookie almost had the car door shut when she heard a harried *Wait!* "What?" Cookie asked, peering inside the Nash Rambler.

"You almost forgot your mama's painting. You get that up in that attic before she finds out you took it, you hear? She's not gonna like that, sho 'nuff," she said, tsking.

"Oh, yeah!" Cookie grabbed the bundled painting from the back seat.

"And Cookie?"

"Yes?"

"Whatever we learn in July, you be kind to yo' mama. Like me, she's worked darned hard to raise you. She loves you. You take that away from her and she gonna look worse than them Dalmatian boots y'all are wearing." And just like that, Beulah howled with laughter, then leaned over and shut the door, waving as she drove away. . . wearing the high heels Trixie had traded her.

12

MITZI STEPPED INSIDE THE GREENHOUSE and felt the wave of humidity engulf her, immediately wilting her hair. She'd been on edge ever since Rachel had shown up on her doorstep the other day. And then Beulah and Cookie had taken off in the late afternoon yesterday with some fluky excuse about needing something at the store. What was up with that?

Then this morning, Dipsy had announced that she needed to go pick up some face cream at the local drugstore before she left for home and Cookie had insisted she accompany Dipsy. But it was clear by the sulkiness of the exchange that they were on the outs.

As soon as they had left, Mitzi rushed Dipsy's two kids outdoors, promising them a trip to the local drugstore when they returned, where she would buy Russell a Tonka truck or a plastic army set. For Rita Mae, she'd offered a Nancy Drew mystery book and one of those silly rubber sea creatures that she was so fond of. But first, she needed to meet with Randall Quid, who lived and worked in nearby Milltown. Fortunately, Rachel had stayed away for the past five years and Mitzi hadn't needed to contact the private investigator in all that time. Now the woman was back. But as the saying went, "the best defense is a good offense," and where Cookie was concerned, Mitzi would do whatever it took to protect her daughter.

She'd planned the meeting with the P.I. in the greenhouse, where she could discreetly keep an eye on the kids and where Ebie would be least likely to look, should he return home early. The greenhouse was Cookie's domain, not hers. She didn't know how long either Ebie or the girls would be gone, so she'd had to pay extra to expedite the meeting with Randall. Anxiously, she entered the greenhouse and peered through the shrubbery -- more like a jungle. She stood at the potting table and watched for Randall's car, the humidity making her hair sag. Nothing.

After pacing for what seemed like forever, she saw his brown station wagon pull to a halt in the back alley and watched as he unlatched the gate as directed. He made his way down the back path toward the greenhouse, stopping momentarily to say something to the kids who giggled and kept swiping at the boxwoods with their nets, in search of bugs.

It was clear Randall had aged in the five years since she'd last seen him. He was no longer paper thin. Instead he had a rounded gut. His hair had thinned as well, and it was beginning to turn gray at the edges. Yet, even as she watched him approach, she could see that he hadn't become stodgy with age, as some men did. No, he wore a permanent dimple as if always smiling. That was one reason she'd hired him over the others. Because he was a man who *cared*. He had understood her predicament immediately when she had first brought her case to him. An orphan himself, he had understood a mother's love, albeit in her case not the biological mother. Besides, he had seen too many cases where the birth mother was unfit for the job. Had thought a child lucky to find a good home. Oh, Mitzi knew it went both ways. Women gave up children for all sorts of reasons, not the least of which was a real love for the infant, so much so that they wanted better for the child than what they could provide. And being the adopting parent didn't guarantee real love and compassion. Some adopted to hang onto a spouse. And maybe that's how it had started out for Mitzi, but one look at the child and she had fallen in love with Cookie, loved her like spring air after a rainstorm, like the dew that lingers long after the sun has risen. No, she couldn't imagine a world without Cookie. Didn't want to *live* in a world without Cookie. She'd been fortunate to have become pregnant a year and a half after they adopted Cookie. And this time she hadn't miscarried. Still, what if she hadn't become pregnant, had never been able to conceive? Would she have enjoyed the life she had? She clasped her hands together in thanks, grateful that she'd never had to face that outcome.

Just then, the door opened with a jingle, and in popped Randall. Mitzi rushed to meet him, ushering him to the potting table where Cookie had a row of stools so she could sit and work while potting.

"Sorry about the mess," Mitzi said, offering Randall a seat on one of the tall metal stools.

The air was pungent with the fecund odors of the indoor garden, the smell of soil and moisture, of tropical flowers and aromas too numerous to name. Though Mitzi hated to admit it, she could almost understand Cookie's love of the soil, her propensity for the greenhouse where she lovingly took cuttings and sank them into the soil, their tips dipped in Rootone.

"Cookie has quite the green thumb," Randall noted, his eyes taking in the sweep of color from the green-and-white spider plant, the many phalaenopsis, to the red-veined prayer plant that closed up each night as though praying, which Mitzi was doing now. Praying that Rachel would give up this quixotic quest to find the daughter she had left at the doorstep of poor black sharecroppers all those years ago. Give up the need to assuage her guilt.

"How did you know the greenhouse was hers?"

Randall had the beginnings of a beard, shaved at the sides so that it formed a banjo shape around his mouth.

"Lucky guess. I don't see you as quite the greenhouse type. And unless your husband has a green thumb, the only one who would spend any time in a greenhouse would be her."

Mitzi cocked her head, appraising the man. No wonder he was a P.I. He thought like a detective.

"So, she's back?"

Mitzi nodded. Rachel had sought her and Ebie out so many times in the past that she and Randall didn't even need to discuss the name. They both knew who he was talking about. And each time the panic in Mitzi's gut grew a little larger, more unmanageable. But this was the first time the woman had come face to face with Cookie. Now the panic had turned into a heavy weight seated on Mitzi's chest. She couldn't breathe. All the questions that had circled over the years began to bear down on her like vultures, watching, waiting: What would Cookie do when she found out the truth? Would she still love Mitzi and

Ebie? Or would she feel betrayed, storm out and never return? Mitzi wouldn't blame her if she did. But she wasn't willing to take that chance.

Over the years, Mitzi had learned a thing or two about Rachel, and what she had discovered had made her more convinced than ever that she needed to protect Cookie from any pain should she learn the truth. Maybe if the woman's life had been less messy, Mitzi might have been more amenable to the idea of Cookie finding out about her biological mother. But what she had garnered had given her pause. Rachel's husband had left her not long after the tornado of 1932 and had remarried, left the past behind. Their house had been spared in the whirl of dust and wind, but the child had disappeared. Much later, Randall had discovered that Rachel had moved halfway across the country, to a tiny little town in Fort Wayne, Texas. Mitzi had breathed a sigh of relief. Rachel was out of their lives. But just as suddenly, she'd moved back. And not only had she returned, but she had moved to the next town over.

Randall removed a file from his attaché case and laid it onto the dusty potting table, tapping it with his index finger. "As you know, I've got a running file on Rachel. She's lived a difficult life, but overall, she's done nothing illegal. Yes, she may move a lot, but that happens when you live on the lower rung of the social stratum."

Mitzi's hackles rose. Why was he suddenly defending Rachel? *She* was the one who had abandoned her child. *She* was the one who was creating havoc in their lives.

"We seem to have lost track of her after this last move. She probably hasn't found a place to land yet, but she will."

"What if she lands here? What then?" Mitzi demanded,

unable to quelch the rising tide of hysteria in her voice.

Randall turned to face her directly. The compassion in his eyes made her feel as though she was falling down a deep, dark abyss. Was she wrong to want Cookie all to herself? Was she wrong to want to protect her daughter from all the ills in life?

"I wasn't going to tell you this, but I think it may help." He peered down at his hands, at his long tapered fingers, which he held together as though in supplication.

Mitzi felt a rising tide of frustration. Wanted him to tell her the words that she longed to hear -- that everything would be okay. That he would see to it personally that nothing would ever enter their world that could hurt her or Cookie, send her family reeling. But she knew that was impossible.

"I met my biological mother this year," he murmured, turning to face her.

Mitzi gasped and flung her hand to her heart, the weight heavier still. God help her.

"Mitzi, I know you don't want to hear this," he said with utmost patience, "but I *like* her. Yes, her life has been tough, but she's a decent person. And it doesn't negate my love for my parents -- not at all. It's just that. . . well, I always felt like there was something missing. A part of me. Sort of like phantom limb syndrome, you know? Now I feel, well. . . whole. There's no other way to describe it."

The pity in his eyes sent her reeling. She rose from her metal chair so abruptly that it tumbled backward with a metallic ring and a crunch of gravel as it landed on the potting shed floor. "Maybe this was a mistake," she said, "to call you. How could you possibly know what it's like for a mother--" She covered her mouth with the back of her hand to stifle a sob.

Randall put the file back in his case and stood. "I'm really sorry, Miss Mitzi. I know this is hard for you. Probably more than anyone else, I know how hard this can be. And I promise to keep looking for Rachel. I'll call you the minute I learn anything new. But I want you to really think about what I said. This woman may not be as bad as you think. And Mitzi--"

Hot tears choked the back of her throat, rendering her speechless.

"You've got to learn to forgive. For your sake, for Rachel's sake, but most of all, for Cookie's sake. I hope you'll think about it."

Then he was gone. Mitzi wiped away her tears with a sheet off a roll of paper towels Cookie kept handy for quick clean-ups in the greenhouse. How could Mitzi possibly forgive Rachel? After all, she'd never forgiven herself for not being honest with Cookie. No, she simply wasn't ready. She breathed deeply of the humid air, allowing herself a moment of self-pity. Then she straightened her spine, put a smile on her face, and walked to the door of the greenhouse, determined to put on a good show for the grandkids.

* * *

Rachel picked up the phone and dialed the number of her landlord, her heart tripping in her chest as she waited for the woman to pick up. Always before, when Ebie and Mitzi had discovered her whereabouts, she had moved on quickly, her bags packed just in case. This time, she had entered their world, had made requests, had pushed the limits by speaking with Cookie, directly going against the contract she had signed when she'd given away her rights. She didn't know what Ebie and Mitzi would do this time, but she didn't want to find out. One thing for certain, they had the protectiveness of a lion when it came to their cubs. *That,* she understood. She might never have the same opportunities in her life as they'd had, but she had the same desire to protect her own. And whether anyone believed it or not, that was exactly what she had done when she'd given Cookie to Rayleen and Chester. Protected her.

"Where are you?" Rachel murmured as the phone rang yet again. Just as she was about to hang up, she heard a voice on the line.

"Who is this? What do you want?" the woman growled.

"Wait, it's me. . . Rachel. Don't hang up," she pleaded. The woman snorted. Rachel could picture her landlord in her moo moo and support stockings that ran midcalf, her hair dirty, her house dirtier. Her expression, even in the best of times, held an air of open disdain. . . for people, for the world in general, and for Rachel in particular, who she considered beneath her despite the woman's lack of finesse. "I have a favor to ask you," Rachel said in a rush.

"Oh, so Miss No Show wants a favor, does she? And what pray tell is that?"

In the background, Rachel could hear a commotion and knew that her landlady was scolding one of her kids, hand pressed over the phone as she had countless times while Rachel had lived there. Despite, or maybe because of, the woman's hounding, the children had turned out just like their mother. Obnoxious and rude.

"Has Ebie Haines or Mitzi Haines contacted you recently?"

Rachel could almost imagine the woman's eyes narrow to slits, hand on hips as she said, "So, what's it to you?"

Rachel took a calming breath to keep herself from going off on the woman as she'd wanted to do most of the time she'd lived with her. How could anyone enjoy seeing people squirm the way she did? Rachel squared her shoulders as if to do battle, then quietly but firmly said, "I need to know because. . ." In her mind she said, "Because I need to know whether to move." But somewhere, in the recesses of her brain, something had shifted and she no longer felt like running, so she simply waited.

"If you want to know whether they're looking for you, honey, I can give you the lowdown. A private investigator called. Says this Mitzi person you're asking about wants to meet with you. . . privately."

Her landlady spoke with such arrogance that Rachel wanted to slap the smug smile she knew the woman was wearing. That holier-than-thou expression that she wore most of the time, even though not one thing about her was holy.

She looked out the window of the phone booth, at her car, wondering where she would go to now. For several seconds, she closed her eyes. She'd been running half her life. If she didn't stop soon, then when? With a quiet conviction, she opened her eyes and said, "Give me the private investigator's phone number." She wrote it down on a spare piece of paper that she fished from her purse, using the glass of the phone booth for support. Then she walked out of the phone booth, heard the satisfying whoosh of the door closing. But what gave her the most satisfaction was the sound of the woman still talking on the phone as it dangled in mid-air. The woman would soon tire of hearing herself speak and hang up. In the meantime, Rachel's destiny lay ahead. It had been waiting for her all along, since the tornado. She knew that now. There would be no more running. She dialed Ebie's number and listened to the harsh rings, determined to speak with him. She would give Ebie two months, two months to do what she was about to ask. Then, whether he was ready or not, she was going to insist he face the truth, just as she had faced that fateful day in September, when the skies had broken loose, their fury changing the landscape of her life forever.

13

RAYLEEN BENT OVER THE ROWS of pole beans, wearing a wide straw hat and overalls and pulling at chickweed. Two months had passed since Rachel had called her and Chester, wanting them to take her in. Now, summer was here -- July, one of their hottest and muggiest seasons. Sweat dripped from her forehead down to the dark, loamy soil below. She stood, rubbing at her aching back. In the distance, she could see a cloud of dust and a big black truck chugging up the narrow road that led to their farm.

"Chester!" she called, never comfortable with strangers, and especially a stranger who came by truck. "Chester!" she shouted, panic beginning low in her belly and rising as it did every time something out of the ordinary happened to change her daily routine.

Chester, who was one field over and weeding between the

cotton rows, looked up and shielded his eyes from the sun. He peered first at Rayleen, then followed her gaze. For a moment, he didn't react. Then he let out a sharp retort to his farmhand and began heading her way, slow at first, then picking up speed so that he was nearly running by the time the black truck neared. Though her husband was a big man, a bulky man, he was quick on his feet, when push came to shove, and he was quick now, thank heavens.

"What do you suppose they want?" Rayleen said to Chester when he arrived panting and out of breath. She kept her voice low, barely moving her lips for fear that the two white men in the big black truck would read her thoughts, her panic.

Chester reached out a meaty hand to steady Rayleen, a large woman in her own right, sinewy. Strong. She'd had to be, to carry such burdens as she had on her broad shoulders. A colored woman didn't get through life without strong shoulders. A colored man, too, for that matter.

The truck skidded to a stop, leaving a set of tracks in its wake. Stopped right in front of them. The two men didn't even bother getting out. For that, Rayleen breathed a measure of relief.

"You Chester Williams, boy?" a curly-headed man with thin lips said through his open window.

Chester removed his cap and nodded. "Yessuh."

"This came for you."

The man held a piece of paper in his hand, waving it. He blew a puff of smoke out the window, his eyes lingering just a bit too long on Rayleen as he sized her up. Rayleen could almost feel Chester stiffening at the affront to his wife. Before he could react, Rayleen rushed to the window and snatched the paper from the insolent man, then quickly handed it to Chester.

"Thanks so kindly for bringin' this here letter to us." Rayleen looked down at the yellow envelope and felt her heart sink. *Western Union. A telegram.* It's then she noticed the Western Union sign in the back window of the truck. Her hands trembled as she waited. Waited for the men to leave. Waited to find out what was in the envelope. Waited for the news that their son, Mason, stationed in Vietnam, was either wounded or dead. Her daughter-in-law, Corliss, and son James, who lived on the edge of the forest and told tales of all sorts of critters of the night stalking their livestock, must have seen the truck headed their way, because they came by mule and buckboard.

The two men in the black truck seemed to recognize their diminishing odds and bid a hasty farewell, but not before the man in the passenger seat took one last draw on his rolled cigarette, then flicked it in their direction with a laugh. Rayleen held onto Chester's fist which, for the moment, was kept safely at his side.

Just then, James and his wife, Corliss, drew the mules to the side of the road, the truck barely missing them as it sped off in a fresh new cloud of dust.

"You okay, Daddy... Mama?" James said, tying off the reins and jumping down, then leaning in to give Corliss a hand. James looked nothing like his daddy. For years, neighbors had teased Rayleen about the differences. Whereas Chester was a big man with massive arms and meaty fists and had only a few years of schooling, James was small-boned and self-educated. Smart as a whip. "Daddy?"

Chester's eyes flashed fury, but beneath it all, Rayleen knew he was just as scared as she was. Finally, as though recalling why the men were there to begin with, he peered down at the offending telegram.

"Mason?" James asked, his eyes falling to the telegram then back to Chester.

"Dunno," Chester said, his shoulders sagging as he let go of his anger.

"Well, read it!" Rayleen hissed all the while intoning *please be alive, please be alive, please be alive.*

Chester seemed to finally come out of his reverie, for he lifted the envelope and slowly opened it, keeping them all in suspense. A hush fell over the group even as the sun baked down on them.

"Well?" Rayleen said with more than a bit of trepidation. "What does it say?"

Chester, who had come to reading late in life, read the words slowly, enunciating each word.

I need to speak with you. Stop. *Will arrive in two day's time.* Stop. *Will arrive by railway.* Stop. *E.B. Haines, Esquire.*

"Mistah Haines? What he want?" But even as Rayleen spoke the words, she *knew*, without a shadow of doubt, that Rachel was back and this time was different. This time she wasn't going to let go of the burr that was even now burrowing its way under her skin. No, this time was different. That woman was dying. And Rachel was determined to get to the truth, to set things right. To reunite mother and daughter.

It's only fair. But fair in 1960s Alabama was a far sight different than fair in other parts of the world. Why, she'd heard tell a colored or an Indian could walk right down the streets of France and no one would give a whit.

Chester shook his head, all the while clucking *hmm-hmm-hmm.* "I think we got ourselves a sit-chi-ation."

"Situation?" James translated. "What kind of situation? You talkin' about Cookie?"

Rayleen wondered how much James remembered about the toddler. He'd only been eight years old at the time she'd arrived, but he'd held a fascination for her. Every chance he got, he'd have her out playing in the garden. He'd sit her up next to him while he weeded and hoed. He'd prop her up against the old elm tree, a quilt beneath her, and keep a running dialogue going. Occasionally, he would stop to show her some plant or other. He would explain its care, and she would talk back in toddler speak, her words often garbled and her lower lip ringed in spit, her little hands looking for all the world like she was "splaining" something to him. When it was time for a break, he would sit out with her and hand her bits of food, then hold her to him, feeding her like she was his own. He would show her butterflies, and walk her through the garden, repeating the names of the flowers and vegetables over and over until she could repeat a handful of words. At strawberry picking season, Rayleen would dress the toddler in overalls, then James would put a little straw hat on her to keep the sun off. Nine times out of ten, she'd pull it off, and James would quietly, patiently, walk over to her and put it back on so that the sun wouldn't beat down on her face. Then he would kneel beside her with his bucket and pick. On tottering feet, little Cookie, as they had named the toddler, seemed to get the idea. She would pick one strawberry, drop it in the bucket, pick another, eat it. Pick one, drop it in the bucket, pick another, eat it. And on it went until Cookie looked like a ripe pumpkin, her mouth covered in strawberry juice.

It took Rayleen a moment to realize she had gone back in time so completely that she had forgotten the conversation until, suddenly, everyone was looking at her waiting for an answer.

"You thinking about Cookie, Ma?" James said.

Rayleen didn't realize she'd started crying until she felt the salty sting of the tears moistening the corner of her eyes. Amazing how quick a little one like that could worm its way into a heart. Into a soul. How she wanted to wrap her arms around that girl one more time. To know that she was okay and cared for. Well, she would have her answer soon. In two day's time.

14

SHIELDING HIS EYES FROM THE intense afternoon rays, Ebie marched over to Union Station. Two months had passed since Rachel had shown up at their house, had seen Cookie. She had phoned him shortly after her visit, had offered an ultimatum, a demand that he had given in to, at least part of what she'd asked. Afterward, she had stuck around Montgomery for a time, but as the deadline neared for the second part of the ultimatum, she'd suddenly gone missing.

Where are you, Rachel?

A police officer, who stood in the middle of 210 Water Street, blew into a shrill whistle as he directed the hustle and bustle of pedestrians and traffic. That sound and the smell of creosote from the railroad ties filled Ebie with nostalgia for his childhood. He, in knickers, waiting for his father to return home from France where he'd served as an officer at the Battle of Belleau Wood. He recalled his father's eyes as he searched the depot for signs of Ebie and his mother. The smell of his father's aftershave as he rushed into their waiting arms, first kissing Ebie's mother, then snapping Ebie up in an embrace and carrying him one-armed through the thoroughfare, his mother holding tight to his father's elbow as though afraid to let go of him lest he fade into the crowd -- once again, gone. With reluctance, Ebie let the memory fade.

He didn't know what he hoped to accomplish once he was in Shardsburg. Would Rachel Aberdeen even be there? He had felt certain she would stick around this last time, but somehow he had lost track of her this past week and a half and it didn't sit well. Everywhere he went, he felt her shadow, but when he turned, no one was there. He'd had trouble sleeping because not only had he lied to Cookie about her birth, he'd lied to Mitzi as well. Why couldn't Rachel let sleeping dogs lie? More importantly, why hadn't he kept her on his radar? On a hunch, he decided to go to Shardsburg, to speak with Rayleen and Chester to see if they knew anything. Over the years, she had touched base with them as often as she had Ebie. If anyone knew something, it would be them, yet as an outsider, he felt certain they would only speak candidly if he met with them face to face.

As he stepped to the side of a stately elm to allow a couple to pass, he berated himself. For some inexplicable reason, he had thought by humoring Rachel's latest request, she would wait patiently until he could decide what to do, which in the end would add up to little. He had simply planned to wait her out. That decision had lulled him into a false sense of hope. It would destroy Cookie if she believed her whole life had been a lie. Dipsy had her family and her church, plus all of her society friends, for support in a crisis. And sure, Mitzi's insecurities would be put to the test, but eventually she would be okay. No, it was Cookie he worried about most. Just like Mitzi, she looked strong on the outside, but she had a marshmallow inside. Mitzi did, too, but it was different with her. In the end, she was a Southerner, through and through. She had the steel backbone that Cookie did not.

Except for that one time, he reminded himself. The moment that had changed all of their lives forever.

He pressed forward, traversing the cracks on the sidewalk, head down. Cookie was so independent, a loner. In a crisis, she had only Ebie and Mitzi to turn to, but would she? And if she didn't? What then? He couldn't take that chance.

No, he had to find a way to make this right, to sweep the past under the rug as he had so many times before. Better yet, put a lid on the past and keep it tightly sealed.

He felt a sharp pain in his stomach, his ulcer acting up again. He reached into the pocket of his suit vest and pulled out a couple of antacids then popped them one by one into his mouth and chewed.

Most people used the Amtrak depot these days. More modern. Quicker, too. But Ebie liked the comfortable old brick facade of Union Station, the line of arched windows that reminded him of wheels on a train. Built in 1898 by the Louisville and Nashville Railroad, it had withstood countless changes to the Montgomery landscape through storm and drought alike. It had carried soldiers like his father, from WWI and again from WWII, through its terminal, seeing them off to places unknown, reuniting the lucky ones with families, but changed by the war. Always changed.

Now, it's my turn for change.

Ebie gazed up at the massive building. F. Scott Fitzgerald had met his wife Zelda here while stationed at nearby Camp Sheridan during WWI. Yes, the railroad and the Train Shed had a long, historied past for so many in this community. Ebie was so focused on his thoughts that he scarcely noticed people passing him, the men doffing their hats and nodding with a brief, "Mr. Haines."

In fact, he'd been *so* lost in thought that he hadn't realized he was in the path of someone until he ran into a man with a loud "oomph"!

"Oh, I'm so sorry, Mr. Haines. I didn't see you."

Ebie looked up to see Winston Cowel who everyone called Winn, his parents clearly an admirer of Winston Churchill, as Ebie was himself. Winn was tall, just a hair over six feet, and had light wavy brown hair. Ebie guessed him to be about thirty years of age. A genial sort. And like Cookie, he seemed to always have his hand in the garden. He was said to have worked hard as a teen after his father died, saving up to buy his own plot of land. A gentleman farmer.

"No, please, pardon me," Ebie said with an apologetic smile. "I, well. . . have a lot on my mind."

"Ditto, Sir," Winn said with a laugh, but his smile quickly turned to a frown. "I know you're busy and all. . . but may I ask you a question?"

"Of course."

"Were you headed into the station?" Winn's blue eyes held a question.

"Sure was," Ebie said. "You want to go inside, take a seat and ask me your question?"

Winn heaved a sigh and nodded. "That would be great, Sir,"

he said, marching over to the door and opening it for Ebie. "You first."

Ebie couldn't help but smile. It had always been him opening doors for other people, but now the early gray must be showing because young men had started opening doors for him. It had never failed to remind him that there was a before and after. Young and old. And as someone who was becoming aware of his age, he knew he had to make things right for Cookie's sake. For all their sakes.

Sometimes he wasn't sure he wanted to be around to see his family pick up the pieces should the truth ever come out. But then on better days, he wished that the truth would come pouring out so that the family could begin the healing process. Yet, what if Cookie hated him -- both him *and* Mitzi -- for the deception? What then?

Well, he would cross that bridge when he came to it.

They pushed through the wide terminal with high ceilings and huge wooden beams. Oak benches lined the marble floor, and wooden railings on the upper story showcased the stained glass windows. Rays of color shone through them, bathing the room in an ambient glow of colored light. Ebie ushered Winn to an empty spot next to a harried mother with three small kids.

He turned to the young man. "So, how may I help you?"

"Well, as you probably know," Winn said, fidgeting, "I have some property just north of town."

Ebie nodded, not sure where the young man was headed with this.

"And, well, I've heard you have land up north." The man peered down at his tapered fingers as though wondering how to proceed. "Former sharecroppers, am I right?"

The skin at the nape of Ebie's scalp tingled. How could this man possibly know where he was headed? Had Max spoken to him? He felt new pangs in his stomach, grabbed another antacid and sucked on the chalky tablet, waiting.

"Well, the thing is, Mr. Haines, I'm trying to decide whether I should lease out a portion of my property." He turned a deep crimson and squirmed in his seat. "Of course, I was never comfortable with the idea of sharecropping. It was just too much like slavery. . ." His words trailed off, unfinished.

"I see," Ebie said, his feet in both worlds, the old one that provided certain advantages for him and his family, and the new one that was challenging the old concepts of status quo. Although Cookie didn't know about the Shardsburg property, she *did* know about his other land holdings. She had called such contracts "debt slavery," even though he had long since given up sharecropping in favor of leasing the land. Each time she had brought it up, he'd used his skills at debate to try to change her mind. Still, she had nicked at his conscience. Worse yet, he had worried that perhaps she'd known something about what had happened all those years ago. But in the end, it was clear that she hadn't. "So, how can I help you?"

Winn rubbed his sweaty palms on the knees of his pants. "It's just that farming that much property would be a huge undertaking for one person, and I don't earn enough income from the portion of the farm that I work myself to hire people to handle the rest. Besides, you know how difficult farming can be."

Once again, Ebie felt a jolt of remorse. Each year his sharecroppers had fallen deeper and deeper into debt. Until the fifties, he had owned the store where they purchased their goods on credit, and he received a third of the prospective earnings from their crops. The sharecroppers bore the brunt of any loss, be it from weather or pestilence, bad health or injury. Cookie accused him of "reaping the rewards off the backs of the downtrodden." Even now, it left a sour taste in his mouth.

"Then renting your land outright would be the way to go," Ebie said, glad to be of help to the younger man.

"Do you know of anyone who might be interested in leasing the land, Sir?" Winn asked, dipping his head slightly to avoid a woman behind him with a rather large handbag.

Ebie put a finger to his chin, his eyes taking in the remarkable stained glass windows as he thought. "You could ask around at church," he said at last. "I'm certain you could find a taker."

Winn sighed, clearly disheartened, but stood. "I see. That makes sense. Well, thanks for your time, Mr. Haines. And say hello to Cookie for me."

Ebie could have sworn the young man blushed when he mentioned Cookie. Ebie had always secretly wondered if Winn had a thing for her. After all, they both enjoyed gardening, tilling the land. Despite Mitzi's mentoring, Cookie seemed to have been born in overalls, which no well-bred woman in Mitzi's family had ever dared to wear in private, much less in public. If only Cookie had been born a man, she would have done well in the nursery business. As it was, it remained little more than a hobby. Winn was about to turn away when Ebie suddenly had a thought and grabbed the other man's sleeve. "Wait! I have an idea. Let me run it past Cookie. She has quite the greenhouse."

Winn chuckled. "That she does. That girl could grow a cactus in a rainforest."

Ebie smiled, certain if anyone could do it, Cookie could. Maybe, just maybe, she *could* have her own business, with the right encouragement. Still, a woman on her own, hoping to run a business, would have a hard time in Montgomery. He shook his head at the ludicrous thought he'd almost entertained.

As he watched the other man finger his shirtsleeves nervously, another thought occurred to him, one that might actually work, if he set his mind to it. Perhaps, with the right leverage, Ebie could point Cookie in Winn's direction, thereby making it possible for her to still dabble in horticulture while forestalling yet another Sunday meal with Mitzi extolling the virtues of marriage along with the fact that Cookie wasn't getting any younger, nor were "her eggs." Ebie had found the whole discussion almost as distasteful as Cookie herself, but there was no talking Mitzi out of her "Sunday sermons," as he had come to think of them.

Turning his attention back to Winn, he said, "Cookie has a growing business and she's running out of space at home. Would you be amenable to leasing the property out for greenhouses?"

"Would I!" Winn all but gushed. "I've even thought of it myself, but I didn't have the capital."

Ebie felt a welling of excitement almost equal to that of Winn, but he held it in check, preferring to play his hand close to his chest. "Let me see what I can do. Now, you do understand that Cookie can be stubborn--"

"I do," Winn said, biting his lip.

"And that she can be willful--"

"That, too," Winn agreed.

Ebie chuckled inwardly. The man obviously knew Cookie rather well. "Then it's settled. I'll speak to her and let her know about the lease. How many acres and how much are you asking?"

"Ten acres. The price is negotiable."

As travelers jostled the pair, Ebie considered the man's words: *I don't have any capital.* Perhaps Cookie and Winn could go into business together. Winn was clearly smart with his money, whereas Cookie didn't have the best business sense. But she did have real talent with plants. And Mitzi was right, she *wasn't* getting any younger.

Ebie frowned and looked over at the ticket window and the growing line of customers. "Look," he said, turning back to Winn. "I have to travel to Shardsburg within the next couple of days. Could you hold off leasing your property until I return? I need to talk to Cookie, but I have business first. It shouldn't take more than a week. I can pay you a holding fee, if you'd prefer."

Winn's face lit up. The man would never make a good poker player. "No need. I can hold the property for a week. And thank you, Sir," he said, taking Ebie's hand and pumping it vigorously.

Ebie patted the young man on the shoulder then pulled out a small notepad and pen that he kept with him at all times, should he run into any of his clients while out and about. It helped him keep track of the many questions they shot his way. He handed the notepad to Winn. "Write down your number, and I'll give you a call when I return."

The man hurriedly scribbled down his number, then gave Ebie's hand a final pump before leaving. With a chuckle, Ebie watched Winn go, the poor man clearly distracted as he ran into passengers, gesturing his apologies. Lost in thought himself, Ebie turned his attention to the ticket counter. Now, he just needed to purchase tickets to Shardsburg. Then he would work his magic on Cookie.

15

COOKIE LOVED THE SMELL OF freshly mown grass in the morning, the sound of the rainbirds tick-tick-ticking water across the lawn. She loved the whistle of the tufted titmouse, the trills of the dark-eyed juncos, and the flute-like voices of the hermit thrush. However, this morning, as she sat in the passenger side of Dipsy's Buick, it was hard to savor the sights, sounds, and smells, because Mitzi had taken to caterwauling, her hands thrown up in mock despair. Okay, so Cookie *hadn't* found the right time until now to tell Mitzi she would be losing her help around the house for the next week.

At least Cookie and Dipsy had made up in the past two months. Unfortunately, Kent and Dipsy hadn't, evidenced by the narrow set of her lips and the fatigue around her eyes.

"Beulah has a sick aunt down in Columbus. Said to tell you she's really sorry." Cookie felt a pang of remorse at the cockamamie story she'd come up with on the fly. Truth was one thing she'd always prided herself on and she didn't like having to lie. But Mitzi was like a dog with a bone when she set to worrying. No. . . better to keep her muzzled for now, until they learned more.

"What am I going to do?" Mitzi leaned into the open window of the Buick and stared across at Dipsy. "I've got two grandkids to take care of, the house. . . and you haven't even mentioned where y'all are going. What will I say to Kent when he calls?"

"He already knows, Mama. I told him I'm taking a few days away," Dipsy said on a sigh, "so just leave it."

Cookie threw up her hands. No one, but *no* one, told Mitzi to "leave it." As tight as Cookie's shoes felt right about now, she felt certain that Dipsy's felt tighter.

"But, but. . ." Mitzi sputtered and fumed.

"Mama," Cookie said, putting a hand on Mitzi's arm. "Dipsy takes care of the kids and a house, and she does all that without help. She's *tired*. She just needs a couple of days away to rejuvenate. . . like that cream you wear on your face at night. You know. . . it makes you feel younger, better about yourself?"

For some reason, that seemed just the ticket, because Mitzi's mouth formed a wide "O." After that, she began smiling and shooed them away, telling them to have a good time. "And call me, girls!" She made a pretend phone with her hand, thumb to ear, little finger next to her mouth.

"You got it, Mama." Cookie wondered if this would be the last time she would be able to call Mitzi "Mama" and mean it.

"Thanks for understanding," Dipsy said, her usually pale olive skin appearing sallow this morning.

Today, Dipsy wore sunglasses to hide her eyes, and a silk

scarf over her curly brown hair, making her seem like a movie star, not the first time Cookie had thought so. Dipsy had that *"je ne sais quoi,"* a certain something that made people imagine themselves with her life. Want to *be* her. Cookie had heard friends of her mother huddled together whispering behind their hands at what a "looker" Dipsy was. Add to that, her sense of style and taste -- a taste that Cookie had bi-passed altogether -- and it was clear that Dipsy had developed a mystique that made heads turn, whether male or female. So why was such a beautiful woman, inside and out, having problems in her marriage? Cookie knew not to poke the bear by asking. Like Mitzi, Dipsy would tell Cookie in her own sweet time and not a second before.

As Cookie leaned out her window, Mitzi yelled, "Wait, stop!" She waved an envelope in the air. "This came for you in the mail. Probably another of your gardening ads."

Turning the envelope back and forth, Cookie inspected it. She could find no return address. Mitzi was probably right. Something for the garden. She stuffed it into her purse, then yelled, "Bye, Mama," as the two of them drove away waving, Dipsy at the wheel.

Cookie fell back in her seat and let the cool wind blow over her. It felt good to finally be on the road, to be dressed in normal clothes again, in white culottes and a short-sleeved burgundy sweater. To peer up at the elms that lined the street. Their first stop would be Beulah's house. Fortunately, by the time they arrived at her two-story brownstone twenty minutes later, Beulah was seated out on her porch swing, a paper sack at her side. The warmth of the summer sun had already set the cicadas humming overhead in the Allegheny Chinkapin with its wooly, reddish round bark.

Dipsy parked the car in Beulah's driveway, then ran around to open the trunk while Cookie went to collect the older woman and to carry her paper sack for her. Inside the paper bag lay a folded dress, shoes, and a nightgown along with toothpaste and a toothbrush.

"Where is your luggage?" Cookie asked, helping Beulah up off the swing.

"You got it," Beulah said as though Cookie had lost her mind.

"You don't have a suitcase of some kind?"

"You're lookin' at it." Beulah fixed her with a stare.

"Okay, but Dipsy has enough space in that bag of hers. You two can share, if you want."

"I'll take my chances with what I have," Beulah said with her typical air of aloofness. She was always careful to hold her head high, throw her shoulders back. She had spent countless years trying to get Cookie to do the same. *That way people know you're someone. That you have value.*

But Cookie had never listened. After her failed attempt to sell her topiaries, she wondered if maybe she *should* have heeded Beulah's advice. She tried the new Cookie on for size. Shoulders back, head up.

"What you doin', girl?" Beulah said when she saw Cookie's antics.

"I'm doing what you've told me to do for years now."

"Well, stop it. You look ridiculous."

Cookie's shoulders slumped. Okay, so maybe she could never be Beulah, a woman who took her role as a strong black woman seriously. Maybe she could only be what she was -- a woman who loved getting her fingers dirty in the garden, who got as much pleasure out of watching a plant grow as most people did watching their favorite television show. Who enjoyed the simpler things in life.

After a somewhat rocky start, the three left in Dipsy's sedan, Beulah in the passenger seat and Cookie seated in the back, acting as co-pilot. She rolled out the map, twisting it every which way until she found the right road. "Okay, here we go!"

They made their way north toward Mt. Vernon, Alabama, two and a half hours north on I-65, three hours now that Dipsy was pregnant and had a squirrel bladder. Beulah handed them each a half piece of Juicy Fruit gum "to keep their mouths quiet."

"Why don't you ever chew a whole piece?" Dipsy asked as she turned on the blinker and shifted into the fast lane, a sporty red Alfa Romeo with two young men pulling alongside them and tooting the horn. Dipsy merely winked, then stepped on the gas.

"Well, I never," Beulah said, but laughed all the same. "And I only chew a half because money doesn't grow on trees, Miss Smarty Pants. Leastways, not for me."

Cookie couldn't tell if an admonishment was in there somewhere because Dipsy *had* married money. Oh, she loved Kent, too. But his lifestyle hadn't hurt anything in Dipsy's book. She followed Mitzi's mantra that it was just as easy to love a rich man as a poor man. And maybe it was. Or maybe love wasn't that simple. Maybe it had to do with caring more about someone else than yourself.

"So what you gonna do once you get to this Shardsburg?" Beulah asked Cookie, pulling a kerchief from her sleeve and blowing her nose. "I mean it's not like the same people gonna be livin' there after all this time."

Cookie had worried about that. What if this turned into the biggest wild goose chase of a lifetime? What then? "I only need to find one person who remembers something."

"And if there is no such person?"

In the silence that followed, the air thickened with anticipation. "Well, at least we'll have had a girls' weekend away."

A pall settled over the trio when, suddenly, Beulah snapped her gum and said in her normal irreverent tone, "The heck with that, girl. We need to make this weekend count. Dipsy!" she ordered, turning to Dipsy and directing her toward a pull-over on the side of the road. "Stop there."

"Wha--? Why?" Dipsy said, but did as told.

"We gonna teach this girl to drive. She can't go an entire lifetime havin' all of us drive her around. Got to learn for herself!"

And so, Cookie learned to drive. Her first attempts behind the wheel were rocky at best. The lane seemed too narrow, and she forgot to watch the road as she periodically peered at either Beulah or Dipsy as she drove. And of course, Dipsy's screams didn't help. But, little by little, as the road straightened and fewer cars served to frighten Cookie, she relaxed. . . a bit. Yet, by the time Dipsy was ready for her next potty break, Cookie was relieved to stand, her hands stiffened into claw-like talons.

"Stretch it out, girl," Beulah urged Cookie as Dipsy hurried inside the Winn-Dixie to pee and to purchase some Twinkies and Hostess Ho-Hos for the road.

Cookie bent her head from side to side and rolled her shoulders several times. It wasn't just learning to drive that had her so wound up, but knowing that somewhere out there her future and past awaited her like a talisman. What she learned could irreparably change her life, for better or worse. But in the end, did she have the courage or even the desire to find out? Until now, she'd had a good life. A life filled with family. Sure it was messy. Wasn't all family a little messy? But this was more. . . so much more.

"I know you're thinkin' 'bout this Rachel woman," Beulah said as she sloughed off the padded jacket she'd been wearing and heaved it into the back seat. She spit her gum into a tissue then peered over the Buick at Cookie. "But, whatever happens, your family loves you. They'll always be there for you."

Cookie wanted to believe that -- more than anything. But what if she *did* find out she was adopted? What then? Would Mitzi feel betrayed that Cookie had gone behind her back? Furthermore, would this other woman accept or reject her? She wished she could ask Beulah to hold onto her a little while longer, as she had as a child heading off to school for the first time. Get her to bend down and tell Cookie everything was going to be alright, that she just needed to take a deep breath and count to ten. Then Beulah would smile, as she had all those years ago, tears glistening in her eyes as she snapped five-year-old Cookie up in a bear hug that made a girl feel as though the outside world couldn't touch her, couldn't chew her up and spit her out like Sunday's liver and onions, which she'd hated on all counts. No, Cookie needed a big dose of Beulah to comfort her.

And the funny thing about Beulah was that she seemed to know just what to do. Because she marched on over, clamped her arms around Cookie and said, "Now girl, don't you go makin' me cry with that pouty lip of yours. We gonna get through this like we done got through everything else, you understand me, girl? And ain't no one gonna hurt my Cookie-girl even if I have to come give 'em what for."

Why that comforted Cookie, she had no idea, because truth to tell, Beulah was even farther down the ladder than Cookie herself in the estimation of her fellow Montgomery-ites, leastways in the white community. But Cookie knew quality when she saw it, and Beulah was a Rembrandt, a Stradivarius, and the Notre Dame Cathedral all rolled into one.

"You'll hold my hand through all. . . this?" Cookie asked, her lip trembling slightly no matter how much she willed it not to.

Beulah looked her in the eye, then reached down and clasped hands with Cookie right there in front of the Winn-Dixie with people gawking and a scrawny woman with a giant mole on her cheek pushing a food cart and glaring at the pair. At that moment, Beulah must have realized they were still in public, because she dropped Cookie's hands and acted all Aunt Jemimy, which she did whenever she was tryin' to keep white folks off her back. But Cookie knew. She knew that Beulah was twice the person that woman would ever be, because she had something *that* woman lacked. Compassion. A compassion big enough to hold up the world for a five-year-old when it was caving in on her. And for a thirty-three-year-old who didn't know where she fit, in a world where girls were to be seen and not heard, where intellect in a woman was suspect, where women were relegated to the back of the bus just as surely as Rosa Parks. For that empathy and compassion, Cookie would be forever grateful.

Before Cookie could dwell on it further, Dipsy exited the Winn-Dixie slurping a drip of vanilla ice cream that was running down her arm. As she neared, she said, "What? The cone's for the baby. Calcium. At least I didn't get pickles to go with, now hop in the car. I want to see Shardsburg before dark."

Cookie shook her head. Leave it to Dipsy to keep them all grounded. "Okay, co-pilot. Where to?"

16

RAYLEEN SHADED HER EYES AGAINST the intense rays of the early morning sun and frowned as a dark vehicle wended its way down the long dusty road. A cloud of dust and debris trailed it as it headed toward the old sharecropper's shack a mile away, on the edge of the field.

Could Ebie be here already? But he wasn't due for another day. No, it had to be someone else. And any unfamiliar vehicle was suspect in this neck of the woods. Strangers didn't just drop in. They had a purpose, and that purpose was seldom in Rayleen or Chester's favor. She grabbed the weathered porch railing and squinted, wishing she could divine the occupants of the large dark sedan.

Odd. No one ever drove down to the other shack except for the curious locals, and those were mostly kids. She'd had to run 'em off more than once. Stranger still, Ebenezer Haines, Ebie for short, had left the shack as it was after the twister of '32. Left it entirely intact. Dishes on the table as though someone might walk in any moment and sit down to some fried chicken and corn pone, okra and biscuits, washing it all down with a glass of whole milk or sweet tea. He'd even gone so far as to pay her to drive down twice a month to clean the place.

She shivered, despite the heat. The place just gave her the willies. . . like she was walkin' on someone's grave every time she marched up the creaky steps and used the old skeleton key to enter the house. She could swear the house groaned when she stepped inside. She always hurried through the job, expecting to see some ghost of the past, all the while wondering why Ebie had insisted on keeping the shack as it was, back in the day. After all, Mr. Ebie could have sold the place, or leased it out like he had their homestead. So, why hadn't he? Was it guilt? That question had nagged Rayleen to no end. There would come a day when she was too old to care for the shack anymore. What then? She removed her straw hat and fanned her face.

"Chester?" she called through the open doorway of her house. "Looks like we got company."

"Um?" he said, clearly distracted as he meandered onto the porch.

Rayleen pointed with her chin to the dust cloud making its way up the dirt road toward the neighboring shack. Mr. Ebie had long since rented out the excess land, allowing them to till the soil. They grew alfalfa and corn, cotton and wheat, whatever the market would bear.

Chester merely frowned.

"You okay?" Rayleen asked. Chester wasn't much for talking in the best of times, but this was worse than usual. "Something wrong?"

"Just wonderin' what Mister Ebie wants." The whites of Chester's eyes grew large.

"You suppose that's him there, that he come early?" she said, once again pointing her chin in the direction of the sedan and the dust cloud that was gathering near the old shack.

"Nah, he won't be here 'til tomorrow. He always comes when he says he will."

"Then who's that?" Rayleen asked, worry settling on her shoulders like one of Chester's woolen army blankets.

"Dunno," he said, "but I 'spect we gonna find out soon." He leaned through the doorway and grabbed the truck keys that they kept on a hobnail next to the screen door. "You comin' with me?"

Though rarely one to hesitate, Rayleen held back this time. The car was too nice, too "city" as they were apt to say around these parts, but only to each other. Who, besides Mr. Ebie, even knew about this lonely homestead in the backwaters of Alabama? Things tended to be a bit sleepy. Most whites had long since moved from Shardsburg, the last of 'em gone following the big tornado in '32. The only ones left were the Snyders, who had purchased the gas station and general store from the Haineses. Soon after, the interstate was built, bi-passing the one remaining establishment. Now, only the few locals still stopped in for the odd item they'd forgotten to buy while in town. Few ventured this far from the main highway for gas or food, despite the signs. The only thing that kept the Snyders going was their interest in many of the neighboring farms. They bought the seed and supplied the harvesting equipment in exchange for a percentage of the profit. And though that might *seem* like sharecropping, the

Snyders had been fair and well-liked. When the harvest hadn't been good, they'd reduced their share of the profits. When the harvest was 'specially good, folks gave a little extra. It worked for all parties. The Snyders had been much appreciated in these parts.

Chester interrupted her thoughts with a loud shrill whistle as he headed toward the old jalopy he had pieced together from various junkers. One fender was blue, the other rusted. The hood of the truck was gray so that when it was seen altogether, it reminded Rayleen of one of her aunt's crazy quilts. Chester opened the passenger door and yelled, "You goin' to check out those folks with me, girl?"

"Almost there!" she called, still lost in a funk as she rushed to climb into the truck.

He shut her door behind her with a loud thunk, then ran around front and climbed into the driver's side.

"Wait!" Rayleen said, peering toward the house. "Where's Charlotte? We're supposed to be watchin' her."

Chester chuckled at the mention of their granddaughter. She was always wandering off somewhere. "We'll only be a minute. 'Sides, knowin' that girl, she's probably by the crick catchin' pollywogs."

Rayleen knew he was right. No one would dare hurt Charlotte or risk Chester's wrath, and Chester protected his own. Besides, he was a big man who had boxed in his day and won near every bout.

"We'll come back for her. Now, buckle up," Chester said with a laugh, because of course the seat buckles had long since rusted shut, the nylon belts gray with mildew and curled into a yarn-like ball that seemed to always get caught in the doorjamb.

Before she'd had a chance to settle, he keyed the engine, and with several loud sputters, the truck sprang to life and chugged forward with a lurch. Chester's arm automatically swung out like a crossing guard at the railroad tracks to keep her from launching off the bench seat. The road, which became more and more rutted with each passing rain, jostled her back and forth as they drove, so much so that she slid in her seat and rested against Chester's shoulder. He took the opportunity to place an arm around her and kiss her on top of her head, all the while keeping an eye on the road ahead.

"You think this visit of Ebie's tomorrow has somethin' to do with selling the farm?" she asked, her mind a scattershot of emotion.

Chester nibbled on his lower lip, a sure-fire sign he'd been mulling that same question over in his mind. "Could be. He ain't a young pup no more and hasn't got any boys to pass this place on to. Maybe he's lookin' to sell."

"We ain't got no money, honey," she said, trying to lighten the mood, even as she was crumbling like a sugar snap inside.

"Maybe he'll give us time to pay. Could be," he said hopefully as he took the dirt road closest to the cottonwood by the river, the road he took near every summer morning when tending the field.

"Wishful thinkin', Little Man," she said, but she liked that about him -- that even in the worst of times he always looked on the bright side. *Hope.* She'd had too many of her dreams dashed to dare hope again. "Maybe he's comin' to talk to us about Cookie," she countered.

"What could Mr. Haines possibly have to say about Cookie after all this time? Don't make no sense."

He shook his head as they neared the old gray weathered shack where two white women and one older black woman now stood. Rayleen leaned forward, trying to place them but failed. As she took stock of the place, her thoughts scrolled back to the first time she'd ever seen Cookie as an infant, out on the front porch with Rachel. Funny how, even after all these years, her throat would catch and her eyes well with tears at the idea of a child she'd raised for a short while. But love was like that. It stayed with a person no matter the time or distance. And there was no greater love than of a mother and a child. Though she'd never technically been Cookie's mother, she'd raised her like one. Heck, she'd taken care of that child off and on since birth, only later coming to keep her after Rachel skipped town. How could a woman of any caliber look at a baby and not be changed? Rayleen conjured up Cookie as a baby, her outstretched hand exploring the contours of Rayleen's face, delicate eyelashes fluttering as the infant suckled a bottle and smiled, milk dripping from the corner of her mouth. A baby didn't see color, only love. Rayleen clucked at the thought. How could one look on the loving eyes of a baby and not be moved?

* * *

Cookie peered out the window of the Buick as it bounced down the rutted dirt road toward the old sharecropper's homestead. Then she rubbed her eyes, still tired after a night at a motel. They could have easily made it to Shardsburg by midday, even with Dipsy's squirrel bladder, but Dipsy had wanted to clean up, to start the day fresh. She had even paid for the motel. . . said she needed to rest up before going out to the

146

homestead, especially after the ordeal of Cookie's driving. Heck, even Cookie felt worn out, though she was nearly getting the hang of it by the time they'd pulled over into the parking lot of the Little Lytle Motel.

Now, as the end of the well-worn path to the Haines' property came into view, Cookie saw a small clapboard building, weathered to a deep chestnut, its front porch sagging. Behind it stood a cluster of cottonwood trees that ran the length of the creek bordering the homestead. Around the shack lay acres upon acres of watermelon that smelled sweet in the early morning July heat. Already, the day was proving to be a hot one, a scorcher as they liked to say in these parts. Through the open windows of the Buick, Cookie could hear cicadas thrumming in a "scritch-scritch" from the line of trees to the west.

As soon as the car rumbled to a stop, Cookie leapt out and ran up the porch, tripping on a loose board and scraping her ankle. Surprisingly, the windows to the shack were still intact, the glass wavy, as though a window into the past.

"Hurry!" she called to Dipsy and Beulah. But Dipsy only grumbled. And nothing would get Beulah moving until she was good and ready.

"I don't know why you're in such an all-fired hurry," Dipsy said, tugging at her skirt, which had ridden high up her thigh, stuck to the sweat from the heat and humidity. "The day's young. Geez!"

Cookie knocked on the door, waiting. No answer. She tried again, this time rapping a little louder than before. Still nothing. From the outside, the place appeared abandoned. Frustrated, she marched over to the window and pulled a handkerchief from her sleeve. She made a circular swipe at the light coating of dust on the window, then peered in. "Ooh, ooh!" Cookie called, ushering the still grumbling Dipsy over to her. "Look!"

"What's so darn interestin'. . .?" Dipsy's words died off as she peered in wide-eyed wonder. She turned to Cookie in amazement. "What on earth?"

17

COOKIE WAITED AS BEULAH HEAVED herself out of the black sedan and slowly marched up the steps of the sharecropper's house. Beulah stopped to wipe her face with a handkerchief, to stave off the heat.

"Come look," Dipsy called, waving her hands with excitement.

Slowly, Beulah traversed the rickety porch and then leaned forward to peer through the circle of glass Cookie had wiped clean. "Mm-mm-mm. Looks like no one has lived in this shack for years and yet it's clean as a whistle. Odd."

"My thoughts exactly," Cookie said, for inside was a time capsule from the thirties complete with an old worn oak kitchen table, a ewer placed in the center as though to serve lemonade on a hot day. In the corner sat a wood stove, an iron skillet on top of one of the burners, a dented coffee kettle on the other. A large basin and ewer offered the only means by which to wash, as she could see no bathroom. A single bed stood off to one side, a crazy quilt spilling over the sides of a white iron bedstead, the headboard done in a fine scrollwork. A hope chest sat at the end, as though waiting for its occupants to return.

On one side of the shack stood a wooden ladder that led to a loft with a single mattress and bedding, and a small nightstand. It, too, seemed stuck in time like an insect trapped in amber.

Cookie was so preoccupied with the sight that she hadn't noticed footsteps until she heard the words, "May I help y'all?"

Startled, Cookie pivoted in time to see a young girl in a plain, threadbare beige dress covered in miniature faded red flowers, her feet shod in dirty tennis shoes with holes near the toes and no stockings or socks. Her skin was the color of dark tea -- no cream -- and fine wrinkles lined her eyes. The top layer of her coffee-colored hair was burnished copper by the sun, and her lively eyes were set deep in her face. Furthermore, her irises were so dark brown as to be a single color. Cookie hadn't realized she'd been staring until the girl repeated herself.

"Uh, sorry, do you live here?" Cookie asked, her cheeks feeling warm as though touched by the summer sun.

"Nah! I live over yonder," she said, pointing far in the distance. "But my grandma and grandad live over there." She pointed to a brown shack weathered by the sun and wind. "I'm visitin' them. In fact, I think I see grandaddy and gran drivin' ol' Willy now."

And true to her words, a truck, as patchworked as that quilt on the bed, leaped and lurched along the rutted backroad toward the house. Cookie quickly turned toward the preteen, fearing that the grandparents might not be as forthcoming as the granddaughter.

"Does an Allister K. Byrd live here?" Cookie ventured, her heart stilling as she awaited the answer.

"Ain't no one's lived here for some time now."

Cookie shook her head, not sure she'd heard right. "But--" She peered toward the interior of the homestead.

"Why is the place kept the way it is?" the girl asked.

Cookie nodded in unison with Dipsy, while Beulah stood back aways, watching.

"The owner asked that we keep it that way until he says otherwise. Gram and Grampa get a cut on their place for lookin' after this 'un."

"May I ask your name?" Cookie said, remembering her manners.

"My name's Charlotte Mae, ma'am. And y'all?"

Charlotte's eyes trained on Cookie's clean and well manicured hands, while Charlotte's were baked by the sun, her nails chipped, dirt rounding the cuticles from digging in the soil.

"My name's Cookie Haines and this is my sister, Dipsy." Dipsy nodded politely. "And this is Beulah, our --" She was about to say housekeeper but thought otherwise.

"Did you say Haines, ma'am?" Charlotte asked in surprise, backing away slowly as if to put distance between them.

Cookie nodded.

"You Mr. Ebie Haines' daughters?"

"Sure am."

She paused, as though considering. "Maybe you should come with me down yonder," she said, pointing to the truck that was even now edging the watermelon patch. "Gram and Grampa will want to meet you."

Cookie looked to Dipsy who seemed just as surprised as Cookie by this turn of events. They started down the porch but before they got very far, Dipsy tripped on her heels, falling unceremoniously onto the soil, baked to clay by the fierce summer sun and overlain with a fine powder of dust.

"Ooh, ooh, ooh," Dipsy wailed. She removed her red high heels and grimaced. "I think I sprained something."

Cookie knelt beside her, touching the mound of Dipsy's stomach lightly. "Is the baby okay?"

"Just twisted my ankle, that's all."

"Can you walk, Child?" Beulah asked, bending down and running her fingers over Dipsy's ankle.

Dipsy shrieked, her eyes closed against the pain and her face blotchy.

"We need to get her out of this heat," Cookie said, bending down and placing an arm around Dipsy, Beulah taking the opposite side.

Cookie and Beulah helped her back to the porch, each shouldering Dipsy's weight as she hopped on one bare foot. Charlotte marched behind them, admiring the bright red stilettos that she carried by their thin straps.

"Reminds me of Dorothy's slippers in *The Wizard of Oz*, only with heels," Charlotte said to no one in particular. "How in Sam Hill can anyone walk on these things?"

Cookie smiled. Anyone besides Dipsy would have known not to wear heels, but she took after Mitzi when it came to fashion, even when pregnant.

"Here." Cookie set Dipsy gingerly onto one of two old cane rocking chairs on the porch, which looked as if they too were waiting for the occupants of the home to return.

Just then, an old International Harvester pulled up beside the shack, loose bits of straw lazily drifting from the flatbed and filling the air with the smell of dried sweetgrass. Charlotte's grandparents hopped out of the Harvester and strode up the steps. Her grandfather was a big man with hands the size of mitts and a face that bore acne scars, while her grandmother wore a wary expression that let Cookie know she didn't cotton to strangers, especially ones who were clearly on her land, or leastways land that she was caretaking.

A look shot between the pair as if to say that because Cookie and the others were all women, they came under the wife's jurisdiction. Charlotte must have recognized that her grandmother's dander was up, because she quickly positioned herself between the women and said, "Gram, this here's Mr. Haines' daughters, Dipsy and Cookie, and their. . . friend. What'd you say your name was?"

"Beulah. The name's Beulah, and you are. . .?" she asked Rayleen, hands on hips, her eyes trained on Charlotte's grandmother.

Cookie witnessed the exchange, but it was as if an entire play was being acted out in front of her, for Charlotte's grandmother stood wide-eyed when she'd heard Cookie's name, and then exchanged a glance with her husband, who shared one in return.

"I'm Rayleen, and this here's Chester," Rayleen said, still eying Cookie with such keen interest that it sent a ghost of. . . *what*. . . whispering through her?

For several awkward moments, they stood in silence, each sizing up the other. Finally, Charlotte seized the spotlight by saying, "They're here looking for an A.K. Byrd. I told them there ain't no--"

"Isn't no," Rayleen corrected with a haughty upturn of her chin. "And yes, A.K. Byrd lived here in the thirties, but he's long gone. Not even sure if he's still alive. That was some thirty years ago. How come y'all are lookin' for him?"

Cookie didn't know how much to tell the stranger. Clearly, this family was living on Haines land and had been here for some time, and yet Cookie didn't know where all the threads led, who remembered what, if anything. For all she knew, she was barking up a tree with no roots, so she chose her words carefully as she reached into her pocket and pulled out the yellowed newspaper clipping.

"Someone gave me this."

She handed the paper to Chester who in turn handed it to Rayleen. "She reads faster," he said, by way of explanation.

Rayleen pulled bulky black reading glasses from her apron pocket. For the next few minutes, Rayleen's eyes scanned the text, her lips pursed and her brows furrowed as she slowly peered up at Cookie.

"Have you ever seen this article before?" Cookie asked, knowing it was a longshot that the woman would recall such an obscure article. But to her surprise, the woman nodded. "Do you know what happened to the baby?"

"Not for me to say," Rayleen said, turning her eyes slightly to the left so as to avoid looking Cookie square in the eye.

Just then, Dipsy moaned and began rocking in pain. "My ankle's starting to throb," she said through gritted teeth. For one brief moment, she turned deathly pale and it appeared she might pass out.

Chester's shoulders slumped. "Ma'am, we best get her inside and lay her down before we have to pick her up off the porch.

Got a pump inside. We'll get her some water. That should get her to feeling better."

He broached no argument. Reluctantly, Rayleen pulled an old skeleton key out of her apron pocket and sauntered over to the door, unlocking it in one swift motion.

Chester said, "You ladies help her in. . . please."

Once again, Cookie moved to one side of Dipsy, Beulah the other, and lifted her to her feet.

"This way, Dipsy. We'll have you fixed up in no time," Beulah said, tsk-tsking Dipsy as if she were a child who had disobeyed one of her mama's orders.

Within minutes, they had her laid out on the bed, an oddly fresh-starched pillow beneath her head. Cookie found her eyes wandering over the place. It smelled of Endust and ammonia, a bouquet of fresh flowers on the sideboard.

"You say this A.K. Byrd lived here?"

"Yes'm." Rayleen shooed away her granddaughter, who had begun picking up knick-knacks and studying them.

"And no one lives here now?"

"That's right."

Cookie felt a presence in this room, as palpable as if whoever had once been there was here now, watching over them. "When was the last time anyone lived here?"

Rayleen peered down at the newspaper clipping and handed it to Cookie. "Not since the tornado."

"You mean since this article came out. . . in '32?" Cookie's head began reeling as she fought her way to one of the four wood and cane chairs that surrounded the kitchen table. Her daddy owned this land. Why would he keep this place in perfect working order all these years, as though a shrine. *But a shrine to what*? And why had he never said anything about this to either her or Dipsy? Did Mama know about this place? Cookie ran a trembling hand through her hair. She didn't know, but she aimed to find out.

18

WAVES OF PANIC FLOODED RAYLEEN as she stood inside the sharecropper's shack, the unaired shack smelling musty as it did every time she entered it despite the many cleanings. After so many years of being empty, it felt odd to have so many people inhabiting it at one time. Willing her hands to stop shaking, she offered Cookie a glass of the water Chester had pumped from the spigot above the chipped porcelain sink, all the while taking stock of the child she had raised for nearly two years. Funny how life could come full circle. The past never stayed the past, not really. Like a white-footed deer mouse, it just went underground for a while only to pop up in some other place, in some other time, from a warren of burrows that twisted and turned beneath the surface of a life. That's the way it was with people, too.

"You feeling okay?" Rayleen asked.

Cookie merely nodded, the news that her daddy had kept the shack just as it was since the '32 tornado no doubt a shock. Did the girl even know what happened afterward? Rayleen bit her lip. Well, *she* certainly wouldn't be the one to say anything. Not if she could help it.

She turned her attention to Charlotte, who had taken to rummaging through drawers until she came across a spam-colored Ace bandage with silver clips attached to hold the wrap in place.

"Here, Miss Beulah," Charlotte said, handing her find to the older woman whose wiry graying hair had come loose from its bun.

"Thanks, honey," Beulah said, then began wrapping Dipsy's ankle to loud protests. When Beulah was done, she dug through her purse and brought out a couple of pills. "Here," she said, handing the white pills to Dipsy and offering her a glass of water. "Drink this down."

"What are they?" Dipsy asked through gritted teeth.

"Aspirin. You'll feel better soon."

Charlotte was still rummaging through drawers, fascinated, it seemed, by the aged contents within. "What's this, Gram?" she asked, pulling out a faded red and white tin with the words *Carnation Malted Milk* written on the label

"A powdered drink," Rayleen said, "and take my word for it, it's good!"

Charlotte, in bare legs and tennis shoes, held up the tin. "How come you never buy it for us then?"

Rayleen had to laugh. That girl had way too much of her grandma in her. "'Cause, unless a cow can give us malted milk, you're not gettin' any. You know we don't have that kinda money."

"Oh," Charlotte said, eyes glistening as she replaced the tin back on the cupboard shelf which had been closed off with a blue gingham curtain. Next, she turned her attention to the loft above. "What's up there, Gram, and how come you never bring me with you when you come clean this place?"

"Because I need you to watch the house for me." Rayleen rolled her eyes.

That child's gonna be the death of me.

Yet, secretly, she was proud of her granddaughter. That girl was audacious and strong, something no girl could afford, much less a poor black girl. But maybe, with this new wave of civil rights, her grandbaby would finally have a fighting chance to be somebody. To stand up and be counted.

Charlotte peered longingly at the ladder that led to the loft.

Rayleen sighed. "Go check it out. No one's stopping you."

Charlotte squealed in delight and scooted up the ladder faster than a bobcat on a red cedar tree. For the next few minutes, Beulah and Dipsy talked softly, while Chester made for the outdoors, uncomfortable, as always, around two white women. Meanwhile, Beulah seemed to be watching Cookie as she peered at her surroundings, clearly just as interested in this place as Charlotte.

"What brought you ladies here, Miss Cookie?" Rayleen asked, but before Cookie could answer, Charlotte appeared from the loft above, lying on her belly and peering down at the first floor, an old picture frame in her hand.

"Hey, Grammy, is this a picture of that A.K. Byrd and his wife?"

Before Rayleen could answer, Cookie's head jerked upward,

her eyes squinting. She stood and moved closer, peering at the sepia photo of the pair in an aged gold frame. "May I?" Cookie asked Rayleen, reaching for the photo.

Charlotte peered over at her grandmother. Reluctantly, Rayleen nodded her approval.

With that, Charlotte leaned as far as she could over the edge, while Cookie stood on tiptoes. For one brief moment, she had a hold of the frame, but then, as if in slow motion, the glass frame fell, turning over and over in midair. And just as suddenly, time once again sped up and it came crashing to the floor, glass splintering in all directions before the frame finally skittered to a stop.

"I'm so sorry," Cookie said, bending down to pick up the larger shards of glass while Rayleen rushed to find a small dustpan and broom, and the blue and white enameled pot she'd seen under the kitchen counter.

"Here, Miss Cookie," she said, handing her the large blue pot. "Put the pieces inside this."

Together, they cleaned the floor of the many shards of glass. Cookie seemed near tears as she picked up the sepia photo and handed it to Rayleen, her eyes drifting longingly over the photograph. As Rayleen took it in her hands, the weight of the frame pulled the picture from what was left of the frame. To her surprise, behind the first photograph was another photograph. Before she could say a word, Cookie grabbed the picture from her, her deep blue eyes drifting slowly up to Rayleen's, a question written in them.

"This is my uncle," Cookie said, her voice trembling. "How did this end up here?"

* * *

Cookie bent over the photograph of her uncle, Edward, who had died in a logging accident in the northwest. Her father had rarely spoken of him. He had died long before Cookie was born, but what she'd heard of him had become folklore passed down through the family. According to her father, Edward had been a brilliant man who could have done anything, been anyone, and yet he had given it all up to ride the rails to Oregon, where he had gone to work in a logging camp. For four years, the Great Depression had settled over the United States. Like a blanket of silt from the Dust Bowl, it swept through the Great Plains in waves -- touched every part of America and its people. The powder seeped into homes had covered everything it touched, chewing up land, crops. . . lives. Entire families packed up everything they had and moved west, hoping for a better life. But why Edward? He had Ebie and Mitzi to see him through the hard times.

Cookie tapped the photo. "What is my uncle's photograph doing here?" she asked again.

The muscles in Rayleen's jaw rippled as she handed the photograph to Cookie. "He lived here for awhile."

"*Here?*" Cookie wasn't sure she'd heard right. "Why did he live here?"

Rayleen tilted her head, her eyes drifting toward the door as if wishing she could talk to Chester before answering. "Hasn't your daddy told you anything, Miss Cookie?"

"Not about this." Cookie plopped down onto one of four cane chairs next to the oak table.

"You *do* know your momma and daddy owned the store and gas station here in the 30's. They run both of 'em."

"The store? What store?"

Rayleen blew out a breath and tsked. "Don't tell me you don't know about that, either?"

Cookie rubbed her face, then pressed her temples against the oncoming headache. A rush of unwanted thoughts flew through her at breathtaking speed, snippets of memory that wallowed in the shadows of her mind, just out of reach.

"Surely they said *something*. . ."

Cookie shook her head, feeling the odd need to laugh or cry, she wasn't sure which.

"Cookie?" Dipsy said, her voice wobbly from the pain, the aspirin not yet kicking in. "Did I hear right? That Momma and Daddy lived here a long time ago?"

"Above the store," Rayleen amended as she walked over to close the curtains to keep the early afternoon sun at bay. "Your daddy's brother lived with them for a while."

"Take me there," Cookie said on a whim, determined to get at the truth, once and for all. "Is it far?"

"Not far, but what will we do with Miss Dipsy?" Rayleen protested. "Surely--"

Cookie turned to Dipsy. "Can I borrow your car?"

Dipsy merely nodded.

"I'll stay with Dipsy 'till you get back," Beulah offered, the strain of the day showing in the shadows beneath her eyes and the weariness of her expression. "We won't be no trouble," she said to Rayleen.

"Well, this place belongs to y'all as much as it does me, so I suppose it will be all right with Mister Haines."

"Wait!" Dipsy said, her expression rheumy. "You don't have a license, Cookie."

Rayleen laughed, her eyebrows lifted. "This here's

Shardsburg, not Montgomery. Ain't no one gonna care if she got a license."

"Gram!" Charlotte admonished, all but forgotten in the loft. "You tell me not to use the word ain't."

Rayleen peered up at her granddaughter and placed her hands on her hips. "Oh, lawd. The one time the girl listens!"

Cookie laughed along with the others. "The day is heating up. We'd better get going if we want to get there and back before we wilt."

"I'm coming too, Grammy!" Charlotte called. Before anyone could respond, she had descended the ladder two rungs at a time.

Five minutes later, after a brief farewell to Chester who promised to look after Dipsy and Beulah, Cookie was behind the wheel of the Buick and trundling down the rutted dirt road through a swath of farmland as far as the eye could see. The cicadas, which had hummed in rhythm when they'd first arrived, had now slowed, coming in intermittent waves of sound. As for the acres of watermelon, they were soon replaced by tall field corn that hid the road from view, the lush swishing movement filling the senses with sight and sound that felt like an ancient choir, chorusing them with a serenade as they drove down the road toward a destination unknown except to Rayleen.

For the next ten minutes they drove, finally reaching asphalt that edged a small stand of white oak and fir. Beside the road, a woman wearing a straw hat walked with two children clinging to her overalls. Cookie watched through the rearview mirror as she passed, the scene strangely familiar.

"Should I have stopped to see if they needed a ride?"

Rayleen raised an eyebrow and gave a shrill laugh, then turned toward the window, her eyes scouting the horizon. "Ain't no black woman gonna take a ride from a white woman, lessen she knows 'em."

Charlotte harrumphed from the back seat, her arms crossed. "You gonna owe me a penny each time you say ain't, if you're gonna tell me not to use it."

"All right now you, pipe down. No one wants to hear flack from a chick with no feathers, get my drift?"

Through the mirror, Cookie watched the girl pout, head down, eyebrows nearly together. They drove on, past field upon field of cotton, the boles not yet forming to a puffy white, the heat of the day cooling the drooping leaves. Finally, the large white two-story building loomed large, the front porch sagging and the screen door opening and shutting with the wind, screeching with rust and age.

Cookie slammed on the brakes, a memory blinding her vision. Of a child -- her, she felt certain -- and a person standing next to her on the dust-filled road in front of the store. "Where we goin'?" the child had whined, her feet blistering in her too-big shoes.

"Hush, Chile, you'll see soon 'nuff."

Cookie turned to gaze at Rayleen. She knew that voice. Knew it like she knew the groan of the floorboards, knew the feel of the moisture from the swamp cooler that bathed her face in a fine mist. Knew the inside of the store she had yet to enter.

She took a moment to collect herself. Then she was about to step out of the car when she saw the envelope Mitzi had given her just before she left home. It must have fallen out of her purse when she'd braked so hard. She bent down and lifted it, one side of the flap open. She ran her finger along the groove then slid a paper out. On it was a flowery scrawl. She quickly scanned it, her breathing growing shallower. Then for one brief moment, she felt her world spin.

19

EBIE NORMALLY LOVED THE EARLY morning train ride to Shardsburg, the rolling hills, the fields of wheat, the eastern redbud and loblolly pines. He loved the swish-swish-swish and the clack-clack-clack of the wheels on the rails. The hum.

But today, he felt unsettled.

Yesterday, he'd gone to work early to deal with an especially long caseload before he left town for Shardsburg. When he'd returned home that evening, he'd learned from Mitzi that both Dipsy and Cookie had left for places unknown. Still uneasy about Rachel's latest return, and worse yet her disappearance, he'd been shocked to learn that the girls were gone, and so suddenly. On a hunch, he'd gone to his study and discovered the Shardsburg deed missing. A chill had settled over him.

Cookie.

She rarely entered his study, but why had she done so this

time? Had Rachel tipped her off in some way? And how much did she know about her birth, if anything? He didn't want to borrow trouble, but the day he'd been dreading might finally be here. The day she learned the truth about herself, her heritage. About his duplicity. He couldn't imagine how she would react in light of what she might learn.

Ebie rubbed his face in frustration, then leaned back against the headrest. He closed his eyes, hoping that the thoughts would fade, replaced by blessed sleep. But sleep wouldn't come. Instead, his mind ran the gamut of scenarios, from Cookie's anger to possible acceptance, from appreciation of the life she'd had, to rejection. Which would it be? He couldn't bear the thought of those brown eyes turned on him with the eternal question *why?* Why hadn't they told her? Why had they gone to such lengths to hide the facts of her birth? Why had they never revealed who her parents were?

Because you couldn't handle the truth, Cookie.

But he knew it was because *he* couldn't handle her knowing. Knowing that he wasn't the great Ebenezer Haines, lawyer extraordinaire who could slay dragons. Just not her dragons. He loved her, but he couldn't help her. Not in the way that she needed most, especially after that near fiasco of a wedding with that bigamist, Jared. After that, she'd lost all faith in people.

No, he couldn't protect her from life's many sins. From *his* sin. The sin of omission.

"Excuse me, is this seat taken?"

He peered up to see an elderly woman in her eighties with blueish-gray hair and rheumy eyes. She reminded him of the wealthy spinsters in Montgomery proper. For one brief moment, he inspected her, her attire. An elegant mustard-colored suit.

Large pearl earrings. Gold bangles at her wrists.

He immediately unbuckled his seatbelt and stood to let the elderly woman in. He stayed standing until she was seated, her large blue-and-white striped bag at her feet. She reached inside and pulled out a book, *The Art of Understanding.*

When she saw him looking at it, she held it up and said, "Have you read this?"

"No, ma'am," he said. He'd never been one for self-help. He preferred figuring things out on his own.

"Oh, you should. I'm almost finished. Then you can have it if you like."

He wouldn't "like," but he would never say that to the sweet old woman. Instead, he thanked her, then settled in for an afternoon of rest, once again closing his eyes. He didn't awaken until he felt a jolt and a rustling as the train came to a halt at one of the many stations.

"Here you go," the old woman said, standing. "This is my stop." She sidled past him, then handed him the book.

"What?" he said, rubbing his eyes and yawning. Then he remembered. The book.

"Read it," she suggested. "I have a feeling you could use it." She lay a wrinkled hand against his arm, her skin paper thin and covered with age spots, then gave his arm a pat. Before he could respond, she turned.

He called a quick thanks, then dubiously peered down at the large blue and yellow book. Hesitantly, he opened it, but the pages were a blur. He reached into the pocket of his woolen jacket and pulled out his reading glasses. The words before him felt as if they had been written just for him.

The art of understanding begins by opening your heart to those around you. To listen. To care. And ultimately, to be willing to change. Because only through positive change can we grow as a people. But to achieve true change, we must first forgive. . . forgive ourselves and others.

Ebie shook his head. "Rubbish," he murmured as he leaned back in his seat. But even as he spoke, he knew he hadn't been entirely honest with himself. In his darkest moments, he *did* feel guilt for what he'd done. Because, in the end, he had taken Cookie not to help her, but to help himself. To save his marriage. For their sakes, not hers. But he *had* come to love her. No, he would not think about the past. It did no good. Look to the future, not the past. That had been his motto. A good one, in his mind.

* * *

Mitzi made the call to Kent to come pick up the kids, explaining only the barest of details, just enough to make him worry, to make him wonder what it would be like to lose Dipsy. Three days alone to juggle childcare and work, and to see everything that Dipsy contributed on a daily basis, would make him think. She hoped. Next, she called to make her motel arrangements. Then she ran upstairs to her bedroom and quickly packed her bags. Something was wrong. First Dipsy and Cookie had taken off to parts unknown, and then Ebie had surprised her last night with the news that he was taking an early morning train to Shardsburg. It couldn't be a coincidence that he had chosen to go there now, of all times. No, something was in the offing and she felt certain *that something* had to do with Rachel. For two months, she'd been lulled into a false sense of security. But now. . . She had three days to get to the bottom of this. Three days to locate Rachel. Three days to prevent her from ruining

Cookie's life. . . *all* their lives.

Mitzi's hand trembled. Something was different this time. Mitzi could feel it in her very bones. Always before, Rachel had respected their privacy, had adhered to the letter of the contract, promising to only contact Mitzi and Ebie, never Cookie. Mitzi and Ebie had appreciated that. But this time Rachel had reached out to Cookie directly. Maybe she hadn't expected to see Cookie in the kitchen that morning, yet something in Rachel's manner made Mitzi wonder. None of them were getting any younger. Perhaps Rachel felt that she had bided her time long enough and now planned to risk everything to finally meet her daughter. Mitzi closed her eyes. *Breathe. Breathe.*

"Okay, Mitzi girl," she whispered to herself and opened her eyes wide. "Time to put on your big girl panties."

With that bit of encouragement, she opened her dresser drawer and felt around beneath a stack of underwear until her fingers touched the stack of bills she'd picked up from the bank yesterday. Quickly, she walked to the luggage lying open on the bed and stuffed them into a side pocket. The taxi should be here to take her to the airport soon.

As she began zipping up the bag, her phone rang downstairs. *Who can that be?* She nearly dismissed it, but then she thought of what she'd told Cookie. . . to call her and let her know she was okay. It was getting late and Cookie still hadn't called. She ran downstairs, huffing as she answered the phone.

"Hello, Cookie?"

"No. . . it's me."

For a moment, she couldn't place the solemn male voice. Then it came to her in a rush. Randall, her private investigator.

"Yes?" She paused to catch her breath. "Have you found

Rachel?"

He wavered, as though choosing his words carefully. "I have. And she wants to meet with you."

Mitzi pressed a hand against her ear. Had she heard right? She sank gratefully onto the chintz-covered Queen Anne's chair. Bless her heart.

"Did you hear me?" Randall said.

Just then, she heard the taxi honk outside and stood to look out the front window. She waved to get the driver's attention, then held up her index finger.

"Where is she?" Mizi asked, her eyes trained on the taxi driver who looked side to side with impatience.

Randall gave a short chuckle. "Are you seated?"

She wasn't, but she decided to humor him. "Yes?"

"She's here. . . in town."

A nervous giggle escaped Mitzi's lips. "Here?"

"Here."

She quickly scanned the possible venue sites for their meeting, but she was too nervous and feared being seen in public with the woman. Finally she said, "Could she come to the house?" She knew it was risky, but maybe if Rachel saw how well Cookie had been raised, how much she and Ebie loved her, she would back off, leave them alone for good this time. Understand that she had done the right thing when she'd given them Cookie to raise. The taxi gave two short impatient honks.

"I'll call you right back," he said.

After he'd hung up, she ran outside and offered the taxi driver twenty dollars to wait until she knew for sure if Rachel would agree to the early morning meeting. Five minutes later, she got word. She thanked the taxi driver and watched him drive away. Then she went inside to prepare a pot of tea and scrounge through the refrigerator for food to serve her guest. Fortunately, Beulah had left her some finger sandwiches and teacakes. Perfect. Now, all she could do was wait.

* * *

The store. Rayleen flushed with shame, a shame laid bare for all to see. Because on these steps she'd left four-year-old Cookie with complete strangers. Broke her little heart. Even now, the cries reverberated through her chest as she recalled that day. How she'd walked away, clutching the baby blanket, never turning back until she heard the screen door slam and the screams muffle to faraway mewls. Never would she forget those final moments. Ebie standing on one side of the porch, Mitzi bent down with open arms to embrace the child she had never seen before. The moment of shy interest until Cookie realized that this woman. . . this stranger, meant to keep her. The look of stunned horror, then the squirming, kicking, Cookie's face gone red as she fought, her eyes trained on Rayleen, arms outstretched.

"*Mama! Mama!*" she cried, imploring Rayleen to rescue her. But she couldn't.

"Go!" Ebie had said, coming forward to shield Mitzi and Cookie from Rayleen.

Rayleen hadn't known what to do. She'd never gone against a white person, and yet Cookie was a child. She didn't understand. Surely these people could see that. But Ebie broached no argument, moving forward so that Rayleen stumbled down the steps, still clutching the blanket and nearly falling to the bare earth below.

172

"Be a good girl," Rayleen called, holding up the blanket.

"I said go!" Ebie shouted, pointing toward the road, toward the fields that would lead to her sharecropper's shack.

For years after, Rayleen had avoided this place, had shunned it for the tragedy it was. To her, it reflected a shame so deep, so impregnated in her that it gave voice to something her grandmother had once told her about being a slave who'd been separated from her parents, sold to a white family. Her title? *Keeping House.* No name on the "property" holdings. Just *eight-year-old Negro.* Now, here Rayleen was doing to Cookie what had been done to Rayleen's grandmother. But no, that wasn't quite right. Not exactly. Cookie would be welcomed into the Haines family, treated like a daughter. At least there was that.

When she arrived home to Chester's waiting arms, the boys gathered around her in reverent silence, she finally shed the first real tears she'd allowed herself. For the next few minutes, Chester rocked her, patting her back and cooing the words, "It's alright, baby. It's for the best."

Rayleen nodded, her head against his chest, his shirt moist with her tears, her hands balled in fists and her chest tight with unexpressed anguish. "I know," she finally whispered.

And she did. A white child raised by a black family would never be allowed by either community. Rayleen and Chester had been able to keep the child hidden for as long as they could. But in a year, Cookie would need to attend school. As long as Rayleen kept the child, she put the black community at risk, and she couldn't afford that. It was the right thing to do.

Then why does it hurt so much?

Now, as she stood outside the store, the adult Cookie at her side along with Rayleen's granddaughter, Charlotte, who was blessedly unaware of that time in Rayleen's life, she wondered what the future would hold? Wondered if Cookie could forgive her, forgive any of them, their secrets.

20

COOKIE'S SKIN PRICKLED WITH ANXIETY as she climbed the steps of the small grocery store. With a wisp of recognition that caused her to shiver, despite the mid-morning heat, it dawned on her. She'd been here before. Once, long ago, she had seen a photograph of herself as a child, one of the few remaining after the basement had flooded that one year in '34, which is why her family had no pictures of her before age four, according to Mitzi. It was taken here. At this store. On these steps. The sign had read Bailey's Mercantile back then. Now it read Snyder's Mercantile, but she felt certain the stores were one in the same. Mitzi had said the photograph had been taken in one of "those little backwoods towns" while on vacation. Was this the town? But if Ebie had owned this store all those years ago, why had it been called Bailey's Mercantile?

Too many questions, and too few answers.

With a raised brow, Cookie turned to Rayleen and Charlotte, who were still at the bottom of the steps. For one brief moment, Cookie read the terror in Rayleen's eyes and recalled the warm dark hand.

Rayleen's hand.

A tsunami of memories washed over Cookie and the shiver in her stomach turned into a torrent of emotion and unspent feelings. So many things about her childhood had been. . . odd. Moments in her life that had felt like a Picasso painting. Disjointed. The man in the alley and her parents' response to it. The lack of pictures, as though she'd been formed out of whole cloth. The artwork Mitzi kept from her. What other things had Mitzi kept hidden. . . had they *all* kept hidden? Even Dipsy, transparent, conventional Dipsy, hadn't let her in on her mother's treasures, her talent. But Ebie. . . he may have kept the biggest secret of all. The truth behind her birth. The lost years. She felt as though the foundation of the life she'd cobbled together -- her messy, unconventional life -- had suddenly been founded on quicksand. That any moment now she could be sucked beneath the water-laden terrain of her childhood.

Who am I?

Cookie's brow gathered in question, but Rayleen merely peered at Charlotte, then back to Cookie. She shook her head slowly in a gesture that said, *Not here. Not now.* Hopefully, Cookie would have time to ask Rayleen later, when they were alone. And she needed to. . . desperately. Because, whether anyone knew it or not, the envelope Mitzi had handed Cookie before she left had contained a letter from this Rachel person asking if they could meet. Telling her it was of the utmost importance that she not speak to anyone. Telling her that what she had to say would change Cookie's life, but that she had some business to attend to first. She'd asked if they could meet in a week. Cookie had read the letter and reread it, searching for some note of explanation. But all she'd sussed from the many readings was a wisp of desperation. A note of despair. Why? Even if this Rachel person *was* Cookie's biological mother, why was it so important that she speak to Cookie now? The woman would have had years to contact her and had chosen not to.

Turning toward the screen door, Cookie willed herself to enter the mercantile. Once inside, she felt the immediate familiarity of the place. It was like walking onto a long forgotten movie set, only snippets familiar. The smell of moist wood, the creaking sound of the aging oak floors and of the ringing of the ancient cash register. The screech then thump of the screen door slamming behind her.

A memory came to her unbidden of an adult opening and closing the cash register, her tears as a child turning to whimpers as she thrilled in hearing the bell and watching the cash register open. She kept walking, her eyes perusing the shelves of overpriced goods, of necessities for the small community. Her eyes lit on the coolers at the far side of one wall filled with drinks of all kinds: Pepsi, Coke, Nehis, Chocolate Soldiers.

Just then, she heard footsteps and turned. "You remember, don't you?"

Cookie turned to face Rayleen who was just inches away, so close that Cookie could smell her clove gum. Charlotte, on the other hand, was glued to the teen magazines below the counter at the front of the store.

"Remember what?" Cookie released the breath she hadn't known she was holding until now. "Why I was here? Why I was holding your hand out in front of the store? It was your hand, wasn't it?"

Rayleen's eyes widened. Then she threw an arm across her stomach, a hand over her mouth, as though she might be ill. Tears pooled, but she didn't speak for several moments. At last, she lowered her hands and said, "Not here, Miss Cookie. Come to my place. We can talk there."

Then she was gone.

* * *

Mitzi was so nervous she'd had to take an anti-anxiety pill as she awaited Rachel's arrival.

"Where are you, Rachel?" Mitzi murmured as she peered around the voile curtains, her eyes moving back and forth searching for signs of life, for signs of Rachel.

For years, Ebie had been the one to deal with the woman. Fortunately, Rachel had kept to the signed contract, where she'd promised to give full custody to Ebie and Mitzi, but most importantly, to stay away from Cookie. To never reveal the truth of her birth. For that, Ebie had seen to it that she received a small pittance to get her by each month. It had assuaged his guilt -- his *and* Mitzi's. But now all that had changed. Why?

Only one way to find out.

Once again she peered around the curtains, waiting. Finally, with an edge of apprehension, she saw movement from the right as one lone figure walked toward her, the woman paper thin, her skin aged by the sun.

Mitzi watched with growing despair as Rachel made her way up the walk past the azaleas and the yellow-and-red dwarf

178

nandina. She couldn't help but recall that day when Cookie had become hers -- the day she had swept the four-year-old up into her arms, the terrible cries of a child who had been torn away from her parents not once, but twice. And now she might be torn away yet again, only this time it would be of her own doing, if she chose. But would she? Or was their bond strong enough to hold her? She hoped it would be the latter.

Taking a stalwart breath and steeling herself for what lay ahead, she waited for the buzzer to ring once, twice, three times before she answered it so that she wouldn't appear too eager, too anxious. When she opened the door, the woman before her wasn't filled with righteous anger, as Mitzi had imagined. Nor did she seem like an avenging angel. Instead, she just appeared tired, sad. As though life had batted her around once too often and she was seeking refuge in a storm, just as Mitzi had all those years ago when she had longed for a child of her own, someone to hold, to love, someone who would forgive all her flaws. Someone who would never leave her.

For some inexplicable reason, Mitzi grabbed Rachel up in her arms in sympathy and hugged her, allowing the woman to cry on her shoulder for several moments before releasing her.

When they finally parted, they stood staring at each other until Mitzi said, "Where are my manners? Can I offer you refreshments?"

Before Rachel could answer, Mitzi took Rachel's trembling hand and ushered her into the kitchen, again not her usual habit. Guests *always* ate in the formal dining room, but Mitzi had a feeling a mimosa and finger sandwiches might relax both their frayed nerves.

For the next few minutes, Mitzi chattered about the weather, about the news: Vietnam, the Kennedys, Martin Luther King and the latest march in Birmingham. About the garden, the latest plantings. Then, without thinking, as she got out two margarita glasses for the mimosas and was pouring the cool liquid into them, she said, "Every year, Cookie gives me vegetable starts from her greenhouse for my garden."

Mention of Cookie brought a startled silence to both women that continued until Mitzi swallowed her courage and said, "Drink up. I have a feeling we're going to need it."

To her surprise, Rachel giggled, an almost girlish sound for a woman who appeared so downtrodden. And in that moment, Mitzi could almost picture her as Audrey Hepburn, had Rachel's life not taken such a harsh and demanding turn. And also in that moment, Mitzi realized that this was a woman who had never been pampered, had never gone to a hairstylist. Who probably always purchased her clothes from St. Vinnies or Goodwill. In a sudden flash of inspiration, Mitzi no longer saw Rachel as her greatest adversary. In her mind, she had built her up to be a formidable challenger, a Cruella DeVille in stilettos. But she was neither. She was a tired, sad woman, who had given her child away and was now filled with regret. And regret was one thing Mitzi had experienced in spades because she knew the toll it had taken on Ebie when she'd lost her mind all those years ago. When she'd demanded a child from her womb, a womb that had been unable to produce a child. When he'd gone to any and all lengths to get her one and had suffered the loss of his integrity, so cherished by a small-town lawyer. It had been his greatest source of pride, his integrity. But for her, he had compromised it. How many times had he been asked to compromise it over the years in order to keep the secret of Cookie's birth? They could lose everything if word got out that the great Ebenezer Haines had lied in order to forge documents that would bind Cookie to them forever. For her birth records hadn't been lost in the tornado, as Ebie had told the lawyer. No, he still had the real birth records locked in his safe. Even Mitzi hadn't seen them. Why hadn't she ever thought to look?

Because I'm afraid of what I'll find.

She tapped her chin, determined to think about that later. For now, she turned her attention back to Rachel, who was staring forlornly at her clothes even as she fingered her wilting hair. And in that moment, Mitzi understood, because she had a secret of her own. She hadn't been born well-off. No. Mitzi, the Montgomery debutante, had been born to a poor Fuller Brush man, who'd found his fortune in advertising. Further, she recalled the moment that turned her life around. It was such a small event as to be insignificant. It had happened when the wife of a rich industrialist, one of her father's clients, had taken a shine to the poor waif and had made her her project, had her maid dress her up and do her hair. But what had delighted Mitzi the most were the shiny red shoes she'd been given. Her father had even bought taps to put on them so she could dance around like Shirley Temple, who now sat on the boards of the Walt Disney Company, Del Monte Foods, and the National Wildlife Federation. Mitzi had never forgotten those shoes or that experience. It had changed her life. Maybe she could help Rachel change *hers.*

Well, Ebie always says I'm a marshmallow inside. No reason to change my s'mores now.

Mitzi, whose tact had never been her strong suit, stopped and tilted her head to one side, a finger on her chin. "You know, you have great cheekbones. You would look good in makeup and a chignon."

Rachel peered down at her hands. "People tell me that, but I can't see spending money on myself." She touched her hair gently as though it were someone else's hair, not hers. "I wish I could. . . you know, dress up." Her eyes grazed her tattered dress, a dull beige.

For the first time since Rachel had shown up on her doorstep, Mitzi felt on solid ground. She may not know how to handle this thing with Cookie and Rachel, but she did know fashion.

"Oh, have I got just the thing for you. It's perfect. Hang on a sec." She ran upstairs and rummaged through her closet until she found an A-line dress, black. An Audrey Hepburn look-alike. She'd drawn pictures of the dress and had taken it to her dressmaker who had made it to fit, back when Mitzi's waist hadn't yet expanded along with her hips. Even now, she knew she had a good figure, but she'd been svelte once upon a time. Rachel could just about pull this dress off.

Frock in hand, she dug through the bottom of her closet until she found some black pumps that might fit, then rummaged through her drawer until she found some silk stockings, still in the package. She looked around for something to put it all in. She grabbed her oversized beach bag with its blue-and-white stripes and red starfish, and then stuffed the contents into the deep interior. Next, she picked her makeup bag off the counter and added it to the pile inside the bag, finishing up with a hair brush, hairspray, and an array of bobby pins. She knew she was being presumptuous, but she and her friends from church loved dressing up and she had a feeling that Rachel was no different. She just hadn't had the opportunity until now.

Just as she was about to scurry out the door, she remembered the stack of bills that she had tucked into her overnight bag before she'd learned that Rachel was in Montgomery. Should she dig it out, give it to the woman, order her to stay away for good this time? Or should she finally give in and agree to Rachel meeting her daughter, though it was hardly for her to say at this late date. Cookie was an adult. She could make up her own mind.

Oh, Cookie. Will you still love me? Think of me as your mama? And can you forgive me?

But she knew Cookie. She'd never been the vengeful type. And even as different as they were in temperament and taste, she knew that Cookie loved her, would forgive her the past. But would she stay in Mitzi's world, or would Cookie's new family take precedence? Would she forget all about Mitzi?

No, a little voice inside her head said. *She won't.* She just hoped she was right.

Gathering her courage, she grabbed the bag and headed downstairs. On her way through the front parlour, she grabbed a Vanity Fair off one of the end tables.

Mitzi entered the kitchen, chattering the whole way. She set the bag next to Rachel, who peered down at it with interest.

"I'm a fashion nut," Mitzi said, feeling in her element now. "My friends and I go through all the magazines. Take a look at this one." She pointed to the woman in black with a very chic red-and-black jacket over her dress. "You would look great in this."

She pulled out the dress and listened with delight as Rachel gasped, her hand over her mouth as though she'd revealed a yearning she hadn't known she had. "That's lovely," she said at last, her brown eyes filled with longing.

"It would be perfect for you, especially if you plan to meet your daughter at some point. Try it on. You can use the bathroom."

"I couldn't," Rachel said, but even as she did, she giggled, the change in her expression taking years off her face.

"Of course you could. I can't fit it anymore, and Cookie, bless her heart, doesn't share my love of fashion. I would be thrilled to see it go to a good home."

"Really?" Rachel asked, her hands together in supplication.

"Sure. It's just gathering dust in the closet."

"But I came to talk about Cookie, not. . . you know." She looked down at the bag once more.

"I know, but there's plenty of time for that. Try it on. If you like it, you can have it."

Rachel stood, nearly knocking over the chair in her haste. "If you're sure."

"I am," Mitzi said, handing her the bag. "And if you feel like it, we can fix your hair up afterward." She pointed to a picture of Audrey Hepburn in *Breakfast at Tiffany's*. "That style would look great with this dress."

"I could look like that?" Rachel said, frowning rather dubiously, her head cocked to one side as though trying to imagine herself as the movie star and having a hard time envisioning it.

"Just try on the clothes, and if you like, I'll fix your hair and do your makeup." Mitzi pointed her toward the hallway. "Bathroom's on the left."

Rachel started in that direction then halted, chewing on her bottom lip. "Why are you doing this for me? I thought. . . well. . . that you. . . you know." She lowered her eyes.

"Wanted nothing to do with you?" The words slipped out

before Mitzi could retrieve them. But now that the truth lay between them, she decided maybe it was for the best. To start fresh. To come clean.

"Well, yes, I suppose."

Mitzi shrugged. Perhaps she was getting old enough that she needed absolution for taking a daughter that wasn't hers to take. And perhaps Rachel needed it, for giving away her daughter without understanding the consequences of her actions. Because who ever did understand at that age? Hell, at *any* age. Life was just so much more *messy* than Mitzi could have ever imagined. One action, one moment, could change the course of a lifetime. For so many people. Tears welled in her eyes. In a husky voice, she said, "Go. . . try it on."

For a second, their eyes met in mutual understanding. Then Rachel nodded, and she was gone. Mitzi could almost pretend she had just imagined it. . . all of it. That Rachel Aberdeen was in her kitchen, and even now was trying on her clothes instead of being shown the door.

"Maybe you're growing up, Mitzi Haines," she whispered, taking a sip of her mimosa and welcoming the wonderful sweetness of it. "About gawd damned time," she added and then laughed.

For the next ten minutes, Mitzi nursed her mimosa until finally she heard an "ahem" and turned. There, in the doorway, stood Rachel, appearing awkward in the chic black dress that showed off her curves. A dark seam ran up the back of her legs from the silk stockings as she pirouetted for Mitzi, coming down from tiptoes in the matching black pumps. She looked almost coquettish.

Mitzi stood, a finger on her chin as she tilted her head from side to side. "Hand me that bag."

Rachel dutifully offered her the oversized beach bag. Mitzi dug through it until she came to the hairbrush, bag of bobby pins, and hairspray. "Let's see if we can give you a chignon."

To Mitzi's surprise, Rachel actually appeared excited by the idea of a transformation. For the next half an hour, Mitzi teased, primped and hairsprayed Rachel's unruly hair into submission until she was a reasonable facsimile of Audrey Hepburn.

"Before you look at yourself in the mirror, let me do your makeup. You might as well have the entire package." Mitzi winked.

Once again, she pawed through the satchel and brought out the cloth makeup bag, laid it onto the table and rolled it out, each tube of mascara, lipstick, and eyeliner, held in by a band of black elastic. "Come sit."

Carefully, she conditioned, then buffed and polished Rachel's face, finding just the right shade of lipstick, pruning her eyebrows so that they arched just so. Lastly, she used liquid eyeliner that swished up at the corners like Cleopatra. Like Audrey Hepburn. The transformation was stunning.

With nervous excitement, Mitzi led her to the full-length mirror in the den, making her close her eyes before she was allowed a preview. "Now!" Mitzi said, enjoying the drama.

Rachel opened her eyes and gasped. "I'm beautiful!" she said, then flushed with embarrassment that she would say such a thing. And to a stranger, at that.

"Don't be embarrassed. You're right. You are beautiful."

"But I've never been beautiful before," Rachel exclaimed, a catch in her voice.

"Yes you have. You just didn't know it."

Rachel seemed to ponder that. "I can keep these... the dress, the shoes?" she said, timidly looking at herself in the mirror.

"Of course you can. Now let's go in the kitchen and talk about Cookie," Mitzi said, unable to stave off the inevitable any longer.

"Okay," Rachel said.

Then, to Mitzi's surprise, Rachel grasped her arm and gave her a hug before backing away shyly. "Thank you," she murmured.

"You're very welcome," Mitzi said, amazed by this turn of events. "Now, let's have that talk."

Before she could move, Rachel put a hand to her shoulder and paused, appearing flustered. "First, there's something you don't know. Something I need to tell you."

"Oh?" Mitzi said. But upon seeing Rachel's fearful expression, she quavered. "What? What do I need to know?"

21

EVERY TIME EBIE RETURNED TO Shardsburg, he felt unsettled, as though the past and the present had caught up with each other, testing him. The first thing he noticed when he crossed the county line was the humidity. It seeped beneath clothing, rode into the dark crevices of a body, leaving a person feeling claustrophobic, as though both God and the weather had conspired to make him as miserable as possible. He knew the signs well. By nightfall, the skies would open up with thunder and lightning, sure as shootin'. As if it knew what he had done. Knew the tangled web of his deceit, even though he had intended it only for good. Always for good. But good and right weren't always the same thing. The law was black and white, on that account. Didn't deal in shades of gray.

No, the law was a fixed thing. It found fault far more often in the colored community than the white. He held no illusions about that. And banking was no better. A white man could get a loan far faster and more often than either a colored or, God forbid, a woman. Some people just got a foot up in the world, while others didn't. Though some people might preach otherwise, he knew there was no such thing as true fairness. A person just made due with their lot in life and got on with it. Wasn't that what his daddy had always told him?

He rolled down the window of the car he'd rented in Huntsville. The smell of pine needles flanked by wet walls of granite and ferns reminded him of that day so long ago. The day that had begun the downward spiral, even as it had made his and Mitzi's lives so infinitesimally richer, for it had brought them Cookie. Tenacious, stubborn, strong, and yet oddly fragile Cookie. That girl held none of the pretenses of high society, even though Mitzi had done her best to introduce her to it, to reel her into it. No, she had followed her own path, just like his brother. And had suffered nearly as much.

"And isn't that where it all started? With my brother?" he murmured, bending over the radio to find a station to drown out his musings. Finding nothing but an occasional word or bit of music that forged its way into the bristling static, he finally turned the radio off and hummed a ditty, giving up in the end.

Visions flashed through his mind in short bursts as he drove the winding backroads. Edward. That girl. The baby. Ebie's father had sent his brother to Shardsburg to work at the store, talk some sense into the errant younger son. Thought Ebie was up to the job of managing his little brother. But who could manage the human heart?

Feeling anxious, suddenly, and in need of a walk, Ebie pulled into a spot at the side of the road next to an old hunting trail that he and his brother had used thirty years ago, when they were hunting white-tailed deer. As in years past, the undergrowth was sparse and the canopy of pines spotted at best, which is why they'd had to build a blind. He wondered if it was still out there, or if it had been carted away by other hunters or hikers seeking firewood.

Only one way to find out.

For the next half hour he climbed the winding trail past large boulders and broad-leafed fern, past the downy serviceberry and two-leaf bishop's cap, mountain spurge letting him know that he'd achieved the higher reaches of the Alabama hillside. Winded, he halted, stoop-kneed, to catch his breath. Funny how this climb had seemed so much easier when he was a young buck. Panting, he pressed on, the memories flooding in now, like shards of light streaming through the lean forest.

"Leave me alone!" This, coming from his brother when Ebie had questioned him about the girl. He'd never used her name, as if that would give her life, make her real, make her a threat to every dream the family had for Edward. But Edward wouldn't listen. To anybody. He never had. He believed it his right to flout convention, to upend the norms that kept the weave of hearth and home tight. He had pulled at the threads, little by little, until they had begun unraveling at an alarming rate.

"What's wrong with you?" Ebie had called all those years ago, rushing to catch up to his brother, whose narrow shoulders and spare body spoke of a summer of hard work -- work that the family had forced upon him hoping that he would "grow up." Ebie grabbed a hold of his brother's backpack and whipped him around, a lank of the boy's dark hair covering one side of his face so that only his one dark eye and tapered nose showed above a squared jaw. "Listen to me, damnit!" Ebie hissed.

Taken aback by Ebie's swearing, which he seldom did, Edward had stopped, his mouth opening and closing like a landed smallmouth bass. "What do you want from me?" Edward had finally shouted, pushing Ebie.

"I want you to give this girl up," Ebie said, winded from spent emotion. "She's underage for God's sake!"

Suddenly, Edward went cold, his gaze appraising, his eyes narrowing. "Tell me what's *really* bothering you, brother. It's not her age. Well, maybe a little," he conceded, jaw set. "She's just not rich enough for you, right?"

"She's a hillbilly, for God's sake," Ebie said and then groaned, immediately regretting what he'd said. That's not what he'd meant at all. What he'd really meant was that she wouldn't fit into Edward's world, and he wouldn't fit into hers. "Look, we're getting off on the wrong foot here. Let me start over."

"Oh, y'all said your piece," Edward said, his dark eyes glistening. He'd taken after neither his father nor mother in regard to his eye color. No, he'd inherited a recessive gene. Whose gene, they had no idea.

"It's just that, well. . . where do you two plan to live?"

With a rueful laugh, Edward said, "Not with you, I gather. Can't have me takin' up with the wrong kind."

Ebie's voice softened. "And *her* family?"

The desperation in Edward's eyes spoke volumes. He worked his jaw as though staving off tears, and then with a renewed anger Ebie didn't know existed in his younger brother, he stormed off so that Ebie had to run to keep up.

They neared the top of the hill, the blind off to one side so that any deer mounting the hill would never know that hunters were nearby, when Edward turned, hands slicing the air. "You're right, okay? You're right. Her parents threatened to shoot me on sight if I ever come 'round her. You happy?"

Ebie wrapped his arms around his brother, but Edward flailed, determined to stave off any empathy on Ebie's part. But Ebie was stronger and held his ground until finally, his brother stopped flailing and fell into Ebie's arms like a limp rag doll.

"I'm gonna marry her, big brother. I swear I am," he said through tears.

Ebie expelled a short burst of air, determined to say the right thing. The thing that would reach his brother, make him understand that this was for his own good. Finally, he hit upon it.

"Listen, I'm not going to tell you what to do. But just promise me this. Get a job. I heard they're hiring green chain pullers in Oregon. I could help you -- provide references. Then you save up. For a year, maybe, whatever it takes. Come to her when she's eighteen and you have something to offer her. . . a home, a life. Promise me that," he said, bending down to look his younger brother in the eye, certain that given a cooling off period, the boy would feel differently.

Edward peered anywhere except in Ebie's eyes, until finally, he could flee them no longer and looked up. "Okay," he said, at last, "but only for a year. And I *am* going to write to her every day. I swear!" he added defiantly.

"I'm sure you will, brother. I'm sure you will." Then Ebie pulled Edward to his chest one last time and felt the weight of what had come between them fall away.

Now, as Ebie came up the rise and searched to the right, the memories fading, he saw what remained of the thirty-year-old blind. There wasn't much left of it. Just some rotting wood and a leaf and dirt covered bit of camouflage breaking the irregular rhythm of the forest floor, a reminder that time had passed. But not the loss. Never the loss.

Emotion that he had kept buried for so many years came bubbling up and he let loose a howl of self-loathing, frightening a brown pine warbler from its roost close to the top of a nearby loblolly pine. He reached for his antacids, but before he could get his hand in his pocket, pain gripped both his jaw and chest and sent him crashing to his knees, sweat dripping from his brow.

"Oh, God," he murmured. "My heart."

He knew the signs. His father had died of it. He searched the forest floor for any sign of a hunter, a hiker. Then he closed his eyes and prayed.

* * *

Mitzi sat down on her bed, still shellshocked from the phone call she'd received. She'd never heard the confession that she felt certain Rachel was about to make. She would have to save that for later. Instead, she'd rushed to get the phone, expecting Cookie or Dipsy on the other end of the line. But it was neither. Her heart had stopped beating as she'd listened to the woman, heard the sympathy in her voice.

"Thank you," Mitzi said. "I'll be there as quickly as I can." Afterwards, she'd hung up the phone, said a hurried goodbye to Rachel, and then raced upstairs to get her keys and purse, her hands shaking.

* * *

In the end, Rachel had told Mitzi only a half truth, she realized as she set out in search of a new place to live. For years she had been unseen, like a shadow, merely existing. She marched down the sidewalk of the suburban street past Ebie and Mitzi's neighbors. Even now, some of them might be peeking out their curtains, wondering who Mitzi had been entertaining for the day. In Rachel's new outfit, hairdo, and makeup, she could almost fit into this world of wide lawns, trimmed hedges, and rainbird sprinklers tic-ticking away the minutes. Almost. But she knew the truth. She would never fit in because she didn't have the name... the breeding. Yet still, she felt happy... happier than she had felt in a long time.

As she continued down the street, she was surprised when those in polite society said hello to her, *saw* her. She swished her purse back and forth like a young woman out for a stroll, and that's how she felt. Like she had rolled back a good twenty years, before life had worn her down so completely she could just about imagine herself part of the scrappy, Shardsburg, Alabama soil.

A twinge of regret left her feeling raw... tired. Who was she to play dress-up? Pretend? She was still that girl, that wounded and terrified little girl who Wes had found huddled in the sharecropper's hut all those years ago. He had picked her up, saved her in his own way. Turned her toward the door, toward the light... forward. Where was he now? She didn't know. All she knew was that he had rescued her on one of the worst days of her life.

It dawned on her, as her feet pounded the pavement and her legs grew weary, that she was looking for rooms to rent here, near Cookie. But just as quickly, she knew that could never be. She could never afford a home here.

Just then, she saw what was left of a newspaper on a park bench across the street. Maybe she could look through the Want Ads. Find a job at least. One step at a time. To her relief, as she sat down on the bench and picked up the paper, she saw that, indeed, the classifieds were still intact. In it was an ad for live-in childcare, for a Miss Dipsy Calhoun placed by Kent Calhoun. Hmm. Where had she heard that name before? Then it came to her. This was Cookie's sister. If she got the job, she could live close to Cookie, see her now and then, as long as she was able. Maybe, after today, Mitzi would feel more inclined to let her. For the first time in decades, Rachel felt a mustard seed of hope. But one thing held her back from making the call. One very important aspect to consider, because she had a debt to fulfill to the person whose life she had stolen through no fault of her own. She had to make good her promise. And she would do that. She had given her word.

22

COOKIE PURCHASED A FEW SUNDRIES for Beulah and Dipsy to share as well as sandwiches for all of them and a six pack of soda. She topped it off with a box of moonpies. That should keep everyone happy, she decided as the cash register opened with a resounding clunk. Cookie took the proffered change and added it to the jar on the counter.

With a heavy heart, she left the store and found Rayleen and Charlotte standing beside Dipsy's Buick. The store's cool interior had been replaced by a blast-furnace heat that instantly wilted Cookie's hair and left her feeling faint. How did people work in this heat, she wondered as she hurried down the steps and struggled to open the trunk of the car? She placed the groceries inside it and rushed around to the driver's side of the Buick. It still felt odd to be behind the wheel of a car. Fortunately, the area was rural and the roads straight, so she had little trouble navigating the flat terrain.

Per Rayleen's instruction, instead of heading toward the shack, Cookie drove a half mile further down the paved road, then turned onto a rutted road that snaked southward.

"Where are we headed?" she asked, feeling an odd sense of déjà vu as she passed barley fields that shushed in the wind, waist high, corn on the other side of the dirt road.

"Our place," Rayleen said, tucking her face forward to catch the wind coming in through the open window.

The Buick bucked and kicked, bottoming out on the ruts then coming up as if on a tide. "Was I ever at your place as a child?"

Rayleen looked pointedly toward Charlotte, who was seated in the back. The girl ran her hand against the stale air currents and stared out the window. With a pained expression, Rayleen turned to Cookie and nodded.

Cookie chewed on this new bit of information. Had Rayleen taken care of Cookie on occasion when she'd lived here as a child, as Beulah had? And if so, why hadn't her parents told Cookie? As she approached Rayleen's place, which was a near twin of the one on the other side of the field where Dipsy and Beulah were staying, she couldn't help but wonder.

Moments later, they pulled up in front of the rundown building that was tidy despite the obvious poverty. Cookie wore anxiety on her shoulders like a mantle, a thread of memory tugging at her. Like still photographs, they came. The willow tree. *Flash.* The side garden. *Flash.* The rose arbor. *Flash.* Little touches that made poverty more bearable, she supposed.

Charlotte jumped out the moment the car came to a stop and yelled, "Baby! Here baby!" And just like that a golden retriever barrelled from the side yard, its muzzle gray. Then to Cookie she called, "Want to come see my rabbits? Grampa made me a hutch and said I could keep my bunnies here."

Before Cookie could answer, Charlotte ran to her, grabbed her hand and began skipping beside her, pulling her along. Cookie was out of breath by the time they arrived at the hutch that stood off to one side of the barn.

"See?" Charlotte pointed first at a brown-and-white one. "It's an American fuzzy lop," she said. Then she nodded toward a large white-and-black rabbit. "That's a Rex. His name is Henny and this one here is Penney."

Cookie laughed. "Aren't those names better suited for chickens?"

Charlotte shrugged. "That's what Mama and Papa tell me, but I like the names."

And Cookie had to admit that the pair seemed to come when called. Charlotte opened the cage and pulled out the lop-eared rabbit, which she handed to Cookie to hold. Then she lifted out the Rex and cradled it in her arms, talking to it in a series of gibberish that only the rabbit could understand it seemed, as it nestled deeper into the cleft beneath her chin.

"Let's go show Grams," Charlotte exclaimed, running ahead.

* * *

Memories flooded Rayleen as she watched Cookie and Charlotte turn the corner of the house and head toward the barn, Charlotte chattering like a magpie. Rayleen pondered the day Rachel had come to her in a threadbare wraparound dress in cotton the color of parched earth. The girl had shown up on Rayleen's doorstep the day after the tornado, appearing disheveled and distraught. Rayleen hadn't opened the screen door, hoping to lend distance between her and Rachel. Besides, she and Chester hadn't even had time to clean up the torn shingles that had come off the roof, much less all the downed branches from the large oak tree out front. Most of the town was still in disarray. What did Rachel want *this* time?

"You don't understand," Rachel had pleaded, her sinewy arms wrapped loosely around the toddler as though she might drop her at any time, so heavy was her burden. "Between the tornado and the baby crying night and day. . ."

Rayleen shot a harried look at Chester, who was listening from the kitchen. Here Rayleen had two children, and Rachel only the one, and yet Rayleen rarely complained. What good would it do?

"It's just that--"

Rachel turned slightly, peering over her shoulder. It was then that Rayleen saw the handprint on Rachel's arm where someone had grabbed her as well as the bruise on her cheek, the cut on her forehead. And she saw what Rachel had been trying to show her -- that the child was far too thin for a two year old. And far too small. Plus, she too had a cut on her forehead and bruises. Quickly, Rayleen opened the door and bade Rachel enter. Rayleen brought the child to her, relieving Rachel of the added weight, then urged the woman to take a seat on the threadbare sofa.

"What do you need, Miss Rachel?" she asked, expecting that the woman would ask her to keep the toddler for the day until things could be sorted out.

"I need you to take Caledonia."

"I can keep her for the night if you want--"

"No, you don't understand," she said, peering down at her fingers which were clasped together in supplication. "I want you to *keep* her."

"Permanently?" Rayleen turned to Chester who had been quietly listening, his eyes widening in alarm. "But, surely--"

"No-no," Rachel said, her voice raised and her eyes desperate. "Just for awhile, until I can figure out what to do, where to go."

"Where did you get those marks?" Rayleen asked softly.

"It's not what y'all think." Rachel seemed to turn in on herself, her body shrinking as though in reaction to what she had to say. "There's a man in town. That's all. Calls us poor white trash. Believes it's his duty to rid the county of people like us. It's not safe anymore. . . for us, or her." At this, she locked her arms around her knees and broke down in silent tears.

But Rayleen couldn't get over the fact that something about Rachel's story didn't quite ring true, or perhaps it was only a partial truth. Was she covering for her husband, Byrdie? And yet some Southerners *did* treat poor white sharecroppers almost as poorly as they did Rayleen's family. Not sure what to do, Rayleen nevertheless urged Chester to get milk for the baby and food for Rachel. Then to Rachel she said, "Why not take the child with you?"

"I have no way to feed her, to take care of her. Once I'm settled, I'll come get her, I promise."

Rayleen knew the sour smell of desperation. Of poverty. Of fear. It was the plight of too many sharecroppers, too many black folks who were only one or two generations away from slavery.

Just then, Chester returned with a ham sandwich and a glass of milk, which he handed to Rachel. "I got the milk warmin' on the stove for the baby. Just be a minute," he said, then excused himself to give them time to talk.

"Wait!" Rayleen called to Chester, then turned to address Rachel. "I need a second to talk to my husband, Miss Rachel. You eat up, and we'll be right back." She handed the toddler to Rachel.

Rachel nodded, her eyes already on the ham sandwich.

Chester followed Rayleen to the bedroom, where she shut the door so as not to be overheard. "What are we going to do? Should we take the girl? It's just for awhile."

"How do you know that?" he demanded, in his deep melodious voice that spoke of honey and cream and all things good. "And what'll happen if folks know we got ourselves a white child? Ain't no one gonna be happy... not our people, not theirs."

"If anyone finds out we're keepin' her, we just tell 'em we're takin' care of the child while her folks are away."

"But what if this man who's been botherin' her hears of it? What then?"

Rayleen closed her eyes. "Lord give me patience," she whispered and then opened them. "First off, we don't know that she's not just coverin' for Byrdie. Secondly, I know it sounds crazy, Chester. But that child isn't gonna live much longer the way things are goin', and Rachel's right. She's got to get settled before she can pay mind to that child. It will only be for a few days. She said so herself."

Chester harrumphed. "You are the gal darndest woman, Rayleen, I swear."

"But you love me."

"Got that right," he said with a deep, guttural laugh. "Wish you weren't born with such a big heart there, girl."

"Yeah, well, that big heart has taken care of your behind all these years."

He produced a rich mahogany laugh, full of hope and promise. Maybe, just maybe, everything would work out this time. But hope had a way of bitin' a person in the butt, if a person wasn't careful. She knew that and had guarded her heart as a result. Yet now, she felt her resolve weakening and sighed.

The memories faded as she watched Charlotte and Rachel return from the barn, each holding a rabbit.

Rayleen heard the tinkling of the wind chimes James and Cookie had put together, lo those many years ago, and shivered. She'd always felt that they were touched with the tiniest bit of magic. Cookie must've thought so, too, because she stopped, one ear cocked, listening.

"Wind chimes," Rayleen said, by way of explanation. "Made of nuts and bolts and baling wire. You and. . . I mean James put them together, hung 'em in the pawpaw tree out back."

"Tell Cookie what they mean," Charlotte urged, the ten-year-old wriggling near as much as that rabbit she got in her hands. "Go on!"

"Don't go gettin' pushy on me, girl. I'll speak in my own good time and not a second sooner, y'here?"

"Okay," Charlotte said, looking down at her sneakers as she kicked at the dust. "Sorry," she added in contrition.

As if in reminder, the wind chimes once again tinkled in the breeze, the melody soft, ancient. . . as though a piece of the landscape that had outlasted many a family over the course of time. Outlasted the Chickasaw and the Koasati too, less than a thousand of the Koasati left, with their broad features and pine needle baskets. Rayleen had traded a basket for a large iron stew pot. The basket had been one of her few treasures, impractical but well-loved.

"So what *does* the sound of the wind chimes mean, if you don't mind my asking?" Cookie said, struggling to maintain control of the lop-eared rabbit as it pawed her with its hind feet, digging needle-like claws into her skin and bringing up instant welts.

Rayleen stared off into the distance, imagining the land as it had once been before the pine forest had been cleared off to make room for arable land meant for crops, the major crop being cotton, back before synthetics had been invented. But the synthetics had soon outdistanced the more natural fiber. Rayleen felt certain that it was this, more than a willingness on the part of the white Southerner, that had opened the way to the freed slave, because the slaves were no longer needed to pick cotton, the plantation system gone. Gone like the. . .

Charlotte cleared her throat, reminding Rayleen to answer their guest. "Well, truth told," Rayleen said, tearing her gaze from the horizon back to the pair waiting impatiently for an answer, "it's said that every time you hear the tinkle of a chime, it's the spirit callin'. Warnin' of a coming change."

"But change can be good or bad, can't it, Grammy?"

Rayleen laughed at the hopefulness of the implied question. "Yes it can, baby girl. Yes it can."

But before they were able to discuss it further, Cookie squealed and out popped the squirming rabbit from her grasp. It scooted across the county, fast as a cricket, the animal zigzagging its way to the corn patch and disappearing, clean as a knife through butter. Under other circumstances, Rayleen might have laughed, had she not known how much a rabbit could eat, given the chance, nor how fast it could populate an area, if it found a mate.

"Well, least somethin' round here is free," she said, then seeing Cookie's furrowed brows, motioned with her head toward the house. "Best get that rabbit before it eats us out of house and home."

23

EBIE AWOKE IN THE HOSPITAL to the hum of a monitor. His eyes blurry and his brain clouded, he searched the room for signs that might indicate where he'd landed and why. Although most hospitals looked alike, he felt certain this wasn't Montgomery. For one thing, the walls were white instead of washed-out, institutional green. Ebie tried to recall his last memory, but all he could remember was thinking about his brother as he drove down a country lane. Had he been in a car accident?

Before the question could be answered, he heard a rustle at the door and turned. There, to his surprise, stood Mitzi, her hair disheveled and dark circles beneath her eyes, but wearing a pale saffron dress with tiny flowers and black high heels.

"Mitzi? Is that you?" Ebie asked as Mitzi rushed to his side, tears filling her eyes. "What time is it? And where am I."

"It's 3:00 pm and you're at the Huntsville Hospital. And thank God you're alive, you silly man," she said, grabbing his hand and giving it a brief shake. "Don't scare me like that again."

Ebie whistled. "You must've flown here in that car of yours. What happened to me?" he asked, trying to sit up. In the end, he gave up and sagged back onto the pillow.

"You had a heart attack, you old fool," she said, pressing his hand against her cheek and giving it a fierce kiss. "Why didn't you *tell* me you were going to Shardsburg?"

"I didn't want to worry you," he said, his memory slowly returning.

She ran her fingers lovingly through his hair, her hand coming to rest on his cheek. "But why go to Shardsburg now, of all times?"

He looked into her questioning green eyes. How much should he tell her? A sudden urgency filled his lungs with a need to share at least a small portion of his burden with her.

"The Shardsburg deed went missing."

Mitzi pulled up a metal and plastic chair next to Ebie's bedside. "Missing? How?"

"I think it was Cookie--"

"But why?" Mitzi interceded, the chair forgotten as she stood to pace. "What would she want with an old deed anyway?" Then she turned sharply on her two-inch black high heels, her hand going to her mouth. "You don't suppose she knows. . . about Rachel?"

"I don't know what she knows. But I worry that she may be headed to the old place. In fact, she may be there already." He peered down at the IV's and the heart monitor that beeped rhythmically as he lay tethered to the bed. For one brief moment he thought of pulling the monitor and IV out, grabbing his clothing that was no doubt stuffed in one of the cabinets, and getting the heck out of Dodge. What if Cookie was in Shardsburg, even now, talking Rayleen into spilling all she knew? One of only two people, besides himself, who knew the truth. The whole truth. What then?

"Mitzi," he pleaded, his voice hoarse. "You have to help me."

"Anything, Ebie," she said, coming to sit beside him on the bed and stroking his hair. "You know that."

"You need to get to Shardsburg before Cookie does." He tried to sit up again but couldn't find the energy and sank back down onto the soft pillow. "Head her off at the pass, talk to Rayleen. I'm certain that's where she's headed."

Mitzi shook her head. "I can't leave you. . . not like this."

"You have to, Mitzi." He reached out a hand, placing it on her arm, his gaze steady, imploring her to listen.

Mitzi's eyes narrowed. "There's something you're not telling me, Ebie. What is it?"

"There's no time, Mitzi. I promise, we'll talk about this later. But you have to leave. Now."

Just then, the door opened and a small male nurse entered in blue scrubs that looked two sizes too big for him. "How are you holding up there, Sir?" he said, pulling down the clipboard from the back wall and scanning it as he did.

"Fine," Ebie said, though he was not fine. Nothing was fine.

"It's time you got some rest," the nurse said, setting down the clipboard, then going over to the counter where he pulled out a paper cup from the dispensary. He filled it with water and produced two pills he'd brought with him, one a dull green, the other white. "Here," he said, handing them to Ebie.

Ebie turned to Mitzi. "Talk to Rayleen. Then come back and I'll tell you everything. Please."

Only after he secured a nod and watched her stand to leave did he finally drink down the water and pills. His eyes felt heavy, as if he'd been awake for hours. He gave Mitzi a brief thumbs up, then he closed his eyes, sleep a welcome relief.

* * *

Cookie looked up in time to see the rabbit skitter into the cornfield, kicking up dust in its wake. Already she felt the sting of the nail marks that ran up and down her arm in angry streaks, but she had no time to dwell on it as she took off at a run.

"Catch her," Charlotte cried, her expression earnest. "She'll get into grammy's vegetable patch, if we don't."

While Charlotte veered off to the right, Cookie moved to the left. She lingered only a moment to see Charlotte enter the rows of corn before she, too, took the plunge. With the sun shuttered behind the tall feed corn, the temperature cooled, and yet the mugginess of an Alabama summer made her sweat instantly. As she ran full out through the corn fields, the hair at the side of her head clotted into moist clumps. Her arms, which still stung from the rabbits claws, now burned fire for a new reason -- the sharp corn leaves biting into her flesh as she raced back and forth through the corn in search of the elusive bunny. Occasionally, she saw movement and ran in the direction of the bent corn, but no sooner would she come within reaching distance than the rabbit would kick up its heels, dodging this way and that. Soon, her heart was pounding in her ears and her breathing came in short, jagged bursts. She was about to give up when she made one last attempt to dive at the bunny. However, before she could slow her movement, she saw the black arm of a man reach out and scoop up the rabbit, which the man clutched to his chest just as she ran into him with a loud thump. For one brief moment, they stood looking at each other in stunned silence.

"You looking for this?" the young man asked.

She could only nod as she took stock of the stranger. She gauged him to be about ten years older than herself, which would make him in his forties, by her reckoning. He was reed thin, had short hair, his features narrow. But his eyes are what drew her to him. There was a gentleness to them that put her at ease.

"This Charlotte's rabbit?"

Cookie gasped. "How did you know?"

He merely laughed. "'Cause she's my daughter. 'Sides, I've caught this little escape artist more often than I care to count." He laughed again, now holding the rabbit by its ears.

"Won't that hurt him?" she asked as the bunny's back legs kicked a furious rhythm.

"Nah!" He looked the bunny in the eye. "This way I won't end up like you." He dipped his head toward the angry red welts running up and down her arms. "We better put something on that before those cuts get infected. Let's go see what Mama's got in her medicine cabinet."

"Rayleen's your mama?"

"Yup," he said, already heading toward the farmhouse. He peered back at her as if to say, "You comin'?" Then he added, "Charlotte looking for this here rabbit?"

"She's somewhere off to the left," Cookie said as she ran to keep up.

He didn't wait for her. Instead, he called Charlotte's name

again and again, until they heard her shout, "Over here, Daddy!"

"I got your bunny, Baby!" he called back.

The young girl let out a whoop. Soon the sounds of her crashing footsteps met up with theirs so that by the time they reached the edge of the cornfield, she was chattering a mile a minute, telling him all about Cookie, where she had found her, where she had come from, and why she was there.

He stopped so suddenly that Cookie nearly ran into him for a second time that day. "Cookie?" he said, his face paling a shade, his eyes scouring hers. Then he turned to his daughter, as though maybe he had heard her incorrectly.

"What, Daddy?" Charlotte asked. "What's wrong?"

"N-nothing, Baby. Just. . . nevermind," he said, leaning into her, the bunny squirming between them. "Let's get this beast back in its cage. Then I'll tell you what. In the next week or so, I'll help build you a new cage, a huge cage so this bunny has room to run around. What'ya say?"

"Thanks, Daddy!" Charlotte said, beaming up at him.

"Okay," he said as they burst through the last of the rows of corn into daylight. Rayleen was still standing where they'd left her, hands on hips and a worried expression on her face.

When she saw the trio, she stilled, her eyes meeting her son's. For a brief moment, Cookie could swear that something had transpired between them, words not spoken, yet passed between them nonetheless. Both of them looked at her. And in that instant, Cookie knew. Charlotte's father recognized Cookie. He remembered.

24

RAYLEEN GUIDED COOKIE UP THE steps of the shack, her heart swelling as her eyes met her son's over Cookie's shoulder. James had asked about the girl periodically over the years. Even now, she could still recall his heartbroken little face all those years ago as it crumbled into tears when she'd told him Cookie was gone. When she broke the news to him, he'd taken off running toward the river. Rayleen had sent Chester after him, but they hadn't found him until nightfall.

A rush of fear wedged between her ribs at the memory, as if fresh instead of long ago. Chester had found James holed up down by the river in a little hollow beneath the cottonwoods, dirty tears staining his brown cheeks. Rayleen had almost lost two children that day. It had scared her more than she cared to admit. She fought down the rising nausea at the thought, then forced herself to remember the good times as she moved Cookie toward the screen door.

Cookie had been *his* little sister, or at least in James's eyes. He had carried her everywhere he went. Cookie had called him JJ, unable to form the word James. The name had stuck for as long as she was there. None of the family had ever talked about why he had taken to her so. But then again, as the oldest child, he'd been the most nurturing of her kids. He had filled in as father to his younger brother, now off in Vietnam, when Chester had left for stints at other jobs that brought in guaranteed money, unlike the farm, which could set them back in a bad year.

Before she could dwell further on the past, James rushed to open the screen door for the pair, pulling Charlotte to his side to let the two women pass. The screen door gave a loud screech. Rayleen would need to have Chester oil it. Again.

Once inside, Rayleen eyed the red welts on Cookie's arms from the rabbit's claws and frowned. "Let's get something on those. James, go get iodine." Then to Cookie she said, "The iodine is going to sting."

Cookie merely nodded, her eyes roaming the interior of their home as though searching for signs of recognition. *Does she know? Does she remember?* Rayleen had only to look at James to realize he had cottoned to the name Cookie when he'd heard it. It was like losing your first pet. . . or child. *You never forget.* Her throat tightened, remembering the first child *she* had lost. At the age of two. James had been four. Four and a half, at most. Surely he couldn't have recalled the incident.

One moment of distraction.

Chicken skin ran up her arms. That was the thing about tragedy, she realized, the familiar ache settling on her chest. It clung to a person just as the hot mashed potatoes had her two year old when she'd pulled the pot off the stove. She could still hear the screams. Still feel the weight of guilt. She had leaned toward the open window to call Chester to dinner. One moment of distraction for a lifetime of guilt. Could that be why James had doted over Cookie so, as a child? Because, as the big brother, he had wanted to keep her safe in a way he couldn't *his* little sister? What a burden for a child to carry.

Soon James returned with the iodine. With alarm, Rayleen noticed Cookie holding a crude wooden carving of a horse, her eyes suddenly alight with recognition.

"Neigh-Neigh?"

The name she had used for the horse as a three-year-old.

A chill traveled through Rayleen and her knees buckled. James rushed to Rayleen's side and threw an arm around her waist to support her. How? How had Cookie remembered such a small detail? Rayleen said a quick prayer beneath her breath then grasped James' outstretched hand. She had a feeling she would need it in the upcoming days.

* * *

As Cookie stood in the small pine shack, the lingering smell of fried eggs and bacon permeating the air, she felt a ghost of a memory pass through her as she once again turned her attention to the roughly carved horse. Though in some ways it was crude, in other ways it had captured the spirit of the horse perfectly, the way its mane blew in the wind, its tail raised, its head elevated and angled to the left, as though in defiance.

Her thoughts turned to another memory. Of her seated in a vegetable patch as a child, playing with Neigh-Neigh, making it rear up on hind legs, then bringing it down with a snort to paw at the dry earth. A memory of her, seated on a billowing blanket, her head shaded by a raggedy straw hat, a voice just off to the side and above her happily chatting, but about what? She forced her mind to concentrate. *Think! Think!* Then, like an apparition, a hand appeared from the sky above, a small, deep mahogany-colored hand holding a plant of some sort. She felt sure the person was explaining the plant as though the little three-year-old could understand. Had this been where she'd learned her love of the earth, of all things horticultural?

Cookie whirled around to face the pair. "Did you babysit me as a child?" she asked, cocking her head slightly.

"I--" Rayleen turned to her son, as if seeking help.

The young man licked his full lips, his eyes darting to his daughter and back again. "What my mother is trying to say is that, well. . ." He turned to Charlotte who was seated on the sagging green couch and had stopped flipping through a magazine to listen. "Charlotte, go out and check on your rabbits."

Her brows furrowed, and she sluggishly rose from the couch, shoulders shrugged in a show of protest. "I never get to hear any of the good stuff," she grumbled as she opened the screen door, letting it slam shut behind her.

James released a sigh and said, "Kids!"

Cookie harrumphed. How many times had she heard her mother use that exact same word? Once Charlotte was out of earshot, Cookie turned back to Rayleen and said, "So *did* you babysit me. . . as a child?"

Just then the whir of a car pulling up next to the house drew their attention away. James walked over to the window and pulled back the lace curtains.

"Who is it, Son?" Rayleen asked.

"I don't know," James said, stepping aside so that Rayleen could take a look. "We don't get many visitors this far out," he said for Cookie's benefit.

Cookie stood on tiptoes, trying to peer over mother and son's shoulders. She twisted her head around and felt her heart still as she saw who had pulled up in front of the shack.

Mitzi.

* * *

Mitzi fished in her purse for her bottle of diuretics, opened the lid and swallowed one, washing it down with a Grape Nehi she'd purchased at the little store they used to own. Walking into that store had been like walking back in time, like looking at old snapshots. Ebie working behind the counter while Cookie played with a tea set placed on a stool. *Flash.* The fear Mitzi had felt every time anyone walked through the door, worried it might be Cookie's mother coming to claim her, or worse, one of the town gossips out to defame her. *Flash.* Unable to contain their fears any longer, Ebie had packed their belongings, the family fleeing in the night. *Flash.*

But what she remembered most was the feeling of weightlessness as they drove away from that place, the darkness of nighttime settling over her like a mantle, comforting her. The Rambler's headlights lighting the road ahead in soft haloes, reflecting the eyes of nocturnal animals edging the forest; deer and raccoons, owls and bobcats that roamed the night. It was then, all those years ago, under the cover of darkness with only the hum of the highway and the sound of crickets to soothe her that she had felt most at home. Away from prying eyes. Away from intrusive questions. Away from cruel stares. Quite simply, she had given up on the kindness of her fellow townsfolk, who had gossiped continuously about Cookie. She had lost faith in mankind. It had taken Mitzi a year in Montgomery to regain her sense of self. And though she put on a good game face, she knew she had never regained her confidence entirely. Probably never would. Cookie had been her one saving grace, she realized with a wan smile. Mitzi had poured her heart into her daughter and was pleased with the outcome. Because Cookie was truly a good person. And *as* a truly good person, she gave Mitzi a mustard seed of faith in humankind.

Mitzi checked her face in the mirror and frowned at her hair, wilted by the humidity. It was fitting though, no? To have to face the woman who had cared for Cookie, by all counts loved Cookie, looking so. . . so. . . *dowdy*. She fingered the cross at her neck and said a silent prayer. *Forgive me, Rayleen. Cookie.* She closed her eyes and took a deep breath, then stepped out of the car.

Already the entire clan stood on the porch, Rayleen, and what Mitzi could only guess to be her son, making way for Cookie, whose expression was one of confusion, worry, and surprise all wrapped up into one neat bundle.

"Mama?" she said, finding her voice. "I mean Mitzi? What are *you* doing here?"

"Where is Dipsy?" Mitzi replied, not ready to answer that question just yet.

"She and Beulah are at the house over yonder," Rayleen said, stepping forward as if in challenge, her chin lifted in the direction of the second homestead Mitzi and Ebie owned, the only two remaining of their holdings in this part of the county.

"Beulah? What is she doing there? I thought she was attending to a sick relative," Mitzi said, reaching into the Rambler and pulling out her sunbonnet, then shutting the car door, glad she'd thought ahead. She fanned her face with it, then placed it on her head, not caring that she probably looked silly and out of place in her Sunday bonnet.

"That's not important, Mitzi," Cookie said, rushing down and helping Mitzi up the steps as though she were a doddering old fool who couldn't walk on her own. Mitzi waved her away, brushing off her sleeves as though she'd gathered dust in the few seconds walk across the barren soil.

"I've been wondering when this day would come," Rayleen said, her voice made of the same steel Mitzi had remembered from long ago.

Now that Mitzi was on the porch, she had time to take stock of the woman. To her surprise, despite the blistering sun and squalid conditions, Rayleen had fared rather well. Her eyes had fine crows feet around them and her hair sprouted wispy strands of gray, but all in all, she seemed rather. . . happy. As though in poverty and family -- and no doubt church -- she had found community from the many storms that had buffeted her throughout the years. How Mitzi wished that she had at least part of that. She'd always worn a mask. As the wife of the great Ebeneezer Haines. As the mother of a child she wanted as her own. As the community organizer who had her finger in town politics, always testing the wind so that her family remained in good stead with her neighbors, unlike what had happened back in Shardsburg. She shivered at the memory. There, she had heard the cruel comments: *She stole that child. Thinks she's better than us.*

Doesn't belong here. And yet no one had spoken out against them in public, too afraid to lose the supplies the store offered. But in private...

Even now, Mitzi felt the sting of those words like a fresh slap to the face. Those had been bitter years, but she had forged her way through, despite ladies and men alike knotted in gossip aimed at both her and each other. Their sharp tongues were like poisoned darts, always seeking the weakest part of a person. Always looking to wound. Not so Cookie. She, of all people, avoided the limelight. Refused to join in at the expense of others. It never failed to amaze her that the very people who espoused "Christian" values were the same ones tearing everyone else down.

No, that's not true. There are decent people everywhere.

But decent people often hid when the pitchforks came out. Too afraid for their own hide to save another's.

You're one of those people, too, Mitzi, she realized, determined to be totally honest with herself. The day, which was already turning off brutally hot, seemed to grow in intensity as she aimed the ire at herself. Well, she may *have* been one of those people, but no more.

"Could I please get a drink of water, Rayleen?" she asked, forcing a smile to her lips.

"Come on inside, Mitzi," Rayleen said with a hollow laugh. "Looks like we're gonna have us an old-fashioned meeting of the minds."

25

FROM THE MOMENT COOKIE HAD first laid eyes on Mitzi, she knew something was wrong. Desperately wrong. Mitzi never traveled outside the small circle of her neighborhood. Plus she was a notoriously bad driver. Either Ebie or Beulah drove her if she needed to go any distance. No, something so important that she had overcome her fear of driving had brought her here to this shack with its dark, smoky interior and threadbare rose-colored sofa.

As she watched her mother take stock of her surroundings, Cookie felt certain Mitzi had been in this small shack before. But why not? After all, she and Ebie owned the two shacks, according to the deeds Cookie had found in Ebie's files.

"Mitzi, what's wrong? Why are you here?" Cookie demanded, heart pounding in anticipation of the answer.

"I. . . I. . ."

Rayleen moved forward, hip out, arms crossed. "Might as well tell her, Miss Mitzi. That's why you're here, isn't it? I'm through keepin' y'all's secrets. My son and I have had to live with 'em every time one of y'all come here askin' about Miss Cookie."

"What?" Mitzi stepped back, as though gut-punched. "No. That's not why I'm here, I mean, who. . .? Who has been here asking about her?"

"You know. Rachel. Her sister. That man!!" She spat the last two words with distaste as though the very thought of him filled her mouth with bile.

"That man? What man?" Mitzi swooned.

For one brief moment Cookie thought she might have to catch Mitzi, but her mother plopped onto the faded sofa instead and placed her head in her hands.

Cookie took a seat next to her. "You alright, Mitzi. . . Mama?"

Humidity had made Mitzi's hair limp and her skin had paled to a dangerous shade of ash. Before Cookie could ask anymore questions, Mitzi murmured, "So he's alive. I always wondered. . . worried."

"What, Mitzi, worried about what?" Cookie didn't know what Mitzi was talking about, but she could feel the tension in the humidity of the late afternoon Alabama air as it bounced through the room. It felt oppressive, as though a weight on her chest that couldn't be freed.

"He doesn't want Cookie," Rayleen said, handing Mitzi the glass of water that James had brought her. "He's after Rachel, mostly."

"The man's a monster!" Mitzi railed, the color returning to her cheeks and her eyes lit with a fire Cookie had never seen before.

"My father?" Cookie demanded, frightened suddenly.

"No, no, no." Mitzi shook her head vehemently.

"Is Rachel my mother? My biological mother?" Cookie felt her world crumbling, as though the ground had opened up beneath her and had swallowed her whole, pulling her down, down, down.

Mitzi's eyes pleaded for Rayleen to help her.

"You made your bed," Rayleen said.

"We all did," Mitzi whispered, tears rimming her lids.

A volcano erupted inside Cookie. She exploded to her feet so fast that she nearly stepped on the tail of a calico cat she hadn't seen enter the house when she'd first arrived. It let out a loud screech and ran under a table to hide. Cookie clutched her hair to regain control of her emotions.

"So it's true. You and Ebie aren't my real parents?" She began pacing, willing herself not to cry. "You lied to me all these years?" Then a thought came to her, a truly horrible thought and she turned on Mitzi. "Is that why I was never allowed to call you mother?" Cookie demanded, anger guiding her words even as she wanted, *needed* comfort from the very woman she was confronting.

"No, never. Cookie, I *wanted* you to call me mother."

"Then why? Why does Dipsy call you mom, but I'm only allowed to call you Mitzi?" Cookie insisted, her voice crackling with emotion. Now that she was finally unburdening herself, she couldn't seem to stop. All the questions she'd had, odd things that had made no sense to her as a child, suddenly resurfaced in one fell swoop. Her love for gardening when no one else cared a fig, her odd memories of light playing through a dirty window pane in a ramshackle house, her stuffed rabbit. . . the one with a missing ear and fur all matted. Is this why she'd always felt different? Because she *was* different?

Mitzi's jaw quivered and silent tears fell down her cheek. "I wanted you to call me mother. You don't know how I craved to hear that word. But you said I wasn't your mother, that I would never be your mother." Pain filled her eyes as she stared first at Cookie, next at Rayleen. Then, in a soft voice, she said, "You said *she* was your mother, not me. So you started calling me Mitzi, and that was enough for me." Tears spilled down her cheeks and her lips trembled. "It had to be," she said in a whisper. Then she sat up taller, her voice stronger. "But know this, Cookie Lee Haines. I have always loved you. And I always will, no matter *who* birthed you."

"Wait! What? I don't understand. Rachel gave me to Rayleen?" All the steam whistled free and Cookie deflated onto the couch once more, her anger spent. Her thoughts swirled in confusion like dust from the surrounding farmland, choking her every pore until she thought she might topple off the daveno and onto the rough oak floor.

"Tell her what happened, Miss Mitzi," Rayleen urged, her jaw set. "Tell her about Rachel, about Byrdie, about the twister, about the deal y'all reached."

Cookie flinched. "Deal? What deal?"

"It wasn't like that, Cookie," Mitzi said, placing a hand over Cookie's. "It was the best for everyone. You don't know what Byrdie was like. He was a hard man with a mean temper. Rachel knew that."

"Why didn't she just leave, take me with her?" Cookie demanded, near to tears.

"Look around you, girl," Rayleen inserted, plopping down

in the hickory rocking chair opposite Mitzi. "We were poor --
poorer than we are now. Rachel was the same. A young woman
with no skills could have never supported a child on her own.
Even a white woman. That's just the way it was back then."

James took a spot behind his mother and nodded in support.
"It's true. I remember Rachel. She was churchmouse poor. Thin.
Hungry."

"She wore worry on her forehead like a bandana," Rayleen
confirmed.

"Her clothes were always threadbare," Mitzi agreed. "Half
the time, she didn't even have a pair of shoes. It was shameful, is
what it was."

Cookie threw her hands up in disbelief. "Do you hear
yourself, Mitzi? It's shameful? What was she supposed to do? She
sharecropped on *your* farm. If she couldn't afford a pair of shoes,
it was because she and her husband were trying to *survive!*"

Mitzi began to cry quietly and James stepped in to offer her
a tissue. To Cookie's surprise, Rayleen stood and walked over
to kneel beside Mitzi. She patted her shoulder and murmured,
"There-there, Miss Mitzi. You did the best you could."

"Y'all think it was easy for us, back then," she said to Cookie,
"but we never broke even at the store, what with most folks
unable to pay. The only thing that kept us afloat was the gas
station, and even that just barely kept us ahead of the creditors.
We scrimped too. Why do you think I made all those clothes
instead of buying store bought?" Mitzi turned to Cookie, her
eyes red, her lashes wet.

"Wait! What? *You* owned the store?" Cookie felt dizzy
suddenly.

Mitzi gave a quick, short nod.

It had never dawned on Cookie that Mitzi and Ebie had struggled too. She had just assumed they had always done well, what with the house and Ebie's practice.

As if she'd read Cookie's mind, Mitzi said, "Even after Ebie's parents paid for him to go to law school, once he started his law business, he took clients pro bono. Did work for young mothers, the elderly, people who had no voice. He doesn't always get paid for his work, but he does it anyway. That's the kind of man he is, Cookie."

Cookie ran a hand through her hair. How had she been so blind for so long? It was as if she'd been living in black and white and could suddenly see color. Then why did she feel so awful?

"Honey," Mitzi said, "I didn't come here to hash through the past."

"Why *are* you here then?" Rayleen asked, struggling to stand.

Mitzi reached over and squeezed Cookie's hands between her own, the warmth of them providing comfort, despite the swirl of emotions that threatened to choke her.

"I'm here because your father is in the hospital."

Cookie tore her hands away and stood. "What do you mean? Why? Where?"

"In Huntsville. He had a heart attack."

Cookie shook her head to clear the cobwebs. "I don't understand. Why would Daddy be in Huntsville?"

Mitzi and Rayleen shared a nervous glance.

"He was looking for you," Mitzi said. "He was afraid of what you might find when you got here. He wanted to talk to you first, to explain."

The dizziness returned and the first thing Cookie remembered was waking up on the floor, her eyes on the ceiling, three faces staring down at her.

26

THEY SAY YOU CAN'T GO home again, or at least that's what Cookie had heard all her life. And yet as she came to, after passing out, three sets of eyes staring down at her -- Mitzi, Rayleen, and James -- all she could think about was that she had spent nearly three years of her life in this home. She didn't know whether to laugh or cry, because according to everyone here, she'd had not two mothers, but three. First Rachel, then Rayleen, and lastly Mitzi. And now, as if that wasn't enough, she had her father to worry about, dear sweet Ebie. From the time she was little she could remember him picking her up to show her all the books in his collection, explaining them as he went, the faint wisp of cherry tobacco filling the air. She loved his office, the large oak desk with its drawers filled with pens and papers and ink stampers. She especially loved the stand-up globe that she'd twirl and twirl, eyes closed, her finger landing on some unknown spot, never opening her eyes until the globe had stopped. Then she would ask her father about whatever location her finger had landed on and he would explain it, the people, what they looked like, how they lived, their form of government. She'd envisioned an entire world from those early talks. In her mind, she had flown to places never before imagined. Even now, she could picture the two of them together in her father's study. Those had been good times, special times.

"We need to go," Cookie said to no one in particular as they helped her to the sofa. "Let's pick up Dipsy and Beulah first. I'll drive."

"*You?*" Mitzi said, reaching for her glass of water and taking one last swallow before standing.

"I learned how to drive. . . on the way here."

"You're not driving, young lady. You just passed out, for heaven's sake! And explain to me again why Beulah is here." Mitzi placed her hands on her hips, one eyebrow cocked upwards. "What else haven't you told me?"

"You're one to talk," Cookie let slip before she could think about what she'd said. But now that she was on a roll, she found it hard to stop. "One lie hardly makes up for a lifetime of them."

Before Mitzi could answer the charge, Charlotte popped through the door. "Uh, Momma? Miss Cookie?" Then she stood back as Beulah pulled a limping, sweating Dipsy past the lintel, her beehive hairdo having listed to the side in the sweltering heat.

Cookie rushed to Dipsy's side and helped her onto the sofa. "What on earth were you doing out in this heat. . . and with a twisted ankle?"

"Dipsy, Beulah?" Mitzi hovered, the shock of what had transpired over the course of the day turning her normally healthy complexion a sallow, almost flaxen color. "What happened to you, Dipsy, and why *are* you here, Beulah?"

Beulah, bless her heart, having dragged Dipsy across the cornfield in the afternoon heat, appeared unready to make any accommodations for Mitzi's bent feelings.

"I'll have you know, Miss Mitzi, that your daughter here hurt her foot because she's always wearing those high-heels y'all like to wear." She looked down at Mitzi's two-inch black and gold Louboutins then gave Mitzi the eye. "As for me, well, *some*one's got to take care of these daughters of yours."

Beulah squared her shoulders in a face-off. But Rayleen stopped her mid-track by saying, "Time's a wastin'. Thought y'all were going to check on Mr. Ebie."

"Daddy?" Dipsy declared, the color returning to her cheeks, and the fatigue suddenly exchanged with fire. "What about Daddy? And where are my kids?"

"Your kids are with Kent."

"*Kent?*" Dipsy tried to pull herself up off the couch but couldn't.

"She had to send the kids with Kent. Ebie's in the hospital," Cookie declared. "Had a heart attack."

"Don't tell them that," Mitzi groused.

"Like you didn't tell me about my mother?" Cookie countered.

"Wait, what?" Dipsy demanded, her dander up now as she tried to stand.

Suddenly, James, who had been all but forgotten in the corner, put his fingers to his lips and whistled to silence them. All eyes turned to him. "Look, Miss Mitzi. . . Miss Cookie. It's clear we have a lot to talk about, but first you need to tend to business."

Just then, the sound of a truck came bouncing up the road followed by the screech of brakes. Moments later, Cookie heard the thump-thump-thump of footsteps running up the steps onto the porch. The door burst open and Chester stood there, filling the doorway, a look of panic maring his acne-scarred face. When he looked around and saw Dipsy and Beulah, he nearly collapsed in relief at the sight of them. Rayleen ran to him and snatched up his large hand in hers and squeezed tight.

"What the heck?" he said, leaning into Rayleen.

"The two saw Cookie's car and wandered over here," Rayleen explained, and then discussed all that had transpired in the past half hour.

"I just went to check on a downed tree south of the property, and when I returned, they were gone." He eyed Beulah with a look of frustration. "Thought something had happened to them, what with Miss Dipsy's leg."

Both Dipsy and Beulah had the good sense to lower their heads in contrition.

Rayleen, who had seemed on edge since Mitzi's arrival, stood to her full height. It was then that Cookie noticed something she'd missed before. A small, well-worn locket, its borders burnished into a fine sheen from years of handling. Rayleen worried it with her hands, absentmindedly flipping it open. And there, to Cookie's amazement, were three small photographs in sepia tones. One James, the other another boy, a brother perhaps, and lastly a little white toddler in overalls, wispy blond hair lifted by the wind as though an echo of the way she had arrived at this shack. . . with the wind. Mitzi must have seen it too, because she gasped, placing a hand to her mouth, her eyes watering.

"All these years," Mitzi murmured, her eyes distant as though seeing into another time.

Rayleen stepped forward in challenge. "That's right, Miss Mitzi. I kept her picture all these years. She was *my* child first."

"Yes, but--"

"No!" Rayleen all but shouted. Her next words were spoken through gritted teeth. "There are no buts. You never let me say goodbye to her. . . to Cookie. You took her from me and never let me tell her--" Her voice ended on a sob. She turned to Chester, who wrapped her in his arms, cradling her now as he no doubt had then, when she'd returned home after delivering Cookie into Mitzi and Ebie's waiting arms.

"Let me say something," Mitzi pleaded, her eyes moving back and forth as she sought to state her case.

"No!" Chester said in a voice so low as to be almost unheard. "You've done enough. Go! Now!" Then he turned his back to the women as, one by one, they filed out, Cookie ushering the others first. She gave a single backward glance and saw only James' apologetic shrug. Then she marched out the front door, her heart heavy with unanswered questions.

27

FOR COOKIE, THE PAST FEW minutes had been a blur of activity... Mitzi white knuckling it behind the steering wheel, as she prepared for the seventy mile drive to the hospital. Mitzi had even tried to swallow some pills "for her nerves." But Cookie knew only too well about those nerve pills, and no way did she want Mitzi driving with those in her. Instead, she snatched them up, put them in a zippered pouch and then placed the pouch in her purse.

"You can have them later, when you don't have an entire car full of people to look after," Cookie said, trying to quell the anger inside her.

In the meantime, Chester helped Dipsy hobble into the backseat of the Buick alongside Beulah. Chester slammed the car door shut, then waved farewell to the passengers, James still on the porch, his arm around Charlotte, who leaned into him. As

Mitzi keyed the engine and the car sprang to life, Cookie waved.

For the next half an hour they drove, watermelon patches quickly turning to cornfields. acres and acres of agriculture soon replaced by pine groves that eventually fell away as the city of Huntsville loomed large. After sharing the food and drink she'd purchased at the store with the others, Cookie dug in her purse for some gum and began chewing, snapping it over and over to calm her nerves as they drove deeper into the city. To Cookie, her father had always been a larger-than-life figure who could leap tall buildings with a single bound. She'd never thought of him as mortal. She rolled down the window needing fresh air. In her mind Ebie would live forever, so the thought of him in a hospital came as a great shock that left her feeling weak.

Once again she snapped her gum while tapping a rhythm on her knee.

"Oh good gawd, Cookie!" Mitzi said, putting on her cat's eye sunglasses, her hair placed in a silk scarf she'd pulled out of the glove compartment at a traffic light. Even in a crisis, Mitzi somehow managed to look cool. "You're driving me crazy with all that snapping. Your dad had a very minor heart attack. It may have just been a panic attack for all we know, what with all his worries lately."

"Worries? What worries?" Cookie spit her tired-tasting gum out the window, a billowing cloud foreshadowing a coming storm.

"Did you just litterbug, Missy?" Mitzi tsked, shaking her head in frustration. "I could get a fine for that. I swear, little girl, sometimes I think you were raised by wolves."

Mitzi must have seen the shock on Cookie's face, because she reached over and patted Cookie's knee. "Pay no attention to the woman behind the steering wheel," she said, flashing Cookie one of her famous smiles. "She's got hoof-and-mouth disease."

Despite Cookie's mix of emotions, she couldn't help but laugh. Leave it to Mitzi to break the tension. Cookie burrowed down into her seat, put her feet up on the dashboard and watched the tips of the trees pass by, a light wind picking at the branches. The sun behind the trees turned them into dark shadows ringed in rays of silver. As a child, scenes such as this had seemed magical. They were magical still.

"Mama, did you ever think your life would turn out like it did?" she asked absentmindedly, as she chewed on her thumbnail. When Mitzi didn't answer right away, she turned to look and saw shiny tears brimming Mitzi's eyes.

Mitzi returned Cookie's gaze, her blue eyes searching, the car swerving out of its lane.

"Look out!" Cookie cried when they weaved onto the shoulder, nearly hitting a post. She sat up, heart pounding. "Jeez, if I had known you'd react like that, I would have waited 'til we were at the hospital!"

Mitzi shrugged. "Sorry, sweetie. I always was a one-trick pony. Hey, speaking of hospitals, there it is!" Mitzi slowed the car in front of a large cream-colored concrete structure and turned into the parking lot, the wind whipping harder than it had before, sending leaves skittering across the asphalt. Mitzi finished parking, then keyed off the engine. She stopped Cookie before she could exit the car. "Honey?"

"Yeah?"

Though usually not at a loss for words, Mitzi stammered now. "It's just that, well -- your dad has a lot on his plate. He always has. Go easy on him, okay?"

Cookie paused, thinking about what Mitzi had said. She peered back at Beulah and Dipsy before answering. Then she chose her words carefully. "I may be mad at you guys for not telling me the truth, but I've always loved you. I always will." And with that, they clasped hands.

*　*　*

Rayleen moved from Chester's comforting embrace so she could stand by the window and peer out the lace curtains at the retreating vehicle with the three women from Montgomery. The lace had been Rayleen's one extravagance in an otherwise ordinary life. It's funny. She knew she should want for more. At least that's what the ads on the TV preached. But she was happy with her home, with her life, but more importantly with her family. They gave her a sense of belonging. Most of the things around her had been handmade, from the knitted throw on the back of the daveno to the willow rocking chair that Chester's papa had passed to them when he died. Above the fireplace was Chester's corn cob pipe he had drilled and fitted with a stem, and over the fireplace hung a painting he'd done of workers in the fields, a basket full of cotton hoisted on the shoulder of a man who looked suspiciously like Chester himself, only without a single blemish. How he had been before life had worn him to a frazzle. She had always loved the bright colors: deep blue, the color of the sky just before dusk, yellow, the color of a duck yolk, and green, the color of the cotton plant itself.

So much of what they owned was handmade... held a piece of each of them. And for that, she cherished each and every bit of her home and the things in it. All she had to do was to pick up

234

the coiled clay pot from beside the daveno and instantly it drew her back in time to James, a shy little boy who had handed her a package wrapped in brown paper and twine. He'd drawn pictures on the paper using yellow chamomile, small purple potatoes, and marigolds. The tag weaved into the twine was shaped like a heart and simply said "Mama" in big bold letters. She had known then that she had a special boy who would do her proud, if the world would just leave him be.

As she turned away from the window, her stomach sank at the sight of James who had walked into the room holding a worn blanket. A lamb had been stitched to the front of the quilt, pale green fleece dividing each and every square. All four corners bore the name of a family member.

Rayleen gasped as she looked from her son to her husband, then back again. "Where did you get that, Son?" She had been careful to keep it concealed behind a brick hidey-hole she'd discovered near the hooked arm of the old cast iron brazier. A large cast iron pot could be hung on the hook and swung into place over the fire. Even now, she used it once in a while for old time's sake. She was the only one who ever dug around in there -- or so she'd thought -- until now.

"You think I don't know about the blanket, Ma? About her people?"

She turned away, unable to bear the pity in those wide brown eyes. Her son had always seen through her. Chester said she could be as hard as Shardsburg's clay soil sometimes, but you had to be hard to live in these parts and survive. Chester, more than just about anyone, knew that. And he had scars to prove it. One ran lengthwise across his left cheek after he'd been involved in a knife fight as a teen. Wasn't his fault, but didn't nobody care whose fault it was. All anyone saw was the color of his skin, not the person inside. Every time she thought of Chester, of his hams for arms stretching wide around her, how tender her bear of a husband could be, why it just made her melt inside like butter pecan ice cream on a hot July day. She loved him. Fully cherished him. How many women could say that about their men? No, Chester had a heart of gold and saved his temper for the outside world, knowing that they could only make it out alive if they stuck together. Like beeswax and honey. Her eyes suddenly regained focus as her son stepped in closer.

"Mama?"

"Mmm-hmm," she said absentmindedly, her thoughts still in the past.

"I been doin' a little research about these here names."

It was as if he'd struck a match and she could still smell the sulphur because she was instantly alert. "What do you mean you been doin' some research? What kinda research?"

"I know about Cookie's mama." His face had gone a chalky white.

Chester stepped in and lay a hand on James' shoulder. "What you mean you done know about Cookie's mama?"

"I know where she's at. But Mama?" He hesitated, handing her the corner of the quilt that bore the name of Cookie's mother. . . the real name.

Rayleen's jaw quivered and she dropped to the daveno, feeling as though she'd been rent in two.

"Don't you think it's time you told Cookie?" He knelt before her, his soft eyes pleading even as he took her hands in his, the warmth of them a healing balm.

28

THE MOMENT COOKIE SAW HER father swallowed up in the hospital bed, she rushed over to hug him, not waiting for the others to catch up. All the way over, she had worried about how she would react after everything that had transpired, but all that fell away when she saw him hooked up to IVs.

Dipsy, who brought up the rear along with Beulah, hurried toward them, then plopped unceremoniously onto the bed beside Ebie. "Daddy," she cried, snatching up his hand in hers.

"Oh, for heaven's sake," Mitzi said, as though she hadn't been just as worried about Ebie, if not more. "Your father's fine. But he won't be if you two yahoos don't quit crushing him."

"They're okay," Ebie said, trying to smooth things over as he had done countless times throughout their lives. "They just missed their dear old dad." He winked at the pair, but Cookie noted the paleness of his skin, the tiredness around his eyes.

Finally, she released him and stood.

"We have a lot to talk about," she said, afraid that if she didn't spit it out now, she never would.

"I know, honey," he agreed, "but can it wait? I'm feeling awfully tired," he said with a yawn.

Just then a nurse entered. "It's time for Ebie's medicine." She handed him a pill and a Dixie cup filled with water to wash it down. He swallowed the medicine along with the water, making a face as he did. The nurse walked over to a chart, filled in the time of the medication, then turned to them before she left. "You may stay a few minutes longer, but afterward he will need to rest. In the meantime, may I speak with you for a moment, Mrs. Haines?"

The pair talked quietly in a corner as Cookie and Dipsy squeezed Ebie's hand one last time and gave him a final hug. When the nurse was finished speaking with Mitzi, she opened the door and with a swoosh, she was gone.

The struggle of the past few days must have taken their toll on Ebie because his eyes fluttered closed. Cookie had so many questions, so much to say, but it would have to wait. And Mitzi would be of no use. She could be downright tightlipped when the spirit moved her, and she had already made it clear that until Ebie was ready to explain, the story was not hers to tell. But why Ebie? Why was his part in this so much larger than Mitzi's that she bowed to him to tell it? Although patience was never Cookie's strong suit, she knew that this time she would have to resign herself to waiting, if she were to ever learn the truth.

Slowly, grudgingly, she kissed her father on the forehead, heard his soft murmur, then opened the door and made her way downstairs, the others trailing behind. She was just about to reach for the door that led to the hospital lobby when the door flew open and there stood Rachel, Cookie's biological mother.

"Oh..." Rachel said, her voice trailing off. She wore the same dress she had the day she had entered the family kitchen, but her skin seemed less sallow, her pale gray eyes clearer.

For one brief moment, Cookie felt as though the world had quit turning. The two stood there, staring at each other. As the others made their way down the last of the stairway, they too stopped in various locations on the stairwell.

"You!" Mitzi cried. "What are you doing here? I thought we had an agreement. You said you would let us talk to Cookie first." She peered up the stairwell as though only now realizing where Rachel was headed. "You leave my Ebie be, y'hear? You've done enough already!"

Mitzi's face had gone a shade of crimson Cookie had never seen before, and for just a glimmer of time, she saw that Mitzi could be formidable when she wanted to be. Cookie would never want Mitzi's wrath turned on her, she realized, shrinking into herself.

"I have no intention of upsetting Ebie, but there's something he needs to know. Something you *all* need to know."

The whites of Mitzi's eyes revealed her fear coupled with a wildness that Cookie had never seen before. Something about them frightened her, made her wonder what more Mitzi knew that she wasn't saying. If, indeed, Rachel was Cookie's mother, then the worst had already happened. Cookie knew about her. Knew that she had been looking for Cookie. Knew that her parents had kept that knowledge from her. So why the unbridled fear now, of all times? Something didn't make sense here. Something that had the pair faced off in a head-to-head.

"What is it, Mitzi?" Cookie said, peering back and forth between the two women. "What aren't you telling me?"

For a moment, silence reigned. Then finally, Beulah spoke up in a voice so low as to be almost unrecognizable. "Tell her, Mitzi. You done held it from her long enough. If you don't tell her I will."

"Tell me what, Mama?" Cookie said, in the heat of the moment forgetting to call her Mitzi.

Again, silence reigned. For several agonizing moments, everyone stood, each looking to the other for the answer. Finally, Mitzi spoke up. "I told you before, it's Ebie's story to tell, and Ebie will tell it. Until then, you will just have to wait. All of you."

29

COOKIE FELT AS THOUGH SHE had been slapped as all eyes turned to her in the stairwell of the Huntsville Hospital. "I'm tired of all the games," she said, plopping down onto the bottom step of the concrete stairwell.

"Now look what you've done," Mitzi admonished Rachel, making her way as best she could on heels to where Cookie sat, head in hands.

"Someone had to tell her," both Rachel and Beulah said in unison.

Dipsy, who had all but been forgotten on the upper landing of the stairwell shouted down, "Well, I've just about had enough of y'all!" She stamped her good foot, then began crying and sat.

"Well this is a fine, howdya do," Beulah said in a huff. "Now you've got both girls upset, Mitzi."

"*Me?*" Mitzi turned to Beulah and scowled. "It was her!" She turned back to point at Rachel, who appeared tired and spent, her newly graying hair as limp as her dress.

To everyone's surprise, Rachel was the only one of the bunch composed. She looked straight at Mitzi with those sad blue-gray eyes of hers and said, "You have forty-eight hours to tell her the truth, Mitzi. Forty-eight hours. Better yet, let's meet at the old sharecroppers homestead at noon, tomorrow. And I want Chester and Rayleen to be there. It's their story too, after all."

Cookie waited, heart thrumming as Mitzi stood clutching her purse. In twenty-four hours she would know the truth of her birth, of the child's disappearance -- *her* disappearance, though at least she knew the outcome of *that*.

Finally, Mitzi gave a short nod of her head. "But I want Ebie to be there. I'm going to see how soon they can release him. Fortunately, the doctor doesn't think it was a heart attack -- just a panic attack. That's what the nurse wanted to talk to me about." She turned first to Dipsy, then Cookie. "I'm going to stay here with Ebie. You three take the car. . . go stay at the old sharecropper's house. We'll meet you there tomorrow."

"How will you and Daddy get there with no car?"

"I can take the girls so you and Ebie can have the car," Rachel said softly.

For several moments, none of them spoke. Then, finally, Mitzi agreed.

"But remember," she warned, "this is Ebie's story to tell, and *he. . . will. . .* tell it."

Rachel gulped down any words she might have spoken, then simply nodded and turned.

* * *

Rayleen hung up the phone, then leaned back against the kitchen hutch. Tomorrow, everything would be revealed. The quilt still lay where James had left it. He needed to be there at the other sharecropper's house too. She would call over there, let him know. It was only fitting that Cookie learn the truth at the place where it had all begun. A story so convoluted that it defied logic. And yet this sort of thing had been happening since the beginning of time. That was the odd thing, Rayleen knew. Life could sometimes be stranger than fiction.

She walked over and picked up the blanket, breathed in the smell. After all these years, she swore she could still detect Cookie's baby scent as though it had become permanently embedded in the fabric. Funny how a scent could take a person back in time. In this case it took her back to the day she'd had to take Cookie to her new parents. She'd bundled her up, dressed her real pretty, combed out her silky blonde hair into little ringlets. Cookie had been a pretty toddler, but more than that she'd been a loving child. And Rayleen had loved her right back. Years ago, if anyone had ever told her she could love a little white baby like her own, she would have laughed. But children had a way of reaching into a person's heart. They weren't born with bias. It was drilled into them, sometimes beaten into them. Rayleen understood that now.

She recalled that day in vivid detail. Picking the little girl up in her arms. Everyone saying goodbye to little Cookie. All except James. He hadn't understood. Later, when she'd returned home without the toddler, he had run out of the house and into the cornfield and beyond. It had taken most of the rest of the day to find him. He'd loved Cookie. Loved her like his own. She would trail after him as he hayed, talking to him in a slur of words, little bubbles of spit marking her words. Then she'd smile at the delight on all their faces that she had put such effort into the words.

But that day. . . that cursed day, Rayleen had cradled Cookie in her blanket. She'd tried to give it to Cookie to take with her, but before Mitzi could take it, Ebie had shouted at Rayleen to "Go, just go!" Even now, Rayleen could see Cookie's puzzled expression as she begged for "blankie," then "mama." Arms outstretched, begging. Her sweet little face balling up in fear and anger at this transition in her life, her chin covered in drool to match her tears. Rayleen had wanted to comfort her, to snatch Cookie up in her blanket and run home, keep her safe. But as long as Cookie was white and Rayleen was black there would be no safekeeping. Only fear, intimidation. Better that she find a home in her own community before something happened.

And yet she could still hear Cookie's cries in her mind's eye. Still see the determination as the toddler leaned as far away as she could from Mitzi who held her fast in her arms. Still see the spit rolling down her chin, the tears blanketing her eyes. And for one brief moment, all the pain that Rayleen had kept buried inside her came rushing out in a river of grief that threatened to drown her in sorrow. She crumpled to the pine floor, the blanket in her lap, the bittersweet smell of memory fresh in her mind, and for the first time in years, she sobbed.

30

AS THEY DROVE TOWARD THE hospital exit, Rachel at the wheel of her old Desoto, she saw a police officer ahead. He was stopping every car, one by one, and speaking with each of the drivers. As Rachel waited for him to reach her car, she thought of what had just transpired. After all these years, she had Cookie at her side, and yet now that the girl was here, she felt an odd distance that she hadn't expected, as though their meeting was too new, too raw to know what to feel or how to act. She wanted to reach over and wrap Cookie up in her arms, but for all intents and purposes, Rachel was a stranger to Cookie and she didn't know how the girl might react after all these years of believing she was Mitzi's daughter. So instead, Rachel gripped the wheel tighter and felt the churning in her stomach that seemed loud amid the vast silence that had taken hold of each of the car's occupants since the group had left the hospital.

When it was her turn to speak with the policeman, Rachel pulled up beside him and rolled down her window, trepidation causing her hands to shake.

"Ma'am, ladies," he said, tipping his hat.

"What's the problem, officer?" Rachel said, feeling more than a tiny bit of foreboding.

"There's a tornado on its way up. It just passed through Jefferson and should be here within hours. Best to get somewhere safe, to a storm cellar if you have one."

It was as if he'd laid bare her worst fear, for it brought to mind that horrible day -- that day when everything in her life had changed. *She* had changed. Her hands began to shake almost uncontrollably. The thought that she would be in the sharecropper's hut when the storm hit, just as she had been years before, was not lost on her. She quailed at the memories the storm might stir.

Please, God, don't let the twister come this way. Make it take another path.

But God hadn't answered her prayers then. Why should he answer her prayers now?

* * *

The moment Mitzi had told Ebie that Rachel had met them in the stairwell and that she was on her way to the sharecropper's hut with Cookie and the others in tow, he'd pressed on the nurse's button, then shouted for the nurse when she didn't arrive right away.

"By God, Rachel is not going to be the one to tell Cookie the truth," he fumed to Mitzi as he pulled himself up in the hospital bed. "She deserves to hear that from us."

"But Ebie--"

"Get my clothes," he ordered. "In that bag."

Mitzi had never seen Ebie like this. He was always so calm and composed, a behavior he had honed in the years he'd been a lawyer. Before the nurse had time to arrive, he was already pulling his IV out, bandage and all.

When the nurse entered and saw what he was doing, she let out a shout. "Hey, what are you doing with that IV?" she demanded.

"I'm taking it out. What the hell does it look like I'm doing?" Ebie snarled.

Mitzi tried to calm him, but there was no calming him this time. She could see that he was hell bent on getting to their daughter before Rachel told Cookie the whole sordid story.

"You can't leave without the doctor's permission," the nurse admonished, trying to push him back into the bed.

"Then get the doctor. NOW!" he shouted.

Fortunately, a doctor must have been nearby and heard the commotion because one entered the room within moments, a stethoscope around his neck. Though he wasn't officially Ebie's doctor, he had been the on-call doctor for the ward. As such, Mitzi knew he had the ability to release Ebie if he so chose. Apparently, he did, as he looked at Ebie's chart, then laid it on the counter.

"It looks like you had an anxiety attack rather than a heart attack, from what we can see. We usually release people at noon, but I am giving special permission for you to be released now, as long as she can show the nurse you can walk on your own. Then, I suggest you meet with your personal physician next week. I will prescribe an anti-anxiety drug for you. You can pick it up at the pharmacy at your convenience, but I do hope that you will try not to get too worked up, Mr. Haines." Here, he looked down his glasses at Ebie.

After he left, Ebie had walked for the nurse, then she had ushered him out in a wheelchair. Ebie had the good sense to appear chagrined for causing her so much trouble, and yet Mitzi knew that for him to react this way, he must feel very strongly about speaking to Cookie. And yet Mitzi had known him long enough to know that something wasn't quite right, that there was something he wasn't telling her, but what? She wasn't sure, but she had a feeling she was about to find out.

* * *

It was as if the storm had unleashed a torrent of feeling Cookie hadn't known she was harboring. Here she was, on the way to the very sharecropper's hut where she was born, her birth mother seated beside her in the old Desoto, and yet all she felt was dread. And as though nature itself had read her emotions, the wind began to blow. At first leaves scattered across the highway leading out of town, then a buffeting wind replaced it as they headed through the cornfields, the cotton fields, the watermelon patch. Not yet a tornado, but frightening nonetheless. Just then, the wind kicked up, howled a warning. Cookie braced herself for what lay ahead as Beulah moaned in the backseat, which she had been doing ever since she'd heard a cyclone was headed their way.

"I never liked cyclones," Beulah mumbled as Dipsy comforted her, instead of the other way around, which was more typical of the pair. "I've seen what they've done when I was a child. Hmm-hmm!" Beulah pursed her lips, as though warding off the fearsome beast.

Cookie felt it too, the building of anticipation. The apprehension. She blew into her hands to keep them warm, for the air, which had been hot earlier, had decidedly cooled. It seemed to whistle in through every crack and crevice, to pour into her very veins until she felt as though she were about to shake apart. For some reason, the only one who seemed nonplussed by the storm was Dipsy. She seemed to revel in it, as though expectant of a needed change. Something to wipe away the old and usher in the new. And yet Cookie didn't know what that "new" entailed. What could she possibly learn that would be any worse than knowing she had been lied to her entire life? By those she loved. She hadn't allowed herself to go there, to dig too deeply for fear of what she might find. But now, she might have no choice. She was going into the lion's den, the place of her birth. The place where life had taken a left turn. As if her fear wasn't enough, she could almost feel it emanating from the very pores of her birth mother, Rachel. It was as if the wheels had come off her emotions and she had begun to shudder as bad if not worse than Cookie herself. Suddenly, Rachel pulled over to the side of the road.

"I can't do this," she said, turning to Cookie. "I can't go back there. The tornado. . ." She let her words trail off, her face ashen and the whites of her eyes like haloes around her irises. Her fingernails dug into the steering wheel and she began to cry.

"You can't stop here, Miss Rachel," Beulah pleaded, imploring Cookie to make her see reason. "A storm is comin'. We need to get inside."

"You. . . don't. . . understand," Rachel said through gritted teeth.

"What don't we understand?" Cookie said, grasping Rachel's right hand and soothing her as best she could under the situation.

"I need help. . . I can't. . ." She began sobbing uncontrollably.

All eyes turned to Cookie for support, but she didn't know what to do. She just knew that she had to do something. She thought of the pills she had absconded from Mitzi earlier. Anti-anxiety pills. They were in her purse. She pulled them out. Benzodiazepines. The "in" drug for high-strung mothers, and Mitzi definitely qualified as that.

"Does anyone have any water?" Cookie asked the pair in back.

Beulah shrugged apologetically, whereas Dipsy harrumphed, then dug into her giant bag. "I have kids," she said by way of explanation. "So I have everything in here but the kitchen sink." She smiled, handing over a plastic fold-up cup with a lid screwed tight, keeping a small amount of water in place.

Cookie gratefully grabbed the cup and held both it and the two yellow pills out to Rachel. "Take this. They're Mitzi's. . . to calm her nerves."

Rachel looked at them suspiciously, then with trembling hands fingered them out of Cookie's palm, washing them down with the entire glass of water. For several moments, no one moved. Finally, Rachel took a deep breath, steeled her shoulders then nodded, peering up at the sky that was growing thicker and more turbulent by the minute.

"We'd better get moving," Dipsy said, sounding fearful for the first time since they'd learned the news of the impending storm. "It won't be dark until eight, but it's almost six and most tornadoes hit between four and nine at night."

"Right." Rachel put the car in gear and they moved out onto the highway.

Relief flooded Cookie, and yet she knew they had no more than twenty minutes before the storm was upon them. They had to reach the sharecropper's hut, or die trying.

31

EBIE KNEW HE SHOULD HAVE told Mitzi the truth before now, he realized as he focused on the shifting weather through the windshield of his wife's Buick. All his life he had protected her, and now he could protect her no more. She had to know the entire story, and she had to know before he blurted it out to the others, and yet how could he break her heart? He felt his resolve slip.

"Honey?" he began, taking her by the hand as she drove.

"What is it, Ebie?" Mitzi asked, puzzling her eyebrows at this sudden display of affection as a tornado approached.

She started to pull her hand away so that she could have both hands on the wheel, but he held fast, determined to speak before he lost his nerve. "I have something to tell you."

The wind began to rise, lashing at the car as though it were a toy that the wind could simply pick up and deposit elsewhere.

He had only moments to explain what he should have explained years ago. In a rush that left him breathless, he laid it all out for her. But before he could comfort her and beg her forgiveness, she screamed, just as the sound of a freight train whirled in and the car pummelled down the side of the road, landing in a ditch with its wheels and headlights slanted upwards. He had no time to contemplate her reaction because before he could say anything further, the metallic scouring of sand screeched across the paint of the Buick followed by a tree limb that seemed to hurtle at the windshield out of nowhere. As if in slow motion, he saw it come towards him, heard it crash through the windshield right to where he sat frozen to the spot. Just before it hit his face, it stopped and the wind passed, the car rocking as if on a stormy sea rather than in a drainage ditch. For one brief second, he couldn't move, couldn't speak. He could only sit there. Then he felt what he hadn't before. Through it all, Mitzi had held tight to his hand. . . with him, even to the end.

* * *

For Rachel, coming back to the sharecropper's hut felt like returning to hell, for it had been here that her life had unraveled, had come undone. *Before*, she'd still held out hope for a good life. Still believed that "happily ever afters" were possible. She hadn't known then that a storm could carry away with it that tenuous thread of hope. Chew it up and spit it out until it was nearly unrecognizable. She opened the door of the hut and took a breath of the stale air inside. All the windows were shuttered. From behind she could see the funnel cloud closing in, meandering slowly across the fields, as though giving her time to fear its arrival. As though drawing out the greatest emotion before it landed to upend lives like hers, to bring out the worst and the best in people. She'd seen both and yet it still frightened her, still left her breathless. Still left her trembling, her legs weak.

"Are you okay?" Cookie asked tentatively.

Heart hammering, Rachel studied her for a moment -- wanted so much to tell her the truth, the whole truth, and nothing but the truth. But it wasn't her truth to tell. It was Ebie's. In the end, only Ebie and Rachel knew the truth. She just hoped that after it was all said and done, Cookie could forgive them. See that each of them, in their own way, were trying to do their best for her. Each of them flawed but all of them caring.

"Rachel?"

Cookie caught Rachel's eye, but all Rachel could do was nod. Just then, the sharecropper's hut began to shudder as though a giant combine was barreling through it. The ground beneath their feet began to buck and roll. Rachel tried to speak, but her words began to slur, the medication Cookie had given her to calm her nerves making her dizzy, nauseous. She fell to her knees. Within seconds, she was trembling, her teeth grinding against each other, panic seizing her throat. She tried to call out but couldn't. Instead, it was as though she'd gone back in time, back to 1932.

"Byrdie," she whispered, seeing him as if he was there, his brown eyes wild with fear, his face burnished from overexposure to the sun.

"Get down!" he shouted.

Before he could say more, the windows shattered inward, shards of glass flying everywhere. The toddler began a slow, accelerated wail that could scarcely be heard above the howl of the wind, the freight train sound of an incoming cyclone. Rachel crawled toward the small bed, lifted Cookie to her, all the while protecting her with her body. "It's okay, baby. Mama's here." But still the toddler wailed. The cabin bucked on its foundation feeling as though it might tear loose at any moment, the entire structure airborne. Jars flew off the shelf and shattered around her. The chairs that surrounded the table began to tap dance across the floor toward her as though dancers that only now realized mother and child lay on the floor.

Byrdie, for his part, had been thrown against the table, his jaw bleeding from the contact. It's then that she saw he'd been drinking, the odd glazed-over shine in his eyes, the smell of whiskey on his breath. And she saw the anger mounting in him at the injustice of his life. As if the storm had somehow encapsulated everything wrong. Every slight at the hand of those with power, money, privilege, while he toiled day upon day, never getting ahead, never seeing daylight in the endless grind of poverty. And she also saw that he had nowhere to put that anger. Nowhere except...

Suddenly, the house shuddered to a halt, the silence deafening, as though merely a lull -- the earth taking a deep breath. But just as she tried to stand, the lull ended and the full force of the storm's fury was upon them, knocking her back, she and the toddler dashed to the floor. She hit the back of her head and felt an instant swelling, but she had no time to ponder what had happened, because at that moment, Byrdie got to his knees and crawled over to the window. She heard glass crunching beneath him. That's when the house really began to buck and roll. All she could do was to hang on... to pray. All the while, the toddler screamed.

Then suddenly, the rolling floor beneath her shuddered to a gradual halt, the wind moving north. Only then did she realize the storm had passed. They had survived the rare September storm. And yet it did nothing to quell her angst or that of the toddler who began to howl louder than before. But her eyes were on Byrdie, on what he was seeing through the now open curtains. For there, in the field, it was as if a colossal rototiller had chewed up the entire field, heaving the cotton this way and that. Some of it lay in swaths of gray-green vegetation, most of it gone, simply blown elsewhere, little white puffs floating in places, as though the cotton had been set free to snub their noses at Byrdie. At their condition. At the very poverty that enchained them.

It's then his eyes went to Chester and Rayleen's place. Not a piece of it had been touched, other than the odd shingle or tree branch. Nothing beside that to reveal that a storm had ever taken place. There was something almost tranquil about it that set Rachel's mind at ease. But to Byrdie, it was a slap in the face. He grabbed the windowsill and pulled himself up slowly, still reeling from the injury he'd suffered at the hands of the storm. In slow motion, he turned his glazed eyes upon her, both his knees and hands bloody from the broken glass.

"God has turned his back on us," he told her in slurred words. "'Cause of people like them." He pointed in the direction of the Williams' hut.

"No, Byrdie," she implored as the toddler began wailing in earnest. "They're good people. They work hard, just like you and me. It's just the way of things--"

But before she could get another word out, he charged, head lowered like a bull, steam coming out of his nostrils as he gathered speed. And before she knew what hit her, he was upon her, yelling for her to shut the child up. Yet he gave her no time to respond. Instead, he grabbed the toddler by the arm, still howling, and tossed her across the plank flooring where she landed against the bottom cupboards with a thunk. Within moments he had Rachel pinned and was on top of her, pounding her with fists until all she could do was cover her head with her hands. Soon she began a low wail of her own.

"No, no," she pleaded, but he wouldn't listen. It was as though his mind had gone elsewhere, replaced by that of this madman. She begged him to stop. Pleaded with him over and over, her screams turning to mewls. Just as she was about to lose consciousness, the door flung open and she felt him being pulled off of her and fists pummeling bare flesh. She crawled to where the toddler lay crying and held her tight. Only then did she look up in time to see Wes, Byrdie's foreman, shoving Byrdie out the opened front door.

"Leave her the hell alone!" Wes yelled.

For one brief moment, Rachel thought Byrdie might force his way back inside. Instead, he swore and gave her one final lingering glare that set her heart racing. Then, with a burst of air, he ran down the steps.

Together they listened to Byrdie open the truck, climb in, and then Rachel heard it go roaring off, in a cloud of dust no doubt. Afterward, Wes came to her, threw his arm around her and held her tight.

"Don't worry," he promised. "I'll never let him hurt you again."

That was the last she'd ever seen of Byrdie.

* * *

257

The room went dark. Cookie heard the storm coming, felt the shudder of the hut as it swept up on its foundation and slammed down, a timepiece falling from a shelf above and landing next to her on the sturdy oak table. She clutched it with one hand, her other hand searching for purchase on the edge of the table.

"Oh, dear god!" she whispered just as the wind from the tornado blew the door open and knocked her to the ground, sending her spinning toward the kitchen on her rear. She could hear it, a freight train rolling off its tracks and heading straight for her, but more than that she could feel it in her stomach as though it were about to open her wide, to do what it hadn't been able to do all those years ago.

Memory flooded her in little bursts from a time when language was still new to her, adults unfathomable. Somewhere, deep inside her, a single word emerged. "Mama!!!" The voice was that of a child, and yet she could feel it swell from inside her chest and out her throat. As if an apparition, a woman appeared to her, a younger Rachel, scrabbling toward her, hands outstretched in desperation. The childish Cookie held a hand out to her -- to the mother she had lost all those years ago. Felt a hand clasp hers. A mother saving her child.

For one brief moment, Cookie felt relief. But before she could quell her fear, she heard shouting, saw out of the corner of her memory another hand, a different hand. A man's hand, tearing mother and child apart. Spinning her in a different direction. And then the volcano that was this man burst toward her, spewing a lava of words Cookie didn't understand. Words that even now escaped her. Eyes wide, Cookie shrank back, trying to make herself as small as possible, her childish brain hoping against hope that she would simply disappear into the small space beneath the kitchen sink. But he reached for her, dragged her by her arm as she slid like a ragdoll across the linoleum, all the while pleading for him to leave her alone.

"You did this to us!" he hissed, his squinty brown eyes just inches from hers, his hot breath smelling of garlic and cigarettes. . . alcohol. "None of this would have happened if it weren't for you."

The man's fingernails dug into her arms, slicing them open with his sharp nails.

"You're hurting her," Rachel pleaded, crawling across the floor toward Cookie. "She's just a baby. She's done nothing."

Still holding onto Cookie, the man backhanded Rachel sending her sprawling backwards on the floor, her lip cut and bleeding. Then he turned to Cookie and fisted his hand around her hair, pulling it so tight that Cookie could scarcely move or breathe, her eyes and ears stretched tight against her scalp. For what seemed like forever, neither moved, as though frozen in amber, the bull of a man heaving his fury and hatred toward her and her mother. Then, with one quick breath, he shoved her back so hard that she went flying, her head hitting the kitchen cabinet with a thump that sent a hot slicing pain running down her scalp. She felt her head, felt the warmth of blood. Heard it trickle onto the floor. Plop. Plop. Plop.

And then it was if she were seeing it through another person's eyes, no longer that of a child but through her own adult eyes. Heard the man shouting at her mother, pushing her. Cookie had retreated then as now, curled into a ball, listening to things she didn't understand, weeping softly for her mama, soon wailing as she had done when the storm slammed through the house like a hurricane.

Then, as though from another life, she heard the door swing open, could feel the salvation of a man coming toward them, hear the bull of a man leave, yelling all the way. Only this time it was Ebie, her father, who had come to rescue her, Mitzi not far behind. He snatched her into his arms. Over his shoulder, Cookie saw Rachel, only she was still youthful. In her mind's eye Cookie saw the younger version of the woman come to her. Hold her, search worried fingers through her hair.

"It needs a butterfly bandage," she had said to someone behind her all those years ago, then deposited a warm kiss on Cookie's forehead. Then one day later, she had deposited Cookie on the Williams' doorstep.

Now, fully in the present again, as her father fussed over her, Cookie thought the tornado was returning, but the tremor was no longer coming from the wind outside. No, this tremor came from deep within her, burbling up like a geyser of pain, spewing forth in a cry of anguish.

"Why? Why? Why?" she shouted, fists balled. "Why didn't you tell me no one ever wanted me, that my whole life was a lie? Why?"

She slid to the floor, even as Ebie held her to him, cradled her in his arms. For several minutes, he sat rocking her, but before she could come to grips with everything she'd learned today, she shoved him away from her, teeth gritted, tears running down her cheeks.

"Honey, you've got it all wrong." He pleaded for her to listen. "You were loved, *are* loved."

Ebie's black hair hung limply over one eye and his cheeks appeared hollow, lacking its normal healthy color. Cookie had never seen Ebie so wobegon, so. . . lost. "But that man--"

"He wasn't your father, Cookie," Ebie said in a rush. "Your father was a good man. He loved you."

"Loved me?" She shook her head, not understanding. "Then where is he? Why did he abandon me? Abandon Rachel?"

Ebie shook his head in frustration. "Let me explain." He turned to Mitzi as though looking for support. They paused, as though needing a moment to come to a decision. Finally, Mitzi nodded for him to continue. He turned back to Cookie, grasped her hands and in a soft voice filled with sorrow said, "Rachel isn't your mother."

Dipsy, all but forgotten in the corner, gasped, Beulah immediately coming to her in comfort. Cookie rocked back on the balls of her feet, holding her head. "I don't understand. Who is Rachel then, if not my mother?"

Once again Ebie turned to Mitzi for support. On a sigh, he turned back to Cookie. Rachel came to stand beside him, her face pale but looking more herself after the ordeal.

"Rachel is your aunt," Ebie said.

"*Aunt?*" Cookie couldn't believe what she was hearing. She held out her hands as if to ward off any further surprises. "I don't understand," she repeated, shaking her head as though that would somehow help her make sense of all this.

"My brother was your father. Rachel's sister, your mother."

"Uncle Edward was my father?" Cookie asked, plopping down on the floor, legs spread out and swiping at her tears. Mitzi searched around for tissues and handed her a few to blow her nose. "How?"

"Yeah, how?" Dipsy said, coming to her feet with help from Beulah.

"You've got to understand. Edward was a good kid, but a bit

rebellious. We figured it was just a stage that he would outgrow, eventually, so we sent him to the farm up here in Shardsburg for the summer. Figured a little hard work would help him grow up. Become a man."

Ebie's Adam's apple bobbed as he spoke, his throat thick with emotion as he explained his younger brother, whom he clearly loved. "It was my fault that he died."

Cookie had never seen her father cry and it tore at her to see him this distraught, but she hadn't yet worked through her own emotions that seesawed between anger, hurt, and relief to finally know the truth. She knew that over the coming days she would come to terms with what happened, but right now she needed time. Lots of it.

"What happened?" she said through a voice choked with tears.

"He wrote to my parents," Ebie began, "told them he was in love with a girl."

"My sister," Rachel said in a voice filled with quiet dignity. "She was beautiful then. Kind. But we were dirt poor. And it was considered a scandal, wasn't it Ebie? A daughter of poor sharecroppers with a family of means?"

Ebie's throat constricted, his eyes welling with tears. "That it was. It would have ruined our family name."

"So you made him go away," Rachel added, much to Ebie's discomfort.

"Just for a year," Ebie protested. "I thought it would give him time to think, for things to cool down."

"But you didn't count on my sister getting pregnant." Rachel's words sounded accusatory.

"No, I didn't." He tilted his head down and to the side as

though unwilling to face them.

"Is that true, Daddy?" Cookie asked, reaching for his hand and feeling his cool touch.

His eyes lifted slowly and he nodded. His eyes never wavered from hers, now that she knew the whole truth, or at least the kernel of the truth. More would be coming in the upcoming days, no doubt, but this was enough. . . for now.

"The family sent him to Oregon, to work in a logging camp."

This part of the story she knew. The family lore. He'd been given the most dangerous job in logging -- that of green chain puller. He had never returned home. The family had spread his ashes near a river. Or at least that's what her parents had told her.

She pictured her uncle. . . rather, her father. No wonder it was so easy to accept the fiction that Ebie was her father. The two brothers looked so much alike, and she shared many of their features, not the least of which was their thirst for knowledge. But where had the green thumb come from? Was that Edward's? Or had she inherited it from her mother.

My mother.

She felt a check in her spirit. "Is my mother alive?"

No one answered.

"Daddy?" Dipsy said, standing firmly beside Cookie, all the while rubbing her tummy as if to soothe the child inside.

Mitzi ran interference for Ebie, placing herself between him and the two girls. "Leave your father be. He's been through a lot in the past few days."

"Okay then," Dipsy countered, "then at least tell me what you told Kent when you dropped off the kids. And what did you tell him about me?"

"I told him the truth, that you needed time away with your sister. I didn't know about Beulah," she added churlishly.

Up to now Beulah had been watching from her spot in the corner. "You're one to talk about truth. You're the one who kept the truth from Cookie all these years."

"You knew too," Mitzi said, bobbing her head back and forth to make her point.

"But it wasn't my truth to tell!" Beulah countered.

Cookie jumped to her feet. "Wait! You *all* knew, even you, Beulah? And you said *nothing*?" She turned to Dipsy. "Did you know? Did you?"

Dipsy tried to speak, but Cookie was too upset to listen. "No," she shouted, hands up, fresh tears flowing down her cheeks. "All of you just leave me be! I want to be alone." She needed space. . . to figure out who she was now that everything she'd believed about herself, about her family, had changed. Anger seared her emotions as she ran outside, slamming the door behind her. The landscape outside reflected her feelings, for as far as the eye could see trees had been uprooted and plants trammeled into the dust of the hardscrabble Shardsburg, Alabama, soil. She set out on foot, tears flowing down her face, fury setting fire to her steps. She didn't know where she was going or care what she looked like. She just needed time to herself, to think, to figure out where to go from here, now that she was no longer the daughter of Ebie and Mitzi, sister to Dipsy. But if she wasn't theirs, who was she?

They say that tragedies come in threes, the first tragedy being the Great Depression. The second tragedy, Vietnam. Yet tragedy dogged the 60's as civil unrest seemed to grow from the very war itself, as though the nation had seen itself at its worst and had vowed to change the inequities that held it in its grip. Into this unrest grew a seed. A seed of hope. For winds of change. Just as the tornado had cleared out what ailed those afflicted by the Great Depression, so too had this new cyclone lay bare some of what had bedeviled the nation. Dogs attacking protesters. Fire hoses ripping at the clothing of black youth. Black children running the gauntlet just to attend elementary school. Into this time of turmoil came growth. A burgeoning equality, an equality that by its very name, means equal. Even. A fair playing field. And so it was, that both women and those of color saw some gains. How long those gains would last, or how close they would come to the virtue of equality, was anyone's guess.

32

"GET DOWN!" CHESTER SHOUTED AS he slammed the front door closed against the oncoming wind. "Tornado! Under the table. Now!"

Rayleen didn't ask questions. She dived under the kitchen table and lay huddled on the floor, hands over her head and neck for protection against the incoming storm. It seemed to last forever, rattling her entire kitchen cupboards, the doors opening and glassware crashing to the linoleum around her. She could do nothing but hang on and pray. The ground beneath her vibrated. She thought it would never end, but finally the bucking beneath the floorboards had ceased, the roll of the linoleum in waves that would have seemed impossible under different circumstances, gone. For several seconds, she held her breath. Although the storm had passed, she feared the eye of the storm. But after several minutes, as she listened to the cyclone veer northward, she leaned on her knees, briefly closing her eyes before taking stock of her surroundings.

"You okay?" she called to Chester.

In response, she heard a grunt and a moan, then moments later, Chester came staggering into the kitchen, holding his head. "Bumped my head on the coffee table," he said, then laughed despite the pain.

Although she knew the mess would need to be cleaned, Rayleen scrambled to her feet and rushed over to hug him, wishing away the pain and yet grateful to have him by her side during times like these. Now that the storm was past, Rayleen took Chester's hand, and together they marched to the living room and peered out the window at the damage done. Downed branches lay strewn across the front yard. The big tell would be in back, where the corn had stood tall only moments earlier. The thought of losing all that made her feel weak in the knees. How many times would life kick them to the ground and force them to get up, only to kick them again?

As she was busy stewing over the possibilities, Chester nudged her and pointed with his chin. She followed his gesture and saw what he had wanted her to see. Two cars parked beside the other shack. Rayleen recognized Cookie's car, or at least the one she'd arrived in. The other was unfamiliar.

"Looks like we got ourselves more company," Chester said, his eyebrows a shelf of confusion.

He disliked any change, anything new. When they'd first married, Rayleen had thought it strange, but as she'd aged and seen the way of things, all the tests and trials thrown their way, she finally understood. Best to keep things small, simple. The older she got, the more she liked being in the nest of her family while keeping all others at bay. That way there were no surprises. No confrontations.

Rayleen frowned as she tried to get a better look. "Think Ebie's here?" she wondered out loud.

"Could be," Chester said. "He was comin' by train, though he probably rented a car out of Huntsville. We'd best check it out."

"What about the mess in the kitchen?" she asked.

"It'll hold until we look in on the others," Chester replied, taking her hand.

Rayleen sighed, wishing she could check on James and his wife first. The cyclone had come from that direction. No telling the damage it might have done in their neck of the woods.

As if reading her thoughts, Chester said, "Let's just quick go see who's over there, then we'll head out to James and Corliss' place. Afterwards, we can come back and clean up." He grabbed his keys off the hobnail by the door and they headed out to the truck with its patchwork of colors.

Before they'd made it halfway to the other shack, Rayleen saw James's truck, his wife at his side. Only then could Rayleen breathe a sigh of relief. And yet she had no sooner relaxed when out of the corner of her eye, she saw something else, something she hadn't expected, for down the winding road came Cookie, dirty tears streaming down her cheeks, her expression fueled with anger.

"Get this rust bucket moving," she told Chester. "A cyclone has done shredded her life into bits. She's going to need someone to help glue those pieces back together."

* * *

Cookie looked up in time to see an old tan colored International coming down the dirt road. She swiped at her tears with the back of her hand. From the Y in the road, she could see that Chester and Rayleen were also headed her way, both trucks climbing over fallen debris to get to her. James' truck arrived first. He stopped beside her and yelled, "Hop in. We left Charlotte with a neighbor while we check in on Mama and Daddy."

She hesitated for only a moment. To the east, past the cornfields, she could see a swath of destruction that uprooted trees as far as the eye could see, as though some unseen giant had simply blown them down on his northern march, lazily winding in and out of corn fields, past houses, taking bites out of a few of them as he went.

James yelled out the window to Chester and Rayleen. "I'll run Cookie to your place. Meet you there."

Cookie sandwiched in next to James's wife, who he introduced as Corliss, a woman in her late twenties. She had kind eyes, her thick wiry black hair a halo around her narrow face, and she wore overalls, like her husband, as though she'd been caught working in the fields when the tornado had hit and hadn't yet changed.

Seeing the tears that Cookie had tried but failed to hide, James and Corliss exchanged a brief glance of concern. Then James said, "You all okay over there?" He jutted his chin in the direction of the other shack.

Cookie merely shrugged. It was as if the tornado had run through her and hollowed her clean of all emotion. Instead, she felt numb, all the tears she had cried leaving her dull, lifeless. Desiccated. How could she put into words how she felt now that everything was gone? Her past. Her present. Her future. She was a blank canvas, her life's story yet to be written.

"No one's hurt, if that's what you mean." And yet even as she said it, she melted into a fresh puddle of tears.

Corliss lay a hesitant hand on hers, her brown eyes full of sympathy. James reached across and lay his hand atop Corliss and Cookie's, letting her know in actions that he understood.

The truck jostled each of the occupants in turn. Cookie barely noticed when the truck came to a halt, nor the door opening as Rayleen came in and scooped her up. She and Chester were about to help her toward the house when James said, "Wait. Let me talk to Cookie for a minute. Outside," he added.

As if understanding what her husband meant to do, Corliss said to Chester and Rayleen, "Why don't I pour you both a glass of sweet tea after we clean up from the tornado?" Then she ushered them inside while James motioned Cookie toward the big vegetable garden near the side of the house.

"Do you remember this spot?" James asked, offering her a seat on a tree stump that rested beside the garden, which fortunately had weathered the storm better than the corn.

Cookie sat, feeling like a small child, as though she'd shrunk in the past day and was shrinking still.

"I used to set you up on a blanket while I tilled and weeded the garden, but you'd always climb off and start playin' in the soil. Mama used to have to give you a bath afterwards 'cause I couldn't keep you out of the dirt. It was like you were born to farm."

A breeze blew up and it was as if it had blown a curtain away from her vision. She, as a child, seated on the ground, intent on digging. She'd thought it a memory of her and Mitzi or Beulah, but thinking back on it now, neither one of them would have ever let her play in the dirt.

"I used to show you the plants from the vegetable garden and the flower garden down yonder. . . tell you their botanical names." He laughed here. "You would always try to repeat the names in baby talk." He looked down at the garden that had been swept away with the wind from the tornado, large gouges taken out of the earth itself. "When you were a toddler, I took you to old man Percy's strawberry patch." Once again, he chuckled, all the while shaking his head. "You ate so many strawberries he said that next time he was gonna weigh you before and after I come to pick."

"I was wearing overalls," she whispered, as though talking about someone else, not her.

"That you were. Momma gave you my hand-me-downs. You followed me everywhere. Do you know how you got the name Cookie?"

Until now, Cookie had wrapped her arms around her legs, her chin resting on her knees, her eyes on the ground before her as though it held the answers to her past, and perhaps it did. But now, Cookie peered up at James and could almost imagine him as a child, hear his voice as he explained the different plants to her. Except for perhaps her biological mother, who she had yet to meet, no one in her family liked gardening. All had thought her odd for her penchant to mother plants instead of people. Perhaps here was where she'd learned her love of gardening.

James didn't wait for her to respond. He pointed toward the house with his chin. "You were feeling mighty low when you first arrived. You were kneehigh to a tadpole, just so big." He made a gesture with his hands, no more than two and half feet, all told. "You were missin' your mama. So *my* mama made you some tea and cookies to get your mind off your mama.”

“That’s why you called me Cookie?”

“Nope,” he said, reaching down and handing her what remained of a sunflower, the yellow face reminding her that there was beauty, even in tragedy. “It’s because every day thereafter, you would drag Mama to the cookie jar and demand a cookie.”

“Did she give one to me?” Cookie asked, shielding her eyes from the sun with her hand.

“Once in awhile. We started calling you Cookie after that.”

Cookie wrapped her arms tighter around her legs and rocked, placing her head on her knees and feeling the sharpness of jaw against bone. “What’s my real name?” she asked, laying her head down and peering up sideways at him.

“Caledonia. I think your mother was of Scottish descent.”

Cookie perked up at the mention of her mother, a figure that seemed no more than a vague shadow in her mind. Since first learning that she’d had a different mother, she’d thought only of Rachel. Now, she would have to reconfigure the image, but when she tried, she discovered she had nothing to replace it, as though the woman was a sepia image shown in sharp relief against an unrelenting sun, so that all that was left to the naked eye was a black hole where the image of her mother should have been.

“So Mitzi and Ebie changed my name on the birth certificate. But what about my mother?”

“I don’t remember much about her,” James continued, “except that she had red hair.”

Cookie nearly tumbled off the stump. “Red hair?” She touched her own hair, saw the red highlights that revealed themselves only when the sun shone brightly, which happened often here in Alabama.

James nodded. "I remember she was pretty. And kind." He peered off toward the other farmhouse, his eyes narrowing. "She wasn't prejudiced like Byrdie." He stiffened at the very thought of the man. Just as with Rachel, Byrdie had left an impression that carried its mark across the decades. "I was afraid of him." He peered down at the stalk of wheat that was now twirling in his hand. "We all were."

A soft wind whistled among the leaves of the cottonwood trees that graced the stream that ran the southern border of their property, or rather her daddy's property. But she was afraid to break the spell that had been woven between them by speaking up, preferring that he open up to her gradually.

"He beat daddy more than once." His expression hardened and his brown eyes became twin marbles.

"What did your daddy do to stop it?" Cookie asked, absentmindedly clutching the hem of her culottes.

He shrugged. "What *could* he do? He couldn't say anything or risk retribution."

"You could have told Ebie," she said, just a little too quickly.

For the past few minutes, James had felt like an older brother, but now he simply closed up like her Mimosa pudica, the "sensitive" plant she grew back home that would close its leaves when anyone came too close to it.

"You don't understand things around here a'tall," he said, frowning.

She could see that she had angered him, for he strode away at a crisp clip. She ran after him and could almost imagine herself as a child doing the same, idolizing her big brother, only he wasn't her big brother. They lived in two completely different worlds, and her words had only proven that.

Frustrated and wanting to make amends, she followed him to the barn. Before she could reach him, he leaped up the rope ladder as though it was nothing more than a jungle gym and climbed into the loft. Minutes later, he slid back down, barely touching the steps of the jute ladder.

"Here," he said, holding out a package wrapped in twine. "I saved this for you. It was yours. We couldn't find it when it was time to leave."

All the emotion of the day felt bundled into this one moment. She was so exhausted from it that all she wanted to do was to sit, to close her eyes, to forget that her life had changed in unalienable ways. As if sensing her fatigue, he showed her to a hay bale and encouraged her to sit.

"What is it?" she asked.

"Open it," he said, his voice much softer now. "See for yourself."

Gently, she tugged at the twine until she'd managed to remove the corners. Then carefully, she unfolded the brown paper wrapping. First, she saw only a foot of matted brown fur. Then, as though a long lost friend had come to life, she opened it further and cried, "Millie!" Tears welled up in her eyes, and once again she sank into a puddle of tears. Her body began to tremble. "How? Mitzi said that this bunny was just part of my imagination!"

James took a seat on a nearby hay bale. "It wasn't your imagination. This came with you the day Rachel brought you to our house. Millie and Tillie."

"You remember!" Cookie shuddered at the realization that her memories were real. All those odd parts of her childhood suddenly appeared like still photos, one after the other, as she tried to process them into something that made sense, something she could understand. "You saved Millie!"

"We tried to find the bunny before you left, but it fell between the bed in your room and the floor. Mama kept it for five years or more."

He reached over and picked up Millie, pretending that it could talk. For the first time all day, Cookie laughed, but it was tired sounding, even to *her* ears.

"Mama finally decided to toss it, but I found it and hid it. . . in case."

Cookie cocked her head to the side, the smell of straw and animals strong inside the barn. "In case?"

James pursed his lips. "In case you came back," he said softly.

It had never occurred to Cookie that maybe she hadn't been the only one who felt as though she'd been cheated, her past stolen from her somehow. Now it was as if the pictures she carried inside her head were someone else's pictures, not hers. Mother, father, a sister. All there. She was the only odd one out. The piece of the puzzle that didn't fit. She lay the sunflower in Millie's lap, a memory burbling to the surface of her setting up a picnic on an old blanket, Millie and Tillie at her side. As a small child, she would talk to them as though they were real, encourage them to drink up the imaginary tea, eat the small plastic food on the plastic plates.

"I always wondered," James said, then paused.

"Wondered?" Cookie echoed.

"If you kept it going. . . the gardening." He snagged a piece of hay from a straw bale and began to chew on it.

Cookie laughed amid the tears that still threatened. James

handed her his plaid kerchief that he'd kept in the upper pocket of his overalls and she blew loudly into it. "I have a greenhouse," she said, her voice sounding nasally. "I have Norfolk Island pines, a fiddle-leaf fig. I have a chain of hearts, a chain of pearls, any indoor houseplant you can imagine. You name it, I have it."

James threw up his hands and laughed. "I've created a monster! I've never done much with houseplants. Just outdoor plants, but I would love to see your greenhouse someday."

"You would?" Cookie didn't know why it surprised her that he would share her love of gardening, so much so that he would want to see her greenhouse. No one had cared much about her plants except for her. He reminded her of a beloved uncle or an older brother, even though he wasn't that much older than her. He had an easy way about him that put people at ease. And he had given her the one thing that could help her survive this past couple of weeks -- her ability to get lost in the garden. If anything could give her the needed time to grieve the loss of her past, of her innocence, it was her garden.

"I know the past few days have been kind of tough," James said, pulling out another piece of straw and twirling it.

"You have no idea," she said, a hard lump in her throat making it nearly impossible to speak. To gather her thoughts and emotions, she peered up at the rafters, at the dusty streams of light playing through the beams. "I don't know where I belong anymore." She hid her face in her hands.

For several seconds, they sat in silence. Finally, James spoke up, saying, "I know you can't see this now. . . but someday, you'll realize you haven't lost a family. Instead, you've gained a whole lot of family and friends, my family included."

Cookie knew he was probably right, but first she needed

time to mourn a lifetime of lost memories. Of broken trust. It had been so hard to learn to trust again after her engagement had fallen through. But this. . . *This* was something altogether different. She loved Mitzi and Ebie, but they had lied to her. Even dear sweet Beulah had lied to her. She knew they all had their reasons, but if she couldn't trust them, who could she trust?

James stood and reached a hand out to her. "C'mon, Cookie. Let's get you inside the house. Mama's probably got dinner going by now. You can stay here tonight. Either daddy or I can call over to the other house and let your folks know that we'll drop you by in the morning."

"You keep a working phone at the other shack when no one has lived in it for the past thirty-odd years? Why?" Cookie asked.

"For your daddy," James said, his expression serious.

"For *daddy*?"

"He stays there when he comes up to look after his holdings," James said, handing her Millie and the sunflower. To her bewildered expression, he added, "I think that's how he does penance." His eyes drifted toward the road that led to the other shack. "For his brother's death."

Cookie felt the need to explain, to set the record straight. "But he didn't *cause* it."

"You know that and I know that. But he blames himself." He stared down at his feet for a few moments, then looked up at her, his eyes never leaving her face. "We all blame ourselves for something or other. But most things aren't in our control." He shrugged.

She could sense some pain there, and she wondered if it had to do with her. If he felt guilty for not being able to protect her, to keep her safe from the world and all its hurt.

"All we can do is our best," he said sadly. "Now let's go get some dinner. Besides, it'll be dark soon."

Then he offered his hand to help her up from the hay bale and they trudged out of the barn, Cookie hot on his heels. Before following him into the shack, she took one last look down the dirt road, to the sunset silhouetting the other shack, and frowned. She hoped that someday she could wrap her head around all that had happened. Pick up the pieces of her life and move forward. How her future would look, she couldn't say. But then again, maybe James was right. Things were never really in one's control. Not really. Today had taught her that, if nothing else.

33

PHONE IN HAND, EBIE PEERED out the kitchen window at the cottonwood that lined the river behind the house. He dialed the Willliams' number, then listened to the tinny sound of the phone as it rang over and over again. Now that Ebie was forced to confront the past, he had thought of nothing else. It was enough that he had blamed himself for his brother's death all these years, but now Cookie blamed him too. As he stood there thinking, Mitzi came up behind him and began rubbing his back in a slow circular motion as she had on countless occasions over the years when he'd been dealing with one crisis or another.

"She'll come around," Mitzi said, but he heard the worry in her voice and knew it was he who had put it there. "She just needs time."

"We don't have time," he said, watching Rachel out of the corner of his eye. Beulah and Dipsy had taken up residence on either side of her after her earlier meltdown. Fortunately, Mitzi had known just what to do to help the tranquilizer wear off after Dipsy had explained what had happened. She'd fed Rachel until he'd thought the poor woman would burst, and yet that wasn't necessarily a bad thing. She was rail thin, and her dress hung loosely over long limbs and bony shoulders. Even her knees seemed too big for her legs. The woman was practically starving.

Mitzi's eyes followed his gaze and she squeezed his shoulder. "Rachel isn't your fault either. She was dealing with demons long before we brought Cookie to live with us. She would have never married Byrdie, if she hadn't."

"I know," Ebie started to say, when someone with a deep voice finally picked up the phone and said hello. "Mr. Williams?" Ebie said in a rush.

A long pause ensued. Finally, Chester answered on a sigh. They had been around this bend before. When Edward had first died, Chester had found Ebie stinking drunk more than once. Had helped him to bed. Had told him that drinking wasn't "going to bring that boy back" as he pulled off Ebie's shoes and socks and stuffed a pillow beneath his head. If it hadn't been for Chester, Ebie didn't know where he would be now. Probably in the cemetery, alongside his brother. In those early days, he'd wanted to curl up in a ball, never crawl out of his bed, get dressed, eat, shower. He'd sat staring lifelessly out the window, pouring over every memory he'd had of his brother. He'd loved him. Had wanted only the best for him. How had it all gone so wrong?

"You there, Ms'sr Haines?" Chester asked.

"I'm here." Ebie worked to quell the emotion rising in his throat. "Is Cookie there?"

Once again, Chester paused. "She's outside. With James," he

added hesitantly.

"James?"

"Our son." He cleared his throat before continuing. "Your daughter seemed mighty upset when we found her walkin' alongside the road."

Ebie sensed Chester was choosing his words carefully, so as not to rile Ebie. He winced to know that the other man felt he had to parse his words after all these years. And yet, if he were in Chester's shoes, he probably would have done the same. Memories of slavery and the lynching of grandparents and great grandparents had kept the younger generations wary of upsetting the status quo. Still, it bothered him that a man he'd known for over half a century felt the need to couch his words.

"Oh, here she comes now," Chester said, clearly relieved to be able to hand off the phone to Cookie.

With dread, Ebie listened to the clatter of the phone and pictured Cookie standing at the doorway, wondering whether to answer his call, whether to speak to the man who had hidden her past from her behind a wall of secrecy as thick and impenetrable as a hedge of Cherokee rose. He hadn't realized how tightly wound he'd been since she left until he heard her voice and felt the tension fade slightly.

"Cookie? Is that you, honey?"

"Yes, Daddy," she said, the unmistakable catch in her throat tearing at his emotions.

"You okay?" He moved away from the others so that he could speak to her in private.

"Yeah," she said. "I didn't mean to take off. It's just that I had a lot to take in."

He bit his lower lip and blinked rapidly. The skyline through the window had already taken on a gray hue as nighttime approached. Outside, the crickets had begun to chirp and the birds had roosted for the night, the sounds of the settling foundation lending an eerie quality to an already difficult day. Even the women had grown silent, as if to speak might somehow bring back the wind, and with it the tornado and its aftermath of destruction.

"I suppose you have a lot to think about," Ebie said. "You coming back soon?"

Ebie could hear a soft rustling over the line but nothing else. Finally, Cookie said, "I'm staying the night here. Then tomorrow, Chester and Rayleen will drive me to the other shack. But Daddy?"

"Yeah, baby," he said, feeling tireder than he had in years.

"I want to meet my mom. Promise me."

Ebie fought down the lump in his throat. She had no idea what she was asking. But still he said, "I promise," knowing all the while that meeting her mother would break Cookie's heart.

34

TENSION FELL OFF COOKIE IN waves as she prepared for the half mile journey to the other sharecropper's shack. She didn't know what to expect, how she would react in the face of everything that had happened yesterday. But there was no turning back. She had stepped through the door, both physically and metaphorically, and now, like it or not, she would spend years reconstructing the past to prepare her for the future that lay ahead. Yet she had no choice but to move ahead. The genie was out of the bottle and she couldn't stuff it back in if she'd wanted to. She breathed in one last breath of the still morning air, the aftermath of the storm leaving dead vegetation everywhere. Chester and James had spent most of the evening repairing damage around the farm, both men no doubt eager to evade Cookie's melancholy. And why not? Even she hated the sadness that engulfed her like a noxious cloud. It was too much to bear. For anybody.

"You ready?" Rayleen said, her eyes drifting to the weathered gray shack northwest of them. "We ladies are gonna take you there, that right, Corliss?"

Corliss had changed into one of Rayleen's dresses today. Though it hung loose, it looked smart on her, the fabric a gray blue cotton. A wide V-neck collar drew the eyes downward to the wide belt that wrapped around her middle, accentuating her waistline. And she'd curled her hair so that she appeared downright stylish, overdressed for what they were about to do. But Cookie supposed that was just Corliss's way of asserting her equality, and why not? The world was changing. Cookie just hoped the cost of change wouldn't be too high. . . and that the change would be for the better, for both blacks and women. A deep sadness settled over her as she thought of the Vietnam War raging through their living rooms each night. So much in life was spinning out of control, both on a national level, and on a personal level. But she supposed that was the way of things. And perhaps she had been lucky. . . for her world to have upended late in life instead of early on.

Corliss must have seen Cookie's hesitation, because she linked arms with Cookie and said, "Let's go say hi to your mom and dad."

Cookie allowed herself to be tugged along. Funny that she had only now met Corliss, and she could only recall James in a rather vague way, whether from memory or simply from the stories he'd told her yesterday, she didn't know. But somehow they had already found a place in her heart. Would she find a similar place in her heart when she met her mother in the coming days? She froze as she reached James and Corliss' truck.

Corliss' deep brown eyes met hers. In a low voice, so as not to be overheard, she said, "James has caught me up on what's going on, and. . . well, I know it's none of my business, but--"

"You ladies gonna get in, or what?" Rayleen demanded, giving Corliss the eye.

Corliss bent down and whispered. "Let's just say that I know what you're going through, and trust me," she said, taking Cookie's hand, "it may take time, but it's going to be okay."

Cookie mulled over what Corliss had said, wondering what had happened in the other woman's life to allow her to commiserate and hoping she was right. Corliss squeezed Cookie's hand then waited for her to slide onto the bench seat of the pickup, both Corliss and Rayleen sandwiching her between them.

Corliss called to James and Chester, who were just rounding the corner of the weather-beaten shack. "We'll be back in a bit."

Both men waved to Cookie. With sadness, she wondered if she would ever see them again. For the next several minutes, the truck bounced along the rutted road, the crows already picking at the downed heads of corn. The storm would be a disaster for Rayleen and Chester, this year's livelihood gone. A weight settled on Cookie's chest. It seemed that no one would survive this year unscathed.

Until now, Rayleen had sat primly, her hands folded together, her eyes on the road, betraying little of the emotion she must be feeling at the loss of their crops. Slowly, she unfolded her hands and placed one hand on the dashboard as if to steel herself for what she was about to say.

"I knew your mother," she said so quietly that Cookie could have sworn she'd imagined it. "She was a sweet young thing. I can see why Edward was taken with her." She paused to give Cookie a chance to respond, but when she didn't, she continued. "The two were in love, clear as crystal. Edward, he wasn't a bad boy. . . just restless. He didn't fit the mold his family set out for him." Rayleen fussed with her green dress as though suddenly uncomfortable in her Sunday clothes. "And Ebie, as the oldest son -- he was all bound up in duty to his folks. It was his job to keep Edward in hand, make a man out of him."

Despite the early morning warmth, Cookie felt cold suddenly and fidgeted with the knobs for the heater only to discover that they didn't work. Frustrated, she leaned back, eager to learn something, *anything* that might help her understand her mother and father, though it felt strange to call people she'd never known that when Ebie and Mitzi had been the ones to raise her.

Rayleen licked her lips. "Ebie tried. Lord knows he tried to fit Edward into that tight little box, but that boy wasn't made of the same cloth as the others. He was artistic." Rayleen brightened here. "If you ever get a chance, you should see his paintings. He was gifted, but artwork didn't count for much in a family of lawyers and businessmen. It didn't pay the bills."

"So they sent him to the country to learn the business," Cookie filled in.

Rayleen nodded. "But he wasn't good with his hands, least not in that way. And he didn't have a head for business." Rayleen rolled down the window, letting in the fresh air as she clucked, a smile forming on her lips as she strolled down memory lane. "No, that man woulda run the business into the ground. He got to know the poor sharecroppers round these parts. Felt sorry for them. Wanted to help them make a livable wage, own their own property. Believe it or not," she said with a laugh, "he actually went up against his daddy and Ebie to try to get his family to sell the property to the sharecroppers for a fair price, allow us to make payments. . . over time."

"Stop the truck!" Cookie said, wanting to hear every word of what Rayleen was saying before she faced her family.

Corliss, who up until now had remained silent, shrugged and said, "Okay." Then she pulled the truck over, leaving the engine running. Already, the heat of the day was settling in, the scent of sweet corn adding a sickly sweet smell to the odor of the baked clay soil beneath their tires.

"And?" Cookie asked.

"And of course Edward's daddy would have none of it. Said. . . well, I won't tell you what he said, not in polite company, but I'm sure you can imagine it. Said no son of his would ever sell off land to a. . ." Her words trailed off and she looked down at her hands which were once again folded neatly on her lap, her nails filed to little half moons.

Despite the years that had passed or that she'd had nothing to do with what Ebie's father had said, Cookie felt the need to apologize. "So Edward was considered the black sheep of the family. . . because of his views?"

Rayleen snorted. "You could say that."

Off in the distance, cattle grazed behind a fence that had been unaffected by the tornado. It amazed Cookie how easily life went on around her when her world had been shattered. She wondered how many other people had thought the same thing during *their* times of crisis.

"They shipped Edward off. . . to Oregon. To work greenchain. By then, your momma knew she was pregnant. She told him before he was set to leave."

Cookie fought back the waterworks that threatened to spill down her cheeks. "But he left anyway?" she said, her voice husky with emotion.

Rayleen glanced over at Corliss, who appeared to be doing her best to stay silent, to let the chips fall where they may. "The family gave him no choice. They gave him an ultimatum. Either he go, spend a year in Oregon with the hope that the relationship would cool during that time, or lose everything, his family included. It was that last part that got him, in the end, because he loved his family. They said if he still felt the same way toward the girl when he returned, they wouldn't stand in his way. Edward figured he would return in a year, marry his sweetheart, and that his family would come to accept things, eventually."

"But he never got the chance," Cookie said, wishing she wasn't sandwiched between the two women so that she could bolt for the door. Whenever upset, she either worked in her garden or walked. To sit idly by had every nerve end tingling with anxiety.

"How did he die?" she asked, fearing the answer. She had always known that her uncle had died in a freak accident, but she didn't know how and had never thought to ask. To her, he'd been an enigmatic figure that her family rarely talked about so that he had faded into the shadows of her thoughts as something akin to a fable trotted out on only the rarest of occasions.

For a moment, Rayleen didn't answer. She patted the seat beside her as if to gather courage before she spoke. Finally, she said, "The new boys were given the most dangerous jobs. So they made him a green chain puller. The line broke and he got pinned between a log and the equipment. Ebie had never forgiven himself for insisting that Edward go."

Emotion tugged at Cookie's throat, but she forced herself to ask the question that lingered in her mind. "What happened to my mother?"

Rayleen's eyes went to the devastation outside and for a moment, Cookie thought she might not answer, but finally, Rayleen stiffened her spine and continued. "She couldn't afford to care for you alone, and Edward's parents were afraid people would learn about the affair. So they encouraged her to give the baby to her sister who was married. That way, Ebie could keep an eye on the child. Her parents thought it a good solution. Mitzi never knew about any of this. Not until she had the miscarriage and Ebie came up with the idea of adopting you. But even then, she thought the baby was Rachel's"

Cookie offered a mirthless laugh at the many layers of deception. But she still hadn't asked the one question that meant the most to her. The one that had kept her up at night since hearing of her biological mother. "Did she want me? My biological mother?"

Once again, Rayleen snorted. "Oh, honey, she wanted you more than life itself. I truly believe that not a day went by that she didn't think about you. When Rachel, bless her soul, brought you to me, she let her sister believe you had died in the storm."

Cookie gasped, shocked by the admission. How could Rachel have been so callous, so cruel? Fire burned inside her at the very idea that Rachel would have kept such a horrible secret from her sister, had lied to her. Had she done it out of guilt for what she'd done? Was it like giving away a puppy that whined too much or piddled on the floor? She ground her teeth together.

Seeing Cookie's anger roll through her like thunder, Rayleen put her hands up to stop her. "She didn't do it to be cruel, Cookie.

Rachel was afraid her sister would take you back if she knew you were alive. It would have ruined any chance she might have for a new life. You have to understand," she added, before Cookie could protest, "this was the Depression. People were sending their children on orphan trains to be taken in by other families, farm families that put the children to work. Your mother and her parents were having trouble feeding themselves. They couldn't have added one more mouth to the family."

"You did," Cookie countered, turning toward Rayleen. "You couldn't afford it any more than they could."

Rayleen looked skyward, closing her eyes briefly before reopening them. "It was only supposed to be for a few days, a month or two at most. Besides, we lived on a farm, so we had food, and our crops didn't blow away in the tornado like Rachel and Byrdie's crops did. We could at least feed you. In those days, to have a roof over your head and food on the table was enough. We considered ourselves lucky."

"Well, you weren't lucky this time," Cookie said about the latest storm, but immediately regretted her words when she saw the look of devastation on Rayleen's face. "Oh, Rayleen," she breathed, "I take that back. I didn't mean. . . I know how hard this is for you."

Rayleen set her jaw, her expression hardened. "You have no idea how difficult this has been for me," she said, her chin pointing toward the drying corn husks that lay bare to the scorching sun that, even at this early hour of the day, drew sweat down each of their brows and caused rivulets to run down the inside of Cookie's dress. "Each time I try to stand up, God knocks me to my knees," Rayleen continued, her voice filled with righteous indignation. "How many times do I have to crawl? Huh?" she demanded, stabbing a finger into the sultry morning air. "Tell me that, Miss High and Mighty!"

Rayleen must have realized how her words had affected Cookie, because she drew back as if shaken by what she had said, and yet Cookie knew this was as close to the truth she would ever get. Sure Cookie had been knocked down hard when she'd been left at the altar by a bigamist. And she had been knocked down again when she'd discovered she'd been lied to her entire life. But she'd never had to deal with the day to day grind of trying to survive, of trying to put one foot in front of the other and hope that tomorrow would bring something better, would leave fewer marks on her to show for the struggle of living. She felt humbled in the face of everything she knew about Rayleen and her family.

"Thank you for taking me in as a child," Cookie said, meaning it. Would Cookie even be alive without the kindness of these strangers? Probably not. "And I'm sorry. About your crops. About how tough it has been for you over the years."

She thought of the deed her family held on Rayleen and Chester's farm and winced, knowing that this, too, was a form of slavery. She'd heard it called redlining, a system by which people of color found it difficult, if not impossible, to get loans, and the few loans they did receive cost them more per loan than for their white neighbors in the same community.

"I suppose we've done enough talking for one day," Rayleen said, her dander slowly dissipating as the cicadas began their chorus in the early morning heat.

Cookie regretted today because she'd seen the mask once again draw over Rayleen's face where before the woman had been open. Honest. She owed this woman the world, and someday she would repay her, though she didn't know how. But first, she needed to meet her mother, for Cookie to see for herself what her life might have been, had things been different.

Corliss, who had been all but forgotten in the shuffle, said, "You two ready to move on?"

The two women nodded in unison.

"Good! And for what it's worth, I like you both." With that, she put the truck in gear and finished the drive to the other shack which, even now, glowed flaxen from within.

But as they approached and put the truck in idle, Cookie turned to Rayleen to ask one final burning question. "What is my mother's name?"

Rayleen bit her lip and breathed deeply of the pine scented air. "Your mother's name is Julia. Julia Broadhurst."

35

JULIA. AS COOKIE STEPPED OUT of the truck and peered up at the sharecropper's shack, she rolled the name around on her tongue to see if it fit. Cookie Broadhurst, daughter of Julia. And yet it seemed unfitting to take a name that wasn't hers, as though she was betraying her family in some way, the family that had adopted her as their own. Besides, Haines had been her name for as long as she could remember. It placed her squarely among the Jebediah Haines family, and after all, Edward was a Haines. She thought of how similar Edward and Ebie looked to each other. Both had black hair, a thin tall build, though Edward was shorter by a few inches. Both were said to have a keen intellect, only in different areas, so it seemed. No wonder she had never questioned her birth.

"You going to be okay?" Corliss asked as the door to the shack opened and Dipsy came tumbling out, Ebie and Mitzi trailing behind her with Beulah bringing up the rear.

Dipsy's ruddy complexion and round cheeks foretold of the coming baby. It was as if she'd been born to bear children, appearing healthier with each pregnancy. And today, she no longer limped, having recovered from her fall on her high heels. As the foursome barrelled toward the steps, Rayleen came around the other side of Cookie, as if to flank her in support.

"Thanks," Cookie told both Rayleen and Corliss, "but I'll be okay." Then she ran to embrace Dipsy, who stepped down gingerly onto the bare earth, Ebie and Mitzi lagging behind. Dipsy smelled of lemons and soap, a scent so familiar as to be an integral part of her sister.

"You scared me yesterday when you took off!" Dipsy admonished, holding Cookie at arm's length, her eyes running up and down her as if inspecting her for defects.

"I just needed time. . . to think."

"Well, I'm glad you're back."

Dipsy swept Cookie into her arms and gave her a final squeeze then released her and stepped away so that Cookie could greet Mitzi and Ebie who stood in stoic silence, waiting for Cookie's cue for them to come forward. Cookie inhaled deeply of the hot July air, still filled with static from yesterday's storm, before continuing her trek up the steps and into her parents' arms. Despite everything that had happened, everything she had learned in the past few days, it felt good to be in their warm embrace. It felt. . . right.

"I'm sorry for not telling you sooner, darlin'," Ebie said, his voice filled with emotion. Ebie was the strongest man she had ever known, always even keeled. Men in the community looked up to him, came to him for guidance. He had advised some of the most influential men in Montgomery in everything from law to child rearing.

"We're both sorry," Mitzi added, but it was clear by the way she cocked her head slightly, her eyes glued to Ebie, that she hadn't been party to all of it, not completely.

A couple of climbing roses draped the farthest porch posts, runners climbing across the wooden beams that led to the roof. Their smell drifted in waves along the summer breeze, unaware that life around them had changed in a single day, the tornado having shorn the crops like a giant threshing machine. But even the rose had fought bravely to survive in the wind that had mowed down trees while plucking others up and setting them down a dozen yards away like nothing more than tiny matchsticks.

Cookie had practiced what she would say to her parents when she finally saw them, but none of that came to her now. Instead, all she could utter were the words, "Can we go see Julia now?"

Mitzi's cheeks turned cherry red, as though she'd been slapped. Without another word, she stormed inside the house, Ebie excusing himself and trailing in after her. Beulah, who had just stepped out on the porch, moved aside so that the pair could pass.

"You look here, Miss Cookie," Beulah said, admonishing Cookie while shaking a finger at her. "You're not too big to put over my knee, girl! I never taught you to speak to yo' mama that way, y'hear?"

It seemed the madder Beulah got, the louder she became and the more her speech reverted to that of her childhood. For her part, Cookie shrank back, the anxiety and fatigue of the past day having loosened her tongue, clogged the internal filters that should have told her she was treading on unsafe territory. Exhaustion made her feel as though she could curl up into a ball right on this very front porch and take a never-ending nap, like Rumplestiltskin, only to awaken as an old, old woman, haggard and worn. Yet she had no replay button, no way to repair the damage done except to keep moving, to see this story to its end, to finally meet her mother. To know, once and for all, *who am I when everything I believed about myself is a lie?*

It took one look from Beulah, snorting and stamping like a bull, her eyes glassy and filled with anger, for Cookie to know what she must do. To set things right. To try to see things from her parents' points of view.

But before she could act, Dipsy snagged Cookie's arm and hissed, "You idiot! Mama and Daddy love you. They love both of us. They didn't hide this from you to hurt you. They hid it from you to *protect* you. Remember *that* when you go in to apologize."

Cookie took a long, lingering look at her sister, then nodded. Now, she just hoped that she could make her parents understand that she loved them, but she had to know the truth. To know *all* of it, no matter how painful.

* * *

Julia had spent the day primping, but when she peered in the mirror that stood on the dresser in her bedroom, she couldn't get over how pale she looked, her auburn hair now faded to an early gray. Although normally skinny, in the past few months her bones had come to frame an almost skeletal body, her skin translucent. And these days she had trouble putting on her polyester clothing by herself. Instead, her clothes hung on her like fake snow on a christmas tree, weighed her down so that she drooped. What would her daughter think of her, seeing her like this for the first time? She sagged, the strain of trying to look pretty for her daughter having taken its toll.

My daughter.

She had only recently learned that her daughter was still alive. All those years she had mourned the loss only to discover that her daughter had been no more than a few hours away by car. Her heart fluttered in her chest like a sparrow's wings, light and fast, as she recalled the day that her sister had told her. It had been a Friday and just a sliver of daylight remained to announce the coming night. Julia had spent her days like every other day, waiting to be taken to the main hall for meals, trying desperately to shuffle what she could into her mouth, most times failing, her arms too weak for even the small effort it took to eat. That day, she'd been sitting at the table, preparing for the food to arrive, her plate set out with a napkin, a fork, and a sippy cup, as though she were five instead of fifty. She'd seen her older sister's car through the window, had listened to her steps up the driveway, the cowbell on the door jingling to announce her entry into the group home. The look of shock as Rachel took stock of her younger sister, at Julia's deterioration since she'd last visited.

"Please take me home," Julia had pleaded. But she knew it was impossible. She needed a full-time nurse these days, all the privileges of adulthood gone. At night, she would often cry herself to sleep, but not now, not with her sister here. These moments were precious, and she refused to waste a minute of her time "caterwauling," as her mama used to call it.

"Julia!" Rachel breathed, a forced smile on her face. But Julia could read the tension in her sister's eyes, see the small pulse in her forehead. When you were dying, you noticed the little things, the things that others missed.

Rachel hadn't asked how Julia was doing. No point. It was too late for that. Instead she kept up a cheery banter as she sat through the meal, her eyes straying periodically toward the clock, as if to be sure the big and little hands were moving and hadn't stopped.

When Julia had finished with a swipe of her napkin, Rachel turned to her and said, "Would you mind if we went to your room? I need to talk to you."

Rachel tapped her feet on the floor and clicked her nails together, so much so that Julia wondered if she had come to discuss final arrangements. She should be upset at the idea, but she was so happy to see a familiar face that she couldn't find it in her to be mad. In fact it might be fun to plan her final parting. She wanted flowers, lots of flowers. Maybe the funeral could be outdoors with a big long table filled with all the foods she could no longer eat. At her parents' farmhouse with the big weeping willow, everyone dressed in their finest, cows munching in the background. Balloons would probably be too much, and yet. . .

Rachel grabbed hold of Julia's wheelchair and began rolling her out of the dining room and down the hall toward her room. Julia was one of the lucky ones. Several of the people at the home had no visitors at all. And Rachel had seen to it that she got the biggest room. It looked almost homey with the photographs strewn on the bookshelves along with her favorite books. Too bad she slept so much and couldn't get through more than a page or two before nodding off. All these thoughts went through her head as Rachel helped her onto the bed and lay her back against the pillow, covering her with one of their mama's quilts.

For a brief moment, she closed her eyes, forgetting all about Rachel or why she was here. But then she felt Rachel take her hand and sandwich it between her own. The warmth felt good. These days, she shivered, even with the heat on. She sank down deeper into the bed.

"Julia, sweetie?" Rachel said, her voice tentative.

"Mmm?" Julia responded, too tired to open her eyes.

"I don't know how to say this except to just spit it out."

"Oh?"

Rachel took a deep breath before plunging on. "Your daughter's alive."

Julia thought she'd heard wrong. Maybe she was only dreaming she'd heard her sister say her daughter was alive. She opened her eyes but everything seemed fuzzy, as though she were at the bottom of a great pool and looking through a lens clouded by water.

"She didn't die in the storm," Rachel continued, her words rushed now. "I told you that because I knew you would want her back. And it was the Depression. When Byrdie left me, I couldn't afford to feed myself, much less her. And then there was the tornado."

Julia heard the desperation in her sister's voice, a desperation that mirrored her own, all the exhaustion of the day replaced by a renewed reserve of energy that she hadn't known she'd had.

"Where? What happened to her, Rachel?" Julia was fully awake now. She rubbed her eyes, struggled to sit up.

Rachel clutched the edge of the quilt in her hand. "I took her to Rayleen and Chester's. It was only supposed to be temporary, 'til I got my life back together." Rachel stood and began to pace, turning back to plead for forgiveness.

"I don't understand," Julia said, running her fingers through what was left of her thinning hair. "Rayleen and Chester kept her?"

Rachel sat back down on the edge of the bed. "For a couple of years."

"Years!" Jula cried, lifting up from the bed but falling back in a fit of coughing. Out of the corner of her eye, she saw two hummingbirds near the feeder outside her window. They bobbed up and down, twirled around each other. She'd enjoyed countless hours watching their flitting movements, watching them chase each other across the lawn, but now they seemed to mock her with their exuberant energy, energy denied her.

"Where is my daughter?" Julia demanded with a steely quiet that belied her condition.

"She. . . she. . . Edward's brother and his wife collected her. They raised her. She's an adult, Julia. A happy, well-adjusted adult."

Rachel waited as though expecting Julia to jump from her bed, to slap her, but what could Julia do? She had little reserve remaining.

"Where is Caledonia, Rachel?" Julia demanded, her eyes boring into her sister. "I want to see her." Rachel reached to take her hand, but Julia pulled it away, her breathing ragged.

"Please listen." Rachel was trembling now. "She doesn't know."

"Doesn't *know*?" Julia said, turning on her with strength she'd never thought possible. "Doesn't know about what?"

"About you, that she's adopted. That you're her mother and that Edward is her father. She doesn't know about any of it," Rachel said, lips pursed and eyes wide.

For several moments, they sat together in silence, the only sound that of the unseasonable rain that had begun to fall on the rooftop. "Well, then," Julia said, dipping her head, "you tell her, okay? Then you bring her to me." She turned to Rachel, snatching her sister's hand up in her own. "Promise me."

Rachel refused to face her.

"Look at me!" Julia demanded. When her sister was facing her squarely, she repeated her words. "Promise me."

Rachel took a deep breath, then nodded her head. "I promise," she said at last. Then they hugged. Now, Rachel had finally kept her promise. In a matter of hours, Julia would get to see her daughter.

With labored movements, she edged toward the bed, using the back of the chair as ballast. Once she'd finally managed to leverage herself into bed, she paused to catch her breath before covering herself with a blanket and then closing her eyes.

She must have fallen into a fast, deep sleep because she didn't awaken until the alarm went off. A nurse, who had been trekking the halls, heard it and entered with such efficiency that it humbled Julia. Not for the first time, she wished herself into the other woman's body. Wished for just one more day, one more week, one more month, of good health. What would it be like to be so young and free? To have your whole life to look forward to instead of your death? Julia would never know. She was just grateful for today -- the day when she would finally meet her daughter.

* * *

The drive home to Montgomery from the sharecropper's

301

hut had been excruciatingly long. So many thoughts had pinged through Cookie's head as she drove that she'd felt exhausted by the time she arrived home. Yet now, two days later, as Cookie prepared to meet her birth mother for the first time, her leg bounced as though pulled by an unseen thread. And as they drove down the sunny lanes, she'd bit her lip so many times she'd drawn blood. Ebie and Mitzi had chosen to stay behind, so that left Rachel, as well as Beulah, who seemed just as eager to learn more about the woman who had birthed Cookie.

Dipsy, for her part, had rushed straight home to collect the kids and to see how Kent had held up under the pressure of work and raising children. Secretly, Dipsy hoped that Kent finally understood how difficult it had been for her, keeping up with the house and the children all these years while he went off to work.

Prior to Cookie leaving to meet Julia, Ebie and Mitzi had been especially quiet, as though they knew something they were determined not to tell her. But what? A chill ran up Cookie's spine to think that there might be secrets remaining that they hadn't divulged. How many more secrets could she possibly bear?

"Has Julia lived in our town this entire time?" Cookie asked, peering across Beulah in the front seat of Julia's car to get a better look at Rachel who appeared tired and worn in her threadbare beige dress.

"No, I moved her here. . . so she could be closer to you." Rachel steadfastly refused to look Cookie in the eye, instead concentrating on the road ahead with its elm-lined roads and wide front lawns. The neighborhood seemed so out of keeping with Rachel's normally haggard appearance. How had Rachel's sister afforded to live in a place such as this when Rachel seemed to have lived a hard life, moving from town to town in search of work? Nothing made sense.

Finally, Rachel pulled up to a house with a large lawn and picture windows that foretold a well-to-do family and kids running around out back. But when Cookie exited the car, through the picture window at the front of the house she saw what looked like a group of adults seated around a huge table. And as she neared the home, she saw a sign posted out front with the words "The Posey House." Cookie frowned, all the butterflies that had been filling her stomach suddenly coming to life and taking flight. Inside the Posey House, she would finally meet her mother, but what *was* the Posey House?

Beulah, who had been silent much of the way here, stopped Cookie with a hand to her shoulder. Rachel, who had gone ahead, noticed them stop and waited. "Miss Rachel," Beulah implored. "You got to tell her about this place. You can't let her go inside thinkin' this is a regular home. It's not right."

"Beulah?" Cookie said, not understanding. "Rachel?"

Rachel jutted out her hip and cocked her head as if to say, "Leave it be, Beulah," but Beulah refused to go along with the charade.

"You tell her or I will," Beulah countered, holding her purse out as though she were about to swing it at Rachel if she didn't fess up soon.

Cookie closed her eyes and took a deep breath before opening them, the air smelling of freshly mown lawn and four o'clocks, a fragrant shrub with pink and white flowers that bloomed in mid-summer.

"Stop it!" she demanded, stamping her foot like a petulant child. "Rachel, what is this place? Why won't you tell me?"

All the color drained from Rachel's face, and for a moment,

Cookie feared she might faint. But at last she spoke, her face regaining color only marginally.

"This is a group home," Rachel said, her eyes imploring for Cookie's understanding.

"A group home? For what? Is my mother…mentally ill?" she asked, fearing the worst.

Rachel's eyes widened. Then, in a rush, she said, "Of course not."

"Then what? Beulah?" Cookie said, turning to the matronly woman who looked as if she had steam coming out of her ears.

"Enough!" said Beulah, hands held up, purse and all, as though she were being robbed. "That's it. I'll tell Cookie if all of y'all are too cowardly." She began mumbling about stupid white folk and how they could never say what they meant, always hiding things from people like they owned the key to the kingdom. Once she had that tirade out of her system, she put her hands down and said, "Cookie?"

"Yes'm," Cookie said, feeling like she was six again and in trouble for sneaking a slice of key lime pie cooling on the counter.

"I'm just gonna say this straight out. Your mama's dying. She's got cancer."

For a moment, the words didn't sink in. It was as if she were overhearing a conversation with someone else, not her. As if her mind had shut the door to any such thinking, she said, "What?" But then it hit her with hurricane force, nearly knocking her off her feet, pushing her back into the arms of Beulah who was waiting to catch her before she fell.

"No!" Cookie screamed through clenched teeth. "No, no, no!" Sobs welled up in her throat, but Beulah turned her around and grabbed both hands, then looked her square in the face.

"We are not doing this now, Cookie Haines!" she hissed. "Your mama's in there facing the battle of her life, and she wants to see her baby. She *deserves* that. She has waited one heck of a long time and you are not going to deprive her of that by crying, do you hear me, girl?"

Cookie sniffled and fought down the tremors of emotion that threatened to spill down her cheeks. Why, after all these years, did her mother have to be dying? Why? She knew it was selfish of her to want her around longer, to want anything from her at all after so much time had passed. But she did. She did!

"You want to fall apart after we leave this place, and I will be there to support you the entire way," Beulah continued. "Until then, you are going to buck up and make your mama proud. Make *all* your mamas proud."

A wayward tear fell to the ground, but Cookie simply nodded her head and wiped at her tears, determined to keep it together as long as her mother was around.

"Now take this," Beulah said, pulling a handkerchief from her sleeve, "and blow your nose."

Beulah held it up to Cookie who blew into it, just as she had at church on Sundays when Cookie was small and Beulah had come to help look after the two girls. How many days, weeks, months, and years had Beulah spent feeding Mitzi's family, cleaning up after them, wiping away their tears? Yes, she had needed a job. Yes, she'd needed the money. But Cookie had no doubt that it had also been a labor of love. And she felt that love just as keenly for Beulah in return. With her nose now dry, she wiped the last of her tears, then threw her shoulders back and nodded.

"Okay," she said with a breathy sigh. "I'm ready."

Rachel's eyes had lost their luster and the crow's feet that Mitzi had done her best to cover with makeup had reappeared, but she managed a weak smile.

"Take me to see my mother," Cookie said, steeling herself for what lay ahead.

A ramp led to a side door hidden behind a half wall bordered in flowers -- red geraniums and trailing blue and white petunias. A little American flag waved in the center. It all seemed so. . . cheery.

A cowbell announced their entry. "Hello!" Rachel called, familiar with the protocol, apparently, for a middle-aged woman appeared, her curly black hair haloing her head and a 100-watt smile on her face.

Beulah immediately relaxed upon seeing one of her own and within minutes they were talking like two lost relatives. Through a pass-through, Cookie could see a group of men and women in various states of decay, seated around a kitchen table. She bent down slightly to inspect the gathering, wondering which of the women was her mother when Beulah grabbed her by the arm and said, "The aide says your mama's in her room. We can go back now."

Cookie lifted her head too quickly and banged it on the upper cabinet with a full array of fine china, the one that the patients and guests would probably never use, merely there for display, no doubt.

She rubbed her head to ease the pain as she trailed the others down the hall to a room at the back of the house, heard the greetings as she prepared herself internally for this first meeting with her mother. But it was as if her arms and legs had become liquid, any strength she'd had deserting her.

When they entered the room all three women cleared a path for Cookie, leaving a semi-circle around the bed for Cookie to enter. As she neared, Cookie steadied herself for what she might see. But she could never have prepared herself for the tiny woman shrouded beneath the quilt that billowed around her. She looked as if she were ninety instead of in her fifties, her skin shriveled like a prune. Cookie tried to see any resemblance to herself. The other woman definitely had her full mouth and pinched nose as well as her hair color. Mitzi had called the auburn highlights part of her "Irish roots," and yet Mitzi had never mentioned having Irish roots herself, nor Ebie, for that matter. Why had Cookie never questioned these small hints at her heritage? Why hadn't she been more curious. . . *she* of all people, who had been nicknamed "curious Cookie" as a child?

"Cookie?" Julia said in a voice made weak by cancer. "Is that really you?"

"It's me, Mama," Cookie said, not sure if she'd earned the right to use the title yet, but putting it out there anyway.

"Let me look at you," Julia said, trying to push herself up on hands that seemed too delicate for lifting. She held the bedding to her, then reached over and patted the bed next to her. "Sit. I've waited all this time to finally meet you." Julia's eyes, which had been dull and lifeless, suddenly seemed to spark with fresh life as she inspected Cookie carefully. "You're very pretty."

Cookie flushed slightly. She didn't feel pretty just now, but pretty was a relative term, and she supposed that if she were in Julia's shoes, she might feel the same, given the circumstances.

"I never knew about you until just a couple of days ago," said Cookie. "I thought Mitzi gave birth to me."

Julia gave a short, raspy laugh. "Why, if I didn't know

better, I'd say you were apologizing, when it's me who should be apologizing for not finding you sooner." Her eyes strayed to Rachel, whose face held a mixture of remorse and sorrow for everything that had transpired over the past thirty years.

Cookie saw it and knew there would be time for apologies and truth telling. For now, she was just happy to finally meet her mother who looked like one of the little apple dolls that Mitzi's mother had given to her as a child. All shriveled and brown.

Just then, Julia pointed to a framed picture on a large bookshelf. With great ceremony, Rachel brought it to her and laid it across the wedding ring quilt. "Do you know who this is?" Julia asked.

Cookie bent down to inspect the black-and-white picture more closely. The man looked like a younger version of Ebie, only a bit more square-jawed, and the woman was pretty. She had curly auburn hair and a cotton dress with low-slung shoes. Her nose was slightly askew, like Cookie's, her eyes quite narrow and she wore a half-smile, as though she knew something the rest of them didn't. In her arms was a baby swaddled in a pale blanket.

"That's Edward," Julia said, in a raspy voice filled with fatigue. "When he came home. . . while on break. . . before the accident. And that's me," she added, pointing to the woman with the half-smile.

"And the baby?" Cookie asked, fingering the infant in the picture as though she could divine the thoughts of the infant by merely touching the antique photo. "Is that me?"

Julia nodded, the half-smile returning. "I suppose you have a lot of questions."

Cookie knew it was wrong of her to want answers when

Julia was busy fighting a disease that held her in its sway. But she also knew that the clock was ticking and if she were ever to have her answers, it must be now or never.

"Rayleen told me about you and Edward. . . about how he died. About me." She paused, choosing her words carefully. "And she also told me that Rachel gave me up." From her spot on the bed, Cookie saw Rachel wince at Cookie's forthrightness. But she forced herself to continue before she lost her nerve. "And that she told you that I had. . . died. In the tornado."

Emotion played at the corners of Julia's eyes as she fought back tears. Unable to speak, Julia simply nodded.

"What happened to you? Where were you all those years when I was with Mitzi and Ebie?"

Julia tried to sit up straighter in her bed, but in the end needed help from the aide, who then excused herself to go check on the others. "It was the Great Depression. Me, Mama, and Daddy. . . we followed the crops. Lived in shacks with dirt floors, no running water. We made do. Rachel helped us, when she could. Daddy finally got a job driving truck, so we moved into a real house. It even had a cistern!" she said with a laugh, coughing so badly afterward that Rachel came around and began patting her on the back until the coughing subsided. "We got our first shower in ages, when we got that cistern. We were pretty proud of that."

The question that had worried Cookie upon her arrival resurfaced and she glanced at the surroundings, taking in the plush white carpets, the green drapes, the closet that made up one complete wall.

As if she understood Cookie's unspoken question, Rachel said, "Your father paid for this. He brought Julia here. . . so she could be near you. He had planned to tell you about her soon, but I couldn't wait any longer. I was afraid if you didn't know right away, well..." Rachel's eyes drifted to the shrunken woman in bed, swallowed up by the down pillow so that only her face was evident. Cookie recognized the love for her sister written in the set of Rachel's mouth, the sorrow in her brown eyes. "Ebie didn't want me involved. He wanted to handle the whole thing himself. We had a signed agreement. In the end, I'm not sure he would have ever told you about Julia until it was too late."

"Or never?" Cookie countered.

Beulah and Rachel offered nervous glances, which told her everything she needed to know.

"Don't be too hard on Ebie, Cookie girl," Beulah rushed to add. "Your daddy didn't know how to tell you. He worried how you'd take it. Worried you would stop--"

"--loving him?" Cookie finished.

Beulah nodded, then lowered her head as if to avoid Cookie's eyes.

Cookie gazed out the window in time to see two hummingbirds spiralling upward before darting off in opposite directions. And she supposed that's how she felt, a spiralling of emotions that were tearing her apart inside, and yet she sat perfectly still, as if in stillness she might regain the equilibrium she had lost in the past few days. But try as she might, she couldn't regain her footing. The ground felt like quicksand, as though it were swallowing her up. She ground her teeth together. She couldn't go on thinking like this or it would destroy her. No, Beulah was right. She needed to buck up, to show what she was made of, to be... what?

Without thinking, she let out a low growl. So much of her

life was out of her control. Everyone turned to stare at her, Julia included. How could she explain it to them? She felt a stinging behind her eyes and nose. Before, her life had been ordered; it had made sense. Now. . . well, now she didn't know *who* she was anymore.

Julia reached out a hand. It no longer felt cold. Instead, it was warm, the touch tender. "I won't be around much longer," Julia said, each word a challenge now as she struggled for breath. "But I want you to know this. I love you. I have always loved you. And Ebie and Mitzi love you too. Never forget that when the days get rough, ya hear?"

With that, she lay her head on the pillow, closing her eyes to signal an end to their first meeting. Rachel nodded, clearly familiar with her sister's needs. As they left the room, Cookie wondered how many visits remained between her and her mother. But she feared she knew the answer only too well.

36

COOKIE EXCUSED HERSELF AS THE car came to a halt in front of her family's large modern ranch-style house. She couldn't face Ebie and Mitzi just yet, so she bade Beulah and Rachel farewell, then made her way to her greenhouse. There, the dracaena competed with the schefflera for space, steam from the condensation of moisture dripping down the inner glass walls, the greenhouse pungent with unnamed odors. This was her haven from the world. Here no one judged her. Here, her life wasn't complicated. She could be herself without the myriad eyes of society reminding her that she wasn't good enough, pretty enough, smart enough. All the things that women were judged by.

As if no time had passed since she'd last been here, she began her routine of watering, then plucking off dried leaves and depositing them in a bin near the back of the greenhouse. She spent the next glorious twenty minutes forgetting. Forgetting that she was adopted, that her father was her uncle and her mother. . . well, it gave her a headache to piece it all together. Better to leave it be for now.

She was so lost in the easy routine of caring for the greenhouse that she hadn't known anyone had entered until she heard the crunching of gravel and someone clearing his voice. She turned in time to see Winston Cowel bent down tying his shoelace. When he looked up, black hair framed his face and light freckles dotted his nose and cheeks. In the prescient light, she saw the grade schooler she'd known all her life. Winn. Winnie Cowel. They had teased him back then, his pale skin never failing to turn a bright crimson. She had offered to pound the boys for teasing him, but Winn let the names roll off his back. He was who he was. . . and exactly what she needed right now. Something to tether her to a known past, to keep her from feeling as though if she lifted her feet even slightly, she might float away like a hot-air balloon. She needed someone solid in her life, someone to anchor her, someone she could count on. The thought of it made her flush, for she had never given voice to needing another person. She'd always thought of herself as self-sufficient. Capable.

"I heard about what happened -- that you met your biological mother."

For a moment, she couldn't breathe. Then finally she said, "How?"

Winn paled, but answered her truthfully. "Your dad. He thought you could use company, a sounding board." He shrugged.

Between them lay a world of words unspoken. Winn would have been the natural choice for a husband -- someone she could talk to, someone who adored her as much as she adored him. And yet he had been deemed unsuitable because his father had died and therefore Winn had been forced to go to work at a young age to try to support his mother. He had worked hard, had gone to school, got good grades. But he would never enter the finest schools, never be a lawyer or doctor, something Mitzi had set her eyes toward early on. That's why Mitzi had been so bowled over by the bigamist. Hadn't done a thorough background search. Because she had wanted him to be the real McCoy, the high society husband that would help their family rise to the top. And yet Winn was twice -- no, *a hundred* times -- the man her fiancé had ever been.

"You want to help me plant some seedlings into a bigger pot?"

Winn removed his jacket and hung it carelessly over a corner of the potting table, then came to stand beside her. "Hand me a stack of pots," he said, as though they had been doing this together for years. With that, he began filling the pots with rich loam and using a popsicle stick she had handy to furrow out the middle so that he could drop the seedling into the hole and then bury the roots. He gave each seedling a quick drink, then moved on to the next one. As Cookie and Winn stood shoulder to shoulder working, Winn said, "I ran into your father at the train station before he left for Shardsburg."

Cookie's eyes widened. After this week, nothing surprised her.

"And we had a talk--"

"--a talk?" Cookie stopped what she was doing, but when Winn glanced toward the pots that were certainly not filling themselves, she busied her hands. "About what?"

"Well, I had a bit of a problem."

"Problem?"

He looked at her with a glint in his shiny blue eyes. "What are you, a parrot?"

Cookie chuckled. It felt good to laugh again. She hadn't been able to laugh since the beginning of all this. Her emotions of the past week had her seesawing in every direction so that now, instead of feeling light as air, she felt weighed down, so much so that she felt fifty pounds heavier, though if anything, she had lost weight.

"See, I have land, but no money to do anything with half of it and no way to get a loan. So, I was looking for someone to lease the land."

Cookie once again stopped what she was doing, but only for a moment. She frowned as she tamped down the soil in several pots, wondering what he had in mind. Had he asked her father for a loan?

Fortunately, she didn't have to wait long for her answer because Winn said, "Your dad thought maybe you would like the land."

"*Me?*" Cookie said, cocking her head back in surprise. "For what?"

"For your greenhouses." This time it was Winn who paused to take stock of her, his crystal blue eyes never allowing her to waver.

"But I don't understand. I have no money for greenhouses." She stood there, hands covered in dirt, a bit of it hanging from a strand of hair where she had reached up to push it away from her face. She must look a mess, but at the moment, she didn't care.

"I think your dad meant for the three of us to work together. He has the money, you have the know-how, and I have the business sense."

He shrugged, as if it didn't matter one way or the other what she decided to do, even though she knew how hard he had struggled over the years and how much this would mean to him. And yet, she didn't have the wherewithal to do anything about it just now -- not with her biological mother in a group home. Her silence was damning, but to her surprise, he grabbed her shoulder and turned her toward him, his eyes searching hers.

"My father died when I was a young teen. I know what it's like to lose someone you. . ." He paused here, his voice thick with emotion. "I should never have brought up the land. You just take all the time you need. And Cookie. . .?" he said, taking her chin into the palm of his hand and tilting her face upward. "If you ever want me to come with you. . . when you go to see your mother, just ask, okay? I'll be there for you. . . for whatever you need."

Cookie's face grew warm and tears dotted her eyes. Her throat felt too tight to speak, so she merely nodded. "Thank you," she finally managed.

Then they turned back to begin potting once more, but something had changed between them. She was sure they both felt it, as though like a sunflower to the sun, they were now bound to each other forever.

*　*　*

Mitzi peered through the kitchen window toward the greenhouse. How long were Cookie and Winn going to stay holed up in there? She'd seen the tears in Cookie's eyes when she'd exited the car earlier, as she said goodbye to Rachel and Beulah, who departed for their respective homes. Then Mitzi had waited patiently to speak to Cookie only to see her trot off toward the greenhouse. She had started to go after her, but Ebie had placed a hand on her shoulder.

"Give her time," he had advised. "She'll come around."

Mitzi wasn't so sure. She had wanted to go with Cookie to meet her mother, to be there for her to help her pick up the pieces, but Ebie had talked her out of it. She'd been kicking herself ever since. Who better to introduce Julia to Cookie than Mitzi herself? But Ebie had assured her that Cookie needed to do this alone, without her mother hovering over her, to give them a chance to talk, to bond. But now, the suspense was killing Mitzi, along with the fear that she might lose her daughter to her biological mother. Mitzi huffed a sigh as she pretended to dry dishes. Cookie had been out there with Winn a good twenty minutes. Before he'd gone in search of Cookie, he had spoken briefly with Ebie. Mitzi had started to follow Winn, when once again Ebie lay a hand on her shoulder to stop her.

"Mitzi," he'd implored. "You've got to stop mothering Cookie. Give her some space. She needs time to deal with this on her own, with the people she chooses."

"But what if she hates us!" Mitzi cried, covering her mouth with the back of her hand to stifle her grief. Cookie had been her saving grace, the person who had most filled her life with joy. Oh, she loved Ebie, with all her heart, and Dipsy too, but Cookie had been a blessing handed down to her by God himself, she felt certain. How many times had she prayed for Him to give her a child, a daughter, someone to love and to love her in return. It was horrible what had happened to Edward. And she felt badly for Julia, she truly did. But Cookie would never have had the life she'd had if she'd stayed in Shardsburg. No, she would have been malnourished, without a roof much of the time, or in a small hovel, chasing the crops. No telling what might have happened to her had they not rescued her.

Who rescued whom?

The thought nicked her conscience, for Cookie had been every bit Mitzi's salvation as well. Cookie had delivered Mitzi from the pit of despair after Edna Farmer, the town socialite, had told her she might lose Ebie if she couldn't give him a child. Now, looking back, she knew that wasn't true. Ebie loved her, always had. But she hadn't known how much back then. She'd just heard Edna's hateful words and had internalized them, made them her own. And it had nearly killed her.

"What if she wants nothing to do with us now?" Mitzi demanded, fighting back tears. "What then? We have to do something. Let her know how much we love her. Please, Ebie," she begged.

Ebie sighed, but took her hands in his all the same. "So, what do you propose I do about it? We can't turn back time. We can't undo what has already been done. Eventually, she'll come to see that we only wanted what's best for her."

"And what if she doesn't, what then?" Mitzi asked, pacing the living room, her feet pounding the oak flooring. "At least make it right for her."

"How?" Ebie said, throwing up his hands. "Cookie is Cookie. She has a mind of her own. Gets that from Edward," he added with a mirthless laugh. "Lord knows she's got nowhere to go, so I think it's a safe bet we're not going to lose her anytime soon."

Mitzi cocked her head and narrowed her eyes, causing Ebie to blanch but she refused to back down. Not this time. Too much was at stake. She marched over to the alcove and stared through the largest of the three window panes. She could just make out Cookie and Winn's silhouettes through the moist walls of the greenhouse. She felt a small pang of remorse to see them stand so close together. It reminded her of the pair when they were in their teens. Cookie had adored Winn then, but Mitzi had steered her clear of him, worrying that he would never be able to make anything of himself with his father gone. Besides, he had his mother and sister to care for. Regret cascaded through her, as she recalled how she'd pushed and cajoled Cookie into marrying a man "from a good family". But she had been wrong. About everything. She could see that now. Hopefully, it wasn't too late. She turned to Ebie, who had been standing silently behind her, watching the pair too.

"They're right for each other, aren't they?" she said softly, reveling in the smell of Ebie's aftershave, the sheer manliness of him. She loved everything about him.

"Come here," he said, holding out his arms and encircling her, making her feel loved, wanted.

For several moments, they stood holding each other, swaying to a rhythm meant just for them. It felt right, somehow. Had she deprived Cookie of the very love that she took for granted? She railed at the idea, but knew she had. Cookie deserved love. Deserved the right to pursue her dreams.

"Ebie," Mitzi said, feeling the warmth and security of Ebie's chin against her hair.

"Hmm?" he said, still swaying along with her.

"Cookie was born with a green thumb."

"Yes, so?" he said, stepping back and taking her hands in his.

"So, *I* don't have to worry about anything. You've seen to that. And Dipsy won't need to worry about anything, not after she took off like she did. I doubt Kent will ever risk their relationship again. He was never so scared in his entire life. We talked, he and I, by phone."

Ebie blinked rapidly, then laughed.

"We've talked a lot over the years."

Apparently, Ebie had never suspected that because he shook his head and said, "Will wonders never cease."

"They have their troubles," Mitzi said, feeling abashed, "but he really is head over heels for Dipsy, and when she didn't beg him to return home. . . well, let's just say he took it hard. I don't think we'll ever have to worry about that again."

"Good to hear," Ebie said, once again pulling her toward him. "So, what do you want me to do for Cookie?"

* * *

Ebie sat in Max's office staring at a bronze antique wall clock that chimed the hour as he waited for the lawyer to be finished with his client. As he sat in the sumptuous office, flipping through a magazine from the stack of *Times* he'd found on the table, he saw an ad for Johnnie Walker. Though he wasn't given to overimbibe, a drink sounded good right about now after this past week. Ebie's visit to the hospital had been a wake-up call. He needed to be sure his family was taken care of in the event. . .

He closed his eyes, recalling his first visit to see Julia after he'd had her moved to be close to Cookie. He'd planned to tell his daughter about her biological mother, but then he'd lost his nerve. Rachel was right to have pressed the point. Otherwise, he might never have told Cookie about Julia, might have allowed Julia to go to her grave without him ever bringing his. . . no, *her*

320

daughter, around to meet her. The guilt hung like the cloud of cigarette smoke from the man seated next to him, a salesman, if his briefcase and cologne were an indicator. That and his slicked back hair. Even his gold watch seemed meant to impress. Ebie had never liked men like that, like Cookie's ex-fiancé. Every fiber in his being had him wanting to go in and talk some sense into Mitzi when she'd foisted that lothario on Cookie. What had Mitzi been thinking? Ebie shook his head at the memory. No, Winn was more her caliber. Ebie had known it from the time they were teens. Winn was smart, worked hard. He reminded Ebie of himself at his age. Shy, but with depth. The kind of man who would prove himself, make a good husband. Before he could explore that line of thinking further, he heard the door open and watched as Max shook the hand of a small man with a handlebar mustache. The man dipped his head then was gone.

Max lifted a brow, then nodded for Ebie to enter his private office. He ushered Ebie to a seat, then shut the door, his footsteps whisper-soft on the carpeting. Behind him, an oak filing cabinet banked the wall flanked by two broadleaf palms.

"To what do I owe this honor?" Max said, once he was seated behind his matching oak desk.

"I want you to do something for me, Max," Ebie said, cutting to the chase.

Max leaned back in his chair and steepled his fingers, waiting.

"I want you to transfer the ownership of my property in Shardsburg."

After a brief lull, Max leaned forward, dropping his hands to the blotter on his desk. "Why?" he asked. "You're still halfway young, in good health. And you have no boys. Are you selling the property, putting it in Mitzi's name?"

"None of the above," he replied, knowing that Max would challenge his decision. Women didn't own property. Often, a man would simply set up a trust and have the lawyer or a close male friend handle decisions when a husband could no longer care for his wife or children. But times were changing, and though Ebie wasn't fully on board with all the changes taking place, he felt it was time. *I owe her that.*

"I want the property put in Cookie's name. Mitzi will receive the house after I'm gone, but Max," Ebie continued, "I want it put in Cookie's name now."

Just as he'd suspected, Max exploded out of his seat and began pacing the length of his office. "Do you understand what you are doing? Cookie has never owned anything. And why now? She's not even married."

How to explain his reasoning? But Ebie was a lawyer, after all. If *he* couldn't explain it, no one could. "Max, I have no sons and Mitzi and Dipsy are well cared for. They will never have to worry about money. But Cookie's different. She has dreams. I want to give her that chance. . . to see them out. To let her see what she's made of." He threw up his hands before Max could protest further. "Besides, I know I can't predict the future, but I have a feeling she's going to end up with that Winn fellow."

"Winnie?" Max said, cocking his head as though thinking it over.

It seemed like everyone knew Winn. After his father had died, most of the men in his family's circle had taken him under their wing, helped him in one way or another. But who helped the women? The thought had never occurred to Ebie until he and Mitzi had talked the other day. He just figured that's what marriage was for, and yet what if Cookie never married? Ebie felt certain that she would come around, but he wanted to hedge his bets. With Winn -- a frugal man with a good head on his shoulders -- to rein her in, they would make an unstoppable team. But both of them needed help to get their dreams off the ground. He was just offering them that small push. Besides, his house was paid off and his investments had paid off as well. He hadn't needed the money from the farm for years. And the earnings were negligible, but they might help Cookie and Winn finance their goals and ambitions. He didn't know when he would present the deed to her, but when he was ready, he wanted to have it available to hand her. . . to hand *them*.

"Max, I've always taken your advice, haven't I?"

With one hand, Max picked up a pipe lying on his desk, and with the other he pinched some cherry tobacco from a Sir Walter Raleigh tin and placed it in the bowl of the pipe. He tamped it down, then lit the leaves from a match he dug from his desk drawer. He breathed in a long draw of the mixture and released the aroma and smoke into the air with a single breath before answering.

"That you have, my friend. But not now, I take it?" he said, eyeing him with one brow cocked as if to suggest that he wasn't happy that Ebie had chosen this moment to ignore his advice.

"Not now," Ebie echoed. "This is my one chance to get it right with Cookie. I. . . I feel like I owe her."

"Because you didn't tell her about the adoption and the rest?" Max swirled his pipe around in the air as though to encompass everything.

Ebie sighed. "I should have told her earlier, Max. I was just. . ."

"Afraid of what would happen if anyone else found out?"

Ebie closed his eyes, the weight of his guilt crushing. Then he opened them and nodded. The truth of it is, the scandal would have cost him business, cost him his stature in society. It was bad enough that he had lost his brother because of his suggestion to work in the logging industry. But he had thought that keeping Cookie's past secret would be the best for her. She could grow up loved, well cared for. Mitzi would have the child she always wanted, and Ebie would have done his duty to his brother for preventing him from marrying the woman he loved, a woman who never would have been accepted in their world. Even now, after everything that had happened, after all the tears and recriminations, he still believed he'd done the right thing for all of them. He just hoped that someday Cookie could come to understand, could come to forgive him, could come to move forward in life, knowing she was loved, had always been loved, by many people.

"You can't change the past, you know, Ebie," Max said, seating himself on the corner of the desk and speaking between teeth clenched around the pipe's stem. He took another puff, the air once again filling the room with a pleasant aroma.

"I know. But I *can* change the future. . . for Cookie. For Winn, if she'll have him, and I'm confident she will. They love each other. It's written all over their faces."

Max pointed the stem of his pipe toward Ebie. "Well, don't go counting your chickens before they're hatched." Then, with a final sigh, he said, "Okay, against my better judgment, I will put the deed in her name. Once they marry, we can put it in both their names. Would that be satisfactory?"

Ebie offered a wan smile. "Thanks, Max. You've been a good

friend over the years."

Max peered at him with those hazy blue eyes. "I have, haven't I?" Max laughed. Then he got to work.

37

FOR THE PAST MONTH, COOKIE had faithfully gone to see Julia at the group home, each time wondering if this time would be her last. As she prepared to leave after yet another day of eking out bits and pieces of Julia's past, Cookie saw that it wouldn't be much longer. For the last few days Julia had been talking to invisible visitors. On the days Rachel had gone with her, she explained that Julia was talking to loved ones who had passed.

Cookie bent down and caressed her mother's cheek and marveled at how soft her skin felt despite all the wrinkles that had formed as she'd aged right before Cookie's eyes and the eyes of her caregivers.

"I'll get stronger," Julia had told Cookie on one of the previous visits.

And to prove it, Julia had jumped to her feet and begun

running circles around the room, even demanding that she be taken home, that she was all better. The staff nurse had explained that often, before a person's passing, they experienced a surge of energy, as though they were trying to literally outrun their body. The memory of that day had chilled her. But a week or more had passed since then, lulling Cookie into a false hope that maybe Julia was right, that maybe she would beat the odds through sheer willpower. That maybe she wanted to be here for her daughter, so much so that she could make it happen through determination alone.

So it surprised Cookie when today, Julia reached up and ran a silky hand across Cookie's cheek, the ailing woman's rheumy eyes inspecting every inch of her daughter as if to commit her to memory. Early into Cookie's visit, Julia had been thrashing, mumbling, trying to walk, to talk, nothing calming her. The nurse had given her a sedative, but even that hadn't settled her for long. But now, as Cookie prepared to leave, Julia seemed more cogent than she had in weeks.

When she was done inspecting Cookie, eyes filled with an almost angelic glow, Julia said, "Thank you for being here for me. Thank you for everything." Then she smiled a tired, sweet smile that Cookie would never forget.

As she stood and walked toward the door, Cookie heard her say, "Say hello to your daughter." Then she giggled.

Goosebumps chased their way up Cookie's arms, for as she turned back, Julia was staring up at some unseen person that had appeared, in her mind only, but for whom Cookie had no doubt she loved deeply. Cookie frowned, then stepped out of the room, but as she walked down the hall, she heard her mother's voice float in on the still air.

"I love you, Cookie."

Cookie was relieved to escape the house and all the trappings of death, glad to breathe in the cool afternoon air, hear the wrens chittering in the trees, see the clouds scudding across the sky in waves that made her want to float away on them. And to her utter joy, she saw Winn waiting for her, as he had since he'd first offered to come with her, waiting in the car so that she could have a chance to say goodbye to her mother in private. She had her own car these days. She'd purchased it with the sale of her entire houseplant collection to a local nursery. She would have to start all over building her plant collection, but she was used to starting over. Now.

"How are you doing?" Winn asked, taking her hand. They had begun holding hands after they'd first visited Julia, and he had come with her every day since. "You gonna be okay?"

Cookie nodded, eager to put the strange events behind her. She squeezed Winn's hand, then let go and turned on the engine. For the next ten minutes, they drove in silence, and that was the thing about Winn. He seemed to get her, to know when to speak, when to stay silent. And she adored him for it.

She entered the interstate, her thoughts still on her mother's peculiar ramblings. The words played over and over in her head. "Say hello to your daughter." Suddenly, it was as if a light switched on inside her and she slammed on the brakes, her car nearly rear ended in the process. She turned the steering wheel to the left, an oncoming car laying on the horn, her tires screeching to find purchase as she whipped the car around to the lanes going in the opposite direction.

"Are you trying to get us killed?" Winn yelled, hanging on to the door handle until his knuckles had turned white.

"She's dying," Cookie cried, her focus solely on returning to see her mother.

"I know, Cookie. We have known that for some time," he said, grabbing her arm and trying to make her see reason.

"No, you don't understand," she sobbed, tears blurring her vision as she drove. "She's dying now."

"You don't know that," Winn said, leaning toward her while monitoring the cars around them for safety.

"I do!" she insisted. "She thanked me, Winn. *Thanked* me! And she told me she loved me."

"She tells you that every time you see her," Winn implored, running his hands through his hair, even as cars all around her swerved as she attempted to stay in her lane but failed.

"No, you-don't-get-it! She told someone standing next to her to 'say hello to your daughter'. It was my father. He came to collect her." By now she was sobbing so hard that she could no longer see.

"Pull over!" Winn cried. "Honest to God, Cookie, *pull over*," he said, grabbing the steering wheel. Through sheer force, he managed to jutter the car's wheels to the side of the road and demanded she stomp on the brakes, which she did, nearly sending the pair crashing through the windshield.

Once the car was stationary, Winn opened his door and ran around the other side. He squeezed in, pushing her so that she moved enough for him to get behind the wheel.

"Take me back to her. Promise me."

"I promise," he said, taking her into his arms and kissing her on the forehead. "I love you, Cookie. I've always loved you. And if you want to see your mom, you'll see your mom, okay?"

His words were gentle, kind. She merely sniffed, tears

streaming down her face. He held her to him, even as he put the car in gear and pulled out into traffic. The drive seemed to take forever. As they finally arrived at the Posey House, Cookie jumped out and started running even before the car had stopped rolling. She heard Winn exit the car and slam the door shut, hot on her heels, but she couldn't stop. She needed to get there, to be there for her mother's final moments. But even before she reached the door to her mother's room, she knew her mother was gone. Knew that Edward had come to collect her. For as she entered the room, the nurse was already there and the sirens of the ambulance were playing in the distance. But what struck Cookie most, what she would remember for the rest of her life was the look on her mother's face. For on it was a smile. At last, she and Edward would be together for eternity.

38

THE NEXT FEW WEEKS WERE a blur. With the help of Rachel and Winn, Cookie prepared services for her mother. Though Ebie and Mitzi had tried to help, their relationship felt akilter, as though a train had come off its tracks and none of them knew how to get it back on, the weight of what had happened all too heavy. So, they stood in silence on an appropriately rainy day as they laid Julia to rest, each of them basking in their separate misery. Despite it all, Cookie was grateful for Winn's support. She leaned on him now, as he held her hand tightly in his, rain dripping down each of their faces, but no one complained. For her part, Mitzi handed an umbrella to Cookie, and mouthed 'I'm sorry' and 'I love you'. Cookie felt the tiniest bit of consolation in that simple gesture, wanting, no *needing* to restore the connection she had lost with her mother and father through all of this. But she didn't have the words.

"They'll come around, Cookie," Winn had told her. "You just have to give it time. You're all a bit raw right now."

Good old Winn. He always knew the right thing to say. She hugged tightly to his arm, noting how he'd become a man over the course of the past couple of years, his shoulders broader, his face sporting stubble that would one day become a beard. Fortunately, he hadn't grown the long shaggy hair that was coming into style, his hair too thick and wooly for long hair. She had even begun cutting it, and if she had to say so herself, it wasn't half bad.

Rachel had chosen the preacher, a tall thin man who wore a suit, despite the foul weather. Cookie wished the sun had shined for her mother as they lay her to rest, but she knew that wherever she was, she didn't care about the weather because she was with Edward. Finally and forever. The back of Cookie's throat tightened at the thought. She had never met her father, had never felt his pride, but as she looked over at Ebie, who stood with his hands folded around the hat that should have been on his head on this rainy day, she realized that she still had a part of her father. . . in Ebie. And for the first time since their falling out, she wanted to run over and give him a hug, tell him how much she had missed him in the silences that had followed Julia's death. But she couldn't, not now. Soon, she hoped. Very soon.

The preacher began speaking. "Dearly beloved, we are gathered here together. . ."

But Cookie was no longer listening because she noticed a man pull up in a green 50's Chevy flatbed with running boards and a windshield visor. When he got out of his truck, Cookie could see that his hair was thinning, and he wore overalls and work boots. Even at this distance, she could see that he was stooped from age. She watched as he crossed the muddy lawn, making his way to the back of the small gathering. In his gnarled hands, he held an engineer's cap. Rachel discreetly moved to the back and took his hand, then brought him ceremoniously to stand beside Cookie and Winn.

"Meet your grandfather," she whispered to Cookie, as the minister removed a spray of flowers on the coffin and placed it on an easel. "This is your grandpa, Jo."

It was clear to see by the love in Rachel's eyes that he had been a good father, a decent man. A wash of emotion swept over Cookie. The old man winked, tears in his eyes for his dying daughter.

"We are here to say our goodbyes to a wonderful woman. A child of God," the preacher intoned even as Cookie wondered why Julia's father hadn't come to see her in all the time she'd been at the group home.

As if reading her thoughts, Rachel said, "Daddy hasn't been getting around much." She peered down at her feet. "He lost his job at the woolen mills, so he's been working three jobs to make ends meet. He was scheduled for some time off. . . to get to see Julia, but she didn't last that long."

The old man's eyes welled, his lip quivering slightly to have his life explained in such a way. He fingered his engineer cap, the brim, circling it round and round in his hands that were calloused from hard work, and gnarled from age, his knuckles enlarged and his nails ridged.

"Mama died a few years back," Rachel concluded. "Consumption."

"Ashes to ashes, dust to dust," the reverend continued as the sky burst down in tears that reflected those of Cookie and the others. "Now we return our loved one to the earth from whence she came. Let us pray."

Everyone bowed their heads and closed their eyes, except for Cookie. She wanted to see where she had come from, whose ancestry had informed her life even though she had never met her grandfather, Jo. Did his blood run through her veins? Were their vestiges of this small wizened man in her attributes and actions? She would have to ask Rachel someday. For now it was enough to recognize small similarities -- the eyes, perhaps, and the chin.

When it was over, the mourners lined up, Cookie heading the line, followed by Rachel, Jo, Winn, and Julia's few friends who had driven the distance to come see her off into the afterlife. One by one, they deposited dirt into the grave as the casket was lowered into the ground. Then the mourners marched off to their cars as Cookie waited in the relentless rain, shaking one hand after another as was her duty and honor as the only child of a woman she had known only marginally... in the final days of her life. She would meet up with the mourners at a place outside of town that Mitzi had suggested, somewhere discreet. The suggestion had set Cookie on a slow boil, but in the name of keeping the peace, she had chosen not to fight it. Mitzi meant well.

When the day was finally over, the mourners all gone and the hall they had rented cleaned and the tables and chairs stowed away, Cookie turned to Winn and said, "Get me out of here."

Winn hadn't asked questions except, "Where to?"

"Just drive," she'd said. And that's how they had ended up in Opelika, in Lee County, a small town just south of Montgomery where the main street was lined with shops and a hardware store. Further down, she saw the Lee County Courthouse, a brick, Neoclassical-style building with large white colonnades and a white clock tower. She saw a couple, a man in a black suit and a woman dressed in white heading to the Justice of the Peace. She didn't know why, but she turned to Winn and said, "Will you marry me?"

Winn laughed. "What, *now*?" Then seeing that she was serious, he pulled the car over and said, "You're not kidding. But. . . what about your family? Your mother would have both our hides if we didn't give her the big wedding she's always wanted."

"Never mind," Cookie said, turning to face forward, her jaw set and anger causing hot stinging tears to form. "If you don't want to."

Winn turned her head his way and said, "Be reasonable. I've *always* wanted to marry you. Since grade school," he added with another laugh that made her laugh too, despite the tears. "But I'm afraid you're doing this on the rebound, because you just lost your mother. I don't want you to do something that you're going to regret."

"There's nothing I would regret about marrying you, Winn Cowley. I've always loved you. I would have married you years ago--"

"--if it hadn't been for your mom?" he finished.

"If you'd asked," she added sheepishly, sweeping at the tears with the back of her hand.

He stared forward, as though thinking about what she'd said, then suddenly he flung the door of the car open and grabbed her hand, pulling her out.

"What are we doing?" she asked, not at all sure his intent.

But to her amazement, he got down on bended knee and

peered up at her. "Would you marry me, Cookie Haines? You won't be rich, and I can't promise you a home. But I can promise that I love you."

"Oh Winn!" she exclaimed, helping him up off the pavement as people gathered to stare at the pair.

"So, what are we waiting for? Let's see if the Justice of the Peace is busy."

Although getting married had seemed a good idea at the time, two hours later, as they pulled up into the driveway of her family's home and stared at the picture window of the ranch-style house, the idea seemed decidedly more half-baked.

"What do you think your parents will say? I didn't even ask your father for your hand in marriage."

Cookie read the trepidation in Winn's voice, but she couldn't be of much help because she was too busy worrying about Mitzi. She and Mitzi usually got on well, but Mitzi could be downright fearsome when her dander was up.

Just then, the curtains shifted and Cookie saw Mitzi peer out at them and then call to Ebie, who came to stand beside her. Without thinking, Cookie ducked.

"We're not teenagers, for cripe's sake, Cookie. Pretend we're adults." Winn winked at her, and she saw that irrepressible glimmer in his eye, but she knew he was just as scared as she was to face her parents. No one in her family eloped. No one.

39

"HERE GOES NOTHING!" COOKIE SAID, then opened the car door, while Winn exited his side of the car. After that, it was as though her senses had gone blank, as though the bird chatter had ceased and the sun had gone behind a cloud for all that she noticed. Instead, the only thing she could think about was what her parents would say. How they would react to the news that she had eloped.

She didn't have long to wait because the door opened and Mitzi came running out, Ebie hot on her heels. "Where have you two been?" she demanded. "Are you all right?" She turned to Winn for answers when Cookie wasn't forthcoming. But when she saw that he, too, was struck dumb, her eyes widened and her voice lowered in an accusatory tone. "*Winnnnn . . .* Cookie? What have you done?"

For a moment, neither spoke, then as if in unspoken consent, they both said in unison, "We eloped."

Mitzi's entire body reacted, as though she had been physically assaulted by the news. For several seconds, she stood there blinking. And then, as if testing out the words for herself, she said, "Married? You're married? You *eloped*?" Each time she spoke, her voice gained strength, grew louder, more angry.

"Mitzi," Ebie warned in a tone one would use for a growling dog. But Mitzi refused to back down. "Let's take it inside," Ebie said, when he realized she wasn't going to remain silent on the subject.

The walk to the house felt like a walk to the gallows, slow and torturous. Once inside, Mitzi turned on Cookie, who had taken a seat beside Winn on the daveno. "What about Grandma Petrie's dress I saved for you. . . the guests, friends, family?" As before, her voice grew louder as she ticked off Cookie's demerits for having gone against tradition. "I won't have it," she shouted, a finger thrust into the air as though mounting a cavalry charge.

"Mitzi," Ebie tried to intercede.

"No, no, no!" she shouted, all the while shaking her head.

"Now Mitzi, stop."

"They can't -- I won't--"

"*Mitzi*," Ebie said through gritted teeth this time. "SHUT. . . UP!"

Cookie gasped, and even Winn held his breath and didn't move as everyone awaited Mitzi's response. No one spoke to Mitzi that way. *Ever*. For several tense moments, the air sparked with currents of electricity. And then, without warning, Mitzi, who had puffed herself up, suddenly deflated with a laugh that started out slow then gathered strength until she was doubled up laughing, tears streaming down her face. And that's how Cookie knew she was back in Mitzi's good graces. Winn took her hand in his and together they breathed a sigh of relief, while for his part, Ebie appeared downright confused by his wife's behavior. And yet Cookie understood. This was Mitzi's way of coping with something beyond her control. Laughter. They could all use a good dose of it right about now.

Once Mitzi had finally gathered herself together and straightened her hair with her hands, Ebie turned and entered his study, returning moments later with a manila envelope. He pursed his lips, as though trying to decide whether to go through with his plan. Then, with great ceremony, he handed the envelope to Cookie.

"This is for both of you -- a wedding present." When Cookie frowned, he said, "Open it."

Cookie carefully unraveled the cord that bound the flap to the envelope. Then she slowly pulled out what appeared to be a deed. . . to the land in Shardsburg. Cookie's eyes went to her father. "What's this?"

"It's for you. . . and Winn. Max is getting the paperwork done on it. Whether you were married or not, I planned to give it to you. . . so you had a place to pursue your dreams."

Overwhelmed with emotion, Cookie struggled to speak, but the emotion got the best of her. Instead she ran to her father and hugged him. For the first time in her life, she would have the wherewithal to make her dreams come true. She gave him an extra firm hug, then ran to Mitzi and gave her a hug as well.

"Thank you both," she said, Winn chiming in. Then she took the deed back to the sofa so that she and Winn could look it over.

"With this property, we could have a home and land," Winn said. Then he frowned.

"What?" Cookie asked, noting the worried expression on his face. "What is it?"

"We won't have the capital to start the nursery business, unless. . ."

She leaned forward. "Unless what?"

"Unless I sell my property and we move to Shardsburg." His voice rang with excitement at the realization that everything they had ever wanted was within reach: a home, land, and the capital to begin building their dream. . . to make it a reality.

"You would do that?" Cookie asked. Sharing his excitement, she took his arm in hers and lay her head on his shoulder. Already she could picture her home, the greenhouses, the land for growing crops. But how many acres were there, she wondered? She reached for the deed, perusing it until she found the acreage. But to her surprise, it included not just one home, but two, each holding forty acres apiece. And with it came the terms for the other property. . . Chester and Rayleen's property. It showed the earlier cost for the sharecropper -- a whopping two-thirds of the yearly produce owed in exchange for rent. Cookie sat back, stunned. How could a sharecropper ever make a living. . . survive? Then she thought of the store her family had owned. Of the IOU's they must have given out to get the sharecroppers through the long winters. The paired usury must have kept sharecroppers, most of them blacks or poor whites, in debt forever, keeping them enslaved in a lifetime of poverty. Suddenly the deed lost some of its luster.

Cookie kept reading, her eyes stopping on two predictably onerous phrases from the original deed. *This building and the land herein shall never be sold or transferred to anyone of non-Caucasian race. This covenant and restriction shall also restrict any heirs, executors, or administrators or other assignee from selling to said race.* Anger welled inside her. She peered over and saw that Winn shared her anger. She knew enough to know that black covenant laws had been overturned in 1948. Still, it left a sour taste in her mouth for an otherwise happy outcome to the day. She was married to Winn, and she had the land to begin her dream. The rest. . . well, she would deal with that later.

40

One Year Later

THE GREENHOUSES WERE FINALLY UP, eight in all. They filled the south corner of the Shardsburg property so that the house had a clear view to the fields of vegetables James had planted. Cookie surveyed the land, all eighty acres of it, and smiled. Today was the big day, the day her parents would come to see all that they had accomplished in the past year. Dipsy and her brood had agreed to come too, to celebrate the Fourth of July with Cookie and Winn, Independence Day. And though the world around Cookie seemed to spasm daily with word about the Vietnam War, the death of John F. Kennedy, race riots, and Beatlemania, she felt cocooned in her small hamlet, far from the uproar that seemed to catch up with her nightly on the black-and-white television set. And yet she felt hints of it when she visited the local store her family had once owned, the whispers, the stares. The wide path whites gave her when they saw her coming, having heard the rumors of her upbringing. But what frightened her most were the threats. They were subtle, *so* subtle that no one would know but her, and yet they were effective at frightening her, some of them so obscene that she had yet to share them with Winn. It kept her up at night, nerves shattered, but she had been careful to keep it to herself, for now. She wondered how many of color had received similar threats. . . a lifetime of them. But what surprised her most was the insidious hatred for her very femaleness and the audacity that she might run a business. She realized now the gift her family had given her by adopting her: the freedom not to have to live in fear.

Now, away from the prying eyes of the community, Cookie tended the flowers she had planted next to the porch and along the walkway that Winn had installed in the past month. She kneeled down and plucked at the broadleaf plantain and spurge, and of course the ever present dandelion, which Rayleen had taught her to pick, clean, and cook along with bacon grease and crumbled bacon bits. Cookie had been sure to invite both Rayleen and Chester to their celebration, as well as James and his wife Corliss, Charlotte and their new baby, Chance. She only hoped that she would be as good an aunt as James had been a big brother to her as a toddler. But the biggest blessing of the day was the news that Rayleen and Chester's son, Mason, was home from Vietnam. He had survived. He had survived.

Rachel, who had applied for and received the job of caring for Dipsy's children so she could chase more philanthropic pursuits, should be arriving any moment, along with Cookie's grandfather. It still seemed odd to think that Cookie had a living grandparent after all these years, and although they had talked by phone only a few times, Cookie was glad she'd had a chance to know him.

As she toiled in the sun, she could barely contain her excitement. Winn should be back soon from the train station, *with* her parents. In the past year, besides helping James build the greenhouses, Winn had added an addition to the shack and had upgraded the insides of the home, teaching her how to wield a hammer and saw. She had felt competent enough, in the end, to build her own chicken coop out back.

When she saw a cloud of dust forming in the distance, she jumped to her feet. "It's Winn!" she cried. Their dog, Jax, leapt to his feet from the spot beside her. Jax was a hunting dog, a black and white spaniel mix, a stray that had arrived on their doorstep one day and had never left. He had become fast friends with Winn's yellow lab, Chick. "They're here!"

She was so excited that she ran to meet them and raced the Woodie the rest of the way home. When Mitzi exited the car, she was shaking her head at Cookie's antics. She held an arm out to her daughter and Cookie fell into her outstretched arms, happy to be back in Mitzi's loving embrace. The year away had taught her how much her parents had done for her over the years. And she also knew now that life was never simple. She had learned that from Chester and Rayleen. Sometimes you had to accept things as they are, no matter how flawed, or work to change the things you could. And maybe that's what she was doing. . . working to change things, in her own small way. She felt the paper in her pocket. She'd been wanting to do this for a year now, but had been waiting for the right time. She supposed Independence Day was as good as any. But before she could discuss her plans with her parents, Mitzi leaned in and handed her a painting of the shack -- Rayleen's shack.

"You painted this?" Cookie inspected it as if for the first time.

"Don't pretend you haven't seen it before, Smarty Pants," Mitzi said. "Dipsy told me all about you sneaking into the attic. And of course I didn't paint it. My paintings look like a child drew them."

"What?" Cookie frowned, head cocked. "But, I thought--"

"Those were Edward's -- at least the good ones were. Oh, I dabbled a bit, but the only talent I have is with my clothing. I've even tried designing a few of my own," she said, "now that I have the house to myself." She stood back and twirled in a circle, showing off a short-sleeved shift, form-fitted at the waist with a wide collar that draped her shoulders.

"It's beautiful," Cookie breathed, and she meant it.

"Good, because I made you one just like it," Mitzi said with a laugh. And that's all it took to fall back into the rhythm they'd developed over the years.

Soon, the others arrived and the house was bursting with laughter, hugs, and children running through the house, Jax and Chick not far behind. Cookie had cooked all day, making fried chicken, buttermilk biscuits, cole slaw, rainbow Jell-o surprise, the surprise being that she used none of the things she'd hated as a child in the Jell-o. Instead, she'd added maraschino cherries and marshmallows, which the kids were sure to like. For dessert she had made a bevy of pies: apple, cherry, pecan, and even a peach pie, the freezer full of French vanilla ice cream to dollop on top of each of the pies, except for the pecan. For that she had whipped up clotted cream.

After the late afternoon picnic, as the shadows began to fall and the sun was fading on the horizon, she stood, whistling until she was able to get everyone's attention. Winn came to stand beside her and placed an arm around her in support.

"I suppose we should have done this in private," Winn said, garnering a smattering of murmurs and questioning looks from the group gathered 'round the table. "I'll go first, then Cookie has something to say. James? Would you stand?"

James peered side to side, looking first at Corliss, then at his parents and Mason, a strapping young man who would no doubt spend the rest of his life trying to process the war. James shrugged when no one else seemed to know what was going on. He had dressed in a clean pair of jeans and a blue cotton shirt, Corliss in a flowing white dress and matching bonnet, the baby in her arms, Charlotte at her side on the wooden bench.

"We would have never made it this past year if it hadn't been for your expertise and know-how."

James chuckled, clearly recalling a few of Cookie and Winn's earlier mishaps on the farm. Chester and Rayleen joined in.

"Well, we would like to offer you the job of manager, and eventually, I hope you'll consider becoming my partner," Winn said with a shy smile. "I could use a man like you."

Taken aback, James blinked but his wife let loose a very unlady-like holler, to which everyone laughed.

"I take it you accept?"

"Yes, Sir!" James said with an enthusiasm that once again had them all laughing.

"Now, my wife has something she wants to say."

Cookie looked nervously at her parents for support. Ebie gave his nod of approval and Mitzi followed suit. "Chester, Rayleen, could you stand?"

Again they turned to each other in confusion but stood, Chester with his fawn-colored fedora held between his hands and Rayleen in a blue dress that Corliss had made her.

"This has been a long time coming. The forty acres should have been yours ages ago. You have worked the soil year after year, paid more than it is worth in crops as a sharecropper, and in rent afterward." She held the paper out to them. "Here's the deed to your land. It's yours. And if it ever becomes too much for you, we would be happy to rent the land from *you* this time."

Everybody laughed. The world was changing. Cookie knew it wouldn't happen in one fell swoop, rather in baby steps. But at least she could make some small contribution to that change. As if recognizing the changes, the sun fell on the horizon and some of the men snuck off to set off fireworks over the river. As if on cue, the first one went up and exploded in the night sky sending sparks flying in all directions.

The words came to her unheeded. *Let freedom ring.*

And so, for one night at least, she reveled in the changes taking place in her community. Tomorrow she would worry about what lay ahead. But not today. Not today.

Acknowledgements

Writing never occurs in a vacuum. So many people help us along the way, far too numerous to name, but I will do my best to thank those who taught me, stood by me, and continue to support me along the way. To my former Lit-Chix writing group: Patsy Hand, Valerie Brooks, and Chris Schofield. Thank you, from the bottom of my heart for your companionship and friendship over the years. You are all amazing writers, and I am so proud of you. To my current writing group, Laine Stambaugh and Elaine Stek, who have offered tons of reading material and advice, you both deserve to be published. To Elizabeth Lyon, who gave me my start at editing. And to literary agent, Natasha Kern. . . I couldn't have had a better mentor.

To Darrin Brenner, whose artwork could be seen on billboards across Georgia in the 2019 primary and who was kind enough to design the cover of my books. To Sara Rolat, editor and interior designer extraordinaire. To Kaylee Baker for rescuing me too many times to recall. You have my undying gratitude. To Kristen Baker, whom I forgot to thank for her read-through of my previous book. Your feedback was invaluable. Many thanks!

Lastly, to my husband Les and daughter Sara, who has made it her mission to come visit us weekly, and who is the one and only person my dog, Parker, adores beyond measure. If it weren't for all of you, I might never have made it to this point. You are the lights of my life.

ABOUT THE AUTHOR

Author Carol L. Craig, has two published novels: *The Great Unraveling* and *A Thousand Bits of Wonderful*. For over twenty years, she has edited for a host of award-winning novelists. She is both owner of, and editor for, Editing Gallery, LLC. She has been a guest speaker at Women Writing the West in Tucson, Arizona, has given one-on-one editing sessions at Willamette Writers Conference, and spent many happy days with friends and fellow writers at Colony House, an Oregon writer's retreat. While at home in Oregon, Carol enjoys reading, writing, and gardening, along with coffee klatches with her husband Les, and her Sheltie, Parker.

BE SURE TO SIGN UP FOR HER NEWSLETTER AT www.editinggallery.com for a chance at free gifts, or to read articles from writers, artists, film directors, book cover designers, editors, and interior book designers as well as professional bloggers, etc.

YOU CAN FIND CAROL AT
www.editinggallery.com
facebook.com/EditingGallery1
Instagram: @clcraig7